Praise for *The Credit Draper*

'An odyssey of cultural confusion and survival. Full of hope, honour and sadness.' JUDGES OF THE McKITTERICK PRIZE

'This is a subtle, beautifully written story. Sad but never sentimental … a truly fine debut which heralds the arrival of a bold new voice in fiction.' RODGE GLASS

'For all the serious issues that Simons' novel raises, it's also a joyous book in many ways, delighting in the fun and ambition of a young boy.' LESLEY McDOWELL, *THE HERALD*

'There is much to admire in this story… This novel has a ring of truth while bravely tackling themes that have uncomfortable echoes today.' THE SCOTS MAGAZINE

'*The Credit Draper* is a rare evocation of an earlier genre: the immigrant novel… adding a most welcome Scottish dimension.' CLIVE SINCLAIR, THE JEWISH CHRONICLE

Praise for *The Liberation of Celia Kahn*

'A modern classic.' DAVID BELBIN

'Emotive, this is a thought-provoking piece of fictionalised social history.' ALASTAIR MABBOTT, *THE HERALD*

'It is always a joy to find a novel which is such an entertaining and compelling read, is faithful to the history of the times and which also explores so many stimulating political themes.' ALAN LLOYD, *MORNING STAR*

'This is a compelling tale with characters who imprint themselves on the streets of Glasgow.' SCARLETT McGWIRE, *THE TRIBUNE*

'A very good read… explores feminism and socialism with subtlety and intelligence.' GUTTER MAGAZINE

ALSO BY J. DAVID SIMONS

The Credit Draper

The Liberation of Celia Kahn

AN EXQUISITE SENSE
OF WHAT IS BEAUTIFUL

J. DAVID SIMONS

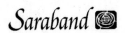

Published by Saraband
Suite 202, 98 Woodlands Road
Glasgow, G3 6HB, Scotland
www.saraband.net

ISBN: 978-190864327-8
ebook: 978-190864328-5

Printed in the EU on paper from sustainably managed sources.

1   3   5   7   9   10   8   6   4   2

For Sofia

The author would like to thank the Society of Authors' Foundation for their generous support in the writing of this novel.

"I saw the waterwheel as a symbol of the divine mechanism of existence as it swept round in its timeless arc, scooping out the lifeblood of the carp-filled pond, carrying its burden to the top and then releasing it gently back to the source in an illusion of quickened pace. The victims of Hiroshima and Nagasaki. Could their souls be returned to their source, or were their essences so obliterated, so totally annihilated at some subatomic level that their very life force disappeared forever from the universal scheme of things? Never to dwell in a godly kingdom or to be reincarnated back here on earth.

And what of their assassins? I sat with them that night in a Tokyo theatre during the early days of the Occupation as they watched and laughed and sang along with the first public performance of *The Mikado* in Japan. On stage, more Americans, as well as British and Canadians – the ABC as the Japanese used to call them – acted out the leads while the locals were relegated to the singing and dancing chorus. There was not blood on the hands of the audience that night but the burnt skin and bomb-blasted souls of the tens of thousands sacrificed in their honour. What of them, these Lord High Executioners?"

THE WATERWHEEL, PREFACE

"And I remembered that famous photograph of the first meeting between MacArthur and the Emperor taken not long after the surrender. The General in simple military attire – no medals, ribbons or starry epaulettes – standing comfortable and relaxed like some John Wayne character, towering over the Emperor beside him. Hirohito, stiff at attention, dressed in morning coat and pinstripe trousers, looking like the Supreme Commander's oriental butler to the ignorant observer. Who would attend the funeral of this Emperor when he passed away? The soldiers stranded in Manchuria? The prisoners-of-war in Siberian labour camps? The fire-bombed homeless of Tokyo? The survivors of Hiroshima and Nagasaki? The widows and children of the *kamikaze*? And I wondered what they would feel as they filed past the imperial coffin, for this man, once so divine and now so human, who had brought the shame of defeat upon their nation, who had caused them to disembowel themselves on the collective sword of surrender. Would they see past the trappings of empire, beyond the Imperial guards, past the wreath bouquets, the thick smell of incense, the chants of the Shinto priests, the coffin walls? Would they ponder on the cold, shrouded, shrivelled corpse within and see that this was just a man? Just a man."

THE WATERWHEEL, PREFACE
(OMITTED FROM THE TEXT OF THE JAPANESE TRANSLATION)

CHAPTER ONE

Hakone, Japan • 2003

'Your favourite season is the one you are born into,' Edward's mother, a bitter child of winter, used to tell him. Edward, an October baby, recalled this statement as the autumn forest flashed by the window of the taxi in its sweep up the hillside. This yellow-brown parade of lacquer trees, poplars and elms marking his journey back in time, trunk by rapid trunk. He used to love this time of year. Now the autumn of his birth day just reminded him of his impending death. The withering, the desiccation, the falling, the decay.

'How long now?' Enid asked.

He leaned forward, tapped the half-opened partition with his cane. '*Nan-pun kakarimasu ka?*'

'*Go-fun gurai,*' the driver grunted, holding up a spread of his white-gloved digits.

'About five minutes,' he told her as he settled back into the leather. His mind still felt fuzzy at the edges, jet-lagged, labouring for clarity in a haze of warped time, half here and half somewhere else. Yet he couldn't really complain. The flight from London had taken only fourteen hours. A modern miracle compared to his first journey on the inaugural Polar Route. Almost two days flying back then. All the passengers rushing to one side to catch a glimpse of the North Pole, the pilot ordering them back for fear of a tilt.

'It must feel strange,' she said. 'Coming back.'

'I don't know. It's a different country now.' He looked at her. Her ringless fingers fiddling with the clasp on her handbag, her head fixed forward, lips tight, her complexion paler than usual. 'Thank you for coming,' he said, his voice still scratching dry from the many airborne hours aloft.

'It's my job.'

'Still, I know you don't like travelling.' He almost patted her hand as he said this, to stop her fidgeting if nothing else. Then as the vehicle began to slow, he felt ripples of panic spread across his abdomen, down his thighs. He gripped the top of his cane.

'The hotel manager's name is Takahashi,' she said. 'He has been very helpful with the arrangements. Please try to remember his name. You forget how heartening it is for people to be remembered. Especially by you.'

The taxi swung off the road, eased up the driveway, stopped in the forecourt. His door was immediately hauled open and cool air swooped into the compartment along with a gloved hand. He shooed away the assistance of the liveried doorman, struggled out of the car. Then steadying himself on his cane, he straightened his back, aware of each aching joint grinding into position until he was fully able to take in the view. A feeling of both joy and gratitude swept through him. The hotel was just as he remembered it. A magical, medieval Japanese castle. Those tiers of grey-tiled roofs cascading out of the hillside. The rust-red balconies. The lanterns.

'Sir Edward, Sir Edward.' An elegant gentleman in dark jacket and pinstriped trousers approached, bowed deep before him. 'How nice it is to welcome you back after such a long absence.' The hotel manager snapped upright, held out his hand.

'Ah, Takahashi-san,' Edward said. 'It is good to be back.' He grasped the offered hand. 'And this is my personal assistant. Ms Enid Blythe.'

Takahashi stepped back, clicked his heels together, bowed again.

'What a beautiful building,' Enid said.

Takahashi beamed. 'Come, let me escort you inside. My staff will take care of the taxi. And your cases.' The manager finger-snapped a doorman into attending to the task.

Edward sighed as he moved towards the revolving doors, grateful for the cane earthing the pulses of excitement racing through his tired veins.

'No need to register,' Takahashi informed them at the top of the stairs, flapping a hand of dismissal at the clerk behind the reception desk. 'You will see that not much has changed, Sir Edward. We have tried not to disturb the original style wherever possible.'

Edward looked around. The spacious salon with its parquet flooring, teak panelling and dull-leather armchairs retained its familiar aura of a gentleman's club. Even the adjoining Magic Room appeared intact, bringing back memories of evenings spent in the company of visiting conjurers and Chinese illusionists.

'My room?' he asked.

'As requested, I have provided you with the Fuji Suite. It too remains almost the same. Ms Blythe has the identical accommodation on the floor above.'

'And office space?' Enid asked.

'You will have your own desk and telephone in our business centre. High speed Internet access, of course. Photocopying on request.'

'Excellent, Mr Takahashi,' Enid said, the colour flowing back into her cheeks at the mention of her favourite accessories. 'Can I just remind you this is very much a private visit.'

'Discretion is one of the hallmarks of this hotel, Ms Blythe,' Takahashi sniffed.

'Even so, it is important that Sir Edward's stay is not made public.'

'I have already briefed my staff. Now, may I show you to your rooms? First, Sir Edward.'

While Enid waited at reception, Edward followed Takahashi down a corridor so much longer and formidable than he had often recalled to reach the open door to his room. His luggage had already been stacked inside.

'Will you be having lunch?'

'I think I will have a nap first. Could you ask reception to call me in a couple of hours?'

'Of course. And if I may be so bold as to suggest, Sir Edward. I thought perhaps we could meet to talk about the old days?'

'Yes, yes, of course. The old days. But not now. Now I must rest.'

'Later then.' Takahashi bowed and left.

With the door shut behind him, Edward laid back against its wooden panelling. His chest ached. He closed his eyes. In a snap-shot instant he saw her. Sumiko. Excitedly indicating the views of the valley from the window. Blinking his eyes open, he almost expected her to be there, the gold thread of her kimono illuminated in the sunshine. He pushed himself off the back of the door and wandered around the room, feeling hunched and frail, like a general stumbling around the battlefields of a pyrrhic victory, poking at corpses, mourning his losses, measuring the price of ambition. He touched the cool fabric of the quilt, ran his hand over the mahogany writing desk. Could this have been the very same desk where he had sat to write *The Waterwheel* all those years ago? The large walk-in cupboard. Sumiko had loved the way the light went on and off automatically with the opening and closing of the door. 'Like magic,' she used to say, replaying her role as conjurer's assistant frozen in presentation pose.

He felt an enormous weariness pressing down on him, immersing his whole body in a fatigue that was almost comforting in its announcement of inevitable sleep. He managed to ease off his shoes and, still in his coat, lay down on the welcome softness of the large bed. As he drifted into a sleep that approached stealthily like the fading past and diminishing future of his conscious existence, he could just make out the sound of temple bells chiming in the distance.

He decided to skip lunch. It appeared Enid was still napping and anyway he had no appetite for a meal that should have been break-fast in his own time zone. Instead, he opted for a stroll in the gardens. As he waited in the lobby for the bellboy to return with his overcoat, he noticed a large glass display cabinet he could not recall from his first visit. He wandered over, took out his reading glasses and surveyed the black and white photographs, captured testaments to the heyday of the hotel. Eisenhower was there, as was Nehru, Einstein, Helen Keller, and Chaplin with tennis racket. There was even a menu autographed by the actor, William Holden. He was surprised to see a photograph of his own younger self standing obvious in striped blazer and white trousers amid a rigid ensemble of staff in the hotel forecourt. The then-manager, name forgotten but remembered for his large spectacles, stood by his side. He searched the back row of chambermaids, bellboys and porters, and there was Sumiko in the far corner, head partially lowered. On the bottom of the case below this photograph lay a copy of his book, open at the title page. A small white card declared: '*The Waterwheel*' by Edward Strathairn. Written at this hotel. July 1957 – March 1958 [Copies available in the hotel library].

He felt quite overwhelmed by the gesture. After all this was a region of Japan quite used to its literary heroes, with its very own Yasunari Kawabata winning the Literature Nobel back in the Sixties. He recalled how much Sumiko had adored the laureate's novel *Snow Country* and quietly mouthed the first two sentences, words that had stayed with him for so long while so much else had faded away.

"The train came out of the long tunnel into the snow country. The earth lay white under the night sky."

He loved that image. From darkness to light. From the torrid urban squalor of Tokyo into the purity of the snow country. Such an image of renewal. Of hope. Kawabata's Nobel citation had read: "for his narrative mastery which, with great sensibility, expressed the essence of the Japanese mind." Kawabata had committed suicide at the age of seventy-two by placing a gas hose in his mouth. Such an ugly death of self-loathing for such a sensitive man. 'What was the point, Kawabata-sensei?' Edward thought. 'What drove you to such an act when death was already so near?'

The bellboy returned, helped him on with his overcoat, held open the door to the gardens. Edward hobbled out into the sunshine. The pure air refreshed and uplifted but also hinted at the gloom of the coming winter. He trod carefully along a pathway strewn with maple leaves, using his cane to brush aside the silky awnings of giant cobwebs spun between the overhanging trees. He passed the greenhouses with their outside trays of bonsai trees, then paused by a rock until his breath came more easily. A young Japanese couple passed, full of bows and whispers. Swivelling on his cane, he pressed on until he reached the pond.

His old haunt appeared unchanged. Lush sprays of ferns and grasses danced among mossy boulders embedded along the banks. Just below the green-slime surface of the pool, he could see the orange-speckled carp gliding through the water.

'Carp can live for two hundred years,' Aldous had told him at a time when even three score years and ten seemed a distant horizon to both of them. 'Oh, to be like them,' he had replied. 'So aged and content.'

He eased himself down on to a low stone wall. There on the opposite bank, attached to a small wooden hut, stood the water-wheel. It greeted him like an old acquaintance, spinning round smoothly, dipping effortlessly into the pond almost as if it were bowing to him in recognition. The newness of the wood declared the wheel was now a reincarnation, the essence of its form remaining while its structure had been renewed. He looked back down at the red-leafed pathway from where Sumiko had come daily, bringing him trays of green tea and biscuits to his workplace. And he remembered something else Aldous had told him, a sentence that had stuck in his mind over the years through the sheer power of its wisdom. 'Great art is the pure expression of our imperfection on the path to truth.' Yes, Aldous. That was it. But so much imperfection. And so little truth.

He leaned forward, dangled a hand over the surface of the water. Immediately, a slew of carp rushed towards his flailing fingers, poking out their heads for the invisible morsels, their pink mouths snapping open and shut like silk purses. A cloud concealed the weakening sun and a cold greyness settled over the gardens. He shivered, regretting his hat and gloves left on the dressing table. But he remained watching the waterwheel, focusing his attention on just one compartment as it scooped out the water from the pond, carried its burden to the top, then released it gently back to the source in an illusion of quickened pace. The sky grew darker. A dried-up maple leaf floated down to rest on the dark wool of his sleeve. Winter was approaching.

CHAPTER TWO

Glasgow, Scotland • 1936

Edward was nine years old when he discovered the miniature sword in his father's pipe-box. The ivory sheath was about eight inches long, simply but exquisitely carved with the figure of an Oriental maiden. Her robed body took up one side of the casing but her head was engraved on the handle of the blade so that when he withdrew the sword from its holder, it had the effect of decapitating the serene face from its body. He loved to let his fingers play along the groove of the carvings, to slip the blade from its sheath, to guillotine that poor young woman over and over again. Such a treasure in the Strathairn family household that contained no ornaments other than a silver-plated cigarette box and a swirly glass ashtray. He asked his father where it came from.

'Japan,' his father replied blandly. As if such an exotic artefact was merely one of an extensive Far Eastern collection housed in their Glasgow flat. 'And be careful you dinnae cut yourself, Eddie.'

'A gift from one of his exotic mistresses,' his mother said in an interruption from her dusting of the sideboard. 'What do you call them? Geishas. Aye, that's the word. Geishas.'

'Haud yer whisht, woman. You'll no be putting nonsense like that in the boy's head.'

'I'm sure he has the sense to know what is true and what is nigh well impossible. Isn't that right, Eddie?' She laughed and shook her yellow rag at him, releasing a burst of dust to drift into the sunlight. He felt a warmth ooze through him, glad to somehow be involved in this easy banter between his parents. It was rare to see his mother laugh. She was normally so distracted by her constant fretting, gnawing the skin off her knuckles with her worry of everything until he feared the white of her finger-bones might shine through the red-raw scarring.

'Dinnae listen to her, lad,' his father said with a snap of his newspaper. 'It was your Uncle Rob that gave it to us. A souvenir of his travels in the exotic East. Your mother wouldnae know the difference between a pair of geishas and a pair of galoshes.'

'And you wouldnae know the difference between a pair of galoshes and a pair of washing-up gloves,' his mother countered, still with laughter in her voice. 'You big lump, sitting there like Lord Muck when there's work to be done.'

'I've done my share of the daily grind,' his father said, slipping further down into his armchair. 'It's my hard graft that puts a roof over our heads. Isn't that right, Eddie?'

Edward didn't know if his father was right or not. All that he cared about was that everything for once seemed to be in order in his little family. That his mother wasn't tense and angry, nor his father sullen and withdrawn. That there was this lightness dancing around the three of them like the shaken-up motes of dust playing in the sunbeams.

'Well, lad, what do you say?' his father insisted. 'Who paid for that Meccano set you got for your birthday? Or the shoes on your feet? Your father with his diligence and sense of responsibility, that's who. Diligence and responsibility. That's what makes the world go round. Your father's hard grind.'

Edward knew his father's hard grind involved working in a shipping office on Clydeside. He'd been taken down once for a visit, recalling all those clerks on their high stools, running fingers down ledgers, inking in details here and there, while his father supervised from a desk at the far end of the long room. Then being escorted on a tour of one of the giant cargo ships by a large, tanned man with an easy laugh and gold braid on his sleeves, helping his mother up the steep steps with a palm to her elbow.

'Do all Japanese women dress like this?' Edward asked.

'Och. Are you still going on about that wee sword? Aye, so I believe. That's how they dress over there. In Japan.'

Japan. If Edward ever reflected on his childhood, it was the only word he could actually hear his father saying in his aural memory. Of course, there had been many conversations between them, pleasant ones mostly, for his childhood had been a happy one until the shadow of the Second World War appeared. But these conversations were all vague noises to him, more a recollection of the overall sound of his father's voice rather than any particular words said. Yet the word 'Japan' remained intact as an entity unto itself, a vocal insect trapped in an amber of sound. He could recall the exact tone and timbre in which it was articulated. Japan. A baritone with a Scottish burr roughed up at the edges by tobacco and malt. Japan. This clue. This signpost. As if his father's sole existence in this world was to no more purpose than to point him eastwards with this one word.

Japan. The name of that country had meant nothing to him at the time. A group of islands on the right-hand side of the map that hung in his school classroom. It was not coloured pink like the rest of the Empire, but remained unshaded, anonymous, like the large mass that was China. In fact, Edward thought Japan was part of China until a small part in the chorus of a school production of *The Mikado* opened him up to a world of Lord High Executioners, Celestial Highnesses, women with knitting needles in their hair, schoolgirls with names like Yum-Yum, Pitti-Sing and Peep-Bo.

This participation in *The Mikado* was just one of the benefits of his senior secondary school. At eleven years old, he had been streamed away from an education by belt and Bible, deemed 'excellent at English' and eligible to spend five years pursuing a Leaving Certificate and the possibility of a university education. It was a time for studying, reading newspapers, listening to the radio as the Germans marched on Europe. And suddenly Japan was there too. And this Japan had a face, but it wasn't the face of three little maids all contrary, come from a ladies' seminary with knitting needles through their hair. This was a cruel face. Fuelled by comic books and newspaper propaganda. He trembled as these Oriental warriors in their airplanes sunk His Majesty's warships, as they scurried through Hong Kong, Malaya, Singapore, Sumatra, Borneo, Ceylon and Burma. The map was changing colour. The pink-shaded countries of Australia and India were threatened. And he was threatened too. As the Japanese and Germans advanced so did his age towards enlistment. Passing time closed around him like a death, like the nights of the dark winter of 1944. But then, there was light. The Germans were in retreat, the British recaptured Mandalay and Rangoon, the American forces landed in Okinawa. And then there was blinding, extraordinary light. Followed by a terrifying heat, branding its victims with its deathly radioactive shadow. First Hiroshima. And then Nagasaki.

The news then was all about numbers, numbers, numbers. Edward heard them tumbling from the radio every night in that disembodied voice. First there were those numbers coming out of Europe. Those many millions. And now these numbers from Japan. When did a number just become a number and no longer a human being? After ten, twenty, a hundred deaths?

'How can we kill so many people?' he asked his father. His mother had gone to lie down with the splitting headache that always seemed to coincide with the evening news.

'We didn't kill anyone, lad. It was Truman and the Yankee bombers that did it.' His father tapped his pipe hard on the wooden chair-arm as if to drive a wedge right through the wartime alliance.

'But they're talking about over one hundred thousand dead. In five days. Almost all civilians.'

'It'll bring the war to a swift end, you'll see. Save the lives of countless American soldiers. And Japs too.'

'But that would have been in combat,' Edward protested. 'This was just… I don't know… a… a massacre. A massacre of innocent people.'

'You're just over-sensitive to these things, Eddie,' his father said kindly. 'Just like your mother.'

'But…'

His father raised a hand to stop him. 'Those bombs could have saved your life too, lad. In far-off Asian places. You'll be old enough to enlist in a couple of months. Your mother and I will be glad if we don't have to worry about that.'

His father was right. The war in the Pacific ended six days later.

Edward went on to take an MA degree at the University of Glasgow, with no more imagination or ambition other than to be an English teacher. He was quite happy to set the rudder of his career firmly on course with his parents' expectations, not realising he had any desires to the contrary nor any choice in the matter until he and his father were called to the reading of his late Uncle Rob's will.

'I still dinnae understand what this is all about,' his father grumbled. 'Rob's got a fine family of his own to be his legal heirs and descendants.'

'Perhaps he's left you a keepsake, father. A memory of your childhood together.'

'To tell you the truth, lad, your Uncle Rob had more of a fondness for you than he did me, his own younger brother. Maybe it was because he only had lassies of his own.'

Edward had really liked his uncle – a towering, tree-trunk of a man with sunny cheeks and a flat cap of sandy hair. A rugby fanatic, always with a sweet in his pocket for his young nephew and a word of advice about getting a decent education. His uncle had also been a traveller in his younger days, setting off for the Orient at a time when Edinburgh was the furthest east most Glasgow men ever went. He had returned armed with a network of Asian contacts that he later leveraged into a highly successful trading company. He also brought back with him an eclectic collection of artefacts. There had been the ivory knife, of course, several miniature toggle-like carvings, cloisonné vases, lacquer bowls and a series of Japanese woodblock prints. Some of these prints Uncle Rob had hung up on his study wall – actors on the kabuki stage, beautiful courtesans running combs through their hair, birds perched on cherry blossom branches. But others he kept in a drawer.

'I see you have to shave the hair off your chin,' his uncle had commented after a rare invitation to join him in his study. 'That means you're old enough.'

'Old enough for what, uncle?'

'These.' And he had unlocked the drawer, taken out a folder wrapped up in a silk cloth, spread the prints across his desk. 'Just dinnae tell your Aunt Cathy.'

Edward had just stood there staring. He knew his cheeks had flamed up but his embarrassment had not been enough to drag his eyes away from what lay in front of him. Naked women bathing, naked women pouring water over each other, naked women douching themselves between their legs. Women with breasts poking out slyly from beneath robes, a fully clothed courtesan pulling on a naked man's penis. He had to press his groin against the desk to hide his own erection.

'Just a taste of what's in store,' Uncle Rob had sighed. 'Oh, how I envy the young.'

A heart attack had now taken his uncle at fifty-five, leaving his Aunt Cathy a widow with two married daughters. Edward wondered what she would think when she found the prints.

'What we have here is a substantial legacy bestowed upon your son for the purposes of his education,' announced Mr Wilson Guthrie, Practitioner of Law at the legal firm of Guthrie, Henderson & Co.

'He's already finished his education,' his father said.

'Is that true, Edward?' Guthrie asked, whirling in his swivel chair to confront him across the large desk. 'Is that true?' the man persisted, as if somehow his father's word was not to be believed. 'Is that true?'

'Yes it is, sir. I graduated with an honours degree from Glasgow University. And I just completed a year at teacher training college. I already have a teaching position lined up.'

'I see,' Guthrie snapped. 'Well, the instructions are very specific. And as executor to your late uncle's estate, I must ensure that funds can only be released in response to receipts issued entirely relating to your educational process.'

'But my brother wrote this will years ago. When Edward was still at school. Surely he would have intended the money to go to him anyway. If he was aware the lad had completed his education.'

'That may well be true, Mr Strathairn. But intention is of no relevance in the case of wills and testaments. Only the written or printed word as authenticated by the testator in the presence of two witnesses.'

'Very Dickensian,' his father grunted. 'And so what will happen to the legacy?'

'It will be returned to the estate and re-distributed among your late brother's family.'

'Excuse me, sir,' Edward said. 'May I suggest something?'

Both his father and the lawyer turned to look at him.

'Go on,' Guthrie grumbled.

'What would happen if I should want to continue my education?'

'Then I shall be obliged to release the funds to you,' the lawyer conceded in a stare over his spectacles. 'Provided, of course, I receive the necessary receipts.'

And in his own distorted reflection, mirrored by a slant of light in the lawyer's spectacles, Edward recognised this moment for what it was. A moment of great clarity. It was like taking part in one of those colour blindness tests when everything appeared as a mass of strange blobs and then, out of the panic of the challenge, a number finally emerged. The truth. There it was all along. How could he not see it? Waiting to be discovered by someone with the correct vision. And here in this solicitor's office, it was not any great decision he had to make, but merely to admit to himself what was obvious. What had been there all along.

'In that case, I will go back to university.'

'To do what?' Guthrie asked.

'Japanese studies.'

'Japanese studies?'

'Yes, sir,' Edward said, even more convinced of the rightness of his decision. Although he had no idea where he might study such a subject.

Guthrie leaned forward on his desk. 'I don't think such studies are appropriate for a young citizen of the British Isles.'

'What do you mean?'

'The Japs. They were our enemy. I know people who fought over there. Perhaps French studies might be more suitable?'

'I thought I only needed to provide the necessary receipts.'

'What about Chinese studies? Or African? Or South American? What do you think, Mr Strathairn?'

'I think the young lad should do whatever he damn well pleases.'

CHAPTER THREE

Hakone, Japan • 2003

A gentle prodding roused him.

'Ah, Takahashi-san. I must have drifted off.'

The hotel manager stepped back a pace, almost stumbling on one of the uneven slabs laid around the pond. He then bowed deeply with an enviable flexibility. He held a tartan blanket over his arm.

'I am sorry to disturb you, Sir Edward. But Ms Blythe asked me to find you. Actually, she asked me to tell a bellboy to find you but I thought I would come personally. I was concerned it might be a little chilly for you out here in the garden.'

'That is very considerate of you.'

'But I see you are wearing your coat.'

'Yes, yes. Now tell me. Is there a message?'

'Professor Fisk called. Ms Blythe said it was urgent.'

'Ah yes, of course. Fisk.'

Edward struggled up from his stone perch, fumbled for his cane and followed the manager back towards the main building. Every so often, Takahashi would pause and point.

'There we have some azaleas, Sir Edward. Such a beautiful early season blossom when it arrives. We will have a tapestry of pinks, reds, yellows and whites here in the garden. Japan is famous for its azaleas.'

And when, breathless, Edward had caught up yet again with the manager, he was told: 'And over there, our wonderful orchard of cherry trees. It is so merry to sit under the pink blossom in the springtime.'

It was with this stop-start procession of botanical inspection they finally reached reception together.

'You may call from over there,' Takahashi said, pointing to a wooden booth in the foyer. 'It will save you returning to your room. And perhaps we can meet later for our chat?'

'Our chat?'

'About the old days.'

Edward took the paper with Fisk's number on it. 'I see. That little chat. After dinner, perhaps.'

'A drink in the bar? We stock a selection of the finest Scottish malts. As well as the hotel's own excellent blend.'

'That sounds fine. Now if you will just excuse me.'

Takahashi smiled, then bowed. 'I will look forward to it very much. There is so much to review.'

Edward remembered the booth from his first visit when it was the only pubic telephone in the building. The whole structure was made of teak, matching the panelling, flooring, desks and stairway in the rest of the reception area. The door boasted one of those concertina designs and as with the closet in his room, the light went on as soon as he folded open the panels. A smell of fresh polish. He settled himself against a stout shelf stacked with directories, set aside his cane, propped his spectacles on his nose. A glass-encased noticeboard displayed cards for local restaurants and taxi firms as well as a small poster in English for the Hakone Open-Air Museum:

"In an incomparable natural setting blessed by sun and magnificent beauty, visitors to the museum can enjoy the enthralling experience of viewing sculptural art combined with spectacular scenery. Founded in 1969, the museum features 26 works by the English sculptor Henry Moore as well as the Picasso Pavilion with exuberant paintings, ceramics, sculptures and tapestries by one of the 20th century's greatest artists."

'Ah yes, exuberant paintings,' Edward muttered to himself. 'How wonderful to be back.' He then read out the number as he dialled. The line connected, then a male voice.

'*Moshi, moshi.*'

Hard to make out if the accent was American or Japanese. 'Is that Professor Fisk?'

'This is Professor Fisk. My God. Eddie. Is that you?'

'Yes, it is. I can't believe I found you.'

'Well, your secretary did a good job tracking me down.'

'Sherlock Holmes has nothing on Enid once she's got her mind set. And you're still here.'

'Remember what you used to say, Eddie? If you start bowing when you're talking on the phone, it's time to leave. Well, I ain't bowing yet.'

'Did you marry a Japanese girl? Was that it?'

'Once upon a time.'

'I see. And you got your professorship? What was your thesis again? Language versus culture? Something about verbs at the ends of sentences?'

'Well remembered. That was a long time ago. In my idealistic days. I'm mostly retired now, of course. But I'm still on the university board. A literature class here and there. Small office on campus. Keeps me off the streets, away from the hostess bars.' A deep chuckle. 'And you're back at the old hotel?'

'It's hardly changed a bit.'

'But you have. I heard they made you a knight of the realm. Do I have to kneel when I meet you?'

'Something like that.'

Another chuckle. 'So, Eddie, everything is organised.'

'Organised for what?'

'The ceremony.'

'What ceremony?'

'You're kidding me? I made all the arrangements with your secretary.'

Edward leaned against the door and suddenly the light went out. 'Damn this contraption.'

'What's happening there?'

'Nothing, nothing.' He pulled the door slightly ajar until the light came back on. 'I don't recall any ceremony. Enid arranged for us to have lunch tomorrow in Tokyo. That was all.'

'Eddie. My university is giving you a doctorate.'

'For God's sake, Jerome. You are ruining everything.'

'Ruining what? What am I ruining, Eddie?'

'This is supposed to be a private visit.'

'Look, I busted a gut arranging this ceremony at such short notice. You must have been told?'

A slight panic washed over him then passed, leaving him with a tinge of nausea. He could almost feel his blood struggle for passage through his hardened veins. He opened the door a little further. 'I don't know. Perhaps I was.'

'Listen, Eddie. There's no need to worry. It will be an informal affair. Twenty faculty, tops. Some of my senior literature students. The dean will mumble a few words about your contribution to Japanese culture. Give you a scroll. Probably a cloisonné bowl as well. That's what they usually present to distinguished guests. Then we'll grab a few slices of sashimi from the buffet and be off. Mission accomplished. Say you'll do it, Eddie. It's all arranged. Lots of face to be lost if you don't.'

'All right, all right. But will we have time to talk?'

'Sure we will. Now I've arranged for a cab to pick you up at ten tomorrow morning to whisk you down to Odawara station. I've also made a reservation for you on the Shink. I sent the tickets to the hotel. I'll meet you at the Tokyo end.'

'The Shink?'

'The Shinkansen. The bullet train. After your time. Hold on to your hat, Eddie, or whatever you knights wear. Forty minutes and you'll be in Tokyo. I'll see you then.'

Edward replaced the receiver. Typical Jerome Fisk. From just this one short conversation, he felt both irritated and warmed by him, and realised that was exactly how the man used to make him feel all those years ago. He opened the door of the booth, raised himself on his cane.

'Where is Ms Blythe?' he asked Takahashi at reception. 'Where is that woman?'

'She is waiting for you in the dining room.'

He stood at the entrance trying to locate her. The place was packed, yet the conversation was elegantly muted, softened by the thick linen tableware and the tapestries hanging from the ceiling. During his previous stay, the diners had been almost all foreigners, mainly American, with evening dress de rigueur. This used to be the only hotel in Japan, apart from perhaps the Frank Lloyd Wright-designed Imperial in Tokyo, where a visitor could find borsht, bouillabaisse, turkey curry and ox tongue on the menu. Now, he saw it was the expensively tailored Japanese who dominated the guest list. Only a few well-heeled overseas tourists could afford to visit Japan these days.

A waiter spotted him and guided him over to where Enid sat. A table by the window, tucked away from the rest of the guests.

'Ah, Sir Edward,' she said, pouring out a glass of water for him. 'Takahashi found you then.'

'I just spoke to Fisk. He says he's organised some degree ceremony for me at the university. Why didn't you tell me?'

'I arranged for you to meet him for lunch. That was all.'

'He told me he made the arrangements with you.'

'He did no such thing.'

'Are you sure?'

'Of course, I'm sure. Why would you think…?'

'I'm sorry. The sly bastard.'

'You didn't agree, did you?'

'What could I do? He said it was all arranged.'

'I'll call him to cancel.'

'No, don't do that. I would really like to see him. Perhaps it won't be so bad. He said it was only an informal affair. A few faculty and some students. What harm is there in that?'

'There could be press. We need to be so careful.'

'Possibly a photographer from the university. These kind of events are always recorded. But the Japanese media? I don't think so. They probably think I died years ago.'

'Oh, I'm sure that's not the case.'

'Well, let's hope it is.' He glanced out of the window. *My goodness. This is my table. This is where I always used to sit. How could they possibly know that?*

This landscape was different from the wilder garden where the waterwheel stood. Here the trees and bushes were trained and sculpted to form a restful backdrop to the large pool in the centre. Tiny lanterns were strung along a wire across the pond while shaded electric lamps guarded the stone steps and the path that ran from the main hotel building, along the side of the water then up towards the annexe. It was here Sumiko would come laden with linen as she moved between the laundry and the guest rooms. She would never turn to look at him, although it must have been obvious to her he was there, and he wondered now if these journeys were orchestrated to occur exactly during his mealtimes.

'Sir Edward,' Enid said gently. 'The waiter is here. Would you like to order?'

He decided to postpone his desire for raw fish and pickles, opted for something more digestible, an omelette and a glass of white wine. But halfway through his meal, he experienced that disembodied feeling that comes with jet lag, as if his soul was still somewhere up in the stratosphere trying desperately to catch up with his body. He put down his cutlery, wiped his mouth with his napkin, pushed himself up from his chair.

'You must excuse me, Enid.'

'Is there something wrong?'

'I'm fine. Please sit back down and finish your meal.'

The corridor was less stuffy and he felt his nausea pass. He decided to return to his room. As he walked, he noticed that the walls of this passageway were lined with another array of photographs of illustrious guests. This time it was John Lennon, in white suit and those tiny round tinted glasses, standing in the entrance hall with Yoko. And there was Thatcher. Stepping out of her limousine, clutching her ever-present handbag, her nose sailing in front of her as if to sniff the appropriateness of her appointed accommodation.

He reached the end of the corridor, opened the bedroom door. The light was already on and he was amazed to see a young Japanese woman in red bra and panties standing by the bedside, stepping awkwardly into a slip. Her long hair hung like a dark curtain over her face as she attempted the manoeuvre. Strange, he thought. He had never seen Sumiko wear red underwear before. He was about to say something but the woman looked up at him and then her mouth contorted to make some kind of noise. A strange gasping sound emerged. A half-dressed elderly Japanese gentleman came out of the bathroom, his skinny legs snaking naked from beneath his shirt. The man began to shout at him. First in Japanese, then in English.

'What are you doing here? What do you want?'

'I might ask the same question.' Edward tapped out his indignation with his cane. 'This is my room. The Fuji Suite.'

'Then it is your mistake. This is the Flower Palace.'

'The Flower Palace? I insist this is the Fuji Suite.'

'Then I insist you read the sign.'

Edward half-closed the door, checked the ceramic plaque but didn't recognise the *kanji* for 'Fuji'. 'Oh. I see. A confusion on my part. My profound apologies.' He took one more look at the young woman. Her legs were crouched and crossed. Like a fawn, he thought. She held the slip to her breast. Trembling. She was quite beautiful.

Back out in the corridor, he turned one way, then the other. The blood beat heavy in his left temple, he could feel the perspiration start to film on his forehead. This was ridiculous. He tried another door. A laundry cupboard. Another. A fire escape. He turned back on himself, hastening along the corridor on his cane until he reached a junction of passageways. A sign. He took out his spectacles. 'Reception'. He didn't want to return there in this flustered state. Another sign. 'Dining Room'. He was back to where he had started. This was no use. An armchair. He sat down, sunk back into the comfortable cushions, closed his eyes, waited for his breathing to settle. An acidic fluid rose in his throat. The taste of milky egg. He swallowed.

'*Ano… Daijyobu desu-ka?* Are you all right?'

He opened his eyes. A porter.

'Yes, yes. My room. The Fuji Suite. Where is it? Fuji? *Doko desu-ka?*'

The porter pointed to the door next to where he sat.

'How silly of me. Of course. *Arigato, domo.*'

He rose from his chair, opened the door. The curtains had been drawn, the bedspread turned down, a lamp conveniently left on for his return. He saw his reflection in the wardrobe mirror. The strands of thinning hair matted to his scalp. His complexion so pale. Stains of sweat on the edge of his shirt collar. Such a fine bespoke suit, crumpled now in his shrinking frame. His mind flirted with the image of the young Japanese woman in her red lingerie. What have I become, he thought? What have I become?

CHAPTER FOUR

London, England • 1952

Uncle Rob's inheritance provided Edward with a well-furnished flat in Bloomsbury, not far from Russell Square and his new college, the School of Oriental and African Studies. From one floor up over a busy junction, looking down on to a shop selling shooting sticks, canes and umbrellas, he could watch the store's clientele, almost always elderly gentlemen, indulge in the same routine as they emerged with their new purchases. A swift tap on the pavement to test the resilience of the tip, a sweep of the head to take in the gaze of an imaginary audience, a neat turn of the heels, then a purposeful stride towards the intended destination to the beat of hard rubber on concrete. It seemed the nation's gentry was turning itself into an imitation of the cane-wielding Churchill as it leaned yet again on the Prime Minister for support.

For the King was dying. In Glasgow, Edward had considered the monarch a remote figure, but here in London, with Buckingham Palace only a mile away, the royal presence was palpable. He could see it in those loyal subjects who crept around the capital like worried relatives pacing a downstairs room, their conversations reduced to whispers. He could see it in everyday commerce as customers and shopkeepers alike handled the coins and postage stamps bearing the head of their sovereign with a deliberate reverence. In cinemas he stood with the audience at the end of each evening performance to sing the anthem and to murmur prayers in wish of a miraculous recovery. And in the daily newspapers he read the dramatic bulletins plotting the cancerous decay of the one remaining lung.

Amid this London gloom, he established a daily routine, his own personal square within the capital, marked out on each of its corners by his flat, his college, the Reading Room at the British Museum, and his local pub, the White Lion. For routine was the legacy of the only child – that filling in of the spaces where a sibling might have been.

At college, he took weekly classes consisting of Gramophone Drill, Structure of the Spoken Language, Speech Work and Romanised Texts. There was also course work on the history of Japanese literature, a discussion class in Japanese, an introduction to Shinto and Confucianism. The Reading Room was where he took refuge from this onslaught of oriental language and thought. And whether it was because of his own loneliness or the sense of misery pervading the capital, he found himself writing poetry for the first time. Reams of it. As if he were compelled to find expression for his own language amid the Chinese characters and Japanese alphabets that crowded for attention within his head. From the Reading Room it was on to the White Lion for a warm pint in front of the hearth, with a copy of the Evening Standard at his elbow. It was a solitary existence. He had made few acquaintances among his fellow students, none he could call a friend. But he was used to being content enough with his own company.

The King's death came almost as a relief from the monotony of his daily existence. Not the surrender to cancer as the nation had expected but a heart attack in the royal sleep after a day's hunting. Edward was amazed at the spontaneous reaction of the public. Drivers stopped their cars, got out and stood at attention beside their vehicles. People wept openly in the streets. Flags drooped to half-mast. Hotels and restaurants closed. Shop owners took down their more colourful displays. Even the Thames appeared to run more sluggish. He went to watch the newsreels showing the grieving but dutiful daughter boarding an aeroplane in Uganda as a princess, ready to return to London as a queen. The pictures – in black and white – possessed a whiteness he had never seen before. The whiteness of an African sun preceding the darkness of a mournful London. He would never forget the princess that day – her transformation from a daughter of the people to the mother of the nation. After all, she was only one year older than he was.

King George VI was to lie in state for three days in Westminster Hall, a quirk of protocol that would allow his ordinary subjects far more physical proximity to the royal personage in death than in life. It was this accessibility rather than any real feeling for the deceased monarch that persuaded Edward to go to pay his respects. But he was sadly unprepared for the enormity of the event. The queues stretched for miles. Newspaper pictures would show them as a mournful and respectful bunch, tens of thousands of them shuffling patiently along the bridges and streets of the capital in the persistent drizzle under a carapace of umbrellas. But in reality the mood was quite cheerful. Some of the mourners boasted about their attendance at the lying in state of the King's father. Others had filed past the coffin of Edward VII in 1910. One old biddy reminisced about the death of Queen Victoria. There was gossip about whether the Duke of Windsor would return from America. A boisterous coach party of pensioners from Leeds, all wearing black armbands, assembled behind him, passed around meat paste sandwiches and thermos flasks of hot tea, offered for Edward to share.

After six hours the procession reached the final corner and he could see the entrance to the Great Hall. Heads around him suddenly sank at the view, hands folded into a clasp, the chattering ceased. At the grand doorway, uniformed ushers paired off the mourners.

'Are you on your own?'

Edward looked up. A young woman about his own age. She was wrapped up warm and pretty in a dark green coat, matching beret and leather gloves. He had noticed her before, standing a few rows ahead of him, chatting easily to those around her, tossing back her head in a wide-mouthed laugh at various comments. He heard her accent now. Of course. American.

He nodded.

'Good. We need to enter in twos. Just like Noah's Ark.' A quick smile, then she drew in beside him, two or three inches shorter than himself, her gloved hand so close he felt he could grab it if he wanted to. Just the thought of that contact – the comfort and warmth that lay so near – highlighting the coldness and loneliness of his everyday life. She bowed her head as did he, their misty breath mingling in the air in front of them. The line shuffled forward and she was pushed closer to him, close enough to smell her flowery perfume mixed with the damp rising off her coat. He felt they could be a couple of newly-weds, she recently pregnant, deciding to call the child George if it were a boy, Elizabeth for a girl, both quietly happy in the thought of this, their own personal contribution to mark this historic event. Moving forward again, he could now see into the Great Hall. He heard her gasp.

They stood at the entrance to a vast medieval building with just its one precious exhibit on display – a guarded coffin on a central dais, resting on top of a catafalque draped in purple velvet. Clusters of lights hung on long chains from the oak-beamed ceiling, casting a ghostly aura over the hall. Four long tapers struggled to illuminate the dais. Colour splashed from the velvet, the uniforms of the guards, the Union flag over the coffin, but otherwise all else was stony grey. The scene was from a royal age when monarchs ruled from draughty castles with steely armour, a testament to the warring heritage that had flowed through this dead king's chilled blood. Slowly, they descended the stone steps, bunching up with those in front, footfalls echoing in the cold, colder than the outside air, colder than death itself. They filed along the edge of the hall, reaching the mid-point, turning to face the coffin, just a few seconds allowed for Edward to absorb the tableau. A large jewelled cross at one end of the coffin, then along the flag-draped lid lay the King's crown, orb and sceptre. Four Royal Life Guards stood at each corner of the coffin, heads and shoulders drooping from the long vigil. And then one step lower down four Yeomen with their pikes, Edward bowed his head. The young woman beside him dipped in a slight curtsy.

Big Ben struck six o'clock. The drizzle had stopped and the other mourners dispersed quickly along the wet pathways. Back to a London life that continued to trundle along despite this dead heart at its centre. Edward lingered self-consciously at the exit of the Great Hall with this young woman Fate had selected for him to share in this historic moment. She was pretty. So very pretty.

'Wow,' she said. 'You could feel the power of your country's royal heritage back there. All those centuries of monarchy stacking up behind that body.'

'Yes, it was impressive,' he managed, clearing his throat. The first words he had spoken for hours. Perhaps for days. 'I didn't think you could still see that kind of thing in this day and age.'

She said nothing. Instead, she took off her beret, shook out her dark, shoulder-length hair, combed through the waves with her fingers. He shivered, stamped his feet, searched for his voice, searched for courage.

'Look,' he said. 'It's been a long day. I don't know... would you like to have a cup of tea somewhere?'

She appeared unfazed by his request, looked him up and down, mouth pursed tight in contemplation. He was about to apologise for his forwardness when she said: 'Something stronger would be nice.'

He took her to the White Lion. Almost bounced along the streets with her as they walked. She told him her name. Macy.

'My parents met in the New York department store,' she explained.

'I'm glad they didn't meet in Marks and Spencer. Or Fortnum's.'

She laughed. That same gutsy, confident laughter he had heard in the queue. He felt immensely pleased with himself.

He found an empty table, tucked away at the rear of the pub, close to the fire. Sean, the barman, looking over his shoulder at Macy as he poured their drinks, his little moustache twitching with curiosity.

'You're a sly one,' Sean said.

'We've just met.'

'All the same. Had you marked down as a loner.'

'Probably still will be after the evening's out.'

'That's not the attitude to take.' Sean tapped the side of his forehead with a nicotine-stained finger. 'Got to think positive. That's the secret. Trap the successful capture of your prey as an image inside of your head. Imagine that you've won even before the game has started. That's what the army taught me.'

'It's not a war I'm fighting here.'

'That's what you think.'

Macy had taken off her coat. Half-turned her chair so she could warm her hands by the fire. She was wearing a cream silk blouse and black knee-length skirt. A simple pearl necklace. Elegant. Too elegant for him, he feared. He slopped some beer on to the table as he laid down the glasses. Back again to Sean for a cloth and some sarcastic comment before he could settle down.

'Is this your usual pub then?' she asked, cheeks reddening in the firelight.

'I live just two doors down.'

'Handy.' She searched her handbag, found a packet of cigarettes. Winston. With one of these new filter tips. She offered him one.

He shook his head. 'Are you staying in London?'

'Near Grosvenor Square,' she said as she lit her cigarette. 'My father works at the American Embassy. My mother stayed in the States but I thought I'd come over with him. Try to do some painting. An American in London, that's me.'

'Oh?'

'You know. Like the movie with Gene Kelly and Leslie Caron. *An American in Paris.*'

'Never heard of it.'

'Maybe it hasn't come over yet.' She smoothed down her skirt over her knee. 'I'm not always like this.'

'What do you mean?'

'This outfit. I did it for the King. I thought it would be appropriate.'

'I don't think he noticed.'

She laughed. 'I meant that I'm a sweater and jeans kind of girl. Thought you should know, that's all.'

He shrugged. 'I don't pay much attention to fashion. Too wrapped up in my studies.'

'So what was the visit to Westminster then?' A long drag on her cigarette, purses of smoke released to the air. 'A night out on the town?'

It was his turn to laugh. And then he dared to say on the first rush of alcohol to his head: 'I did get to meet you.'

'You certainly know how to flatter.'

He had no idea how to flatter. He had gone to an all-boys grammar school. His first year at university had been spent in a daze at actually having female students right there with him in the lecture rooms. Later on, he had managed a few heavy petting sessions at parties and rag balls, one girl masturbating him until he ejaculated inside his trousers. He was more embarrassed than relieved by the event, eventually finding a handkerchief so she could wipe her hands clean. He never saw her again. He was still a virgin, with all the blood of his sexual interest preferring to flush his cheeks rather than to fortify his penis.

She stubbed out her cigarette in an ashtray, quickly lit another, her fingers moving with a fussy energy, the painted nails scratched clean here and there. Her head leaned in towards him, elbow on the table, chin cupped in her hand. Brown eyes, flecked with bronze. Dark smudges of tiredness below the rims. The sleeve of her blouse slipping down slowly off her wrist, letting the silky down of her bare forearm flicker in the firelight. 'What about you?' she asked. 'Who are you?'

Edward thought that if he had been a spy, he would have confessed everything to her there and then. Take all the documents, the names, the codes, the microfilms. The secret radio. The frequencies. Just be my lover. Please be my lover. Instead he told her about his studies with an enthusiasm he hadn't previously believed he possessed. He spoke about the intriguing formality of the Japanese language. The ephemeral quality of beauty in *The Tale of Genji*. The witty delight of Sei Shonagon's court diaries from *The Pillow Book*. How the simple poetry of the *haiku* could compress the essential qualities of nature into a few syllables.

'That's what I like the most,' he gushed, caught up in his own excitement, in her apparent interest. 'The subtle awareness. The attention to detail. Just look at *shodo*, the calligraphy. All that intense energy. Concentrated on a single brushstroke.'

She ran a finger through a small pool of beer, tracing her own private design on the tabletop. 'I like to see passion in a man,' she said, looking down at her handiwork.

He reddened to the comment, hastily gulped down the rest of his beer, not sure if she was referring specifically to him or just to any male of the human race.

'My father spent a few years in Tokyo,' she continued. 'He expects great things from the Japanese. He says they are absorbing all things American, refining them with their own aesthetic, then selling them back to the West. They've already started with the shipping industry. Manufactured items will follow next. He believes the Japanese economy is set to boom.'

'I hope he's right,' he said, relieved the conversation had turned to more practical matters. 'I was thinking of a job in international commerce after I've finished.'

'Smart thinking. Most young men in your situation choose the diplomatic corps.'

He broke off the conversation to fetch another round of drinks, his head already beginning to spin light from the first. Apart from a meat paste sandwich in the queue of mourners, nothing to eat all day. Macy appeared unaffected by her half of bitter, happy to tackle another.

He asked her about her painting. She turned out to be more serious about her art than he had imagined. It was not just a little rich girl's hobby, the diplomat's daughter dipping into bohemia before daddy's trust fund fully kicked in. She had a degree in Art History from some Ivy League university, she was passionate about the new Abstract Expressionism breaking through in the States, spearheaded by the man she cited as her greatest influence – Jackson Pollock.

'He just spreads his canvas on the floor, drips his paints on to the surface direct from the can,' she explained. 'Action painting. No composition. No relationship between parts. Just the pure expression of the artist's unconscious mood. No space between the self and the work. It's angry. Aggressive. Arrogant. Screaming to be heard.'

He watched her as she talked. Red-painted lips animated over those so-white, even tributes to American dentistry. Her arms open, describing Pollock's techniques, pulling slightly at the silk of her blouse, revealing just a peek of bra strap, the shadow of cleavage.

'I wonder how similar they are,' he said.

'What? Who?'

'These artists on canvas. This Pollock with his abstract expressionism on the one hand. And the Japanese calligrapher on the other.'

'You must be joking. They couldn't be further apart.'

'Don't be so sure. What you describe seems to be very manic, releasing the subconscious through lack of control. Painting without thinking.'

'So?'

'Well, on the face of it, *shodo* seems to be the opposite. Calming the mind until reason and emotion are one, allowing for a deeper spirituality to emerge. Yet both are about truth. One is truth achieved through a state of agitation. While the other is achieved through a state of calmness. The difference between Western and Oriental thought perhaps.'

Macy sat back in her chair, grinning.

'What's so funny?' he asked.

'Well, first I thought you weren't listening. Second, I was ready for you to dismiss Pollock as a madman. But you've got an open mind, Eddie. I can call you Eddie, can't I? Edward is too formal. Too much like that dead king. I like that about you, Eddie. An open mind. And a sensitivity to go with it.' She sucked on her cigarette, then waved away the smoke, clearing the space between them. 'I've got a little exhibition of my work coming up in a week or so. Nothing much. A space in a gallery of a family friend. You should come.'

'Has it lots of dripping paint in it?'

'More like sloshing.'

'Good. I prefer the sloshing.'

'That's exactly what this beer is doing in my stomach. I'm usually a gin and tonic girl.'

'So why the beer?'

'I thought I'd try to impress you.'

His fingers wandered to her cigarette lighter, flicked open the lid, sparked up a flame to the empty air. 'Would you like to get something to eat?'

They picked up two fish and chip suppers in Soho. Her idea. After all she was still an American in London who relished the idea of her food wrapped up in newsprint. He insisted on walking her back to her flat, choosing a route along the broad pavements of Bond Street and Mayfair, past Georgian porticos, windows with flowerboxes, balconies with sawn-off wrought-iron stumps. Consular buildings, luxury hotels, private apartments and gentlemen's clubs. It was a London still confident of its own elegance, deluded by its sense of importance in a post-war world. Clear sky, full moon, dead king, princess pining in the palace, this woman by his side. Feeling it more appropriate in the cold to take her hand than not to, yet still managing to keep apart. The formality of space. Very Japanese. At Grosvenor Square, he had expected the American Embassy to dominate, to be lit up grand like a southern plantation mansion with Uncle Sam rocking back easy on the porch. But the chancery was just the same as the other embassies dotted around Mayfair, hidden away behind the broad doors, brass plates and flagpoles of a block of terraced Georgian houses.

In silence they wandered into the large open square in front of the embassy. A barren space with just a few trees, the scattered survivors of wartime bombings. She directed him towards a statue, standing pale in the moonlight. "Franklin Delano Roosevelt 1882 – 1945". Dressed in his cape, propped up by his cane. Then suddenly, from a corner of this quiet plot of parkland, a figure came hurtling towards them along one of the pathways, surprising them, gliding, too fast, too smooth, to be running. A young man on roller skates.

His torso arched in a forward prow, hands clasped behind his back, scarf trailing in his slipstream, he slid past them and around the statue. Expressionless, the skater executed one loop of the plinth, then another and another, wheels grinding rough on the concrete, passing them each time, performing this private dance for them, wreathing them in some fantastic web before breaking away and disappearing back along the path.

'You can leave me here,' she said, her voice breaking the spell.

'Oh. I thought I'd see you to your flat.'

'Here's fine,' she said. She fumbled in her coat pocket. Found him a flyer, pressed it into his hand, her fingers red from the fry. 'It's my exhibition. Try to come.'

He pulled his coat in tighter. Rocked back and forward on his heels. Noticed her lips greasy and flecked with salt. Two beers and the skater making him feel he might be brave enough to try a kiss.

'I had a nice time, Eddie,' she said, stepping back and away from him. 'Don't spoil it.'

CHAPTER FIVE

Japan • 2003

Edward had arranged a wake-up call with the front desk but it had proved unnecessary. He awoke well before the dawn, remarkably clear-headed for only four hours sleep. As his life became shorter, he slept less and less, until he wondered if there would come a time when he would not require any sleep at all. The achievement of a perpetual state of awakeness, of constant awareness, before the reward of permanent sleep.

A quick shower before sitting down in his robe at the writing desk. He ran his fingers over the mahogany, letting his palms be lightly scored by the corners and edges. The rectangular, olive-leather inlay had been replaced and the space for the inkwell was now sealed off with a circle of wood that just failed to match the original. But he was sure it was the same desk. He turned on the reading lamp, opened up the notebook he had bought for the trip, began to write. No longer fiction, for what stories had he left to tell? But poetry. Just like he used to write in the early London days. Except then he wrote about youth, about love, about hope. Now he wrote about nature. About death and birth. Poetry had become his literary garden of retirement where he pottered about in his withered skin, pruning that branch, choosing to pick that flower, hacking out that stubborn weed. Writing *haiku*.

He paused from his scribblings to watch the day break over the hillside, the sunlight rising to glint on the grey tiles of the hotel's outbuildings, to melt on the dewy branches of the poplar trees. Lights flickered on in the kitchens, steam churned out of the fired-up boilers, giant extractor fans started to whirr. The crisp, oily smell of grilling fish, the baby-milk aroma of boiling rice. Bird tracks on the frosted grass. The cold ring of a temple bell. The waterwheel off in the distance. Life beginning anew. Rebirth. Renaissance. Reincarnation. Such a sense of it, deep in his belly.

Lark tracks scratch the frost
Marching fast away from me
Winter's death tolling.

He ordered a light, Japanese-style breakfast to be delivered to his room. A waiter brought a lacquer tray laden with an array of dishes. Miso soup, sweet omelette, pickles, barley porridge, broiled fish and a pot of green tea. Each in its distinctive, ceramic bowl. He marvelled at the delicious combination of tastes and textures delighting his tongue and palate, each one sparking off a flash of memory, too fast for him to harness in conscious thought before the next one appeared and then also died. And then the next one. Pickled radish. What did that sour yellowed root remind him of? Sugared egg. So quick. Impossible to grasp, these disappearing images from his Japanese past. But the sensation pleasant nevertheless. Until the telephone interrupted this grand fireworks display of fleeting recollections.

'Are you angry with me?' Enid asked.

'Why would that be?'

'I thought you might have joined me for breakfast.'

'I took it in my room. I was writing.'

'Well, then, a taxi has been ordered for ten. The *Shinkansen* tickets are at reception.'

'Oh God. Jerome Fisk and his damned award ceremony. I'd almost forgotten. What about back home?'

'No news is good news.'

'And other stuff?'

'Yes, there's other stuff. The usual requests for your attendance at events I will politely decline. It is the Poet Laureate's birthday though. Would you like me to send something?'

'What do I usually do?'

'Depends on who's *in situ*. This one's new.'

'Well, send him a bottle of malt then. He writes better when he's pissed. Anything else?'

'All quiet on the western front. It's past midnight in the UK. Enjoy your trip to Tokyo.'

By the time he had dressed and was walking along the corridors towards reception, his mood was still upbeat. It was the breakfast that had done it. Enid would have disapproved of the grilled fish. And his bowels were sure to pay for it later. But it was just like eating kippers really. He began humming some vague melody as he walked. A slow, ponderous fugue. He tapped his cane to the beat. As he caught sight of Takahashi in the lobby, he believed the tune was the Japanese national anthem.

'I trust you slept well, Sir Edward,' Takahashi said, breaking off from talking with a staff member to greet him.

'I did indeed.'

Takahashi straightened. Not a strand of his thick, dyed-black hair out of place. 'And did you enjoy your breakfast?'

'A good Scotsman likes to start the day with his kippers.'

'I am afraid I don't understand.'

'Nothing to be afraid of, Takahashi-san. Just my exuberant spirits.'

'I see.' A little cough into a clenched fist, then the manager said: 'I did not recall seeing you in the bar last night.'

'I was feeling slightly unwell. I went to bed early.'

'Perhaps it was jet lag?'

'No doubt.'

'And will you require dinner this evening? On your return from Tokyo?'

'I imagine I will dine in Tokyo.'

'I see.'

The hotel manager lingered.

'There is something else, Takahashi-san?'

'Perhaps you remember our desire to have a little chat?'

'Our desire?'

'About the old days.'

'Yes, yes, of course. Tomorrow. I am sure I can manage some time tomorrow.' Edward looked around the lobby. The door to the telephone booth was open and he could see inside to the glass-encased poster advertising the Hakone Open Air Museum and its exuberant paintings. 'Now where is that damn taxi?'

'It has just this second arrived in the driveway.'

Edward pushed through the revolving doors into the crisp morning air. His dry cheeks felt the chill. He put on his hat. A lone birdcall echoed hollow in the valley with such a sadness it actually pained him. That ache in the centre of his chest. He touched the spot, kept his hand there until the tightness had passed. The taxi driver – a small, chubby man wearing a dark suit and white gloves – quickly stubbed out a cigarette, opened the passenger door. Sheets of white cotton covered the seats. The interior air freshened with aerosol lavender.

The driver took his place, adjusted the electronic screen displaying a map, then began to fuss annoyingly with the buttons on the radio. Channels tripped by on loops of sound and blurry green numbers. A classical music station.

'OK?' the man asked, turning round slowly. His fat neck strained at the tight, bright-white collar. 'OK?'

Edward nodded and sat back happily in his seat. The boundaries had been set. No tortured conversations in primitive English or Japanese. Just pure Mozart.

The taxi began its winding climb down the tree-lined hillside, swinging and swerving through a tunnel of dappled light. The area was famous for its hot springs and every so often the hedges of leaf and timber would clear to allow a glimpse of a driveway dipping down to a spa resort. He recalled a trip with Sumiko to one of these *onsens.* Twenty-four hours of sleeping, soaking and making love until his body had dissolved into a hot, rubbery mass.

After about twenty minutes, the road eased out, straightened, broke away from the wooded slopes towards Odawara. What he remembered as a simple, tiled-roof town noted for its plum trees and medieval castle had now become engulfed by urban blight. Japan poured more concrete than any other nation on earth, and here it showed. Concrete river beds, road bridges, rail bridges, hillside buttresses constructed against potential landslides, all waited patiently on the plain, knowing the time would come soon enough to spread their tentacles of cement upwards into the hills.

'*Odawara no eki*,' the driver announced, leaning his head back but keeping his eyes on the road.

'Ah yes. The station.'

Edward felt the extra buzz as he stood on the elevated platform, set above the comings and goings of the ordinary trains below. Everything up here was more streamlined – the uniforms, the benches, the signs, the kiosks – as if their designs and architectural lines had been pressure-moulded by the passing trains. For the Tokaido bullet train stopped here. The Shink. The tracks began to hum. A fluttering in his stomach. Good to know that there were still experiences left in life to excite him. The announcements became more frequent, more frantic. The train was high speed, and so the waiting passengers must be too. Ready to board in seconds. Arched down for a sprint rather than stood up for a middle-distance race. Children were assembled. Luggage stacked with handles sprung upright. Time was at a premium here. Targets had to be met, standards had to be maintained. He tapped his cane around his designated area as the seconds flicked down to arrival. He was prepared. Feeling sprightly. Not the usual aching in his bones. And there was that song again. The Japanese national anthem. Or was it the theme song for the Tokyo Olympics? Dah, dah, da, da, da. A glance down the tracks. It was coming. A rush of displaced air. The metallic-silver wingless Concorde, this beautiful, aerodynamically perfect beast, swooshed into the station. Breathtaking. It slid to a halt in front of him. A carriage door appeared exactly opposite. Number Eight. Corresponding to the number on his ticket. Whoosh. The automatic release of compressed air to open the door. Excellent. Such exactitude in an increasingly chaotic world.

The train took off again before he had time to find his seat. He swayed in the aisle, struggling for balance, searching the overhead sills for his seat number. There it was. A window seat. A middle-aged salary man stinking of hair cream stood up to let him in. Off with the coat. His fellow passenger kind enough to place it on the rack. At last, he could settle. He was looking forward to reacquainting himself with the landscape between Odawara and Tokyo. So much must have changed. Tokyo and its environs back then had been only ten years in recovery since the fire-bombing.

He took out his notebook, ready to record his impressions. But everything flashed by too quickly. He tried to focus on buildings, clusters of trees, fences and fields, follow a car along a country road. But it was hopeless. Just a blur, his eyes sore from the trying. Then a tunnel. Thud. Sudden darkness before the interior lights came on. Pressure forcing the inside wall of the train to squeeze against his shoulder and forearm. His ears clogging.

He practically skipped along the platform at Tokyo station, with hardly a lean on his cane. While his actual body was earthed solid on the concourse, somehow his molecular structure was still vibrating at a rate of one hundred and fifty miles an hour or at whatever speed these trains were capable of. He hadn't felt like this since he was a schoolboy. A June sports day, sprinting free on a hundred-yard dash, blood flowing easily, limbs moving smoothly, lungs clean and fresh, shorts flapping. Parents watching from deckchairs on the sidelines.

He scanned the crowd beyond the barrier. Was that Fisk coming towards him? His hair white now, but still plenty of it. Colour in his cheeks. Looking solid but youthful in a beige sports jacket, grey flannels and grey polo. Like a retired senator with golf as a hobby striding down the fairway. How should he greet this man after all these years? A handshake? A hug? His hand grasped his cane more tightly. Fisk in front of him now, taking the initiative, clutching him tightly by both shoulders as if to show off his vigour. The man's hair was thinner than he had first thought, scalp red and flaky under the white waves. Skin shining, teeth too white to be real. Fisk was a year or two older. But Japan had treated him well. Must be all that raw fish and tofu. Edward used to think it was something in the genes that made them the longest living race on the planet. But it had to be the diet. Definitely the diet. He had never been so lean, his bowels had never worked better, than when he used to live here.

'Eddie. Are you well?'

'What do you mean? Do I look ill or something?'

'No, no, no. I just mean...' Fisk stood back. 'How are you, for God's sake?'

'Not too bad. Considering I have endured both a long-haul flight and a bullet train in the last couple of days.'

Fisk laughed. 'And the cane? You always said you wanted a cane. "When I am old enough for it to be an appendage and not an affectation. Like our illustrious leaders Winston and Franklin D."'

'Did I say that?'

'Sure did. So what is it then?'

'What is what?'

'An appendage or an affectation?'

'It's my hip. I should have had an operation years ago.'

'You gotta attend to these things, Eddie. Or you'll end up hobbling around like an old man.'

'I am an old man.'

'It's all in the mind. I'm older than you are. And look at me.'

He didn't want to look at Fisk. At his precision-pressed flannels and casual deck shoes. At the cashmere collar, flashy wristwatch and expensive dentistry. He just wanted to turn around and head back to the hotel faster than a speeding bullet train. But instead he found himself asking in an enthusiastic tone:

'Now what about this ceremony you've roped me into?'

'We'll talk about that on the way. First, we need to get you up to the next level and out of here. Tokyo is waiting.'

CHAPTER SIX

London • 1952

Edward sat on a bench in Russell Square. He had been writing poetry, pathetic recollections about his first meeting with Macy, but broke off now to read his newspaper. He had been aware for some time of the gentleman who had sat down beside him. Especially since most of the other benches in the square were vacant. He was a well-dressed man of around forty wearing one of these overcoats with a velvet collar, slung about his shoulders like a cape. His hair was slicked back from a widow's peak, pale skin stretched over long cheekbones, displaying the occasional tendril where a deep groove made shaving difficult.

'This country needs a penis substitute,' the stranger said. 'Now there is a young queen on the throne.'

'I'm sorry?'

The man tapped a finger against the headline of Edward's paper. *Government Confirms Atomic Deterrent*. The article featured Churchill's announcement that Britain now possessed the capability to produce an atomic bomb. 'This bomb. A penis substitute, don't you think?'

'Yes, yes. The bomb.'

'I see I have embarrassed you,' the man said, more in observation than in repentance.

'No, sir. I understand what you mean.'

'Good. The King rotting, not yet a fortnight in the ground. And here we are cheerfully boasting of a giant prick for a nuclear deterrent.'

'Churchill blames the last government. He said they started the project. And it was too far gone to stop.'

'I can't believe the old warmonger found it a hard decision to make. I bet the Americans will be pleased.'

'Why is that?'

'Oh. Just that they will have a nuclear ally in the fight for world peace. Now what is your opinion of this… this deterrent?'

Edward eyed up his questioner. 'Well, if these bombs are truly meant to be just deterrents, then why waste all this money building them? We could just pretend to have them. Mock-ups of atomic bombs. Everywhere.'

'Yes, yes. What an excellent idea. Cardboard cut-outs on the beaches and along the cliff-tops. All fenced in. "Danger. Keep out. Nuclear Deterrent." No one would know the difference. I like that.'

The stranger slipped his hand into a coat pocket and brought out a brown paper bag. Rough crusts of bread were cast aggressively across the ground. The response from the pigeons in the square was immediate. Edward turned over from the offending page, leaving his companion to feed the pecking horde at his feet. He noticed the announcement for a new picture starring Gene Kelly. Not Macy's *An American in Paris*, but *Singin' in the Rain*. A gloved hand appeared across the newsprint.

'Aldous.'

Edward shook the offered limb, surprised to feel such a limp grip from such a bold gesture.

Aldous snatched the open notebook off the bench. 'So what do we have here, young man with no name?'

'Please, sir… that is private.'

But Aldous continued to scan the page. 'Writing is not a private matter. We all have some kind of audience in our heads.' He read on, muttering to himself as he went. 'So you want to be a novelist then?'

'It's supposed to be poetry.' He tried to grab back his notebook but Aldous held it out of reach.

'Too much narrative for poetry. Too much like Homer, Virgil and Milton. If you want to tell a damn story, then bloody well write one. Now what is your name and I shall return your property.'

'Edward. Edward Strathairn.'

'Well, Edward Strathairn. There is nothing wrong in dabbling with verse. It is a good way to limber up for novel writing. It gets you in the mood.' Aldous smiled as he handed over the notebook. His teeth were yellowish, like old piano keys. 'Forgive me. You may now have your revenge.'

'And how would I do that?'

'By leaving me.'

The challenge made Edward stay. He pretended to read the newspaper while Aldous tipped out the rest of the crumbs.

'Are you a writer?' Edward asked when the silence between them had become awkward.

'No, I am a reader.'

'Oh.'

'Don't be disappointed. I only mean that I am an editor. Of the illustrious literary magazine known as *The Londinium*. Circulation one thousand, six hundred and forty-three by last reckoning. My meagre offices are across the square.' He waved a hand in the general direction, his thin wrist poking out like a chicken bone between cuff and glove.

'But you write as well?'

'Alas, I am not a masochist, but a sadist. I prefer to slash and burn the work of others. It is more fun. Much more fun. Now what about you?'

'I'm over there,' Edward said, with a nod towards his college on the other side of the square. 'Studying Japanese.'

'So you will join the diplomatic corps then?' Aldous asked, rather disappointingly.

'I was thinking of international trade.'

'Pity. Literary translation might be more satisfying. I hear there is a lot of good writing coming out of Japan these days. Kawabata. Mishima. All needing good translators. Now, if you will excuse me, I must return to my duties. Lesser writers require attention.'

Aldous rose, gave a casual salute, then walked off in the direction of his office. His coat and suit hung loose off his thin frame as he skipped along the pathway, hardly seeming to touch the surface with the soles of his feet. Dancing. Not like Gene Kelly. But like Fred Astaire.

The gallery was in Albemarle Street. Mayfair posh. Large bay window set in an expensive wooden frontage displaying a solitary canvas on an easel. The painting was an abstract. Strong blues, blacks and reds colouring different geometrical shapes. An unsettling yellow eye in the centre. Miro? Edward could see visitors mingling inside. A bell announced his arrival but thankfully no one looked round. The sweat started to creep across his brow and he cursed his haste for not waiting until he had cooled down from his walk. Thick carpet. Waiters with trays. This had to be a private view, not a public exhibition. He was about to leave when he saw Macy pushing towards him.

'You came,' she said, pointing an empty wine glass at him. Her face was flushed, her skin tinged red where her neck and collarbone broke free from the loose strangle of her baggy sweater. Her jeans and canvas shoes were speckled with paint. Very casual compared to the formal attire of the other guests.

'I'm sorry. I didn't realise it was a private party.'

'Don't be so... so... I don't know... so British. You're more than welcome.'

She grabbed his hand. Cool fingers curled around his own damp flesh. He followed her through the clusters of guests hovering, drinking, clinking and chattering around the large canvasses. Such bright colours. Disconnected. Floating. Just as he was in Macy's grasp. They arrived at a triptych of paintings at the far corner of the room.

'What do you think?' she asked.

He detected a vulnerability in her voice that made him want to say something complimentary. Something positive and intelligent about these thick sworls of colour on canvas, these intricate webs of random design. Layer upon layer. Structureless. Aggressive. Drips and splashes. The texture showing him what had been thrown fast, what had been thrown slow. Reminding him of what? Of nothing. Of drips and splashes. He sought assistance from the index card pinned to one side. "Fugue. Nos 1, 2 and 3. M. Collingwood. 1951." No help. Yet this was Macy staring back at him from the canvas. Her mood. Her spirit. Aching from her heart, acting from her uncluttered mind. He suddenly felt himself touched by the honesty, the intimacy, the openness, by this glimpse inside of her.

'Well?' she prodded.

The emotion scraped at his belly, quickly working itself up his throat, swelling into his eyes.

'I love them,' he said, knowing he could just as easily have said, 'I love you.'

He steeled himself for some scathing response to what she surely must regard as a banal comment. She screwed up her eyes, scrutinised him as if she too were searching for what lay inside of him.

'You know, Eddie. I'm really glad you turned up. I really am. Now, come meet my father.'

Ensconced within his coterie, Mr Collingwood stood tall and shiny. Shiny grey-black hair, shiny smooth cheeks, shiny grey double-breasted suit. A good-looking man in that cool, confident, easy, American way. Perfect poster material for Uncle Sam's embassy overseas.

'So you are a friend of my daughter's,' Collingwood said, gimlet-eyed, assessing Edward over the crystal rim of a whisky glass. Then a strong handshake.

Edward tried to return the man's grasp. 'We only just met. At the lying in state.'

'Good. Macy needs to meet new people here. She tells me you are studying the Japanese language.'

'Japanese history and culture as well.'

'I had a stint there during the Occupation. A fine people. Extremely kind. Extremely diligent. My wife hated it there.' Collingwood sent a quick, professional smile towards his daughter. 'So what do you think about her... her stuff?'

'You mean her art?'

'Yes, her art. If that's what you can call it.'

'I love it.'

'Hmmm. Well, it keeps her busy I guess,' he said, before turning back to his circle.

With the man's grip still fresh on his flesh, Edward felt Macy take his other arm, easy as you like, leading him away as if they were newly-weds making the round of their reception guests.

'Don't mind Daddy.'

'I thought he was all right.'

'Liar. He can be a bit sharp. But he doesn't really mean it.'

'All the same...'

'Look, it's nice of you to stand up for me,' she said. 'But you don't need to stay for all of...' She waved a hand around the gallery. 'For all of this. Why don't you go off and have a drink somewhere? I'll meet you outside. Say in about an hour.'

He found a pub nearby, a pint of bitter, a discarded newspaper and a table by the window. He tried to calm himself down, anchor this floating feeling inside of him, swirling and sworling away like those colours on the canvas. He felt alive to these new sensations, not just within himself but all around him. New queen, new art, new friend. Dare he think it? New girlfriend. What he read in the paper confirmed his mood. National identity cards to be abolished, the coronation scheduled for next year. People were now liberated from government supervision, temporarily orphaned from monarchy. An unfettered population capable of great things. London seemed such a delightful, welcoming place now. Through the misty panes, he could see arm-in-arm walks along the embankment, visits to the cinema, picnics in the park. Gene Kelly and Leslie Caron. Singing in the rain.

The fog was coming in thick as he stepped outside the pub. He felt a tug at his sleeve, sensed a shadow slip out of the murkiness.

'Tuppence for a cup of tea. For an old soldier.'

The beggar was dressed in an army greatcoat, one of the sleeves hanging loose where an arm had been. Thin wisps of hair spread across his scalp like winter weeds, eyes jaundiced, imploring him with such a sadness that Edward felt obliged to search his pockets for some change. He gave the beggar what he had asked, received a salute in return. He didn't know why, but the gesture moved him terribly, and he thrust some more coins into the man's open palm.

Macy was a silhouette waiting for him outside the gallery. The same dark green coat and beret from the day at Westminster. Leather satchel off one shoulder.

'I sold a painting,' she said. Her face shone just like her father's.

'You are now an artist.'

'No. I was always an artist. Now I am a painter.'

He laughed. 'What would you like to do?'

'Nothing. Just walk.'

'In this fog?'

'Yes, in this fog.'

Again he felt her arm in his, fingers tightening to claim possession, making him feel warm and wanted from the attention. They were in their own world now, cocooned by the fog, where he could protect her from lampposts, pavement edges, reckless pedestrians, strange shadows emerging into their private space before disappearing again. Hazy orange glows from headlamps, street lamps, torches and table lamps. Cold, sharp voices. People humming or whistling to be heard. Car horns. A bus creeping by, passengers with the faces of the dead staring out at them.

'We're living in exciting times,' he said.

'Yeah, I feel that too. But why do you think so?'

'I think we are finally shaking off the drudgery of the war. People are looking to the future now. With fresh ideas.'

'It's different for you. For you British.'

'Why do you say that?'

'You didn't wipe out two cities with atomic bombs.'

'I never thought the Americans felt too guilty about that.'

'That's the problem. They don't. People like my father feel it was just cause to vaporise tens of thousands of civilians.'

'What about your mother?'

'She could never understand it. That was why she hated Japan. People were killing her with kindness yet she felt so guilty. Anyway, we're here now.'

'Where?'

'Where I live.'

He was amazed to discover there had been a direction to their meandering. Now, he stood in a pillared doorway of what must be a grand Georgian mansion. He could just make out the black-and-white tiled steps.

'I'd like to see you again,' she said, searching in her satchel for a pen. 'Do you have a telephone at your digs?'

He shook his head.

'OK. You can telephone me then.' She wrote down the number on one of her flyers. 'You can find your way back?'

'I think so.'

'Just keep going east. That way.'

Her lips brushed his cheek. Then awkwardly, they were face to face, her eyes darting nervously. Her fingers played with a button of his jacket. He kissed her. It was such a spontaneous action. For if he had thought about it, he would never have done it. But there he was. Kissing her. Full on the mouth. Her lips cold and dry, yet wonderfully pliant. The sensation ethereal. Like wisps of fog.

That brief kiss lingered for days. He thought he could still feel the imprint as he lifted the receiver of the public telephone at the White Lion, fumbled with his coins, pressed button 'A', then 'B' on connection.

'I'm afraid Miss Collingwood is not at home,' said a cool female voice.

He felt a droplet of sweat trickle down his ribcage. 'Do you know when she will be back?'

'I do not have that information. I am only the housekeeper.'

'Will she be back for dinner?'

'That I do not know.'

'Well, when would be a good time to call?'

'That I also do not know. Sometimes she is here. Sometimes she isn't.'

'Can you tell her Eddie called?'

'Is there a number where she can reach you?'

'No, that's the problem. Wait. Give her this number. It is a public telephone at the White Lion. She knows where it is. I will make sure I am here. At nine p.m. Can you tell her to call at nine p.m.?'

'Miss Collingwood knows of such a place?'

'Yes, she does.'

'And you want her to call this White Lion tonight at nine p.m.?'

'Yes. But it doesn't have to be tonight. Any night this week.'

'I will pass on the message.'

The White Lion became his study and his observation post. A table by the fire, the very same table where he had first sat with her. But the telephone never rang for him. After three days, he called once more only to be rebuffed again by the housekeeper. After five days, the end of her exhibition closed off another avenue of opportunity. He became more agitated as his mood rapidly disintegrated from hope to dejection. After a week, he decided he had no choice but to visit her at home.

It took him a while to find the house. He had remembered the number, etched in elegant black on both pillars, from the night of the kiss, but in his excitement he had forgotten to search for the street name. Just as he began to panic that even this connection had been snatched away by the fog, Mayfair revealed her secret to him. For an hour, he set up a vigil across the street. He hunted the lighted windows for a glimpse of her, imagined her in one of the topmost rooms busy at her easel or with canvas stretched across the floor. When that endeavour ended fruitless, he went back into Mayfair until he found a flower-seller, purchased the finest bouquet he could afford. Suitably armed, he approached the impressive Georgian doorway and rang the bell. Where he had expected a housekeeper, an elderly gentleman in a maroon smoking jacket answered the door.

'Is Miss Collingwood in?' Edward asked.

The man looked suspiciously at the bunch of flowers. 'Are these for my wife?'

'I am looking for a Miss Collingwood.'

'No one of that name lives here.'

'A Mr Collingwood? He is on the staff at the American Embassy.'

'I am afraid you have made a mistake.'

'But that is impossible. She brought me to this door.'

'A mistake.'

The door began to close on him. He wanted to push by this doddery gatekeeper, to announce his arrival, to demand to be seen.

'A mistake.' And with a final click, Edward was left standing alone on the step.

'Misery loves company, does it not?'

Edward looked up from the Japanese textbook, which had become no more than hazy scratches before his eyes. Aldous stood before him in a pinstriped suit spattered with raindrops. A pink rose hung limp from a lapel. A raindrop ran down his cheek.

'Aldous. I didn't know you drank in here.'

'I don't. But I saw your glum face as I passed by the window. I bring you more of the same poison.' He placed a pint of bitter on the table, a glass of whisky for himself.

'So what ails the young these days?'

'I don't want to talk about it.'

Aldous laughed. 'Then it must be a woman.'

He refused to answer.

'Young men pine for only one thing. The illusion of love. Am I right?'

'I grudgingly admit it.'

'Then please tell.'

And he did. To an almost complete stranger. But who else had he to narrate his tale in this lonely metropolis? Unfortunately, Aldous was not a sympathetic listener.

'So that's it?'

'What do you mean?'

'She deceived you with the wrong address and you consider this to be the end of the world?'

'She hasn't returned one call in two weeks. And the house-keeper refuses to give me the right address.'

'Have you tried the embassy?'

'The guards won't let me get near Collingwood unless I am on official business.'

'I think this Macy is just trying to weave a little web of mystery.'

'A little web of misery is more like it.'

'That may be the case. But look at the bright side. She gave you the right telephone number. It seems she is reeling you in with the one hand, pushing you away with the other. The classic ruse of seduction.'

'Well, it's working.'

'So, I see. Well, let's have another drink to celebrate your tortured soul. This Scotch is rather nice. More of the same, Edward. More of the same.'

By the closing bell, Edward was quite drunk. His companion suggested a nightcap at his place, offering commodious yet warm rooms above the meagre offices of *The Londinium* as the lure. Along with a decanter of the finest single malt.

The stairway to these apartments was dark and steep, rendered more treacherous by the smoothness of the well-worn steps. Using a hand-over-hand grip on the banister, Edward managed the first landing to the door of *The Londinium*, then needed Aldous to haul him the rest of the way.

'Onwards and upwards, dear boy. Onwards and upwards.'

Edward had not asked if there was a Mrs Aldous, assumed for some reason there wouldn't be. And he was proved right. Instead there was a ginger cat, which leapt to greet him, almost tripping him over on the threshold.

'Don't mind, Macavity,' Aldous said, stroking the creature into a purring frenzy. 'He is the most read-to cat in Christendom.'

The flat was large with doors leading off the hallway into cavernous, high-ceilinged rooms. But any sense of space was reduced by the presence of books. They appeared everywhere, not just on the layers upon layers of shelves but on every vacant surface, tucked into every available niche, slotted into drawers, bowls, even footwear. The floor of the living room was stacked with several tottering towers of magazines, copies of *The Londinium* mostly, presenting a serious obstacle course between Edward and the sofa, which at this point was his necessary destination. He just had to sit down, settle the wooziness inside his head.

He watched Aldous stoke up the coals in the grate until a fierce fire blazed – the only light in the room apart from the glow off the street lamps through the windows. A hand stroked his shoulder, then a glass brimful of whisky appeared. Aldous settled in an armchair opposite, lit up a cigarette, and for a while they did nothing but sip at their malts, gaze into the fire.

'What you should do is write about it,' Aldous said. The fire had tired and the man was a lean shadow in his chair, located by the purring cat, the arc of his cigarette describing the movement of his arm.

'Write what about what?' Edward's head ached, his eyes drooped heavy, giving him little patience for Aldous' circumlocutions, which he had discovered marked the man's discourse style. Either that or the complete opposite. Direct and downright rudeness.

'A short story. About your... how can I say...? Your little tragedy.'

'You are making fun of me.'

'No, I am merely making a creative suggestion.'

'I should write a short story about Macy?'

'No, no. That would be terribly boring. An awful self-indulgence. No, first you should choose your overriding feeling. For all good fiction must be about something. Some underlying theme.'

'Well, that's easy. Anger. That is my overriding feeling.'

'And why are you angry?'

'Because I have been rejected.'

'Good. Then write about rejection.'

'About Macy rejecting me?'

'As I said, that would just be autobiographical slush of no interest to anyone but yourself. No, you must find a vehicle for your rejection. A disguise through which you can vent your feelings.'

'I don't understand what you are saying.'

'I think you do. It is just that you are a little worse for wear.'

'Aldous?'

'Yes, my dear boy.'

'I am tired. Awfully tired.'

'Then you must sleep here. That sofa has a well-used history. I will bring you some blankets.'

Edward adjusted into a prone position, closed his eyes. The movement inside his head, the swaying darkness, began to settle, find its balance. Like waves inside a tub coming to rest. Lipping and lapping into stillness. A warm bath. The water settling gently over him. Playthings floating on the surface. Suds like clouds. A bar of soap slithering around his body. He let himself submerge into the liquidity and then re-emerge baptised with cleanliness. His mother stroking his wet hair. Yes, he liked that. Stroking his hair. So gentle. So soothing. Then a kiss upon his forehead. So light.

'Goodnight, Edward.'

'Goodnight, Aldous.'

Edward didn't remember much of that drunken night but he did take Aldous' advice. He wrote his story, found a vehicle for his narrative, a platform for his wounded voice. Rejection was his subject, and rejection was what he received. Nine times he submitted the manuscript to his new-found friend and nine times it was returned scarred with the red marks of aggressive revision. But the tenth effort Aldous accepted for publication in *The Londinium*. It told the story of an ex-soldier, rendered socially useless by the loss of an arm, who had taken to a life of begging on Brighton seafront. Each day, he watched a beautiful woman from one of the nearby Regency houses glide down to the promenade on her roller skates to perform elaborate dances in front of him. Of course, he fell in love with her. And she used that love to cruelly humiliate him in ways that Edward found hard to believe he was capable of imagining. Until she eventually rejected that poor beggar. As did the sea. For his body was found washed up with the pebbles on the shore. *The Girl on Roller Skates* was Edward's first published work. And Aldous never paid him a penny for it.

CHAPTER SEVEN

Tokyo, Japan • 2003

It was all around him. This ping-ding, flashing, Hello Kitty, Softbank-Sony, *pachinko-pachinko*, vending-machine, giant plasma screen, cartoon, Shibuya girls, 100 Megabits per second, nonsense. And the cars. Of course, he knew all about the cars. Even in alphabetical order. Daihatsu, Fuji, Hino, Honda, Isuzu, Mazda, Mitsubishi, Nissan, Suzuki, Toyota. The taxi driver had a stop-start Buddha patience for them while beside him Jerome appeared oblivious to the crazy world outside. It was noon yet electric lights rippled and spangled through the windows, staining the vehicle's interior in shades of synthetic colours. Salary men in identical raincoats brushed past them. A girl with pink hair. A gigantic, lurid-green octopus painted on to the side of a building, its tentacles strangling the concrete. What was that all about? He didn't belong in this jingle-jangle world. How did Aldous describe it? 'The Japanese have an exquisite sense of what is beautiful and no sense at all of what is ugly.' That was it. How these two sensibilities could exist in one culture was an enigma to him. He wondered how Jerome felt about all this rampant consumerism. After all, he had been in MacArthur's advance party. He had seen first hand how Tokyo used to be. A burnt-out firework with a few charred buildings left standing in the central district, most of which were instantly corralled by the military for their headquarters. It was an opportunity to build again, to create something magnificent.

'What do you think of all this?' Edward asked, waving a hand at the madness beyond the window.

'A moment.' Jerome blew loudly into his handkerchief. 'It's the air-con. Gets me every time. What were you saying?'

'I was asking about Tokyo.'

'Youth has taken over, Eddie. It's not meant to be a place for old men. We've no right to criticise.'

'All right then. But if you had to comment, what would you say?'

'The crows got bigger.'

'Is that it? The crows got bigger.'

'You should see them now. They're like vultures. Giant black eagles. Stealth bombers. It's frightening.'

'You exaggerate.'

'Don't bet on it. One of these days an enormous black bird is going to pick up a child, whisk him away. A shrieking, flapping figure fading away into a sky-high blot. That's when the shit will hit the fan. When people will finally sit up and take notice.'

'Are you serious?'

'Damn right, pal. That's my metaphor for the free-market experiment. A population under attack from giant crows. Pure sci-fi. And you know how the Japanese respond to this airborne threat?'

'I don't know. Shoot them down with air rifles. Poison them.'

'They lay out plastic bottles of water by the garbage collection points. Rows of fucking bottled water. Can you believe that? The light glinting off the liquid is supposed to scare off the predators. You gotta laugh. Talk about treating the symptoms and not the cause.'

'So why stay?'

'I'm used to it, I guess.'

'You're used to it,' Edward said resignedly, sinking back into the seat. 'Never thought you'd get used to anything. Especially Japan.'

'Why are you so critical? You were here at the beginning. You knew what was coming. The motor industry was probably the start of it all and they moved on from there. *Wakon-Yoshi*. Remember? Japanese spirit, Western ability. They've made a very rich living out of that, thank you very much. And what you see before you is the reward.'

'That's not what they do best at all. What they do best is find the beauty in the spaces, in the silences, in what's in between. Not all this... how do you New Yorkers say it...? All this crap.'

'Hey, Eddie, I know you're a great author and everything. But you're being a bit too Zen. You always had a very romantic notion of life here. Very *haiku*, shmaiku, you were. Yeah, you can still find what you're talking about. You've just got to look much harder these days, that's all. Scrape the surface with a bulldozer. Lob in a few grenades. Get underneath all this crap, as you say.' Jerome leaned forward, tapped the driver's shoulder, said something in Japanese. The driver just shrugged.

'If we don't get a move on, we'll be late,' Jerome said, turning back to him. 'Don't want to keep the dean waiting.'

Edward closed his eyes, breathed in deep, tried just for a few moments to shut out the noise and the lights, still himself against the anger that seemed to rise so quickly these days. And this sudden tiredness bearing down on him. So heavy and irresistible.

'Are you OK, Eddie?'

'Yes, yes, I'm fine,' he mumbled, shaking himself back into consciousness. 'Must be the jet lag. Look, Jerome. I wanted to ask you a favour.'

'Shoot, your lordship.'

Edward smiled. 'Remember how you used to take all those photographs? With that little Brownie of yours?'

'Still got it. Collectors' item.'

'What about the prints? Or the negatives? Do you have them too?'

'Sure do. All filed away in my office on campus. They're collectors' items too. Sell a few every now and then.'

'What about that day we went to Kamakura?'

'Hey, Eddie. You were here a million lifetimes ago. How am I supposed to remember that?'

'But if there were photographs, would you still have them?

'Should be there somewhere.'

The taxi lurched forward, almost knocking down a bent-over crone who passed close to the window. It was the first elderly person Edward had seen since they set out from the station.

The campus actually boasted some trees. Even tall ones, which was so unusual for Tokyo. The fallen leaves forming a damp mat under Edward's feet as he struggled out of the taxi in front of the Old Library, which according to Jerome had survived not only the fire-bombing but also the Great Kanto earthquake. Not surprising given the sturdiness of the red-brick building with its turrets and eaves that would not have been out of place on an English university campus. The air smelt sweet with decomposing foliage, resounded with the conversation of students as they moved purposefully towards their lecture halls. Universities always produced the same effect on him. A sense of hope gleaned from these young faces – the hope that maybe this was the generation that could really make a difference. He suddenly no longer resented Jerome bringing him here. This was where he needed to be. In the presence of fertile minds with fresh ideas. To suck at the marrow of their potential.

'Eddie. This is our dean. Professor Watanabe.'

Where Edward expected to find some doddering relic of Japanese academia, he was confronted instead by an urbane gentleman, perhaps in his mid-fifties, immaculately fitted out in a blue mohair suit. The dean's round face glowed with a healthy tan and bore a neatly trimmed goatee. His eyes glinted with bright intelligence, with humour. He looked like an affluent businessman at the helm of some company that would never go bankrupt. And no polite bows either. Watanabe's hand was immediately offered in handshake.

'Delighted to meet you, Sir Edward. We are so glad to have you attend our campus. Professor Fisk here said he might be able to persuade you to come, to accept our patronage, but I never dreamed it would be possible.'

Edward made the usual humble responses and, detecting the dean's accent, inquired politely about it.

'Stanford. I did my postgraduate work there. Education and linguistics.'

'We couldn't attract you to our shores then?'

Watanabe chuckled as he gently led him forward into the library building. Jerome had fallen a step or two behind.

'Actually, Sir Edward, this university has strong connections with your Oxford. Certainly I could have conducted my research equally as well there as I did in California. But the United States presented me with a challenge. A young republic with a directness that is both frightening and exhilarating for us Japanese. I chose to take that challenge.'

The conversation had taken them to the bottom of a wide stairway. A large stained glass window dominated the mid-landing, demanding some attention, particularly as the oblique sunlight cast itself on to their little party. The design on the panes was an abstract, weak yellows surrendering to bold blues. Watanabe tilted his head slightly in the direction of the light, his skin no doubt drawn to the memory of some recent winter skiing trip or a holiday in Saipan. Jerome had closed his eyes to the glare and was gently rocking back and forth on his heels. Edward observed the veins of his own hands as they rested on his cane and they appeared to him not gnarled and ugly, but softened by the angle of illumination into the smoothness of youth. The light had lassoed them into a silence, warming them temporarily but profoundly with its rays. He felt it as an exquisite, uplifting moment, a holy pause in the hectic flow of life. But the beam dimmed and was gone, leaving him to shiver in the shadows.

'Now, Sir Edward, let me explain our little schedule.' Watanabe touched him lightly at the elbow, guiding him forward. 'I have made it brief as I understand you only arrived yesterday. You must be tired, although the mountain air is so refreshing. First, my own speech and presentation of the honorary doctorate. If I may be so bold as to suggest, this will then be followed by a few words from your good self?'

'Jerome did warn me.'

'Very good. English for these guests will be quite appropriate so there will be no need for any tedious translations. A buffet lunch. Then, I believe, Professor Fisk has arranged a short question and answer session with some of our English Literature students. After that, we must allow time for the two of you to catch up. There will be many good memories, I am sure. And the early evening entertainment, Professor Fisk has also arranged.'

'All arranged,' Jerome confirmed.

'Excellent,' Watanabe said. 'And now I would just like to say something of a more personal nature before we continue, Sir Edward. You did a great service for this country. We were demonised and demoralised after the war. Some of that was quite deserved. But you helped restore some of our self-esteem in the international realm. I will always be grateful to you for that.'

The guests clapped politely as Edward entered the Old Library. There must have been about fifty of them, faculty mostly, but also a generous attendance of students. The room, it appeared, had survived as a library in name only, the spacious hall being completely devoid of both shelves and books. A large table stood in the centre, on top of which rested a giant ice sculpture in the shape of a swan. Plates of sushi, sashimi and other cold dishes lay against the base of the frozen bird. As Dean Watanabe strode towards a microphone stand, Edward sat down, settled into position, careful to rest forward on his cane, to show his host the attention he deserved.

He had taken to the dean immediately. As he listened to him speak, he could see clearly how correct this man had been in his educational choice. Watanabe possessed all the refinement and grace of a Japanese gentleman, yet without the tightness and restriction that usually went with it. America had loosened him up, made him confident rather than reticent about his qualities, created a warm and direct human being. He wanted to befriend this man. And he realised it had been a long time since he had felt this way about anyone. When had he stopped trying to recruit new friends? Was it laziness that had kept him from forming new relationships? Had he become so complacent with the creation of his social orchestra, he was prepared to let them die off one by one without replacement? Or was it mistrust that kept him aloof on his ever-depopulating island?

Watanabe finished his speech, called Edward to the floor. There was an awkward moment after heaving himself up on his cane when he had only the one free hand to accept both the doctorate scroll and the cloisonné bowl. He turned to the microphone, managed a small joke about how old age restricted the number of prizes he could receive, added his thanks to the dean, Jerome and the university. Then he found himself saying:

'The time I spent in Japan has greatly informed my life and work, not just obviously as with *The Waterwheel* but in more subtle ways too. My Japanese experience added a broader dimension to my perspective on life, a different way of looking at things, a diminishing of the self in favour of the collective thrust of a civilisation. Sometimes that is not always a good thing, especially in an extreme form. But balanced with the overemphasis on the individual in my own culture, I feel I have become a better person for it. Thank you.'

He sat down, feeling quite moved by his own oration.

After lunch, Jerome led him to the classroom where the question and answer session had been set up. About twenty students sat around on chairs laid out in an informal horseshoe-shape. Again a light applause greeted him as he took a seat at its apex.

'Mostly *kikokushijo*,' Jerome whispered.

Edward stared back at him. 'I don't understand.'

'Returnees. Fathers were diplomats, industrialists or just company employees sent to live and work overseas. The family went with them, and the kids studied either at an international school or the local school. Now they have returned. They're a special breed of student, struggling to get back into Japanese society. Some of them never do. Especially the women. And by the way, their English is excellent. This is the top class.'

Jerome gave a short introduction, then asked for questions. One brave soul put up his hand, an intense-looking youth who asked what advice Edward would give to a young writer.

'Make sure your story or novel is about something,' he replied, trotting out his well-worn response. 'By that, I mean some underlying important theme that guides the narrative. Not some outpouring of personal angst, but something meaningful, like moral or personal conflicts. And something you feel passionate about. Really passionate. After all, unlike creating a poem or a painting, you have to live with the creation of a novel for at least a year or two if not more.' At this point, he often felt tempted to add Aldous' observation that while everyone has a novel in them, most are just a pile of self-indulgent, self-deluding shit. But better not discourage the young and aspiring of this world.

'I don't have any experience of great conflicts,' the questioner complained.

'Then you have two choices. Make them up or wait until you get older.'

'And may I ask, Sir Edward, what choice did you make?'

'I waited until I grew up. And it was coming here and seeing Japan after the war that gave me the moral conflict that created *The Waterwheel*.'

There were other questions – the usual ones about his body of work or advice on being a writer. He fended them off easily, which was just as well, as he was beginning to tire. His class seemed to be running out of steam too when a young woman at the back raised her hand.

'Motoko,' Jerome said.

Motoko stood up. Unlike the rest of her classmates who had dressed up formal for this occasion, Motoko wore a pair of ripped jeans and a loose T-shirt that fell off one shoulder.

'Sir Edward,' she said boldly, one hand on a hip, the other clutching a glossy Japanese magazine. 'I hope you don't mind me asking this question… but there was something in this publication that intrigued me.' The accent was Australian. Such a strange combination – that serene, moonlike face coupled with the lazy Antipodean drawl.

'I didn't realise I am still of interest to popular Japanese magazines.'

Motoko smiled. 'I'm sorry, Sir Edward. It is not really about you directly. It's about the artist Macy Collingwood. She was here in Tokyo a few weeks ago and she gave an interview for this magazine. *Tokyo Art Lover.*' Motoko held up the issue. She had attracted the turned heads of her classmates and was wilting under the pressure. 'I am personally a very big fan of Macy Collingwood. I really love her work... and she did mention you, and I was wondering... I was wondering if you could tell us something more...?'

CHAPTER EIGHT

London • 1953

The Reading Room at the Brtish Museum was Edward's favourite building. He had a nostalgic affection for the Gothic style of his alma mater, Glasgow University, with its cloisters and quadrangles. And a pride in the stark, rugged walls of Edinburgh Castle in its craggy dominance of Princes Street. But when it came to useful interiors, the Reading Room inspired his greatest admiration. He loved the circular design, the womb of books, the arched windows, the magnificent lantern dome trapping for eternity the risen thoughts of its many illustrious readers. He imagined himself among these ghosts, touched by their presence, in awe of their anarchy, as they sat at the spokes of tables within this great wheel of literature. Hardy, Wilde, Browning, Twain, Dickens, Kipling, Tennyson, Yeats and Bloomsbury's very own Virginia had all held tickets. Over there was Karl Marx wriggling bad-temperedly on his boils, behind him Lenin and Trotsky, heads bowed in conspiracy. He had even composed a little ditty to these revolutionaries who had once basked in the splendour of the room's Imperial beneficence.

Lenin and Trotsky
What a pair of sharks
Used to utter Spenser
Now they work for Marx.

And who could blame them for searching out such a sanctuary? Who really wanted a freezing cold, dim garret to host their work when the Reading Room was there for their comfort? 'Come in, find a quiet spot, sit down, hook your toes around the warm, heating pipe passing by your feet, and we'll bring you what you need. What is it that you are doing? Writing the definitive novel? Penning the epic poem? Planning the great revolution?' Edward loved this respect paid to the readers. The little details. The black leather desktop, a hat peg, hooks for his pens, a book rest that unfolded magically from the wooden panel between the rows of desks. The polished mahogany chairs.

He only wished that all this pampering could help him with his own work. Since he had published the one short story in *The Londinium*, he had written nothing else. Aldous had passed on some favourable responses to *The Girl on Roller Skates* and one scathing criticism. 'Clumsy, infantile twaddle' was the phrase that had stood out.

Aldous had laughed at the comment. 'You have nothing to learn from someone who still uses the word "twaddle".'

But it was his Japanese studies that took up the bulk of his time within this sacred space, although he always kept a notebook at his elbow in case the seed of an idea came to him. He looked at the open page beside him. He had written one word. Macy.

'Excuse me, sir.' A leather-aproned attendant stood over him, face fixed in a smile of polite irritation. 'I was asked to give you this.' The man quickly passed over a folded-over piece of paper, grunted dismissively and was off.

Edward unplucked the tight wad and read. 'I'm at the White Lion. Macy.'

How was it that six words could make such a difference to a life? Twenty letters and two full stops. Lines on a piece of paper, scratched this way and that to create such a conflict of emotion. Joy. Anger. Insecurity. Resentment. Even the great novelists who had graced this very room couldn't inspire him with such a range and rage of feeling. He looked at her signature, then the solitary word on his own notepad. Perhaps he possessed a secret gift for conjuring up people just by writing their names. But if that had been the case, Macy would have appeared to him a hundred times by now. He re-read the note. Minimal. Not a 'sorry' or a 'please'. He would let her wait.

Within a minute, he was dragging on his coat, rushing out of the Reading Room, through the wrought iron gates of the Museum, across the road and into the pub. She was sitting at their table. Smoking, dressed in her usual sweater and jeans, her legs corkscrewed around each other in a tension. A pint glass of bitter waited for him.

'Hello, Mr Serious,' she said, stubbing out her cigarette, immediately reaching for another.

'Where have you been? I called you for weeks. I even tried to visit.'

'I've been busy.'

'Busy? What does that mean? Busy? You didn't have five minutes in your precious bloody life to telephone me?'

She shrugged. 'Why don't you sit down, Eddie? Relax.'

'I don't want to relax.' But he sat down anyway. Hands shaking as he took a couple of hurried sips of beer. The fact he was so glad to see her annoyed him even more. All these weeks of nursed anger disappearing in an instant just because she was there in front of him looking so damn beautiful.

'You said you wanted to see me again and then...' Now there was a whine in his voice.

'I did. And I do. So here I am.'

'Why didn't you return my calls?'

'Because I want to be in control. Those are my rules. If you want to see me, then it will be on my terms. No telephone calls. No visits. If that doesn't suit you, you can leave now.'

'But this is my pub.'

She smiled weakly. 'You know what I mean. Well?'

'Why?'

'My reasons are my own business.' She quickly finished her drink, began to pack away her purse and cigarettes into her bag. He reached out across the table, grabbed her wrist.

'No... wait.'

She laid her hand on his, stroked it gently. She might as well have been stroking him between his legs, because under his coat he had the most powerful erection.

'So another drink then?' she suggested.

'No... not just yet.'

'Well, I'd like one.'

He let her fetch it herself. Fortunately, his physical desire for her subsided quickly, but he still felt enthralled by her. He took off his coat, fumbled with her cigarette pack, wishing he smoked, just so he could do something with his hands. She was back with her gin and tonic.

'I read your short story.'

'Oh. Where did you see it?'

'The reading room at the Anglo-American library takes a copy of *The Londinium*. That's where we Yanks go when we can't get a ticket for that wonderful place across the road.' She played with the cocktail stick that snared the lemon slice in her drink, twirling and dipping it, until she pulled out the piece of citrus fruit from the glass, sucked the gin from the flesh, licked the juice from her lips. 'Writers are like magpies, aren't they? Stealing the glittering bits of people's lives when they're not looking.'

'What do you mean?'

'Well, that whole roller skate thing. That was from the first night we met, wasn't it? That guy who ran circles around us in the park.'

'I suppose it was.'

'So, what else was about me? About us?'

He felt himself redden. 'Nothing.'

'I see.'

'I don't think you do see, Macy. You shouldn't presume that everything I do has to be about you.'

'Even if it is.' She sipped from her drink, looked at him steadily over the glass, reminding him of the way her father had looked at him at the gallery. 'Come on, Eddie. I know you like me. You shouldn't be ashamed to admit it.'

'OK. I surrender. I admit it.'

'Well?'

'Well what?'

'Aren't you going to ask me if I like you?'

'You're here now, aren't you?'

'Touché.' She leaned back in her chair, her sweater tightening over her breasts as she stretched. 'Anyway, I liked the story. It showed promise. You should take your writing more seriously.'

'How do you know that I'm not?'

'What else have you written then?'

'Nothing.'

'Are you waiting for me to give you more material?'

'I hope so.'

She laughed, put down her drink, moved in towards him. Her fingers began to trace light sworls on the back of his hand and he felt the sensation all the way down to his toes. Her touch moved to his wrist, tickling him under the cuff of his shirt. He felt himself stir again, amazed at how such tiny pressure from the hands of another human being could arouse such lust.

'Do you still live near here?' she asked.

'Two doors away.'

'Can we go back there?'

'What? Now?'

'Yes. Now.'

He emitted some kind of gargled sound. Then tried again. 'Yes. Of course.'

'Good. Do you have anything to drink?'

'I'll get something from the bar.'

He bought two bottles of porter for himself, a quarter bottle of gin for Macy.

'Anything else?' Sean the barman asked, nodding towards Macy.

'No. That's fine.'

'Are you sure?'

'I said I'm fine.'

'Something for the weekend?'

'It's only Tuesday.'

Sean smiled. 'I could slip you a packet of three.'

Edward couldn't believe it. Half an hour ago, he was sitting miserable in the Reading Room and now he was being asked to plot the loss of his own virginity. 'I don't know. Yes. Do it. Please.'

'Right you are. I'll pop them in with the booze, easy as you like, so no one needs to notice. That's Sean for you. Always willing to oblige. Good luck with the lady.'

'I'm not counting my chickens.'

'This one will hatch. Trust me. Sean knows these things.'

The cold air hit Edward like a slap. Macy shivered, swayed on her feet, then snuggled up against him. It occurred to him it may have taken more than one gin and tonic for her to send over the note, another to invite herself round. He struggled with his keys to the front door of the building as she giggled and flopped all over him. He felt her lips press against his neck. He heaved the door inwards with his shoulder, then pulled Macy inside. They were only three steps up the communal stairway when she stopped him.

'Kiss me,' she commanded.

Her lips tasted sharp from the lemon. Then hot, as she pushed herself into him. He felt the cold tile against the back of his head, her fingers on the buttons of his coat as she pulled it open and pressed herself hard against his chest. He wanted to concentrate on kissing her but so many other thoughts were fighting for his attention. The paper bag with the bottles and condoms slipping and tearing in his grasp. And what should he do with his other hand? Bring it in under her coat? Smooth down her hair? Grab her hip? And what if a neighbour should enter the hallway? And what of the books he had abandoned at his desk in the Reading Room? It was hard to breathe. When would she realise he had little experience in these matters? That he was no Cary Grant or Humphrey Bogart. That he was the virgin product of a Scottish grammar school for boys. That he was completely out of his depth yet so completely desirous of her. He could feel her breasts against his shirt, not just the wool of her sweater but the ribbed cup of her bra. He was growing between his legs. And he knew she must feel him too.

'Good,' she said, pulling away from him. Her eyes smiled at him. 'So where is this flat of yours?'

'First floor.'

'Then take me there.'

His rooms were freezing. As he drew the curtains, Macy flounced around, opening doors, until she found his bedroom. She yanked a blanket off his bed, wrapped herself in it and returned to sit on the sofa in the living room. He liked the way she did that. Making herself at home, as if she were already a part of his life. He busied himself at the hearth, trying to act calm, feigning a relaxed humming as he worked, crumpling up newspapers, adding the coals, until he had a decent fire blazing.

'So what's this then?'

He looked up to see her with the bottle of gin in one hand, the packet of condoms dangling in the other like a piece of sexual mistletoe. His humming came to an immediate stop.

She laughed. 'I like a man who is prepared.'

'Excuse me,' he stammered. 'The coal. I have to wash my hands.'

He hurried past her to the bathroom, locked the door, ran the cold water over his hands, watched the sooty liquid swirl away. His reflection stared back at him from the wall cabinet. He drew in closer, examined his face, the fearful innocence in his eyes, until his breath misted over the glass. He unbuttoned himself over the toilet, urinated into the bowl, careful to adjust his stream on to the ceramic so she wouldn't hear him. He shook out his penis, shrivelled in the cold, attempted a few practice strokes. Women do not know of such things. How so much can rest on the performance of this one fickle organ at this crucial time. He regretted not having snatched the condoms away from her, taking one out now to experiment. He pulled down the toilet lid, sat down and stared at the door. God, he was so unprepared for this. Yet this rite of passage had always been there. Lurking. With the promise of so much pleasure if only this one threshold could be passed. He wanted to be a man but he felt so much like a child. He had read about fathers who took their sons to prostitutes to experience sex for the very first time. That was what he needed now. Professional help. 'Hold me here. Touch me there. Let me help you put this inside of me. Now.' His father had never taken him to a football match, never mind a brothel.

'What are you doing in there?' Macy at the door. Tapping.

'Just a minute.'

'Do you have a lemon?'

'No.'

'Tonic?'

'No.'

'How about a kiss?'

He opened the door. The blanket had dropped around her like an open cape, her hands occupied with the bottle of gin and a tumbler from the kitchen. He clasped her face, kissed her hard, forcing her to step backwards as she tried to return his embrace. They stumbled back across the room like this until they reached the couch and he pushed her down.

'Wait,' she gasped. She put the bottle and glass on the floor. 'Now. Start again. Slower. Take your time with me.'

The big things in life give us pressure, he thought, but it is the small things that give us pleasure. Love, death, marriage, family, health, work are all sent to torment us. To wrack us with their conflicts and their complexities. But the tiny details, the minutiae, they exist in themselves and for themselves. Just for pleasure. Like the delicious curve between Macy's neck and collarbone. There he could place his lips and she would arch her head towards him with a languid tilt. Or the wonderful twists and scallops of bone and cartilage that made up her ear, the dangling lobe of flesh beneath, just right for the nip of his teeth. Then the dense forest of her hair, like a thatcher's layered, sweet-smelling weaving. Or the way she clawed at his clothing, releasing the tail of his shirt so he could first feel the cold air then the warmth of her palm. The scratch and trace of her fingers as they snuck beneath his waistband, the gap too tight to allow her to venture further. He ran his hands over her skin, like a calligrapher with his brush, each gentle stroke infused with meaning. While she was the wild abstract impressionist, splattering him with the rake of her fingers.

'I want us naked,' she demanded. She sat up, quickly drew her sweater over her head. Then with a double-armed arch behind her back, she released the clip of her bra, allowing her breasts to spill out of their cups. He stretched out his hand towards a nipple.

'No,' she said, pushing his arm away. 'I want to see you first.'

He felt more confident now, trusting in his concealed hardness, poised to spring out at her nakedness. He wanted her to see him erect. To let her know how ready and capable he was. With not much finesse, he hurriedly stripped off his clothes, then stood before her. She reached out her hand and touched him. He shuddered and thought he might spill his seed there and then. Then she drew into him, as a ballroom dancer might return to her partner from an outward spin. The soft pouches of her breasts against his chest. His penis pressed up into her belly. Her pubic hair rough against his upper thigh. He wanted to remember these moments, to somehow watch, feel, taste, smell, then register them even as he was a part of them. To be inside them and outside them at the same time. But it was an impossible task. And so he surrendered totally to the experience, knowing he would only be able to recall this momentous occasion in his life as a sensual blur.

'You are in lust, my boy,' Aldous was pleased to inform Edward at every opportunity.

'No, it's more than that.'

'It is written all over your face.'

'Then you're misreading the signs.'

'Nothing to be ashamed of. Lust will get you through the first six months of any relationship. I should know.'

Whether it was lust or love, what Edward did know was that he was fully in Macy's control. Somehow he liked that, in an almost masochistic way, as he relied on her whim as to when she would or would not visit him. He allowed his life to become dependent on these occasions, hardly ever going out for fear he might miss her. He had never felt this way before. So consumed by this surrender to someone, moving from moods of extreme despair to overwhelming happiness when finally she appeared at his door. He started smoking. He couldn't concentrate on his studies. She gave him a book of Byron's poetry with a lipstick imprint of her kiss on the flyleaf. She told him how much she enjoyed his taste, his smell, his touch. She said she could never have enough of him. And then she would disappear for days.

But on this gloriously hot summer's day, he lay by her side on a blanket on a grassy embankment leading down to Regent's Park lake just above the boathouse. One of several couples spread out across the slope. He had often been a passer-by along the water's edge, looking enviously at these entwined bodies sprawled out on the grass, skirts hiked, shirts loose, faces merged. Now he was one of them. A satisfied member of the couples' club. He raised himself up on one arm, looked to where his old single self might have stood. Out on the water there was a solitary rowboat powered by a large man in a turban while a boy passenger sat and watched from the prow. The weight of the Sikh as he pulled back on the stroke took the front of the boat out of the water so the boy skimmed along on air. The lad's face bore a certain arrogance, like a young prince being ferried across the lakes of his kingdom. Beyond the boy and the pond, a mist had settled on the borders of the park above the Grand Union Canal. He turned over on his back and stared at the haze of the sky. Macy scraped her toes up and down the bare soles of his feet, tickling for his attention. Cool, wet blades of grass between his own toes. The air teeming thick with pollen, cut grass, swarms of flying insects. The heat of her limbs beside his. He felt a strong sense of contentment. And yet the moment he became aware of this sensation, it was gone. As though he could never be content with his own contentment. He leaned over, plucked the lit cigarette from between her fingers, sucked in greedily, then placed it between her lips.

'Do you know what I like about you?' she said on an exhale of smoke.

'Tell me.'

'Your acceptance of me. As a woman. And as an artist. Most men view women, especially independent, creative women, as a battleground. Something to be beaten into submission otherwise they feel compromised. Intimidated even. You're not like that.'

'You've got it wrong. I'm just being selfish. I'm prepared to put up with all your nonsense because I love what you bring to me.'

'Like what?'

'Little things.'

'Go on.'

'Putting flowers in my room.'

'That's it?'

'Buying me a new toothbrush when you saw I needed one. Rather than just telling me to go out and get one myself.'

'My God. You're easy to please. Tell me more.'

There was so much more he wanted to tell her. Yet the words wouldn't come, they were lumpen, not in his throat but in his stomach. Held down by a fear that stretched far back into his past. To the sudden flash of an image of a little boy, nine years old, turning up uninvited to the birthday party of a young girl in his class. Fiona, her name was. Fiona MacLeod – he would never forget that. Fiona wearing her fluffy pink cardigan and her chiffon party dress with its layers of petticoats. And as he stood there shaking on the front step, seeing all his classmates running around inside the house, the coloured balloons and the streamers, the little gift bags all lined up in the porch, it was Fiona's mother who told him that he and his pitiful present – a well-thumbed comic – were not welcome. When he had returned home that day bewildered, rejected and feeling lonelier than he had ever done, he recalled how he had found solace in the discovery in his father's pipe-box of the small sword, how he could decapitate the figure of the Oriental maiden engraved on the casing just by sliding the blade out of its sheath.

'I've told you enough already,' he said.

'I'll go then.' She leaned over, kissed him on the cheek, then rose to her feet.

'What's the hurry?'

'I want to do some work in the studio. While there's still natural light. And remember. We're having dinner with my father tonight.'

'God, I had forgotten about that. When is it?'

'Eight o'clock in Soho. Kettner's in Romilly Street.'

'Do I have to go?'

'I don't really care. It's my father who wants to meet you.'

'But he's met me already.'

'Well, he wants to meet you again. That's what he does. He wants to take control of my life. The same way he did my mother's.'

'So why put up with it?'

'He pays the bills, stupid.'

Edward wore his only suit – a blue worsted three-piece affair his father had bought him for his graduation – the jacket too tight now but passable if he kept it unbuttoned. He arrived ten minutes early but Macy and her father were already there, Macy in the cream silk blouse and black knee-length skirt she had worn for the king's funeral. Jack Collingwood looking more film star than Yankee diplomat, with his elegant good looks and immaculate double-breasted suit. Skin shining. Like a star in the firmament of less confident, less attractive men. His host rose to shake his hand. The grip was tight, professional.

'Edward. Glad you could make it.'

'Thank you for the invitation, sir.'

Macy cast him a weak smile, warding off any inclination he had to kiss her. He sat down and Collingwood passed him a menu.

'The calves' liver with bacon is excellent.'

Edward looked at the elaborate script in its red leather folder, the rows of cutlery, the napkin in its silver ring. He could feel the thick nap of linen under his nervous fingertips. He had never been in such an expensive restaurant before. He took the recommendation. Macy ordered fish. Collingwood let the *maître d'* choose the wine.

'So how are the studies doing?'

'Classes are finished for the summer, sir. I still have a few written assignments for next term. Cultural comparisons that sort of thing. Japan and Great Britain.'

'I spent a few years out there, you know. During the Occupation. I was a budding young lawyer then. Full of ideals. Investigating war crimes. Thankless task. Put me off the law for good. Drove me towards diplomacy.'

'What exactly put you off, sir?'

'What exactly put him off,' Macy interrupted, 'was that my mother didn't approve of what he was doing. 'Once she saw...'

'Now, Macy,' her father said.

'Once she saw what her dear compatriots had done to Tokyo, Hiroshima and Nagasaki, she began to wonder who the real war criminals were. Or at least she didn't think one side was in any position to take the moral high ground over the other. She wanted to come home immediately and...'

'Macy. I said that's enough.'

'And that's what she did. Without my father.'

'Your mother came home because she was worried about you.'

Macy tore open the roll on her side plate, struggled to spread a cold pat of butter. 'What Daddy means is that I was about to be expelled from boarding school for having an affair with my art teacher. That was what my mother gave as her excuse. But it wasn't the real reason.'

Collingwood smiled indulgently at his daughter. 'Have we finished our little scene? You don't want to hear any of this, do you, Edward?'

Edward could easily imagine Collingwood now as the diplomat. Smiling and unflustered. Playing one party off the other. He didn't want to be sucked into his game, this father-daughter dynamic, nor did he want to hear anything of affairs with art teachers either. He shrugged a reply to Collingwood, tried to smile at Macy but his lips contrived to betray him, contorting into what he was afraid emerged as a horrible smirk. He was saved by the waiter, who arrived flourishing a bottle of wine. Collingwood busied himself with the tasting while Macy sat tense in her seat, her front teeth cutting into her lower lip. The waiter filled his glass with the ruby liquid and Edward anticipated some sort of painful toast to break the silence but instead Collingwood said:

'Macy says you are a writer as well.'

'That's very kind of her. But I've just had one short story published.'

'He's got potential,' Macy said, her unaccustomed praise surprising him. 'Naive. But good.'

'I'm sure he is. I think it's healthy to have a creative hobby. Macy paints, of course.'

'It's not a hobby, Daddy.'

'Languages. That's what I wanted her to do. She has a natural linguistic ability, did you know that? She should have gone to Rome. Improved her Italian. But no. She wanted to come here to London. Play around with her paints at my expense.'

'You just can't take me seriously, can you?'

'Well, you surely don't expect to make a career out of all that abstract stuff? All that random throwing of paint. I mean it's just not art.'

Macy rose from her chair, threw down her napkin and walked off, just avoiding the waiter who had turned up with three plates balanced on his arms.

'Gone to the powder room,' Collingwood said, his gaze following his daughter's direction, as he tucked in his napkin, sat back to let the waiter serve him. 'So like her mother. Highly strung. Hope you have what it takes to keep her in check, Edward. Well, do you?'

Edward had cut off a nice piece of calves' liver and was tempted to pop it in his mouth, try to chew himself out of a response. But politeness forced him to put down his fork. The dead eye of Macy's unattended fish observed him accusingly.

'I really like her work, sir.'

Collingwood grunted. 'That's not what I asked. Do you have what it takes?'

'I don't know.'

'Well, you'd better find out. Or she'll run circles round you. Her mother was the same. Got to keep her on a tight leash. Keep her under control. Or you'll be the one to suffer. Mark my words, boy. Just mark my words.'

This time Edward did let his fork complete its journey to his mouth, chomped down on the tender, juicy organ, praying that Macy would return. Which she did. Red-eyed and trembling. She remained standing, gulped down a glass of wine.

'Come on, Eddie. We're leaving.'

Collingwood cocked an eyebrow at him, as if to say: 'Well, have you got what it takes?'

Edward stood up, tried but failed to button his jacket. 'I'm sorry, sir. But I must leave. Thank you for...'

Macy grabbed his arm and led him away.

Outside, he took off his jacket, slung it over his shoulder, tried to keep up with her as they walked towards Berwick Street. The pubs were full, forcing sweaty-faced customers out on to the pavements with their pints. Jazz music filtered up into the street from a basement club. The smell of thick, sweet coffee. There was a definite pulse to the evening, a noisy, frantic, sexual beat. He tried to take Macy's hand but she pulled away.

'Why didn't you support me in there?' she snarled.

'What?'

'You heard me.'

'It was all about you and your father. What could I do?'

'You could have stuck up for me, that's what. Just like I did for you.'

'What did you do for me?'

'I said your work was good.'

'So did I. But you'd rushed off in a tantrum before you heard me.'

'Yeah, sure you did.'

He stopped walking, stood looking at her. Her face had twisted into an angry-red ugliness. In that moment, he hated her. He felt it right down to the core. A deep, all-consuming hatred. Yet when she turned and walked away from him, he never wanted her so much.

CHAPTER NINE

Tokyo, Japan • 2003

He awoke. Slowly. Very slowly. Dragging himself out of the fuzzy pit of his subconscious. Gripping the dark edge of exit with his fingers, then trying to struggle up on his elbows. He could see over the rim. The slatted blinds were half-open casting a dull light into the room and a striped shadow on to the floor. But he couldn't recognise where he was. Panic. His legs scrambled to find a grip, to push himself up and out. He must be in a ward. That was always the default mode. 'If I do not know where I am, I must be in hospital.' But at least he was alive. His mouth felt terribly dry. He shifted his head. His neck hurt. There was a desk. A dead computer. A sink. A magazine on the floor. *Tokyo Art Lover.* His head clearing now. The veil of death and illness disappearing. He lifted off the blanket, noticed he was without jacket, tie or shoes. Collar and cuffs unbuttoned. He then raised himself to a sitting position on the couch. The cushion on which he had lain was dusted with flecks of dried skin. Another layer of him had died, shed itself while he slept.

'I will get up,' he thought. 'I will go over to the sink, splash water on my face, drink from that tumbler, and return here to read that bloody magazine. Find out what she said. That shall be the order of events to remember. I will now get up.'

But he couldn't find his cane. He slid over to the edge of the couch where an armrest afforded some leverage. He managed to hoist himself to his feet, then in a half-crouch followed the ledge of the desk, hand–over–hand against the wall with its diplomas and degrees until he reached the sink. He splashed water on his face. So convenient to have a sink in an office. So typical of a Japanese university to ensure this comfort for its staff. He must remember to install one in his own study. He could have a drink of water anytime. Or make some tea. Or rack up some phlegm as he was doing now, spit out the green–yellow gunge and wash it down the plughole. Just like that. So undistinguished for a man of his stature. There was a handtowel too with a little university crest embroidered into one corner. A glass of cool water. Just the slightest taste of fluoride. He dabbed his lips. He could stand up straight now. And there was his cane. In the umbrella stand by the sink. He moved over to the window, played impatiently with all the different lengths and loops of cord until he managed to shift the blinds halfway up and on a slight tilt. Then there was light. He had an easier task with the lever to open the lower half of the window, let in some much needed air. Gulped in a breath, then looked around the room, knowing there was something else to do. He massaged the heel of his palm into the tightness in his neck. That felt good. Ah yes, the magazine. Where was the damn magazine? He eventually found it hidden away under the blanket. Then he had to get up again, fetch his glasses from his jacket slotted into a hanger on the back of the door. So much moving about. He sat down behind Jerome's desk quite breathless.

He thumbed through the pages until he found the article. It was one of those interviews with the page split in two between the English and the Japanese translation. And there was Macy. "*The abstract expressionist Macy Collingwood.*" In Tokyo for a retrospective sponsored by some high class department store. Looking pretty smug about it too. Silver hair still thick and lush. He could see that even from the photograph. She had fattened out a little, gone a bit jowly and sun-dried but she looked healthy. Faded denim shirt. That Native American jewellery with those little turquoise pebbles setting off her colouring nicely. She had turned ethnic. Or Californian. Or vegetarian. Or whatever it was the Yanks did these days to keep so damn fit. He nervously scanned the text, looking for any mention of his name. There it was.

Interviewer: "*I understand you first met Edward Strathairn in London in the early 1950s. Could you tell me something about that first meeting and if the two of you were part of a wider circle of artists and writers of the time?*" He could imagine her laughing at that. Throwing her head back the same way she did the first time he saw her in the queue outside Westminster.

"*Yes, I first met Eddie back then. But no, there wasn't a clique or anything like that. All the real writers were in Paris. Camus, Sartre, Beckett, de Beauvoir. It was just a coincidence Eddie and I got to know each other. To be honest, I can't even remember where and how we met. He was just starting out at the time.*"

Interviewer: "*And did you influence his work in any way?*"

"*His first published story was about me. 'Roller Girl'. Something like that. Stupid title really. I doubt if it is available anywhere. So, yes, you could definitely say I influenced his early work.*"

The sexless interrogator continued: "*And what about Sir Edward? What kind of influence did he have on your work?*"

"*None whatsoever.*"

Edward flinched at that. Not at the truth of it but at such assuredness. She still did those Jackson Pollock lookalikes. There was one propped up beside her in the photograph, resting right up beside her scuffed leather boot, which probably spent most of the day looped up in a stirrup or engaged in some other West Coast outdoor hobby. Macy might have moved right across America after her mother died but she had never moved on from abstract expressionism. She had stayed exactly where she was, let all the fads come and go until they came round to her again. That was Macy. Immutable. And unforgiving.

He read on, fearful of what she might have said next. But thankfully the interviewer had moved on to her more recent work.

He heard the door open. Jerome's face in the gap, eyes narrowed in a scan of the room.

'Still alive then?'

'Just a short nap.'

'A bit more than that, Eddie,' Jerome said, still lingering in the doorway. 'I was worried sick about you.'

'What are you talking about? I feel fine. Quite invigorated.' He performed a half-swivel in the chair to show off his vitality.

'Relieved to hear it. But you had a real nasty turn there.'

'I still don't know what you're talking about.'

'You don't remember?'

'No.'

'During the question and answer session. I think you had a dizzy spell or something. You kind of half-fainted. We had to drag you up here. The nurse even came. Temperature. Blood pressure. All that sort of thing. Perfectly normal as it happens. In the end, we just let you sleep.'

'For how long?'

Jerome looked at his watch. 'Must be two hours. You still don't remember?'

He shrugged. 'Just a bout of tiredness. Or jet lag. Or that bullet train. Travel is very energy-sapping at our age, don't you think? Anyway, as I said, I feel fine now.'

He rocked back and forward in his chair as Jerome moved over to a filing cabinet, began to drag open drawers. Dusk outside. The crisp voices of the young crossing the campus. Final lectures to attend. Tutorials. He had read all about Tokyo teenagers. Ginza coffee shops. Snatched hours in love hotels. Sumo on TV. Pornography on the Internet. Hooked on computer games. No plots of revolution for this generation.

'Got them,' Jerome announced, placing three small boxes on the desk. Grey cardboard containers, stapled at the corners to form their loose rectangular shapes. Jerome plucked off the lids, laid out the photographs in an orderly fashion on the desk. Like cards stacked for a game of patience. Edward noticed the slight shaking of the hands as Jerome positioned the prints. He had an overwhelming urge to touch him then, to place an arm around his shoulder, to ask him so many questions. Has your life been a happy one, Jerome? Did you find love? Are you frightened of death? Does anything have any meaning for you these days? Are you angry? Are you bitter? Are you simply waiting for the end? Do you know what happened to Sumiko? But instead, he looked along the line of photos.

'There are so many of them.'

'Well, I always was a bit obsessive with the camera. Still am.'

'Never owned one.'

'Never owned a camera? How in hell's name do you remember anything?'

'I write it down.'

'What do you mean? In a journal?'

'No. In my novels.'

'Thought that was all fiction.'

'The narrative is. But the feelings underneath are real.'

Jerome turned to face him. 'Photographs are my memories,' he declared. 'They are my narrative. Without them I have nothing. *Zilch. Nada.*'

'Are you telling me if you hadn't taken these, you wouldn't remember any of this?' Edward swept his hand over the desk.

'Yeah. That's exactly what I'm saying.' Jerome folded his arms, leaned back against the desk in what must have been his practised lecture mode. 'I'll tell you something, Eddie. I don't know about you but it's not death that scares the shit out of me. It's the fear of forgetting. If we knew we could carry our memories to wherever we go next, then there would be nothing to fear. It's just the thought that all this life might be forgotten totally, that's what frightens me. And therefore the photographs. Problem is...' He laughed, a watery, almost sobbing kind of laugh. 'I can never remember where I put them.'

Jerome had laid out the prints in chronological order in three columns, each according to the year on the lids of their respective boxes. 1956, 1957, 1958. Good strong, black and white images, still quite glossy despite their age. Jerome had a way with contrast, with composition, always fussing with his posers to position them just right. A lot of the usual tourist shots, friends larking about, but also the occasional artistic effort. There was one of construction workers, padding around in cloth boots on the iron skeleton of a high-rise building, heads wrapped in towelled bandanas, skinny arms sinewy with muscle, lips clinging aggressively to cigarettes. Hods, wheelbarrows, mixer. A homage to the new Tokyo, to the new concrete skyline.

'I like this one,' Edward said of the photo.

'Yeah. Me too. That one was published. *National Geographic.*'

'Impressive. And this one too. The Imperial Hotel in Tokyo. The one designed by Frank Lloyd Wright.'

'The Imperial's gone, I'm afraid. I mean there's still a hotel there by that name but all the Frank Lloyd stuff's been dismantled. Too many earthquakes, too many bombs. Probably wouldn't have lasted another tremor. So they took it down, re-assembled parts of it somewhere. Nagoya, I think.'

Edward liked what they were doing. Just the two of them. Picking out photos, chatting easy, a laugh about this one, glassy-eyed over that one. He had forgotten what this could be like. Remembering a shared past. All the more precious as the end approached for both of them. Exciting too, as he waited for the shots of Sumiko to emerge. And there she was. In her kimono. Standing in the crook of his arm, head rested against his shoulder, head tilted to the camera, the shyest of smiles. In the background, the Great Buddha statue looking serenely down at them, heavy-lidded eyes closing out the obvious non-Buddhist attachment being displayed in front of it. She wouldn't have liked the outward display of affection either. Tense in his arms, leaning in against his clasp just to please him.

'Yeah, that was a great day,' Jerome said, peering over his shoulder. 'The three of us, down by the sea in Kamakura. That was the first time I met her. I remember us walking along the beach together. Trying to find Kawabata's house.'

'That's right. She loved his books.'

'She hurt her ankle and we had to carry her back. A goddamn pity. She so much wanted to see the great man's house.'

Edward looked again at the photograph. 'Is that the only one of her from that day?'

Jerome picked up the print, squinted at it. 'Yeah, that was it.'

And that was the end of the matter. Sumiko had pressed herself into their minds for an instant, before disappearing again. Like a curious butterfly. Edward was desperate to talk more about their day together, to resurrect her memory in shared conversation, perhaps even to ask to keep the print, but a shadow passed over the window, distracting him. The bony swoosh and creak of a broad span disturbing the air. He saw a large crow swoop down across the yard to perch on the edge of a metal bin by the library. It was a monster of a bird. Arrogant. Fearless. It dipped its head into the bin opening, a few tugs, then flew off with a tied-up plastic bag in its beak. By the time Edward had returned his attention to the room, Jerome was already packing the photographs back into their boxes.

CHAPTER TEN

Brighton, England • 1953

From his deckchair at the tip of the West Pier, Edward could just make out the noise from the beach. The laughter and shrieks of children playing in the waves. The musical grind of a merry-go-round. Seagulls screeching in delight at the potential for scraps. He closed his eyes and opened them again, the sheer breadth of the horizon forcing his gaze to widen from its usual scope of narrow city streets. The sun bounced off the water, bleaching the Regency facades of the grand hotels along the esplanade. Pleasure boats ferried day trippers over to the Palace Pier. The wooden planks scraped rough and sandy under his bare feet, the slats between them the ideal trap for halfpennies dropped from over-excited hands. Aldous sat beside him, sunk deep into the canvas – panama hat, white suit, thin gloves, sunglasses, concealing him mummy-like from the ageing glare of the rays. Macy off somewhere to fetch cones of ice cream along with Aldous' nephew – a twenty-year-old youth from Manchester called Robert. Their joyous little party grateful for the opportunity to escape to Brighton from a London steaming and stifling in the heat.

'I think it is time *The Londinium* received another contribution from you,' Aldous said, his thin lips oily and pink-white with cream.

'I have some ideas.'

'Well, just make sure they don't amount to some emotional gush. Given your situation with that girl.'

'Her name's Macy. As you well know. And my situation with her is perfectly fine.'

'Well, she seems to have reeled you in very nicely. Running hot and cold as she does.'

'She makes me very happy,'

'Then you very are lucky, Edward. The state of happiness is only possible when you are young. It requires a certain innocence. A certain naivety. When you get to my age, one has become too world-weary, too cynical, to experience happiness. Or should I say "a state of happiness". I may experience a moment of happiness as I do now, in the company of my friend on this noble structure, jutting into the ocean like the erect penis of this wonderful town...'

'Channel. This is the English Channel. Not an ocean.'

'Please do not interrupt. As I was saying, I may experience happiness as I do now, but only for an instant, before the sense of hopelessness sinks in and destroys it. Whereas for you, Edward, with your heart, belly – and may I add your loins – full of hope, can extend these moments of happiness into a state of being. A state of being that may last days. Weeks even. I envy you.'

'For God's sake, Aldous. You're talking like an old man.'

'It has nothing to do with age, my boy. It has to do with experience.'

'And what kind of experience would that be?'

But Macy was back with Robert, their hands filled with dripping cones.

'Little Mo's won Wimbledon again,' she reported excitedly. 'We just heard it on the radio at the kiosk.'

'Little Mo?' Aldous grumbled as he tried to receive his cone from Robert without dripping ice cream on to his suit. 'Who or what is this Little Mow? A miniature lawnmower?'

'Maureen Connolly,' Macy informed him. 'An American tennis player. She's only seventeen.'

'See?' Aldous snorted. 'The triumphs of the young.'

'What are you so grumpy about?' Robert asked. He had stripped off his shirt since going off with Macy. The braces of his trousers looped loosely around his skinny, white torso, already glowing red in patches.

'Ah, Robbie,' Aldous sighed. 'If only you knew.'

In a departure from her usual casual mode, Macy wore a dress. Summery. A simple floral pattern, the light cotton fluttering slightly in the breeze. Bare legs. Edward gazed at those treasonous limbs flaunting their nakedness, exposing to the public what was usually reserved solely for him. She came to kneel beside him, draped an arm over his leg. He let his fingers play over the warmth of her neck as he watched her tongue sworl around her cone.

'I'm hungry,' Robert said.

'You've just had an ice cream,' Aldous said. 'I thought we might promenade on the esplanade.'

'That was just a starter,' Robert continued. 'I would like some fish and chips. Isn't that what we're supposed to do, down at the seaside? Have fish and chips. With vinegar and sea salt. Don't you want to eat something?'

'I suggest a walk first to build up an appetite,' Aldous insisted.

'I'm hungry now.'

Aldous sat up in his deckchair, drew his sunglasses down to the tip of his nose with an index finger. 'What's the consensus?' His blue eyes flashed in the sunlight.

'Walk,' Macy said.

'Edward?'

'Me, too.'

Aldous looked at Robert who scowled back at him. Aldous sighed then sank back in his chair. 'Then I am afraid Robbie and I must leave you. We are going to stay overnight in Brighton. I will take this undeserving youth for his fish and chips. Then we will need to look for a guest house. We will allow you young lovers a few hours alone before your train.'

The sun was dipping in the sky but the evening was still warm. The crowds on the beach had eased to leave scattered islands of young couples huddled close in the wait for the sunset. A few bored parents watched their tireless children rushing in and out of chases with the tide. Macy had taken off her sandals to walk across the pebbles, letting the waves wash across her bare feet. Edward observed her from behind – her sunburnt shoulders, the way her dress clung to her back, curved tightly over her buttocks, then flowed out to let her legs run free. He could imagine the sea-worn stones rounding into the soles of her feet, massaging pressure points, forcing her toes apart.

She stooped to pick up a shell resting like a jewel within a bed of seaweed, held it to her ear, turned to beckon him towards her. He took her hand and her fingers fell into an easy clasp around his own. Moments like these pleased him so much they hurt.

'Would you like to stay?' he suggested, unable to disguise the fearful inflection in his voice. This was what she had done to him, brought him to that point where he felt insecure in anything he wanted from her. He could almost imagine the scared animal look in his eyes as he asked the question. But he didn't mind. The rewards were too great.

She examined the shell, plucked out a frond, shook it out for loose stones, reapplied it to her ear.

'I don't hear anything,' she complained. 'Just the sound of my own heartbeat.'

'Macy?'

She let go his hand, skipped ahead of him, her dress rising above her knees in her crunching dance over the pebbles.

'Yes,' she sang. 'Yes. Let's do it.'

'We'll need to find a guest house.'

'A seedy, sleazy hotel. Just like Robbie and Aldous.'

'Yes. Just like them.'

She had moved back to him now, grasped his arm, her body hot from the day. 'Robbie's not his nephew,' she said. 'You know that, don't you?'

They eventually found a guest house in a Regency square just opposite the West Pier. Two previous establishments had refused them for a lack of a ring on Macy's finger. The manager of the third might have thrown them out too had it not been for a cancellation just before they turned up.

'No luggage then?' the manager asked as Edward signed the register under the name of Mr and Mrs Pollock.

'No luggage,' he replied, thinking that given the tremor in his voice he might as well have just said, 'Not married.'

The room had a salty dampness about it that clung to the quilt, the curtains, the carpet. Macy flung open the windows and he followed her as she stepped over the sill on to a small balcony littered with pots of red hydrangea. Starlings swooped over the pier as dusk began to creep in. The town seemed to be sighing as the heat finally gave out and the crowds began to trip home. He ran his finger down the bareness of her back and she shivered. He couldn't remember ever feeling so happy.

They went back inside, stretched out side by side on the bed. Her body was hot and sticky, he could taste the salt on her skin. The air, the sun, the feeling of youthful power all contributed to the vigour pumping in his blood, ready to burst. He moved into her. And his world became liquid. A sea of saliva, sweat, semen and her own sexual juices. It was over too quickly.

He turned over on to his back. The silk of the quilt clung to his skin. Voices in the street below the open window. Gulls squawking. Seaside tang. His heavy breathing subsiding.

'There's something I want to tell you,' he said dreamily.

'Yeah?'

'I love you.'

She broke away from his side, raised herself on an elbow. Her breasts hung white under the reddened yoke of her skin, freckled from the exposure to the sun. 'No, you don't.' She laughed, and he felt that part of himself momentarily opened, cruelly close down.

'I said, "I love you".'

'No, you don't.'

'You can't tell me how I feel.'

'Oh, yes I can. This is not love, Eddie. This is just lustful play. Just be clear of that. You just want this.' Her hand strayed from her breasts to between her legs where her pubic hair was matted by their lovemaking. 'And it's only because I won't let you have me when you want me that's driving you mad with desire. Or with what you sweetly misinterpret as love.'

'That's just not true. It's more than that. Much more than that.'

'Well, what do you really know about me, about what's inside here?' She tapped the hollow between her breasts with her fist. 'This you don't know. So how can you love me?'

'I've seen your paintings.'

She calmed for an instant. 'Those are just one part of me,' she conceded.

'I only know that I love you. Why can't you believe that?'

'Then we have a different idea of love.' She twisted away from him, reached over for a cigarette pack on the bedside table. 'Damn.' She crumpled the empty packet, let it drop onto the carpet.

'Forget about the bloody cigarettes,' he snapped. 'What are your feelings for me?'

She smiled. 'Of course, I care about you,' she said, patting his thigh. 'I wouldn't be here if I didn't. I just don't have any illusions about my feelings. I know why I'm involved in this affair.'

'Is that all this is then? A dirty weekend down in Brighton?'

'Poor Eddie,' she teased. 'So very British, aren't you?' She sat up on her side of the bed, bent over in a search for her discarded clothes. The ridge of her spine noduled the pale skin of her back. He wanted to pull her back down beside him, penetrate her again, lose his anger inside her. Instead, he swung his feet off the bed, stood up, walked over to the small sink and ran the rusty tap. In the mirror, he saw his cheeks red – whether from the sun, his anger or the after-flush of sex he did not know. He leaned over the bowl, splashed cold water on to his face.

'So British?' he said to his reflection. 'What's that supposed to mean?'

'Oh, you know. So constricted. So serious. So serious about love. No wonder you like the Japanese. They're just the same.' She had slipped on her sundress and was moving towards him. 'Now, button me up,' she said. 'I need to go out for some cigarettes.'

He had only meant it to be a slap. Even that would have been a surprise to him. Surely it wasn't a clenched fist? More like a playful punch. But his knuckles had definitely come into contact with her face, just above her cheekbone, he could feel that now as he bit down on to his fingers, not quite believing what he had done. Her head had spun sideways from the blow, and she had staggered backwards until she could sit back down on the sheet-crumpled bed, her skirt drawn way up her thighs. He half-expected her to scream, but she just sat there, rubbing her face with the back of her hand, glowering at him, the bruise already beginning to swell on her cheek.

'God, I'm sorry,' he stammered. 'I'm so sorry. I didn't mean to do that. I'm sorry.'

She reached down for her handbag, picked it up off the floor, then raised herself off the bed. 'You bastard,' she said as she strode past him.

He grabbed her by her bare shoulder, turned her round to face him. 'Don't leave.'

'Go on, go on,' she goaded. 'Hit me again. Yes, yes, you'd like that, wouldn't you?' She tried to wriggle herself away from his grip. 'You're hurting me.'

He raised his other arm but then let it drop, released his clutch of her shoulder. He saw the blood-red marks left by his fingernails. And she was gone.

He didn't stay at the hotel. Instead, he took the last train back to London. The carriage was full of cosy, snuggled-up couples, their whispered intimacy only aggravating his own plight even more. He watched the lights of the south coast disappear as the train steamed comfortably into the darkness of the Sussex countryside. He stared at his own reflection in the window, this cruel stranger capable of an anger and a violence he never knew he possessed. 'Is this what she has turned me into?' he thought. 'Or is this who I really am?' Then he remembered what Aldous had told him only a few hours previously. That happiness was such a fleeting thing.

He moved his desk sideways to the open window, so he could turn easily from his books to observe the Bloomsbury streets below. He lit a cigarette, blew the smoke out into the world. These past few evenings had been beautiful, hot, late-light stretches of time. But the heat rising from the street stifled him. The sky was cloudless, a brilliant blue, but for him all of the colour had been sucked out of it, out of the leaves on the trees, the flowers in the window-boxes. Drained of vibrant, bursting summer hues.

From his perch, he could view the tops of the heads of the shirt-sleeved patrons on the pavement outside the White Lion. But the chatter from the drinkers only made him feel worse. Such tinkling, clinking, mindless conversation. Imbecilic laughter. Especially the women with their casual shrieks about nothing. More than a week had passed since the trip to Brighton and he had not seen or spoken to Macy.

He then did what she had always forbidden him to do. He went down to the White Lion, pushed his way through the merry crowd and telephoned her. That damned housekeeper with the cool, haughty tones answered.

'Miss Collingwood is no longer with us,' he was told.

'What do you mean?'

'She has returned to the United States.'

The way the housekeeper said the name of that country made it sound like a fortress against him. His knees buckled at the news and he had to lean against a table edge. Beer slops soaked into the seat of his trousers.

'That is not possible.'

'I can assure you it is very possible, Mr Strathairn. She left by ocean liner yesterday.'

'But she didn't tell me.'

'It was a last-minute decision. I was surprised myself. I was not allowed the time I would normally need to arrange the packing. All that washing, ironing and folding. Those duties require proper planning. Mr Collingwood was sympathetic, of course.'

'Was there a message? A note? A letter?'

'Not one word,' she said. The tone was triumphant.

He bought six bottles of porter from the bar, returned to his flat. Lined them up along his desk like dark brown sentries guarding his heart, getting ready to move off duty one by one. This was what people did in the films, he thought. Or at least someone like Humphrey Bogart or Ray Milland, with their feelings buried deep beneath crusty exteriors. Turn to the booze. Such an appropriate word – 'booze' – starting hard before softening into its slushy sound. Booze. Rhyming with 'lose'.

Each consumed bottle changed his mood, as if it were an emotion he was drinking and not beer. First there was anger. Then the hurt of rejection. The third bottle brought him a sense of loss. The fourth bottle introduced him to guilt, a feeling that lingered long as it chastised him over and over again until an overwhelming feeling of loneliness took him well into unit number five. Utter despair was what he felt last before stumbling over to the bed and drifting into drunken sleep.

He awoke late into the morning. His head felt as if it was filled with concrete, cracked in places to let only the slightest of thoughts emerge. There was an instant when he didn't know what day or time it was – just like those moments of childhood innocence before he had been taught to understand the minutes and hours of the day, the days of the week. Those moments when the structures of the outside world had not yet imposed. And then he remembered Macy. Mid-Atlantic. Sailing further and further away from him.

He managed to heave himself out of his bed, drag on his dressing gown, stand over the toilet bowl. He watched with a certain detached awe the powerful stream of urine that seemed to go on forever. He made himself a pot of tea, drifted over to his desk, sat by the open window, lit a cigarette. The morning was hot but the sky was full of clouds. A clammy haze draped the city. The smell of stale beer hung over his room.

He stood up, moved over to the side of the bed, knelt down on the floor. He felt he was suffocating. His breathing came heavily, in deep uncontrollable gulps, trying to shift the painful knot of emotion tight in his abdomen. And heat. So much heat. Sweat pouring out of him. His lungs finally pushed out a huge cry of release as he pummelled the mattress in a frenzy of self-hatred.

His landlady asked him politely to move out the following day.

Like the slow clunk of a grandfather clock, its pendulum grind somehow heavier in the moist heat, the hot summer dragged on for Edward in post-Coronation London, minute by lonely minute. Aldous had gone off to a rented cottage in Cornwall with Robert, leaving him the vacant possession of his flat until he could find new digs, but his heart wasn't into any property hunting in Bloomsbury. Instead, he set himself the task of learning twenty Japanese *kanji* a day as a useful way of using up this dead time, but after a week he had even given up on that personal challenge. In a rare moment of creative enthusiasm, he knocked back a half decanter of Aldous' whisky and tried to write fiction, but the pen scratched wearily in his hand until he fell asleep at his desk, his cheek resting against the cushioned nap of the unstained blotting paper. The next morning, hungover and despondent, he packed his bags, took the Tube to Euston Station. He would return to Glasgow to visit his parents for the first time in nearly a year.

His father had retired in the interim, a lifetime of total dedication to his shipping firm leaving him devoid of hobbies. He now moped around the house in the loose cardigan and worn slippers he usually reserved for Sunday slovenliness, spending hours on the crossword or in front of the wireless set. His paternal stature had somehow disappeared with the loss of the weekday suit and tie.

'You've got to get that man out of the house, Eddie,' his mother said as she stamped the steam iron on a shirt stretched tight across her board. 'I cannae stand him under my feet a minute longer. Go on. It's a beautiful day.'

Deep-seated in his favourite armchair, his father shook his newspaper noisily. But he put aside his reading and his pipe, reached for his jacket.

'Come on, son. Let's go out where we can breathe more easy.'

They walked through Kelvingrove Park, past the university with its Gothic spires, then further on to the Botanic Gardens. Mothers and nannies were out in force with their batteries of prams, couples were smooching on the slopes. As if the outdoor heat wasn't enough, his father took him into one of the Victorian glasshouses where the climate ranged from temperate to tropical to cater for the city's famous collection of ferns. They found themselves an empty bench under a glass rotunda surrounded by palms snaking high for a grasp of the sunlight.

'I often come here,' his father said, picking out a plug of tobacco from a leather pouch. 'This is my kind of climate. Not your usual wearisome *dreich*.'

'Why did you never go somewhere warmer then? Your company could have posted you overseas.'

His father busied himself tamping down the greasy-black tobacco into his pipe bowl. 'I just never had the courage, lad. Or maybe it was just laziness. Bit of both, probably.'

'But you volunteered for the Front. That took courage.'

'That wasnae courage. That was just patriotic stupidity. If I'd known what I was letting myself in for, I'd never have gone. In the end, it was pure luck that got me through.'

His father had received a shrapnel wound in his left arm early on, sent back from the trenches before the real tragedies at Sommes, Arras, Ypres and Amiens had begun. The wound had never properly healed but with the Clydeside shipyards in full swing by then, it hadn't been difficult to be assigned a job at one of the shipping companies. And that was where he stayed for nearly forty years. The stiffness in the arm remained too. Edward could see it now as his father lit a match, drew it awkwardly to the bowl.

'And how is life in London?' The first clouds of smoke hung in the humid air, the aroma sickly sweet and heavy.

'It's all right.'

'All right? Is that the best you can muster from my brother's legacy?'

'I'm afraid so.'

His father sucked noisily on the whitened stem. 'There's not a lassie involved, is there?'

He didn't reply.

'Well, just remember what I told you.'

Edward did remember what his father had told him. Almost nothing. He had been sixteen years old when his father had sat him down in the front room, asked him if he knew the Facts of Life. Being one of the youngest in his class, he had already gleaned from the older boys what he felt was enough knowledge to avoid the conversation. He had nodded to his father's question, and the man had sat back relieved in his armchair, lit his pipe in the same patient manner as he had done now. 'Good,' his father had said. 'Just don't get anyone in the club before you're married.' And that was it. The only advice his father had ever given him. Except to dry thoroughly between his toes after a swim in the Corporation baths.

'Anyway, I'm glad I've got a few moments alone with you,' his father said. 'There's something I want to say.' Another few sucks on his pipe until a young couple had passed by, pushing a pram with a sleeping bairn tucked up inside. 'It's about your mother.'

'What? Is she ill?'

'I wouldnae say that. At least, not just yet. It's just that she's become awful forgetful. It may be that she's always been like that and I've just never been around to see it.'

'Isn't being forgetful a part of getting older?'

'Aye, maybe. But it's not just about forgetting to lock the back door or bringing back a pouch of tobacco from her shopping. It's just things you wouldnae imagine anyone not remembering.'

'Like what?'

'Simple things. Dates. The other day she couldnae remember her birthday. And simple arithmetic. I caught her with a box of matches spilled out on the kitchen table. She was counting them out as if she was testing herself. You know, two add another three equals five. She kept repeating the exercise. I heard her talking to herself. Sometimes she got it terribly wrong. It was the smaller numbers that seemed to bother her. Fours and fives and sixes. Not the larger ones as you might expect.'

His father's eyes glazed over and Edward noticed how the colour had drained out of them. They used to be such a vibrant brown, like leather freshly polished, now they had faded down to a pale dun, worn-out by the years. The shaving wasn't clean either with a few patches of stubble forgotten by the razor. Tufts of hair grew out of his ears and nostrils. The shirt collar hung loose around his neck.

'Anyway I'd appreciate it if you'd keep an eye on her while you're here,' his father said. 'See if I'm mistaken.'

His mother made a similar request about his father. She had called Edward upstairs to where she sat on her bed with an opened shoebox on the quilt beside her.

'It goes under there, back in the corner by the shoehorns,' she said, repeatedly wringing at the knuckles of one of her fingers. 'Just so you know.'

'Just so I know what?'

'Where the few things of value are hidden.' She plucked her silver evening-watch out of the box, began to polish the glass with a corner of her apron. 'My mother's wedding ring is in there too. And that miniature sword from Japan.'

He sat down on the bed beside her, picked out the sword, ran his fingers along the carvings on the ivory sheath. 'Will you stop talking like this? There's a long life in you yet.'

'It's your father. He's got me awfully worried, Eddie,' she said. 'He gets these pains in his chest. The doctor's given him tablets for it. He thinks I don't notice when he takes them.' She reached out, stroked the back of his hand. 'Why don't you keep that,' she said. 'You were always fond of it. Play with it for hours, you would. Like it was the most precious thing on earth.'

'You remember that?'

'Aye. It's funny the things that stick in the mind. Anyway, watch out for father. Make sure he doesn't overdo it, always wanting to lift things, drag the furniture around when I'm cleaning.'

For the rest of his stay, Edward was on a constant worried vigilance over the two of them. Previously, he had always thought of them as one entity. A single operating unit bound by the vows of marriage and the birth of a son. A bundled package. The Strathairns. His parents. His ancestors. Who looked after him, fed and clothed him, gave him his bus fare, took him on holidays, dabbed his spots with calamine lotion, told him when to get his hair cut, signed off his homework, wrote him letters, bought him birthday presents, kissed him goodnight, came to wave him goodbye. Now they were like separate countries with a shared border, and he was some kind of spy running the checkpoint between them. The onus of care and responsibility had shifted from them to him. And it made him feel both resentful and compassionate at the same time. Resentful for the loss of this taken-for-granted haven that had always been behind him, supplying him, backing him up. Resentful that the son had been forced to become the father of this man and this woman. Compassionate for their vulnerability and vincibility in the face of death.

When he left three weeks later, they came to see him off at Central Station. He held the grip of his father's hand longer than usual until the man's fearful gaze strayed away to the station clock. He tried to seal up the memory of his mother's perfume as he kissed her powdered cheek. He boarded the train, took out his notebook and wrote all the way back to London.

It was hard for Edward to believe Aldous could have had a father and a mother. It was as if the man had arrived on this earth self-contained, self-opinionated and totally developed at the age of forty without the need of a childhood or adolescence. Never younger and never to grow older. Continuing on his merry way, impervious to the slights and slurs of others, exhibiting only the very thinnest cracks of hurt at some of the childish yet sadistic actions of Robert, who this morning had stormed off back to Manchester all because his eggs had not been cooked just right. Or some other petty excuse. Leaving Aldous tied up with rage, quivering lips barely containing the fury backed up behind them, standing by the light of the window in his silk dressing gown, paintbrush attacking the canvas on the easel. It was not easy to assault a still-life painting. Fruit bowl, silver candlesticks and a stuffed pheasant on the sideboard. Absolute realism. No wonder Aldous couldn't get on with Macy.

'It's strange that I've known you all this time, Aldous, and I don't know if your parents are alive or dead.'

Aldous grunted, continued painting.

'I just wondered. You've never mentioned them.'

'Alive and kicking in Devon,' Aldous conceded. 'Kicking each other, no doubt. It's what's kept them in this world so long.'

Silence again. But this time an easier quietness. Aldous' cat Macavity entering the room, a purring slink and slide against his master's calf before leaping on to the window sill, stretching out in the sunlight. Aldous reaching over, stroking the obscenely proffered belly.

'I've written something for *The Londinium*.'

'Ah, finally, some creativity arises out of the misery. What is it called?'

'Don't you want to know what it's about first?'

'Personally, I do. But my readers these days like a good title to pull them in. Publishing is becoming so crass, so commercial these days.'

'It's tentatively called *Against The Odds*.'

'Hmmm. So-so. What is it about?'

'A man in the twilight of his life. Frustrated, disappointed, full of regrets.'

'Sounds predictable.'

'A man who has lived his life according to what has been expected of him. Played by the rules of his parents, his class, his religion, his workplace. Until he realises he has not lived at all.'

'*Bo-ring*.'

'He bets all his life savings on a horse.'

'Ah. Now it gets interesting. So what happens next?'

'You'll have to read it to find out.'

'Ah, I see.' Aldous pecked away with his brush. 'It is the visit home that has inspired. Not the rejection by the beast.'

'Macy may have been many things. But she was not a beast.'

'All women are becoming beasts. It was the war that changed them. All those jobs giving them financial independence. They used to be such pleasant creatures before that.'

'What about men?'

'Men have no excuse. They have always been beasts.'

The advertisement was tucked away at the corner of the notice board. Normally, Edward wouldn't have paid it or even the board much attention. But he was looking for an offer of decent rented accommodation among the tacked up scraps of papers announcing the meetings of clubs and societies to which he was not a member. The School of Oriental and African Studies was full of these activities for happy, energetic, well-balanced, sociable human beings who liked to discuss matters relating to Colonialism and the Commonwealth, who were eager to hike in multi-ethnic packs the pathways of the South Downs, who played cricket, football and tennis, who wanted to swap lessons in Swahili for conversation in Hindi. But there was never any bright chit by one aspiring writer craving the companionship of another. Edward was an outsider. And he wondered if he was an outsider first and a writer second. Or whether wanting to write drove him naturally to being an outsider. An observer. Spotting the advertisement which read as follows:

"Argos Motors requires an English copywriter and general liaison officer for position in Tokyo. Some communication skills in Japanese essential. Excellent conditions. Would suit young graduate of Japanese studies. Please contact Mr Peter Digby, General Manager, Argos Motors."

'I'm not a young graduate,' Edward told Digby over the telephone.

Digby laughed. 'What does that mean? You're not young or you're not a graduate?'

'The latter.'

'I wish people wouldn't use that former and latter stuff. It means I have to go back over what they said, which I've forgotten anyway, and then try to figure it all out.'

'I'm sorry, sir. I'm not a graduate. I've only just completed my first year in Japanese studies.'

'That actually suits us better. You see this job is not about translation. That's what I have discovered most graduates want. Spiritless translation work. No, we don't need a translator. They've got a Jap chap doing that over there already.'

'Who's "they"?'

'Tokyo Autos. That's the company we're licensing our engineering technology to. We just need someone to put his formal translations into normal English. So I can understand what it all means.'

'What kind of translations?'

'Company stuff. Brochures, reports. Maybe some legal and technical papers. There's a big motor show coming up in Japan next year. I'd like to see material in both Japanese and comprehensible English for that. Then there would be correspondence to edit. Annual reports. And to be honest with you, I wouldn't mind having one of my chaps over there on the ground so to speak, just to keep an eye out, keeping Argos Motors' best interests at heart, if you know what I mean? Does it suit?'

'Perhaps.'

'Think about it. Then come over and we can talk conditions.'

Peter Digby turned out to be exactly as he sounded on the telephone. A no-nonsense man in tweed sports jacket who was really an engineering genius specialising in the field of crankshafts and gearboxes but had ended up administering his own successful automobile company.

'This licensing deal is easy money for Argos,' Digby told Edward over his second pint at a pub near to his office. 'Let the Japs pay us so they can tinker with their tiny little cars away over there on the other side of the world. Argos is not interested in the Asian market so we're only too happy to help them out with our technology. Do you know how many cars they made last year? Not even five thousand. And we're too entrenched here for them to ever challenge us with their Isuzus and Nissans, no matter how much they up their production and exports. Mark my words, fifty years from now, and you'll still be driving around in an Argos. This deal is money for old rope. Money for old rope is what I say.'

The conditions were good. A company-paid flat in Tokyo. Monthly subsistence allowance in yen, balance paid in sterling direct to his bank account. Annual bonus. Two years minimum commitment.

'Anything less than that and no sooner you'd be out there, than you'd have to hop on the ship back. It takes nearly a month to sail there. What do you think?'

'I'll take it.'

Digby held out his hand. 'Sealed in flesh. Now before I buy you another drink. Tell me something. Adventure? Or escape?'

Edward thought about this for a few moments. 'The latter,' he said.

There had been a narrow street with high walls. The ground was littered with crushed petals, cut-off flower stalks. The odour of a market packed up and gone home, lingering like the perfume of a departed loved-one. Then a large thoroughfare with traffic. How Edward had managed to catch a bus from there he did not know. More of a miracle that he had caught the right one. He couldn't remember if he had voluntarily disembarked at Tottenham Court Road or whether the conductor had assisted him on prior instruction, but he did remember vomiting into a flower bed in Russell Square. Then standing there, bent over, dry retching for what seemed like an hour. He had felt better after that. His eyes watery and aching, his head throbbing but clear from the effect of God knows how many pints he had downed with Digby at the Bricklayers Arms. Up the narrow stairs to Aldous' flat, fumbling with the key but Aldous opening the door anyway. So wonderful to see his friend standing there in his pyjamas.

'So, if I hear you right,' Aldous said, his blue eyes bearing down on him as twin lamps of interrogation. 'If I hear you right, you went out to find a flat, which I have to commend you for actually managing to do, but this flat it turns out is in Tokyo rather than Tottenham.'

'I have a contract sealed in flesh.'

'So nothing has been signed?'

'My handshake is my bond.' Edward held out his hand to Aldous. It was shaking. 'This is my first job, Aldous. Can't you be pleased for me? After all, I'm now a man from Argos Motors.'

'You look more like a man who's been run over by an Argos Motor. It is not as though I am not pleased. I am just slightly surprised at this sudden career change.'

'It doesn't feel sudden. It feels as though little events have been gradually pushing me in this direction. It was the easiest decision I've ever had to make.'

'East or west, Tokyo is the furthest place away from a certain young lady in New York.'

'This has nothing to do with her.'

'And what will your dear parents say?'

'I shall not tell them until I am on my way. On my way. Onwards and upwards.'

Aldous was the only person to see him off at Southampton on a grey, blustery, hold-on-to-your-hat afternoon. The kind that summed up Edward's current feeling about the life he was leaving. Aldous came up the gangplank with him, pressed an envelope into his hand when they reached the top.

'What is it?'

'Payment for *Against The Odds*.'

Aldous then grabbed him by the upper arms, shook him affectionately, his eyes teared from the wind or from emotion or both, then turned quickly and grappled his way back down the gangplank, his long coat flapping madly in the breeze. About halfway down, he turned back round, waved and shouted:

'Don't forget to write, Eddie. Don't forget to write.'

CHAPTER ELEVEN

Tokyo, Japan • 2003

Edward went out on to the terrace for some cool air and to admire the ambassador's lawn, all lit-up into an unnatural AstroTurf-green by the bathe of arc lamps. Surrounded by those high hedges. It might be the only lawn of such a size in Tokyo. Such a large tract of empty space spared from the clutches of a high-density population. It was probably a pre-requisite for the purchase of the embassy site. Enough room for a good-sized lawn. "We British must have at least a half-acre for our garden parties. You never know when Her Majesty might turn up for a game of croquet."

He sipped on his malt whisky. He felt quite perked up by the alcohol. He had been so tired earlier on. Such a long day in such a long life. The nap in Jerome's study had helped, yet he was all ready to take the Shinkansen back to Hakone when Jerome mentioned these invitations. An early evening reception to celebrate the 500th anniversary of Scotch whisky, hosted by the Scottish Malt Whisky Distillers' Association at the British Embassy. What self-respecting Scotsman could resist? A pure marketing ploy, of course. Who could possibly have known when the first malt whisky was distilled? Was there a plaque somewhere? One of those blue heritage circles nailed into the wall of a tiny Highland croft? "The first whisky was distilled here by Angus MacPherson in 1503". Perhaps there was a dated recipe written down by a monk, crouched by his still in a freezing Lowland monastery. Or a pot excavated from the spot where a moonshiner had fixed his first brew. Another sip. An excellent idea to come to this little reception. On one condition though.

'I'll only go if I can do this incognito,' he had told Jerome. 'I absolutely insist on it.'

'OK, I won't tell anyone who you are,' Jerome had conceded.

'You can introduce me as Aldous. Professor Aldous. A former colleague.'

'But surely people will recognise you anyway?'

'Of course they won't. I'm a writer.'

One or two had stood out in the past. Ernest, of course. But that was because of his other antics. And the suicide. Kingsley, in certain circles. Graham, because he was so tall. But who would have recognised Camus, Boll, Pasternak, Steinbeck, Sholokhov walking along a Tokyo street? The Japanese might even have had trouble with their very own Kawabata. Nobel laureates all. Nowadays it was different. Photographs on the inside cover. Book tours. Interviews. Festivals. He had seen Kingsley's son a few times on television. And then there was that Rushdie chap. Ten years or whatever it was in hiding, yet the most recognised writer on the planet.

'Hey, Eddie.' Jerome calling to him from the patio doors. 'Come and see this.'

It was quite a sight. A parade through the entrance hall headed by a piper, then the ambassador and his wife, the chairman of the Association holding a plate of steaming haggis aloft, followed by a troupe of Japanese men and women in full Highland dress. In his malt-fuelled mood, Edward found the whole bizarre scene quite entertaining. He even joined the guests in their rhythmic clapping and whooping as together they crushed into a large chandeliered reception room. A butler announced the ambassador would make a toast, which he did, flushed in the cheeks no doubt from his own libations. Then the British national anthem sung boisterously by the guests, irrespective of their nationality.

'The Queen,' the ambassador said on its conclusion.

Edward raised his own glass in salute as the kilted band of Japanese took up position in two lines spread out across the parquet floor. The piper pumped up his bag. There was going to be a Highland reel. And then he felt it. A powerful, jagged, jarring thud. Just like the Shinkansen hitting a tunnel. The whole world jolted a fraction then back again. A sudden silence, except for the dying drone of the pipes. An audible gasp from one of the uninitiated. The grasp for a table top. Whisky lapping at the insides of bottles. The swaying of the chandelier. The smash of a glass. Edward had forgotten what this could be like. The waiting to see if this was the big one. That awful moment when the solid ground underfoot could no longer be relied upon. When there was no place to run. When the jaws of the earth threatened to open up and swallow its tormentors in one horrifying act of divine retribution. Another tremor. Longer but not so intense. He looked around. The terrified faces of the Scottish distillers and their staff. The ambassador calm and still, head cocked in readiness for another ripple. Edward could hear the sound of his own heart. A lesser tremor. Fading away. Another minute of held-breath stillness. And the experienced knew it was over. The ambassador with his glass in the air.

'Music, maestro, please,' the Queen's representative shouted. 'Let there be music.' And everyone clapped, happy to slap away their fear.

Edward found himself an armchair in one of the smaller reception rooms, glad to sit down, legs wobbly on his cane from the whisky and the quake. Jerome came in too, ruddy-faced and sweating, parked himself on a hard-backed chair beside him, glass gripped in one hand, bottle in another.

'Never got used to them,' Jerome said. He looked really old and tired now, the flesh on his face hanging loose like burnt skin.

'I thought the buildings were better designed these days.'

'Until the big one comes along.' Jerome knocked back the contents of his glass, poured himself another, hand trembling. 'Damn good stuff this. So, tell me, why did you come back? A little adventure while you still can? Or escape?'

'The first time I came to Japan, someone asked me that too. The manager of Argos Motors. Good man. Can't even remember his name.'

'So what's the answer?'

'If you must know. Escape.'

'What do you need to escape from? Your knightship must have a glittering life back there in good old England.'

'It's too complicated.'

'Go on. Spill the beans to your old buddy.'

'I don't want to talk about it.'

'Just tell me, for fuck's sake.'

'This is what I'll tell you. I think you should ease up on the drinking.'

'You know what, Eddie? You and my doctor agree on that one. But you know what I say? I say – what do you think it's gonna do? Fucking kill me? Cut a few years off my life? I'm already past the average age of life expectancy. I'm living on rented time, don't you know.'

'We all are.'

'All right. I'll ask you something else then. What do you think of the new Japan?'

'Are we going to argue?'

'We always used to.'

'And now?'

'Depends.'

'On what?'

'If you've changed.'

'The truth doesn't change, Jerome.'

'Don't be so self-righteous. Just tell me what you think.'

'No comment. I've only seen some crass commercialism from the back of a taxi.'

'You gotta have some opinions.'

'What do you want me to say?' He knew where this conversation was headed, didn't want to go there, but the whisky would take them both there anyway. 'That modern Japan is just one big American success story?'

'You could at least give us some credit.'

'I give absolutely no credit to a nation that wiped out a quarter of a million civilians with firebombs and atomic weapons. I didn't do so then, and will not do so now.'

He could hear the sound of the bagpipes filtering through from the other room. More clapping. The irreverent stamping of feet. As if to show this fragile earth who was really boss. He just wanted to close his eyes, sink back into the comfort of this armchair and fall asleep. But Jerome was close in, shouting above the music.

'Those atomic bombs saved a million lives.'

Even in his weariness, Edward had to rise to the bait. 'Look, Jerome, why don't you forget about that tired old argument. Do you know what really bothers me now? It's that you Yanks refuse to take a good look at what happened here. Even the Germans went back and took stock of what they did during the Holocaust. But the Americans... the Americans never batted an eyelid over Nagasaki. That is what I've never forgiven. Until they confront the tragedy of Nagasaki, we will never see any enlightened foreign policy coming out of your country.'

He saw that Jerome had stiffened quite dramatically. Patterns of behaviour. So hard to break. Jerome ending up apoplectic and defensive over Nagasaki. It was a blind spot. His American friend was an intelligent man, there was no doubt about that. But when it came to Nagasaki, he just seemed to shut down his brain, turn off his compassion.

'Can't believe you said that,' Jerome spluttered.

'I stood up for the victims. Now you know why *The Waterwheel* didn't sell well in America.'

'Don't be flippant. How can you compare us with the Nazis?'

'That's not what I said. I just said it would help if America did some public soul-searching over Nagasaki, the way the Germans did over the Holocaust.'

'And you think the Japanese have done any soul-searching over what they did? I don't hear a lot of apologies being made from this corner of the globe for all the atrocities that occurred. You might think you're some kind of hero over here. Christ, you've even got the dean fawning all over you. But a helluva lot of Japanese used you and your stupid novel as propaganda to cover up their own misdeeds.'

'All right, Jerome, that's enough,' he said, struggling up from his chair. 'There's nothing more to be gained from this.'

Jerome pulled at his sleeve. 'Sorry, Eddie, no offence meant. Come on, sit down, stay for another. One for the road.'

'No, I'm leaving. Please thank the dean again for his gift. Wherever it is.'

'You left it in the cloakroom.'

He waited for Jerome to stand too, but he didn't move from his chair. 'Come on. We can't part like this.'

Jerome stretched out a limp hand in a half-hearted wave. 'Nothing's changed, Eddie.'

Edward turned his back, felt his entire body taut with rage as he strode off to the cloakroom. His blood pressure must have been right off the scale. There were some tablets if he could only remember where he had put them. An elderly Japanese couple approached as he fumbled at the desk for his ticket.

'We're very sorry to trouble you. But my wife believes you are the writer Edward...'

'Leave me alone, will you? Just leave me alone.'

CHAPTER TWELVE

Japan • 1956

When Edward first arrived in Japan, he imagined himself as this tiny, isolated dot of a soul lost among millions of other souls. And after eighteen months, that was how he remained, not joining the dots, but carving out a lonely existence for himself between his little box of an apartment and the offices of Tokyo Autos. Japan happened all around him, and he wondered at it, absorbed it, learned from it as he added another perspective to his way of thinking. But he kept apart from it. And he found he liked it that way. When he wrote to Aldous about his propensity towards contented isolation, he received the comment: 'You are very fortunate to possess the most important quality for being a writer.'

The First Tokyo Motor Show propelled Edward slightly more into the limelight. The show was a great success with over half a million people attending, and he enjoyed his assignment dealing with the few English-speaking customers at the Tokyo Autos stand. He felt proud of his contribution as a bridge of cultural understanding, his edited brochures in both English and Japanese outlining "the outstanding co-operation in licensed technology between Tokyo Autos and Argos Motors as a cornerstone for the future development of the Japanese automobile industry". Although Tokyo Autos still manufactured many of its passenger vehicles simply by welding car bodies on to the chassis of small trucks, "the company was seriously committed towards producing cars according to international standards and held a long-term belief that it could compete in the global export market". He reported these views back to Digby in London who replied with the letter he now held as he leaned back in his chair, feet up on his desk, in the small office allocated to him by his Japanese hosts. "International Officer" was the sign on his door, ostentatiously describing his position as an English copywriter. The room's tiny window allowed him a view over the skyline of a central Tokyo that seemed to be growing by the minute.

"I am delighted to hear of the contribution our beloved Argos is making to domestic production in Japan," Digby wrote. "But I dismiss as totally fanciful the idea that Tokyo Autos might be able to come up with its own car to compete in the export market. Such a thought is madness, but humour your hosts anyway."

Edward didn't think the idea was madness at all. The American army of occupation had departed, leaving the Japanese to fall back on their boundless capacity for hard work, their resourcefulness at adapting the inventiveness of others to their own ends. They even had a phrase for it. *Wakon-Yoshi*. Japanese spirit, Western ability. And what a combination those qualities were proving to be. He just had to look out of the window to see the result. High-rise office and apartment buildings, department stores, nightclubs, pachinko parlours, all springing up like wild mushrooms in the humid streets below while underfoot new subway lines were being hacked out of the scorched earth. He could even walk out of the front door of Tokyo Autos, cross the road and order an American-style pizza and a half-bottle of Chianti at a newly established Italian restaurant. A new Japan was rising out of the ashes and debris. It was already beginning to hold its own in the global shipbuilding and textile industries and the automobile industry would be next. The country was experiencing strong economic growth, the demand for good quality cars was increasing. Only the lack of paved roads dampened enthusiasm and with a new national highway construction plan underway Edward expected even that obstacle to expansion to fade away rapidly. The success of the motor show had shown that consumer confidence was on the up and up. Digby would be proved wrong. He was sure of it.

A knock on the door. Ah, the tea girl, Edward thought, providing her customary round of green-leaf refreshment. He relished the cleansing taste of her brew as he called out for her to enter. But it was not the delightful kimono-clad Mie who appeared, but the grim and very male Kobayashi, the English translator whose formally worded texts Edward spent all his working days revising. He hurriedly whipped his feet off the desk, knocking over a pile of brochures in the process.

Kobayashi smirked at the chaos, his tiny caterpillar of a moustache twitching above his upper lip. The translator bowed, then ceremoniously held out an envelope balanced on open palms. 'Specific delivery.'

'Special delivery,' Edward corrected. He felt he could easily be employed editing Kobayashi's whole being, not just his translations. The moustache could go for a start. And something needed to be done about the bad breath, the dirty fingernails and the ill-fitting suit. Yet this was an unusual interruption. Edward normally collected his mail from his pigeonhole in the main staff room. And this envelope that Kobayashi proffered was not made from the usual flimsy onion-skin material either, but from thick brown paper stamped all over by some enthusiastic postal worker. Edward plucked it from the man's outstretched hands and turned it over. It was from his Aunt Cathy in Edinburgh. He thanked the retreating Kobayashi and hurriedly slit open the envelope with the Japanese knife his mother had given him.

They had gone quickly, one after the other, like a pair of dominoes flicked over by the fingernail of God or whoever else was responsible for masterminding these events. First his father, then his mother three days later. "*A blessing in disguise*" his aunt wrote in a small, tight script that immediately conjured up her mean lips, bitten hard into concentration over her composition. "*I do not know how she would have coped without him to look after her. After your father died, I was just about to telegram you to come back but then when your mother passed away so soon after I felt it was pointless. A letter is so much more comforting than a telegram anyway, I think. And there was nothing really you could have done, so far away from home.*" It was strange to find Aunt Cathy in such a consoling mood towards him. She had been far from compassionate when he had taken up the educational legacy provided by her late husband, his Uncle Rob. "*You can be reassured that both your parents passed away quickly and with little pain.*" His father had died of a sudden heart attack, while his mother "*had just given up on life. Her memory had deteriorated so much recently that I am not even sure if she knew who your father was. I took care of all the necessary funeral arrangements. That solicitor chap, Wilson Guthrie, who was also your Uncle Rob's lawyer, is the executor and will administer the estate. No doubt he will get in touch with you in due course about the sale of the house and its contents. I have given him your address. I'm so sorry. I have enclosed a few keepsakes for you in the meantime. There are some valuables – watches, jewellery and the like – but I did not want to entrust these items to the international post. Love…*" Included in the bulky envelope were two handkerchiefs, one embroidered with his father's initials, the other with his mother's. A photograph of his parents on their wedding day. Another with him sitting between them on a spread-out picnic blanket.

He stared out of the window. Dark clouds were pushing in quickly from the east. It was the rainy season. The Japanese had officially decreed it thus and it was so. Just as there were days that marked the beginning and end of summer, irrespective of whether the sun was actually shining or not. He could see the delineation of the weather front quite clearly, bright sunshine on one side, a sheet of rain on the other. Workmen who had been padding across girders on a building site in front of his office began scurrying down from their positions, skipping across planked walkways, sliding down ladders, hardly touching the sides as they went. He didn't really know what to do with himself. Except to sit there on the corner of his desk, the edge biting quite uncomfortably into his left buttock. His parents had died. One after another. On the other side of the world, so remote from where he was now, that he felt as if the fact of their deaths must surely be within the domain of another person and not his own.

The day grew blacker and he observed the first streaks of rain cut across the windowpane. It would be both wet and warm outside. An interesting combination so unlike the damp coldness of the British weather. Such an odd thing for his aunt to do, sending these two handkerchiefs. He picked up his father's. Plain white linen, except for the blue-stitched initials in one corner. He imagined his mother doing the stitching, nimbly working her fingers and the needle, then a quick cut of the thread with her teeth. 'Done' she would have said. He put the material to his nose. Freshly laundered. Nothing of his father. No pipe tobacco. No hair oil. No shaving lotion. No starched shirt. No hidden sweets in the pocket. No towel rub-down at the swimming pool. No waiting by the window for the hand upon the gate. No footstep on the stairway. No Scottish burr overheard from the bedroom darkness. He put the handkerchief aside and picked up his mother's. Cream silk with a pale green border. He brought it to his nose and smelt it also. His mother's perfume. And then he felt the tears on his cheek, hot like the monsoon raindrops on the other side of the pane. They came quickly in a sudden burst, then they were gone. He wiped his face with his mother's handkerchief, sat down behind his desk.

Tokyo Autos supplied Edward with an office, secretarial support, commissioned work and organised his apartment, but in actuality he was an employee of Argos Motors. Argos paid his salary, his rent, his transportation and his bonus. It was to Argos he owed his allegiance. He expected nothing from the Japanese firm, yet when news of his parents' death spread throughout the company, he became the recipient of a tsunami of sympathy and kindness from his co-workers. It was the miserable Kobayashi who had been the conduit. The translator had returned to the office later that afternoon with the rain hammering against the window to enquire politely whether the package of special delivery had contained any important news. When he had told Kobayashi what had happened, the black-bordered cards of condolence began to arrive almost immediately. They were followed by small gifts. Boxes of chocolates. A selection of soaps. A set of hand-towels. Bundles of incense. All accompanied by the corresponding business cards of the senders. People he didn't even know. Two days later he was led by a solemn Kobayashi to the office of Mr Tanaka, the company's general manager.

'We just wondered whether you wish to return to London in consideration of your recent tragic loss,' Kobayashi told Edward in a translation of his superior's words. It was an unnecessary role for Kobayashi to play, given that Edward understood very well every word Tanaka had said. But he also understood that the proper procedures had to be acted out. That the foreigner could not be seen to speak better Japanese than his boss could speak English. Tanaka sat behind his desk, pulling at his brilliant-white shirt-cuffs as he waited for his reply.

'That will not be necessary,' Edward responded, with a short bow towards the general manager.

Tanaka nodded then asked in Japanese. 'Perhaps a few days' compassionate leave?' Again Kobayashi translated.

The deaths of his parents still seemed far off in another time zone and all Edward wanted to do was keep on working, keep up a rhythm, keep up his emotional guard. But Tanaka's question presented an interesting cultural dilemma to which he did not know the correct answer. Was it more important to continue working, thereby exhibiting the proper stoicism and loyalty to the company, or was it better to take time off in order to show the proper mourning and respect towards his deceased parents? Edward chose the former.

Tanaka sucked in his breath, quickly conferred with Kobayashi.

'In that case,' the translator said, 'we wonder if you would like to join us tomorrow on the company's summer coach trip to Hakone? The colourful hydrangeas will surely lift your spirits.'

'I am sorry about parents, *sensei*,' Mie the tea girl told Edward in a practice of her English as their motor-coach, the leading one in a convoy of three, moved away from the coastline. Mie was also one of his students in an English conversation class he taught one night a week for some of the staff under a private arrangement with the company. She was a bright young woman, far more adept at picking up the language than her male classmates, but unlikely ever to rise above the level of tea girl. One hand half-covered her mouth as she spoke, the fingers of the other fluttered over the fan in her lap. Edward had always imagined the Japanese fan to be some kind of fashion accessory until he experienced the first few days of summer in this country. The humidity was unbearable. Even now, at nine in the morning, he could feel his shirt cling to the seat fabric as he turned to speak to her. Mie with her round face and very flat features, almost no contours at all, no shadows, no secrets. Just this wide openness waiting for his reply.

'Thank you,' he said, not knowing what else to say in these circumstances. 'It is very sad,' he added.

'Yes. Very sad.' Then her face brightened as the coach cranked down noisily into a lower gear and began to climb the steep road up the hillside. 'Soon we can see Fuji-san,' she said, then dipped her gaze. 'But Fuji-san never lets herself be shown to tourist. Only person who stays in Japan long time will see Fuji-san with no clouds. Perfectly.'

'Then I am sure Fuji-san will show herself to me,' he replied. 'Perfectly.'

She smiled at his remark and he had an instinct to touch her then, just briefly, on the back of her hand. To connect physically to the comfort of another human being. It had been so long. But he turned his attention back to the window where the scene was set for a cat-and-mouse journey as he strained to catch a glimpse of the famous mountain through every break in the treeline. So many different kinds of trees. Maple, elm, cherry, dogwood, magnolia, others he couldn't name. The steamy, earthy smell of the leafy forest floor caught in the draft through the open coach windows. He greedily sucked in the pine tang as the bus continued its crawl above and away from the suburbs of Tokyo and Yokohama. Up into the undulating greenery that appeared to shrink back from the encroaching urban sprawl below. So unlike the wild, craggy and domineering landscape of Scotland.

He thought of the photograph his Aunt Cathy had sent him, the picnic with his parents somewhere in the Scottish Highlands. He had absolutely no recollection of the holiday at all. Now that his parents were dead, even their corroboration of the event had disappeared. Only the photograph remained as the solitary evidence he had ever been present. Without the photograph, there was no memory, no past, no childhood. He wondered what happened in the eras before photography. Did people lose their past to the erosion of time or did they concentrate more clearly on remembering the present? This picnic he knew must have taken place in the Highlands due to the intrusion of a long-haired cow into the corner of the photograph. Quite comical really. He must have been about eight years old, the three of them sitting together on a blanket, so ignorant of their bovine observer. Being a family. The Strathairns. Staring at the lens of some unknown photographer. A family friend or relative? An obliging stranger. His father leaning away slightly from the group, supporting himself on his good arm. He wore a suit while his son sat beside him in his school uniform even though they were on holiday. Only his mother seemed relaxed and casual in cardigan, blouse and skirt. He wondered what the colours of these garments were. His uniform would be dark blue, he knew that, of course. But what was the colour of his mother's blouse? Or her cardigan? Or her eyes? For God's sake, what was the colour of his mother's eyes? And suddenly through a clearing in the hillside woods there was Mount Fuji. Free of cloud cover. Totally naked. That sacred, snow-capped volcano. Too symmetrical to be carved out by the randomness of nature but rather by a benevolent God with an eye for geometry. He felt blessed by the sight of it. As did the rest of the coach party who gasped collectively at this glimpse of their mountain god. A tap on his shoulder. Mie. Indicating Kobayashi, who had leaned over from his seat on the other side of the aisle.

'Many woods make Hakone craftwork,' Kobayashi said, smiling at Mie as he spoke. She drew away as politely as she could from the stale breath of the translator.

'I am sorry but I don't understand,' Edward said.

'Many woods make Hakone craftwork,' Kobayashi repeated. '*Yoseki-zaiku zougan.*'

'I still don't understand.'

'I will show you later,' he said. 'I will show you *yoseki-zaiku zougan.*'

Along with his co-workers, Edward visited Owakudani for a scenic view of Mount Fuji, now covered by cloud. He trudged through a volcanic valley where the grey mud still bubbled and sucked in rock pools. He bought black-shell eggs boiled by crafty locals in the water leaked out from crater cracks. Their whole party hired a boat to sail out on to Lake Ashi, visited the Hakone Shrine, wandered among the ruins of the toll-road checkpoint, then walked the avenue of ancient cedars into Hakone itself. There on the shores of the lake, Edward came across the craft Kobayashi had been talking about. *Yoseki-zaiku zougan.* Marquetry. Hakone it seemed was famous for it. Intricate wooden inlays fashioned from the many timbers Edward had witnessed on the surrounding hillsides to produce boxes, trays, small chests and picture mosaics. Even wooden eggs, in sets of twelve, ever decreasing in size so one fitted inside the other like Russian dolls. Although Mie insisted it was the Japanese who gave the idea to the Russians rather than the other way around. It was the must-have souvenir of the region and Edward bought a set to take home.

After supper at a lakeside restaurant, the Tokyo Autos coach party was in a buoyant mood for the return journey. Amid this collective corporate spirit and bonhomie Edward realised he was quite enjoying himself. As was Mr Tanaka who during the meal had managed to drink copious amounts of sake poured with great diligence by Mie. The red-faced general manager now stood at the front of the bus directing a sing-song.

'I have something for you,' Kobayashi said, moving in to sit beside Edward in place of Mie who had been commandeered into singing a solo by her boss. The translator was also flushed from drink, his eyes bloodshot, his little moustache glistening with sweat. 'A gift from Hakone.' Kobayashi handed him an elaborately wrapped square package.

'May I open it?' Edward asked.

'Of course, of course. Please. Go ahead, as Americans say.'

Edward restrained his instinct to tear off the wrapping paper as quickly as he could, instead peeling off the layers carefully to reveal one of Hakone's famous marquetry boxes with a wooden mosaic picture of Mount Fuji on the lid.

'*Himitsu-bako*,' Kobayashi said, looking very pleased with himself.

Edward made the translation in his head. Secret box. 'Why secret?'

'It is like safe. You need to move panels in special order to open. This is seven-move box. Seven moves to open. It is a puzzle box. In old times, people pass along road through Hakone to Edo will buy puzzle box to keep them busy in journey. I do the same for you.' Kobayashi took the box, slid open a secret panel, and handed it back. 'Only six more,' he said. 'I have instruction paper if you need.'

Edward pressed his hand over the shiny smooth surfaces, trying to find the slots that slipped open like pins in a lock. This was going to be a long process but he wanted to show Kobayashi he was genuinely appreciative of the gift. The gesture had quite moved him. He had always assumed Kobayashi resented him for having to see his hard-worked translations constantly revised, the daily editing that must have sent a message back to the translator saying – what you do is not good enough. Yet here was a completely spontaneous gift. And an expensive one too. He searched for Kobayashi's hand and shook it. 'Thank you,' he said. '*Arigato*. Thank you.'

'Not to mention it.' Kobayashi stood up. 'Please excuse me. I feel a little unwell.'

Edward sat back in his seat, closed his eyes, let the dappled light flash across his face as the coach moved in and out of the evening sunlight on its tortuous ride down the hillside. He heard Kobayashi retch into a paper bag on the other side of the aisle, Mie's thin voice piping out some Japanese folk song from the front of the bus, he smelled the viscous stench of petrol fumes from underneath the floor boards. He opened his eyes. The coach had just rounded a corner swinging his window round into a direct confrontational view with the building wedged magnificently into the rock face. The sensation of familiarity was immediately apparent even though he had never been down this road in his life before. It was as if the hotel had always been there waiting for him. Just as he had imagined. The curved grey roofs flowed naturally down the contours of the hillside, like an architectural waterfall, moving effortlessly from level to level. Red balconies traversed the facade along each floor, moths flitted around lamps already lit to welcome the dusk. White-gloved bellboys stood at attention on either side of the main entrance while one storey above, guests in evening wear lingered on the terrace in the shade of an enormous white pine. Edward had seen this building before. He knew it was impossible but he was convinced he had. In a Japanese story book. In a dream. In a previous life. The feeling of *déjà vu* was very strong. Mie had returned to sit beside him and answered his question before he had time to ask it.

'It is the first hotel Japanese build for foreign guest,' she said. 'You must stay there some time. I believe it is very comfortable inside. Both Japanese and foreign style. Very high class. Very beautiful.'

'Yes, yes,' he said. 'It is very beautiful.'

Once he had received confirmation from the lawyer Wilson Guthrie that his parents' estate had been wound up, Edward telegrammed his notice of termination to Digby at Argos Motors in London. The next day, at the office of Tokyo Autos, and with Kobayashi in attendance, Edward executed a series of low bows before general manager Tanaka.

'I regret to inform you, Tanaka-san,' he said directly in Japanese, 'but I have decided to leave the company.'

'I see,' Tanaka responded in English, with a smug nod to Kobayashi. 'You are returning to London?'

'Actually, I'm not. I've decided to stay on here in Japan.'

'To do what, may I ask?'

'I would like to try writing. Writing a novel.'

Kobayashi, who stood stooped in front of his boss, slowly raised his head, stretched his lips across his teeth in such a curious way Edward wasn't sure if the translator was snarling or smiling at him. But the gesture had unnerved him. Edward knew his idea of a literary career was both a vain and a fatuous one and he felt Kobayashi could see right through to that. After all, his decision was not based on much – just two short stories published in *The Londinium*. For this he was grateful to Aldous, who unwittingly had also been responsible for this sudden career change in one other small way. It had derived from a sentence in a letter his friend had sent him not long after his parents had died. Perhaps it was a throwaway line, perhaps it was truly meant to inspire. The line read: "*All creativity comes from loss.*"

'I did not know you were a writer, Mr Strathairn,' Tanaka said.

'I'm not really sure if I am. It's just that I'd like to give it a proper try.'

Edward then bowed his head towards the general manager – a simple gesture in this minefield of gestures that he hoped conveyed his humility for even entertaining such a lofty notion.

Tanaka nodded thoughtfully. 'We Japanese have great appreciation for our artists,' he said eventually. 'Only last year, we created these...' He fired off some Japanese at Kobayashi.

'Bearers of Important Intangible Cultural Properties,' the translator said.

'Do you know of them, Mr Strathairn?' Tanaka asked. 'These... how did you say...? These bearers of...?' A wave of the hand left lingering in the air for a reply.

'With respect to Kobayashi-san,' Edward said, 'but I believe Living National Treasures is a simpler translation of the Japanese phrase.' He had read about these appointments in the Japanese press. They were some kind of reaction to the Occupation, the fear of losing the traditional crafts amid the deluge of American culture swamping the country. A public trust fund set up by the Japanese government to protect the country's great artists and master craftsmen, designating them as living national treasures, providing them with grants to support their work, to help them train apprentices to carry on their skills. Edward thought of them like knighthoods with stipends attached. Awards had already been made to a potter, a bamboo weaver and a swordmaker.

'Do you know what it takes to be a true master, to be one of these Living National Treasures, Mr Strathairn?'

'I'm sorry but I do not.'

'It requires two things,' the general manager said, holding up one finger, then another. A gold ring flashed on the second raised digit. 'Just two. A lifetime committed to hard work. And an open heart directly to your art. Do you possess those qualities, Mr Strathairn?'

'I don't know. I suppose this is what I am trying to discover.'

Tanaka grunted then spoke rapidly in Japanese.

'Tanaka-san wishes you luck in your journey of discovery,' Kobayashi translated. 'You are fortunate to have both the time and money to find the answer to these questions.'

He took up residency at the hotel that had so fascinated him on his trip to Hakone, the hotel that had been specially built to welcome the first foreigners to Japan, the hotel that on first glance had felt so familiar, as if it were his destiny calling out to him. He rented out on an indefinite basis the Fuji Suite, which consisted of an enormous bedroom with an equally large adjoining bathroom situated at the rear of the main building. The beauty of his accommodation was in its outlook – from a stout mahogany desk by the window he had a view of the hotel gardens and the wooded hillsides beyond.

His father would have liked the hotel. He would have sat quietly in one of the ample armchairs in the lobby, smoking his pipe among the potted palms, as he admired the craftsmanship in the wooden parquet flooring, the intricate designs carved into the teak reception desk or the cloisonné bowls on the window ledges. For his mother, it would be a different experience. With an eager staff to take care of the cooking and cleaning, she would be restless, nervously scratching for work to busy her idle hands. Perhaps she would find solace, even a blossoming talent, in some handicraft like needlework or a flair for horticulture, helping the gardeners with the seedlings in the greenhouse nurseries. Edward sensed the spirits of his dead parents lurking in the corridors, nestling high up in the eaves of the dining room, brushing past him as he sat in the tea lounge, watching him as he sipped an evening cocktail by the giant white pine on the terrace, protecting him, guiding him on his path, not just with the blessing of their inheritance, but with a gentle hand on his shoulder, a whispered word of encouragement in his ear. 'We are with you,' the voices would say. 'We are watching.'

During his first few days of residence, Edward kept his daily strolls to the immediate pathways of the grounds but as he began to explore the full extent of his new home, he followed a track that took him beyond the tennis courts, under an awning of trees that almost concealed his route with the thick bend of their branches, then through veils of cobwebs defending his approach. At the end of this secret tunnel, he emerged into a clearing that hosted a secluded pond. And in the far corner of this delightful spot, attached by a shaft to a thatched hut at the edge of the pool, turned a giant waterwheel.

He sat down on a low stone wall, closed his eyes, tilted his face to the sunlight. He could hear the wheel creak around in its cycle, scooping the water into the troughs on the one side just as it released its liquid load on the other. Not the pumping heart of passionate existence, but the continuous ebb and flow of the natural circle of life. Birth and death and birth and death and birth. The recycling of energy. This constant stream. This yin and yang of grasping and releasing, grasping and releasing, grasping and releasing. He opened his eyes, let himself be hypnotised by the movement of the wheel. It was a fine piece of carpentry, all mortises, spokes, struts and hoppers, with just the minimum of metal gearing. He wondered if the device performed any actual function, whether within the hut a millstone still might grind away at rice husks. But there were no barrows or sacks or anything else lying around to suggest the building was a working mill. He leaned forward, ran his fingers across the slime of the pond. Away from the churn of the wheel, he noticed schools of carp just under the surface. It was so peaceful here. He would ask the hotel manager if he could bring out a chair. For this was his spot. This was – weather permitting – where he would write.

The manager not only arranged for a chair but also a small wooden desk for his typewriter and an umbrella for shade. Tanaka-san was right. The Japanese did appreciate their artists. And even though he was a foreign artist, Edward realised he had been ascribed a certain status within this hotel. He was the writer-in-residence. The foreign penman supposedly successful enough to rent a suite indefinitely. To be pointed out to guests as he sat reading in the lobby or eating alone at his table in the dining room.

It was with such comforting thoughts he readied himself for a late evening glass of malt that he had arranged with the obliging manager down in the hotel bar. A thank-you drink for the provision of the desk and umbrella out by the waterwheel. A young American, Jerome Fisk, would be joining them. Fisk had arrived in Japan after the war, stayed on after the Occupation had ended, inveigled himself into a university position and was now holed-up at the hotel for a few weeks finishing a research paper. A brash New Yorker with strong patriotic views, but a sharp conversationalist nevertheless. Edward was looking forward to the evening. He put aside his pen, closed his notebook, washed the ink stains from his hands and slipped back into his shoes. He hummed to himself despite the frustrations of another unproductive day.

He opened the bedroom door just in time to glimpse one of the hotel chambermaids scuttling down the corridor. An American naval officer, no doubt on R&R out of the nearby base at Yokosuka, was following her with long strides. He was a close-cropped blond man, tanned, his big, shiny-pink lips grinning sloppily over his big teeth as he chased after the girl. Without thinking, Edward stuck out his foot as the officer passed. The American stumbled but did not fall completely to the ground. Instead with hands spread-out in front, he stalled into a crouching position, like an on-your-marks sprinter, hanging there for a few seconds. And then he was on his feet, swivelling round quickly for such a heavy man, pushing his hands hard into Edward's chest. It was a solid blow and Edward was knocked back a few steps into his room, just managing to claw the top of the dresser for balance. His breath full squeezed out of him so he had to suck in quick and loud for air. The American was also breathing heavily, scrutinising him in this sudden male stand-off.

'What the fuck happened there?' the American snarled.

Edward stared back at the officer. The man was bigger and stronger and no doubt combat-fit into the bargain. A full-on fight would be pointless.

'They're pretty fast on their feet,' he said.

'Wha'?' The big American looked at him puzzled. 'Wha' dya say there?'

'Fast on their feet. These chambermaids. Dashing around here and there. Hard to catch one when you need one.'

'Yeah,' the officer said, his attention now on the lapels of his own uniform, which he started to brush into some kind of imaginary straightness. 'Yeah. Just like you say. Hard to catch.' Then he just grunted, turned round and left in the direction from which he had appeared.

Edward watched him go, feeling the fear that had rushed through him begin to subside, leaving him giddy with relief. He clutched his neck, felt the pulse there, waited for his breathing to return to normal.

'I just saw one of your guests chasing a chambermaid down a corridor,' Edward told Ishikawa-san, the hotel manager, down in the bar. Ishikawa-san was a remarkably small man who wore enormous, thick-lensed glasses. It was like talking to a shop window. 'He was an American officer.'

The hotel manager typically shrugged off the criticism of any of his clientele but Fisk rose to the defence.

'Just a case of high jinks, pal. That's what it sounds like to me. High jinks. You know what these guys are like.'

'High jinks, Fisk? If a Japanese man did that in New York he'd be arrested for assault.'

'These men get cooped up in the base for weeks on end. I'm sure he was just letting off some harmless steam. Sure he was, pal.'

'That's not an excuse to terrorise a poor chambermaid.'

'Like I said. Letting off steam.'

'It reeks of American colonialism to me.'

'Perhaps you should write about it, Eddie,' Fisk countered. 'If it causes you so much concern. Man's injustice to woman, something like that, eh? How the Americans screwed the Japanese. No offence meant, Mr Ishikawa.'

And he did write about it. The next day, with the gentle creak of the waterwheel providing the backbeat to his work, he suddenly found creative ideas come easily to him. Little mushrooms of fresh thought popping up here and there. It was such an exhilarating feeling, it made him breathless. For the first time he was experiencing a kind of creative flow, what Tanaka at Tokyo Autos must have meant by an open heart direct to his art. He had found his big theme and the context in which to place it. Rough parts of the narrative began to unfold, as well as sketches for one or two of the characters to drive it. He abandoned his typewriter to write longhand. He was sweating from the frenzy of it all, desperate to get everything on to paper while he could. For as much as he might have wanted to will it, he knew this cloudburst of creativity couldn't last. After several hours of concentrated work, he had written almost four thousand words. He had counted every precious one of them. He read the manuscript through again. And as he did so, he became aware of an unusual understanding about what he had written. He sensed that the whole process contained in the last few hours was not one of creation, but of uncovering. As if the work of fiction he was about to embark on already existed somewhere fully completed and in its perfect form. His task was therefore not to make something new, but to somehow scrape away the dust and the sands of his conscious mind in order to discover the inscriptions of his novel that lay underneath.

'Excuse me, sir.'

He looked up from his papers to see a young kimono-clad woman standing before him, holding a black lacquer tray.

'I didn't order anything.'

'I thought perhaps you will like some green tea and biscuits,' she said, the ease of her English surprising him. Most of the staff could manage their greetings and their thank-yous and that was about it. 'It is quite hot and you work a long time.' She took a step forward, looked round about where he sat. He quickly gathered his manuscript from the table and she put down her tray. She then gracefully crouched down beside him, poured out the tea into a tiny cup. He could see the curve of her neck as she bowed over her task, a few tendrils of hair loose from their clasp running back into the collar of her robe. A small mole graced the space just above her upper lip. Light pads of make-up on her cheek, her flowery scent, just the tiniest dots of perspiration on the side of her nose. There was an obvious grace to her, but also a toughness. He had detected that in the slight insistence in her voice, the way she had confidently moved into his space. She finished pouring, turned to him and smiled. 'Biscuit?' she asked.

'Just the tea will be fine,' he said. 'Thank you. It is very thoughtful of you.' As he sipped at his cup he realised the aroma from the tea was not that dissimilar to her own scent. He was about to remark on this when she said:

'I must thank you.'

'I don't understand.'

'Last evening you stopped American soldier for me.'

'Ah, so that was you.'

'Yes, that was me.' She stood up from her crouch and bowed elegantly before him. 'My name is Sumiko.'

He returned the bow from his seating position. 'And I am Edward Strathairn. Pleased to meet you.'

'I know who you are,' she said, smiling. 'You are famous writer.'

He laughed and wagged a finger at her. 'No, no, no. I am not a famous writer at all. Just a beginning writer.'

She looked puzzled. 'But you live in Fuji Suite like home?'

'That's not because I am a famous writer.'

'Oh,' she said. Another smile, then she bowed quickly. 'Now I must go. Or manager will look for me. I will return later for the tray.'

'Before you go. Tell me, where did you learn to speak English so well?'

'From the Americans,' she said, blushing. 'From the Americans.'

CHAPTER THIRTEEN

Hakone, Japan • 2003

'Ah, Sir Edward,' Takahashi said, looking up from a ledger spread open on the reception desk. The hotel manager appeared just as fresh, alert and impeccable as when Edward had left him in the morning. 'I trust you had a pleasant trip to Tokyo?'

'No, I did not.'

'I am sorry to hear that.'

'Nothing for you to be sorry about. Now, are there any messages?'

'Yes. Ms Blythe asked if you could contact her immediately on your return. If you were not too late. Are you too late, Sir Edward?'

'No, I am not too late.'

'Shall I ring her from here?'

'No, I will call from my room, thank you. I would dearly love a bath.'

'Ah, in that case, you may like to take advantage of the hotel *onsen*. The pools and washing areas have been very much modernised since your last stay with us. Very fine Italian marble has been used in the refurbishing.'

'I shall proceed to my room, Takahashi-san.'

He was just about to leave the reception area when Takahashi came out from behind his desk, caught up with him.

'You may recall, Sir Edward,' he said, almost in a whisper. 'You may recall there was an arrangement to have a little get-together.'

'Oh for God's sake, Takahashi-san. Not now. Please let me be.'

Edward didn't even turn round to see the hotel manager's face. He just set off along the corridor, thrashing out with his cane at the leaves of a pot plant on the way.

The bath boasted a giant brass funnel of a faucet that produced a disturbing, clunking sound way back somewhere in the pipe network, an enormous wheeze, then a tremendous gush of water. Good, he thought. This will be full in a few minutes. He noticed a small bottle of bath oil in a scalloped soap dish, poured the full contents into the torrent and retreated into his bedroom. The plan was to see if the telephone would stretch all the way into the bathroom. After much bending, unfurling of wire and tipping up of table legs, he found that it did. He undressed, turned off the raging flow, scrubbed himself clean in the shower, then slowly eased himself into the scented water until he was submerged chest-high in bubbles and blessed heat. He felt better already. Remarkable how at his age he could still haul his aching body in and out of various transport systems, institutional buildings, badly designed chairs and deep baths. He reached for the receiver, punched out the room number.

'Did I wake you?'

'No, no. It's fine.'

'You sound sleepy?'

'I'm fine. How was your day with Professor Fisk?'

'It had its ups and downs.'

'You didn't argue, did you?'

'A leopard doesn't change its spots.'

'And which one of you two was the leopard?'

'We both were unfortunately.' He eased himself even lower in the bath so that both his chin and the receiver remained just out of the water. He noticed that his other hand had strayed unconsciously beyond his milky belly to between his legs to fondle his penis. 'Well, not to worry,' he said. 'At least, there was no press.'

'And I have some good news for you. The BBC has been in touch. They want to know if they can include you in a series of interviews. It is to be called *Conversations with Wise Men*. For next September.'

'That's nearly a year away. Do they need a reply now?'

'I'm afraid they do. Autumn scheduling, I believe. And they would like to know if you're on board. They said it would help reel in others.'

'Well, tell them "no". The last thing I need right now is to have the BBC poking into my life.' Quite remarkably, he noticed his penis had grown under his ministrations. Not a full-blown erection. Not even half-mast. But a stiffness he hadn't been able to create for as long as he could remember.

'They will be very disappointed. I understand Sir David is to conduct the one-to-one interviews. The two of you seemed to get on so well last year on his show. I thought you would be pleased.'

'Pleased. Why should I be pleased?'

'Well, it means the Beeb hasn't heard the rumours. Perhaps everything has blown over.'

'For the moment.'

'And if something does happen, then this would be an opportunity to put the record straight. To tell your side of the story.'

'I appreciate your concern, Enid. But as I keep telling you, there is no "my side to the story".'

Silence.

'Enid?'

'I'm still here.'

'All right. Tell them I'll agree to some interviews. At home, mind you. Not in some scorching studio. And only with David. And I want some sort of final editing approval.'

'Sir David has already sent over a list of topics he would like to discuss. Would you like to hear them?'

'As long as there are no bloody questions about my ex-wife.'

'There are none.'

'Good. And by the way, I've found the most beautiful cloisonné bowl for you.'

'That's very thoughtful of you.'

He realised his erection had become quite pronounced. Was it the malt whisky? Or the sushi? Had he eaten oysters at that lunch-time buffet? Or was it Enid? She was still an attractive woman. In her late fifties. Devoted to him. Would do anything for him. Perhaps it was the heat of the water coupled with the excitement of his trip and a female voice in his ear. He could feel the hardness fade now anyway. It had reached its apex and was now a mere tortoise head returning to its carapace of crumpled skin. But what a little triumph!

'Sir Edward? Are you all right? There is such a strange echo? Where are you?'

'I'm fine. Just tired. I must go now. I must sleep. It has been a long day. A very long day.'

CHAPTER FOURTEEN

Hakone, Japan • 1957

It was like a game of cat and mouse. Except he didn't know if he was the cat or the mouse. He would be eating his breakfast and suddenly, there she was, just beyond the dining room window, carrying a basket of linen across the stepping stones of the pond. He couldn't remember if she had always performed this task at this time of day and he had never noticed, or whether this was a completely new occurrence. He would go out to his workplace by the waterwheel and a tray with tea and biscuits would be waiting. He would return to his room after dinner and the bed would be turned down, a lamp conveniently left on and the scent of her green tea perfume still lingering. Each swish of kimono or pad of footsteps in the corridor had him turning his head or rushing to the corner for a glimpse of her. But she evaded his capture. Until one evening he decided to stay in his room rather than go down to the dining room. He sat by the window in an armchair, the curtains cracked open to reveal the shadowy outlines of the furniture. As he waited, he realised how excited he was at the prospect she might turn up. It reminded him of the times he used to wait for Macy. Heart racing, mind restless, limbs restless, until the thrill of anticipation peaked and he was left with the disappointment of her non-appearance. But there was a sweetness in Sumiko's toying with him while with Macy there had been a vindictive edge to the way she drew him in then pushed him away.

A light tapping on the door. His body tensed. He regretted not having a glass of Scotch by his side, a cigarette between his fingers. Lock turning, door opening slowly. A glow from the hallway. A petite female figure entering. The light snapped on. Sumiko. A large ring of keys in her hand. He leapt out of the armchair. That had not been his intention. Rather he had depicted himself casually delivering some Japanese bon mot from his chair. But a baser instinct had prevailed, propelling him from his seat. He grabbed her. And she screamed. Another instinct forced his hand over her mouth. She was shaking so much he thought she might collapse to the floor. Keys jangling. He pulled his hand away from her mouth. A speechless, choking sound in her throat. Her eyes bulging. What was he doing? Why had he not thought this through?

'I'm sorry,' he stammered. 'God. I'm so sorry.'

She shook her head from side to side. Like an hysterical puppy. With one hand, he reached out for the door, pulled it wide open. She spun out of his grasp, ran out of the room.

He slept fitfully, the episode with Sumiko making him feel no better a person than her GI pursuer he had tripped in the corridor, reminding him of how he had behaved in Brighton with Macy. He twisted and turned so much during the night that at one point he fell out of bed. The tight wind of the blankets had saved him so that he burst awake to find himself dangling in mid-air with his shoulder swinging just above the floor. His subconscious had betrayed his body. It had ignored the usual boundaries and taken a leap into the void. He hauled himself back into bed. The incident had scared him, making him suspicious of his own nature. If it happened again, he would have to sleep on a futon.

At breakfast, he remained tense to her possible appearance in the garden outside the dining room window. He ate too quickly, spilled tea over his newspaper. He could now add indigestion to lack of sleep as part of his condition for the day. He wondered how she felt, what she thought he had been trying to do to her. What had he been trying to do to her?

'Mind if I join you?'

Jerome Fisk. In his cream suit, the American looking more colonial servant than academic. Without waiting for a response, Fisk pulled out a chair, sat down. A waiter swiftly moved into attendance, laying out a second place.

'The American breakfast,' Fisk said, ignoring the menu. 'You look like shit, pal. Are you ill or something?'

'Slept badly.'

Fisk peered over at his tray. 'Could be all that Jap food making you restless. Miso soup, *natto*, grilled fish. At this time of day. You gotta be kidding.'

'An acquired taste,' Edward said, looking down at the fish skeleton left over from his own breakfast. 'Just like kippers really.' He picked up his knife and fork, scraped a last remnant of flesh off the bones, popped it into his mouth as if to prove his point. 'How's the wonderful world of academia?' he asked.

'For you writers, it's a case of publish and be damned. For me it's publish or be damned,' Fisk said, laughing too loud at his own joke, causing a Japanese couple at the next table to visibly stiffen.

'What's your research about?'

'Really interested, Eddie? Or just being a polite Brit?'

'Bit of both.'

Fisk cleared his throat. 'A linguistic theory I'm putting forward about the Japanese. The way they put the verb at the end of the sentence.'

'Meaning?'

'The Japanese want to know all the details first before they take action. Same with the Germans and their verb.'

'And we English-speakers?'

'Oh, that's easy. We're all about "I" with a big capital letter. Even in the middle of a sentence. Only culture to do that. But usually it's "I" right at the beginning followed by the verb. We put our big selves first, then we do the action, then we worry about the details later. I, I, I, I. That's what we English-speakers are all about. But does our grammar create our culture of egoism? Or our culture create our grammar?'

'Well? Which is it?'

'Haven't decided yet. What do you reckon?'

'I'd need time to think about it. But it's an interesting thesis.'

'Thanks. I believe it explains the obsessive deliberation of the Japanese before they decide to do anything. They want to know the who, where, how and why of everything before they move their asses. We Yanks and you Brits. We just jump on in, work out the details later.'

'Seems accurate.'

'You think so?'

He was about to answer when Fisk suddenly placed a hand on his arm.

'Hey, look at that little doll.'

That little doll was Sumiko. She had emerged into the garden from one of the side doors, holding a large pile of sheets in both hands. Despite her load, she walked remarkably upright. Edward could just see her face above the top sheet. Her steady forward gaze, eyes showing no sign of a sleepless night. Fisk's presence was a fortunate distraction. He could focus on the man's striped tie, the leery eyes, the throat purple-raw and noduled from shaving. He could feel his own skin become hot as he struggled to hold his gaze away from the window.

'Don't know what to make of them,' Fisk said, shaking his head as if in a memory of some previous encounter. 'Do you?'

'Not really,' Edward responded, not sure whether Fisk meant Japanese women or just women in general.

'Excuse me, gentlemen.'

Ishikawa, the hotel manager, had arrived at their table along with the waiter and Fisk's breakfast. The manager bowed, the morning sun reflecting blindingly on his thick lenses. 'I am sorry to disturb you. But I must announce that lunch will be served in the terrace-lounge today. The Honourable Prime Minister of India, Jawaharlal Nehru, will be hosting a private luncheon in this room on behalf of the Indo-Japan Friendly Society from twelve o'clock. I trust that this will not inconvenience you in any way.'

'I'm sure we can cope, Ishikawa-san,' Edward said. 'I read of the Indian Prime Minister's visit to Japan. But I didn't realise he would be staying at this hotel.'

'Regretfully, Mr Strathairn, that will not be the case. I believe the Honourable Prime Minister has to return to Tokyo this evening.'

Ishikawa remained by the table, rubbing his hands together in what appeared to be gleeful anticipation. 'And if I may also inform you,' he continued. 'Tonight there is to be a performance by the great Chinese illusionist Hu Wei in the Magic Room. Your attendance would be most welcome.'

'The staff call him *binzoko*,' Fisk said after Ishikawa had left. 'Bottle bottoms. Because of the specs. Not to his face, of course. Coffee?'

'No, thanks.' Edward glanced out of the window. Sumiko had already completed her passage across the pond and was gone, the door of her exit left half-open. To add to his misery, a fish bone had wedged itself between two of his back teeth. He tried to dislodge it with his tongue.

'What about your novel?' Fisk asked.

'Yes, my novel. I am working on the first draft.'

'Well, what's it called?'

'I don't know.'

'That's an odd thing. Not having a title.'

'Not really.' To his relief, the bone had wriggled free. He picked it out of his mouth, wiped it on to his napkin. 'I believe that anyone who ever says he's got a wonderful title for a book will never write it,' he added, stealing one of Aldous' many pronouncements on literary endeavour.

Jerome looked chastened. As if he had such a wonderful title stored up there in his brain beside all his linguistic theories.

'So what's it about then, Eddie? Can you at least tell me that?'

'I took your advice. It's about American colonialism in Japan.'

'I suggested that?'

'The night I caught the soldier chasing the chambermaid. Coincidentally, it was that girl we just saw in the garden.'

'Can't blame him then.'

'Actually, I think it's going to be a love story. But the underlying theme concerns the Tokyo fire-bombings, Hiroshima and Nagasaki. Especially Nagasaki.'

'Why especially Nagasaki?'

Edward knew he should back off but there was something about Jerome Fisk and his American breakfasts that made him want to continue. 'Yes, Nagasaki. A monstrous act.'

'It brought the war to a quick end, Eddie. Saved tens of thousands of lives. Both American and Japanese.'

'That's the official narrative. But the fire-bombings had already brought Japan to its knees. They were ready to surrender even before the atomic bomb was dropped on Hiroshima. But even if I could forgive you Yanks for Hiroshima, Nagasaki was completely unnecessary. An utter disregard for civilian life.'

'You really think so?' Fisk chomped down on a piece of toast. There were buttery crumbs on his chin. 'So why did we evil Americans do it then?'

'To finish off the Japanese before the Russians got involved in the war in the East. And to show off your devastating weaponry, thereby proving who'd be in charge in the post-war world.'

'That's a dangerous thesis, Eddie. I'd keep that one to yourself. A lot of our boys who were fighting in the Pacific are still based here. They wouldn't take too kindly to what you're suggesting.'

'I'm not suggesting anything. I'm telling you straight. Bombing Nagasaki was an act of pure evil. The Emperor was ready to surrender. Then seventy thousand civilians wiped out for no reason. What was that all about? It's about time you Yanks did some soul-searching. Instead of hiding behind this "saved so many lives" story.'

'Like I said, Eddie, there are a lot of guys who wouldn't take too kindly to what you're suggesting.'

'And like I said, Fisk. It's a love story.'

Fisk dabbed his lips with his napkin, rose to his feet. 'Well, don't make it a love story to the Japanese. They had their fair share of evil acts too. Just ask the residents of Nanking about that. Or any of the survivors of the Bataan Death March. Hey, maybe I'll see you tonight in the Magic Room.'

The Honourable Jawaharlal Nehru had returned to Tokyo but several members of his entourage remained. Edward had seen them loitering in the dining room, milling around in the corridors, strolling in the gardens. A noisy, animated bunch enveloped in clouds of pungent tobacco smoke as they got down to the serious business of politics. Divided strictly by gender and colour of garment – the men in their baggy white cotton clothes, the women in colourful swathes of silk. By the time he arrived at the Magic Room almost all the seats were taken by these distinct groups of Indian men and women.

Earlier in the day, he'd caught a glimpse of Nehru in his trademark frock coat and white cap, addressing the packed luncheon. He marvelled at how the presence of just this one man could create such a stir among the staff and guests. The hotel so puffed up for the event, Edward imagined he could hear the beams and plaster crack with pride. Limousines stacked up in the forecourt, their capped drivers, arms folded, leaning carelessly against the expensive paintwork. Journalists, photographers, police officers, all adding to the excitement. An excitement that remained and carried over as a palpable buzz to the Magic Room, this salon off the main reception area, where the guests chatted and smoked as they awaited the commencement of the evening's entertainment.

He scanned the room, trying to locate Sumiko among the few members of staff in attendance. He had not seen her since her morning cameo in the garden. She had not come out to the water-wheel to deliver his afternoon tea nor had she had attended to his room while he had been at dinner. He worried that he had scared her to the point of leaving her employment.

'Hey, Eddie.' Fisk shouting, pointing frantically to the empty seat beside him. 'Come sit here.'

Edward pushed his way through a bevy of Indian woman to the front of the room.

'Kept one for you, pal.'

'Very considerate.'

'Just being an evil American. Did you see him?'

'Who?'

'The great man. Nehru.'

'Only in passing.'

'I gotta shake his hand.' Fisk wriggled his palm at him as if it still retained some essence of the Indian leader.

'Did you speak to him?'

'Wished him good luck.'

'Good luck for what?'

'I don't know. That's a big country he's running.'

'The show's about to start.'

'Yeah, like I'm going to see the Great Houdini or something.'

'Maybe you will.'

Ishikawa performed the task of master of ceremonies, introducing Hu Wei to the audience first in Japanese then in English. The internationally-acclaimed illusionist was a thin, elderly gentleman who bore all the usual characteristics of his trade – the wispy beard, the pantaloons, the wide-sleeved silk coat embroidered with gold dragons. More impressive was the Chinaman's air of aloofness, as if he were here this evening to pass on the mysteries of his ancestors, but only if he deemed the audience worthy of receiving them.

The illusionist started off modestly. Rings were linked and unlinked with ease, silk handkerchiefs changed colour, a needle was passed through a balloon. Edward had seen a similar performance at the Glasgow Hippodrome with his father just before the war. It was all very ho-hum. He was just about to slip away when Hu Wei announced in English:

'Many of you may have seen an illusionist cut a woman in half. But tonight I will go one stage further.' He stretched out an arm to beckon the arrival of two of the hotel staff carrying a long, pale-green wooden box, which was placed on top of a covered table.

'Tonight I will cut a woman into three parts. Please. My assistant for this evening.'

And there she was. Sumiko. Shuffling on to centre stage, dressed in her traditional kimono, her face painted with thick white make-up. She bowed to the audience, her eyelids fluttering, the stage lights reflecting the perspiration on her upper lip. She really did look like someone who was about to be cut up into parts. Edward genuinely feared for her – not for her safety – but for her ability to carry out the performance. Surely she had never done anything like this before.

At Hu Wei's beckoning, she entered the box from one side, sliding in until her quivering feet appeared at the far end. There were three flaps across the front that Hu Wei lifted and closed in order to show the three sections of her body. A saw was produced and flourished high above the audience. Sumiko's head and feet settled into tense stillness. The audience hushed. And the cutting began. It wasn't the illusion of the sawing that enthralled Edward, or the grind of metal teeth on wood, the sawdust gathering on the floor, the collective imagining of torn flesh, blood, organs and entrails. It was when Hu Wei separated the three sawn sections, moving them on their individual tables about the stage, that he became the most excited. Sumiko's head on one side of the stage, her torso on another, her legs in the middle. He found the whole performance to be extremely erotic, as if each part of her was being served up for him, and for him alone. Of course, Hu Wei re-formed her, held her hand while she tip-toed front stage, bowed to the audience. Edward clapped loudly, too loudly, in the hope of attracting her attention. But she remained impassive, caught up in an almost trance-like state that may or may not have been part of the act. She bowed again and disappeared behind a rear curtain.

The audience had hardly re-settled in their seats when the illusionist moved into his finale – shooting flames from the tips of his fingers. It was a spectacular display of digital fireworks, provoking loud cheering until one of Hu Wei's ribbons of fire hit a pelmet to the side of the stage. The flame flickered then caught hold of the curtain fabric. Edward assumed, as must have everyone else in the static audience, that the incident was part of the illusionist's act, until he saw a young reception clerk rush from the back of the room, rip down the flaming fabric, throw a bucket of sand over the fiery heap. The poor lad appeared to burn his hand in the process.

'I am a doctor,' declared an Indian gentleman emerging from the audience. 'Ice. Get me a bucket of ice. Please. I will need some ice. And make way for our young hero.'

There was a burst of applause as the crowd parted. Edward saw Hu Wei pick up a piece of the burnt fabric from the stage, shake his head, then follow the doctor and his charge downstairs to the kitchens. Someone opened a window to let out the lingering smoke.

'Quite a performance,' Fisk said, flushed in his cheeks.

'The sawing or the burning?'

'The whole goddamn show. Fancy a nightcap?'

'Another time. I think I'll go back to my room. I feel like writing.'

'Wouldn't want to disturb the muse. And the untitled novel.'

Edward really did feel like writing. The events of the day and evening shaking him up into a state of creative agitation. He needed to get it all out, get something down on paper.

She was waiting for him. In the semi-darkness. Sitting in the armchair where he had sat the night before waiting for her. Fingers of blue moonbeams lighting up her pale make-up. That porcelain face.

'I am trembling,' she said.

He walked over to where she sat, drew her off the chair. She really was shaking. She held her face up to his. That white, expressionless mask. The corner of her eyes bloody in irritation from the make-up. What did she want? He really couldn't tell. He held two alien cultures in his hands. The culture of woman. The culture of the Japanese. He could not read the signs, these strange hieroglyphs of need, desire, fear. Then instinct or passion or some other invisible force took over. And he kissed her.

At first, Edward feared he might be acting merely in the spirit of the times, the lingering *zeitgeist* of the Occupation – another arrogant, foreign victor come to take the spoils now that the Americans had departed. Or even more simply, that he was the honoured paying guest taking advantage of the poor chambermaid. But it was not like that. This was not an unequal partnership. Sumiko possessed as much power over him as he did her. His life became dictated by the possibility of her turning the handle of his door as he waited, caught on that emotional ledge between anticipation and disappointment.

Sumiko confided their liaison to no one. And neither did he. The Fuji Suite served as the sole location of their relationship, and by making herself responsible on the staff rota for the cleaning of their love nest, she gradually sneaked in more and more of her belongings into his rooms. He loved these almost daily additions to his surroundings. When she was not there, he would go over to the wardrobe just to smell her scent on the sleeves of her garments or play with the jars of mysterious creams and unguents on the dressing table. There was something comforting in seeing her robe draped over the foot of his bed, discovering a long strand of her hair in the basin or flicking through the pages of the book she was reading just to feel where her own fingers had been.

'You should read this book,' she said. She was sitting upright and bath-clean on the bed, wrapped in a blue and white *yukata* courtesy of her employer. Her feet were bare. Such tiny feet. He abandoned his manuscript just to go over and kiss their soles. Her skin hot and scented from the soak. She giggled and wriggled and kicked at him to stop.

'What is it?' he asked, sliding up to lie beside her.

'*Snow Country*. By Yasunari Kawabata. It is both sad and beautiful. It is my favourite book.'

'My Japanese is not good enough to appreciate such a novel.'

'I will help you translate.'

'What is it about?'

'About a cold man from the city. He goes once a year to an *onsen* in the snow country. There he meets a hot-spring geisha. Are you such a cold man?'

'Why do you say such a thing?'

'Because sometimes you are mean to me.'

'When?'

'In little ways.'

'Tell me.'

'It is hard to explain.'

'Try.'

'I don't know. Sometimes you make me feel I am not perfect for you.'

'How do I do that?'

'I can see it in your eyes.'

Winter closed in, wrapping the hills in an icy mist. Gone were those wonderful days of writing by the waterwheel. Edward stayed in his room all day, radiators boiling, hardly changing out of his pyjamas and robe, ordering meals to his door. His whole world of sleep, work and play narrowed down to this one set of rooms. His cave in the mountains. He was hibernating. And he loved it.

It began to snow. He watched the plump flakes fall, purifying his world into a muffled silence. Until a crow flew off a branch, loosening a white trail in its wake. The hotel boilers stoked up into a frenzy. Black smoke from the few village houses grazing the sky. No one ventured out. No footprints in the snow. No snowmen. No snowballs. Or the joyous laughter of the young. For there were no children here. No vehicles could make it up the hillside either. The hotel was cut off from the plains below.

'Supplies are dwindling,' Ishikawa told him with all the worried seriousness of a military officer at the front. 'We can only last a few more days if this freeze doesn't break. Let us pray the pipes do not break first.'

Edward kept on writing, inasmuch a reaction to the blank canvas outside his window as from any inner inspiration. The snow made everything clearer, more defined, more true. Being stranded added a further dimension to his urgency. Page after page emerged from his typewriter. Accompanied by the sound of a clarinet, the soulful rehearsal of a member of the touring Japanese National Orchestra snowbound in the room above. Sumiko curled up on the bed reading her novel. She had found her own snow country and she was happy.

'I want to go out of this room with you,' she said sleepily. 'It would be very great fun.'

'It's better for both of us that we aren't seen together. You know that.'

'Then let us go somewhere else.'

'Where?'

'An *onsen*. I have a day off next week. If the snow goes away.'

He didn't want to go anywhere. He was locked into his magical world, why would he want to break the spell? But she persisted. The snow began to melt into marbled slush, the local bus company was getting vehicles through with fresh produce from the plain. He arranged to meet her at an *onsen* further down the hillside, away from the usual orbit of the other members of staff. Just before he left, he received a letter from Aldous delivered by the first mail-van to reach the hotel in ten days.

"Eduardo, mon chère,

I am delighted to inform you I have decided to sleep with the enemy. I am now a literary agent. A natural progression from my nurturing of neurotic writers at The Londinium *which I continue to edit, of course — readership now close to two thousand and counting. I do believe people are beginning to read serious fiction again. I wonder if you have finished your own manuscript. If so, please send it over post haste. I am eager to read it. Love, your friend as always. A."*

Typical Aldous. Short and sometimes sweet. Edward tucked the letter into his pocket, concentrated on his walk down to the bus stop from the hotel. Bellboys worked ahead of him shovelling salt on to the icy pathway. The ponds were frozen. The trees frosted white. As his eyes widened to take in his new horizons, he glimpsed a hawk trace a hungry path in the sky. It felt strange to move away from his base. He had spent months at the hotel hardly venturing outside its grounds. He thought he had hidden himself away in order to write. But as he stood waiting for the bus, his lips and cheeks already chaffed from the cold, he realised he was also emerging from a dark, womb-like period of mourning for the death of his parents. He felt like an invalid learning to walk again. He felt re-born. Aldous' letter also cheering with the opportunity it presented. He clapped his gloved hands, stamped the cold from his feet, began to hum to as the bus appeared, cautious in its slippery descent, but remarkably, still on time.

Sumiko was waiting for him at the entrance to the spa hotel. Rosy-faced and smiling. She wore a fur hat, a long woollen coat and a matching muffler. He had never seen her in street clothes before. He had never seen her look so beautiful.

'A friend borrowed to me,' she said, touching her hat. She then linked her arm in his, and he let her lead him to their room.

'However much time you spend washing your body at hotel,' she told him as he changed into his robe. 'Multiply by three.' She nibbled on the tip of a finger in contemplation of this thought. 'No, multiply by four. Only then can you enter the common pool.'

He did as she advised, soaping and rinsing himself in the men's washrooms until his skin emerged prune-wrinkled from under the foam. Yet still the other Japanese male bathers took longer with their ablutions. He felt like a dirty foreigner polluting their water. He would soak in the naturally heated pools until his skin bristled pink, his blood thawed, his limbs dissolved into a rubbery mass. And then plod back to his room to lie on the futon where his body merged with hers into a constant mineral heat. The kneading of sweaty flesh. His blood boiling into fists of erections. Spilling his seed and still he was hard. Pores open. Heart open.

'I love you,' she said.

He watched her as she sat cross-legged on the *tatami*, towel-drying her hair in front of a low mirror. She turned to look at him. A tiny muscle twitched at the corner of her mouth. But he couldn't bring himself to repeat her words. She turned back to the mirror, dragging a large comb so harshly through the tangle of her hair that he saw her eyes water from the pain. 'I am not your *panpan* girl,' she said.

He knew what she meant. *Panpan*. A prostitute served up by the Japanese government during the Occupation to soothe the invading American hordes. The remark hurt him. He knelt down beside her on the *tatami*. A slither of space between them but it felt like a chasm to cross. He could hear her gulping for breath.

'I am very happy here with you,' he said. 'I don't ever remember being so happy.'

'You make me feel like your *panpan* girl.'

'That's not fair.'

'Tell me then, Eddie. Tell me what is fair?'

Back at the hotel, he began to prepare his manuscript for posting to Aldous. A few last-minute pencil edits but generally he was satisfied. Except for the title. He had kept that for last. But really he had known from the beginning what it would be. *The Waterwheel*.

CHAPTER FIFTEEN

Hakone, Japan • 2003

He had slept very late. He could sense that from the moment he awoke. The full morning light behind the drawn curtains still managing to filter through the fabric. The sound of a vacuum cleaner in the hallway. There was something reassuring about that hum. A feeling of order, of being looked after. A memory of his mother performing the same task. If he slept – which could not always be guaranteed – he was always a seven o'clock riser. On the dot. With or without an alarm clock. Then a movement of his bowels, a shower and a shave. Such regularity. Yet this morning, a deeper self had demanded more sleep, had overridden his usual methodical being. He liked that. There was still an ounce of anarchy left in him. He reached over to the bedside table, located his glasses. It was quarter-to-ten.

He washed and dressed quickly but by the time he reached the dining room, he realised it was too late. The tables were already stripped down, the chafing dishes removed, a team of cleaning staff in motion between the chairs.

'Ah, Sir Edward,' Takahashi said, appearing so quietly at his side as to startle him. 'I am afraid you have missed breakfast.'

'So it seems. Such a pity as I am quite famished.' He tried to remember when he had last eaten. A few canapés at the embassy party.

'I am sorry. But the dining room must be prepared. There is an Old Boys party coming for luncheon. But I could organise something for you in the tea lounge overlooking the garden. It is quite pleasant to sit there. And I can arrange for the radiators to be opened.'

'That would be very kind of you.'

'My pleasure. Would scrambled eggs and toast be sufficient?'

'And a pot of tea.'

'Of course.'

'And Ms Blythe. Where is she?'

'I believe she is hard at work in our small business centre.'

'Perhaps you would like to join me then, Takahashi-san? We can have that little chat I have been so looking forward to.'

'That would be most pleasant. I shall let you eat in peace. And then arrive to share some tea with you.'

Almost as soon as Edward had popped the last slice of toast into his mouth, Takahashi appeared at his table, bowed, pulled out a chair.

'Some more tea,' the hotel manager said, wriggling his starched white cuff high on his forearm and pouring out two cups with a measured efficiency. 'So refreshing this particular Indian blend. We have it specially prepared for the hotel, you know. For many years now. It is quite famous.'

As he watched Takahashi sip his tea, Edward knew he was look-ing at the face of a lifelong smoker, the lines etched in the flesh holding a slightly grey tinge, the eyes bleary from years at the front line of such a habit. He could see the stained fingers edgy without their usual wedge between them. And on the back of one hand, the dried-up welt and blister of what appeared to be an old burn mark. Perhaps it was the taste of the hotel's own quality brew that set him off or the mid-morning peacefulness from his position overlooking the gardens, but he suddenly felt an overwhelming curiosity about this man sitting in front of him.

'Tell me, Takahashi-san. Was it hard for you after the war?'

Takahashi gently replaced his cup on its saucer and smiled. 'Hunger, Sir Edward. That is what I always remember. An empty stomach and a constant desire to fill it. But we were lucky. Although we lived in the city we had relatives who were farmers. My mother often walked miles out into the country to visit them, threw herself at their mercy so we could be fed. Traded heirlooms for handfuls of rice. Sometimes I had nothing to eat but grasshoppers.'

'Grasshoppers? I really thought that was only a fiction.'

'I can assure you that poverty drove my mother to such extremes. My brother and I were often sent out to catch them. Excuse me, but do you mind if I smoke?'

'Please go ahead.'

Takahashi turned to a waiter lurking by a far wall, mimed the flicking of ash into an imaginary dish.

'You must forgive me, Sir Edward. But I do like a cigarette with my morning tea. My only vice.'

'I fully understand. I was once a smoker myself.'

'Fortunately you have had the discipline to forsake such an addiction.'

'To be honest, now that I am in my seventies, I wouldn't mind taking up the habit again. Now, to continue with your story, did you find it difficult coming here to attend to all these foreigners? After all, they had been the occupying power. The enemy. The very people who had caused your starvation.'

'I'm not sure if that was true. I prefer to blame the lack of food on the poor way our own government dealt with the gangsters running the black markets. But to answer your question, I was quite happy to serve the Americans. I admired them very much. I still do. They dragged us out of a culture of imperialism and helped to modernise our country. I have always been very grateful to them for that.'

'I hope you don't mind me asking this. But did you ever read *The Waterwheel*?'

'Of course. Although it was many years ago. We retain several copies in our library here. In both English and Japanese.'

'And what did you think of it?'

'That is not for me to say, Sir Edward. I am just a humble reader. Your many awards and prizes speak far better on your behalf than I can.'

'But I am interested to know what you think.'

'I liked the love story with the *panpan* girl very much. I recall it was very moving.'

'But did you feel the novel was balanced? Balanced in the way it portrayed both the Americans and Japanese during and after the war?'

'Ah, Sir Edward, you always were interested in such ideas. Ishikawa-san, the manager when you were first here, do you remember him? He sadly passed away many years ago. He often talked of his conversations with you. Late into the night, a shared bottle of one of our fine malt whiskies from the bar. I was often envious of such occasions. And here I am now, faced with the same opportunity, yet I am at a loss for words.'

'Yes, I do remember Ishikawa-san. He wore such large spectacles.'

Takahashi nodded vigorously and slapped his thigh. 'Yes, yes. Those spectacles. They were extremely large. And thick. They kept falling off his nose. We used to call him *Binzoko*. Bottle bottoms. Affectionately, of course. And never to his face.'

'So you knew Ishikawa-san. How long have you been here then?'

'Forty-eight years, Sir Edward. I retire next spring.'

'My goodness. That means you were here during my first visit.'

Takahashi tilted his head in acknowledgement. 'Yes, I remember your stay very well. All the staff were very impressed that a person could take up residency here for such a long time in order to write a book. We all thought you were a famous millionaire.'

'No such thing. I had just come into a small inheritance after the death of my...' And then it struck Edward. A flash of a memory. A magician's fiery fingers. 'Now I know who you are. You're the young lad who put out the fire. During the performance of the Chinese illusionist. That's the burn mark on your hand.'

'Yes, that is very true. It occurred after the visit of the Honourable Jawaharlal Nehru. Do you remember that? I was very fortunate an Indian doctor was in the audience to treat me so quickly. Otherwise, the scar could have been much worse.'

'You were something of a hero that evening.'

'Just performing my duty, Sir Edward.'

'And so you must remember Jerome Fisk from that time?'

'Of course, I remember him. Fisk-sensei went on to become a professor at one of our famous universities. Only two days ago we chatted when he called about the Shinkansen tickets.' Takahashi brought his cigarette slowly to his lips for a deep inhalation, then turned to look out of the window as the smoke curled out of his nostrils. The tea lounge overlooked the pond with its backdrop of trimmed shrubbery and then across to the dining room. Edward couldn't tell if Takahashi was merely enjoying the view or spying on his staff as they prepared the tables for the Old Boys luncheon.

'This has been an extremely pleasant conversation,' Takahashi said eventually, turning his attention back to the room, squashing out his cigarette in the ashtray. 'But there is one question you have not asked.'

'I'm sorry?'

'Forgive me, Sir Edward. But one thing I did learn from the Americans was to speak directly when the situation demanded.'

'Well, please do so.'

'You asked me if I knew Ishikawa-san and Fisk-sensei from your first visit here. But you haven't asked about one of my co-workers. Sumiko-chan. Why don't you ask about her?'

CHAPTER SIXTEEN

Japan • 1958

'I'm going back to Tokyo,' Jerome told Edward over a glass of Scotch and a game of draughts in the Magic Room. 'My research paper is complete. Time to return to the real world. Do you remember that place?'

'You think academia is the real world?'

'For some. And you?'

'I sent my manuscript to an agent about a month ago. I am presently residing in limbo land.'

'Not a bad place to be. And your manuscript has a title?'

Edward told him.

'Aha,' Jerome said, snatching two pieces off the board. 'The waterwheel in the garden.'

'The very same. That is the symbol I have chosen. The metaphor.'

'For your anti-American diatribe?'

'It's a love story set during the Occupation. It would be hard to avoid the Americans in that situation.'

'In a negative way?'

'In a balanced way.'

'Well, I hope so, pal. Another game?' Jerome had cornered his sole surviving piece with his crown.

'No, thanks.'

'Coward.'

'Merely aware of my own limitations.'

Jerome swept the draughts into their box. 'Listen, Eddie. I've planned a little farewell trip to the coast tomorrow. To Kamakura. Home of the Daibutsu, the Giant Buddha. And a bunch of other temples and shrines. Want to come along for the ride? I've rented an automobile with a driver.'

'Kamakura is also home to Yasunari Kawabata.'

'A pal of yours?'

'No, not at all. He is a well-known Japanese writer.'

'Do you want to meet him?'

'Not me. But I know someone who would like to.'

'Yeah. Who?'

'One of the chambermaids.'

'You sly bastard.' Jerome scratched his head as if he were genuinely puzzled. 'You think you got a guy figured out for being straight-laced. And all the time he's been warming his bed with the female staff. Are you going to tell me who she is? Or is this one of these novels-without-a-title kind of game?'

Edward sipped on his whisky, excited by the prospect of finally revealing her name. Objectifying his relationship so that it would exist outside his head. Outside his room. 'Sumiko,' he said.

'I knew it. Can't blame you. She's a looker.'

'I am only involving you because you are leaving. Not a word to anyone, you understand?'

'Yankee's honour.'

'It so happens she has the day off tomorrow. You will need to pick her up in the village if she agrees to come.'

'Our automobile leaves at nine.'

Edward felt it was going to be a great day as soon as Sumiko entered the car, settled herself between him and Jerome in the rear seat. The chemistry immediate, that peculiar alchemy of human personalities destined to relieve tensions and to create a heady mix. Rough edges, old wounds and unfulfilled needs all disappeared. The dynamic of this trio would be full of humour and easy banter, he was sure of it. Even the sun was shining for them on this early spring morning, so fresh and full of potential.

'"*Kamakura lies host to more than eighty Buddhist temples and Shinto shrines*," Jerome read from his guidebook. '"*It was chosen as the capital of Japan in the 12th century by the Minamoto shogunate because of its natural defences. The sea on one side, hills on the other three so that even to this day any entrance unless by boat means a train or road journey through tunnels. Fifty miles south of the modern day capital, it is a place where Tokyoites come to pray and play*." Get that. Pray and play. I like that.'

Fifty miles south of Tokyo. By the sea. Where Tokyoites come to play. Those were the facts that caught Edward's attention. Kamakura sounded like the Brighton of Japan. Brighton. That was the last time he had been to the seaside. The last time he had seen Macy. He had not thought of her for a long time. Yet as soon he ventured out of his little cave into the real world, there she was. Ahead of him on the pebbled beach, her sunburnt shoulders, summer dress drawn tight over her buttocks, shell to her ear. Dancing. He moved his hand close to Sumiko's, scraped gently at the skin of her wrist with his little finger.

'I want some photos of the Giant Buddha,' Jerome said, declaring his intentions early, like a young child on a family outing. He had brought his Brownie, held it tight on his lap. 'I think I could get some really good shots if the light keeps like this. Yeah, this is excellent light. More than I could have hoped for at this time of year. Class A light. What about you, Eddie?'

'I'd like to see the sea.'

'That can be easily arranged. And Sumiko-chan?'

'I want to see the house of Kawabata-sensei. If we can find it.'

'Sure we'll find it,' said Jerome. 'That will be our mission for the day. To give Sumiko-chan whatever she wants.'

'The head looks too big for its body,' Edward muttered as he sat there observing the Giant Buddha, Sumiko beside him, Jerome in a crouch snapping away at the statue with his camera. The Giant Buddha stood forty feet high according to the guidebook, but appeared much taller in reality. Big and squat. That was what was unusual about the structure. Its squatness. Edward had seen his fair share of towers and columns and steeples and statues on plinths. All reaching for the sky. For immortality. But this Buddha was very much of the earth. Solid. Mortal. Its bronze coating oxidised blue-green from six hundred years of wind, rain, beating sun, storms and quakes, as well as the curious touch and disrespectful buttocks of strangers. Cast in lotus position, hands clasped, eyes closed, that too-large head bowed in meditation.

'That is because of where we sit,' Sumiko said. 'If we stand in a special spot just in front of Daibutsu, it is a perfect shape.'

'How do you know that?'

'I came here before on a high school trip.'

'I can imagine you as a schoolgirl. Uniform and pigtails. Little white socks.'

'Blue. Dark blue socks.' She smiled, walked him over to the location to show him what she meant. She was right. The Giant Buddha now sat facing him in proper proportion. Such a serene icon compared to the agonising Christ of his own religion.

'Smile for the camera.' Jerome in front of them, box Brownie tucked into the pit of his stomach, head bowed to the view finder, shouting instructions, waving them closer. Sumiko giggling but Edward feeling her awkward and tense in his grasp at this public display of affection. A Japanese couple stopping to stare at the *gaijin* and his mistress. At the loud American. 'Say cheese.'

'Cheeeeese.' Click. Frozen in time.

'Can I have a copy?' Edward shouted over to Jerome.

'For Sumiko?' Jerome shouted back.

'What do you think? For Ishikawa-san?'

This made Sumiko laugh. Edward couldn't remember having done that before. Then Jerome doing the same with his antics and his pathetic Japanese jokes. The two men getting loud and worked up into some kind of competitive frenzy, Sumiko laughing at the stupidity of it all.

She took them to a soba shop she remembered from her high school trip. Old beams, counter bar, enormous pots of scalding water steaming the windows wet. A gnarled old man with black teeth serving warm sake out of a kettle. Edward made sure he had a seat beside Sumiko while Jerome talked to his driver, a cheerful little Buddha of a man, sending him off to the nearest police box to find out where Kawabata lived.

'What do you want to do when we get there?' Edward asked her.

'Jerome-san can take photograph for me.'

'You should knock on the door. Tell him how much you like his book.'

She looked shocked. 'You would do that?'

'We Americans would,' Jerome said, pulling up a stool. 'Ask the man for his autograph. A cup of Joe. No problem.' Making Sumiko laugh again.

The driver came back with the address and directions. Jerome clapping him on the back, buying him a bowl of noodles, telling him to sit and relax. They would abandon the car for the next few hours, walk along the seafront to the house.

The beach was empty, apart from a few bored fishermen drying seaweed on racks, the dark green fronds blowing like bunting in the breeze. No seagulls, just a couple of crows foraging for food among the stranded fishing boats. The island of Oshima just visible in a haze on the horizon. Sumiko took off her shoes, hitched up the hem of her kimono, to walk barefoot in the dark sand. Edward strolled beside her, Jerome up ahead, trousers rolled up, kicking up a splash in a stream.

'It will rain soon,' she said.

'Looks likely.'

'Your friend is a funny man.'

'He's leaving tomorrow for Tokyo.'

'*Kawai so*,' she said. 'It's a pity.'

And here was Jerome again, full of exaggerated bows, making a big show of leading Sumiko by the hand, taking her to the edge of the stream, helping her over on the conveniently placed rocks like some American Walter Raleigh. But halfway across, one of the stones rocked on its side, and she slipped. Jerome reached out, tried to grab her, but she fell, landing half in and half out of the shallow water.

'*Bakka ne*?' she said, holding her ankle. 'I am so stupid.' Her body lay sideways and twisted, the bottom of her kimono soaked, sand in her hair. Edward tried to haul her up, Jerome too, but she winced with pain.

'*Itai*,' she whimpered. 'It is sore. I cannot stand.'

Edward crouched down, lifted her up like a bride, so light in his arms. She leaned her head into his neck and he felt the warm breath there, the wetness of her lashes on his cheek. It was too far to carry her back to the soba shop, so he eased her down on one foot. With one arm around his neck, the other around Jerome's, she managed to hop back along the beach to the car. Jerome had to wake up his driver, told him to take them to a local hospital, which he did, swinging the car through the narrow streets like a field ambulance on a mercy mission. A nurse bound up the swollen ankle, lent Sumiko a pair of crutches.

The buoyant mood that had infected the start of the day was gone. Their trio was split, deflated. Jerome had moved up front to sit by the driver, Sumiko sat huddled in a corner in the back, her injured leg stretched across the floor, across Edward's feet. He stared out at the choppy waves of a murky sea as the car hugged the coastline before peeling off for the hills.

'*Bakka ne*?' she said. 'I ruin your day.'

'These things happen,' Edward said. 'It's no one's fault.'

'Blame me,' Jerome said, turning round. 'I should've paid more attention. Everything was going just fine until I had to do my big goofy routine.'

'You didn't hear me, Jerome. No one's fault. Leave it at that.'

'Yeah, that may be. But she didn't get to see the house. I feel bad about that. You really wanted to see that house, Sumiko-chan, didn't you?'

'We'll go to Kawabata-sensei's house next time in Kamakura, Eddie? Next time?'

'Yes. Next time.'

It started to rain. Mount Fuji should have been visible some-where ahead, but its presence was obscured by low clouds. There seemed to be no bright colour anywhere. Only the drab browns and greys of seaside homes out of season, shutters battened down against the weather. No one spoke. All of them hunkered down into their private worlds, the rain lending a kind of legitimacy to the solitude. For that was what people did, didn't they? Listen to rain. Edward listened to it himself, pelting the bodywork, drum-ming a natural beat to his thoughts.

On Jerome's instruction, the car stopped to let Sumiko off at the entrance to the staff annexe rather than in the village. The driver got out, pulled open the passenger door, held out an umbrella for her.

'Thank you for such a happy day,' she said, bowing in her crutches to each of them. As Edward watched her hobble inside, an intense sadness took hold of him. He wanted to rush after her, grab her, shake her, tell her something. Tell her what? That he loved her? Too late he noticed she had forgotten one of her shoes in the car.

Back at the main hotel building, he said a tepid farewell to Jerome. He genuinely liked the man although their political differ-ences had prevented any kind of real friendship. Disappointment. That was what he felt now. About Jerome. About Sumiko. About the whole day.

'Mr Strathairn. Mr Strathairn.'

Ishikawa. Edward feared the hotel manager had found him out for kidnapping and wounding a member of his staff. The incrimi-nating shoe stuffed in his pocket.

'Ah, Mr Strathairn. I have been looking all over for you. It is so unusual not to find you in the hotel.'

'I have been to Kamakura. With Mr Fisk. Is there a problem?'

'Not a problem, I hope. Only a telegram.' The manager handed over the envelope. Edward tore it open and read.

"I love MS. Publishers interested. Come back immediately. A."

It took Edward a few moments to realise MS stood for manu-script and not the initials of one of Aldous' lovers.

He sat in the armchair by the bedroom window, the lights dimmed, a glass of malt whisky in one hand, the telegram in the other. He could hear Sumiko coming down the long hallway, the thud, thud, thud of her crutches on the carpeted floor, not unlike the heavy beat of his own heart. He rose from his seat, walked unsteadily across the room, opened the door just as she arrived on the other side.

'Come in, come in,' he said, trying to sound cheerful. '*O genki desu ka?*'

She swung herself across the threshold. 'I am fine. Just so sorry to spoil everything.'

'Don't be silly. These things can't be helped. Accidents happen.' He felt he would be happy to go on like this, just spouting clichés. 'Did you enjoy Kamakura anyway?'

'It was such a lovely day. And I laughed so much. Jerome-san is very funny. Thank you for taking me.'

'You must have some tea,' he said. 'I insist.'

'Please don't fuss, Eddie-chan. I just want to sit, thank you. My foot is still sore.'

'Of course, you must sit. Here take my armchair. And I'll get some pillows to prop up your ankle.'

She sat down and he brought her a footstool, some cushions off the bed. Then he topped up his glass from the decanter on his desk. He tried to keep his hand steady as he poured.

'What is wrong, Eddie-chan?'

'Nothing is wrong.'

'You act very nervous.'

He sighed. 'There is something I need to tell you.'

'What is it?'

He looked around for the telegram, he had put it down somewhere while fetching the pillows. There it was on the bedside table. He picked it up, waved it at her.

'This has come,' he said.

'Oh no,' she gasped. 'Someone is dead?'

'No, no, it is nothing like that. It is good news for a change. No, I didn't mean it like that either. It is good news for me. No, not that. I have to go. To go back to London.'

'You will be away for a long time?'

'I am leaving Japan for good, Sumiko. This is a telegram from my agent.' Again he waved the document at her, as if it were a divine calling rather than Aldous' probably over-optimistic words of command. 'Publishers are interested in my book. I have to go back. I need to think about my career. I am not coming back.'

'But you told me you are happy here.'

'Yes, that is true.'

'Why are you leaving then?'

'Because happiness is not enough.'

She let out a horrible wailing sound, dropped her head. Her shoulders began to shake. He found himself on the verge of crying himself. That leaden ball of emotion in his stomach all wrapped up inside of him waiting for release.

'Take me with you,' she said, still not looking at him. 'Please take me with you.'

'That's not possible.'

'Why not?'

'I just can't.' He gave her a whole list of reasons. Logistical reasons. Cultural reasons. Consular issues. Everything except the truth. That she was of this time and place in his life. She was of Japan. It was not a relationship he could transfer, just like that, exchanged like currency from one country to the other. How could he tell her that?

'You see,' she said. 'I am just your *panpan* girl.'

'I've told you before. That's not true.'

'You are just like the Americans,' she hissed. Then she began to struggle out of the armchair, pulling herself up on her crutches.

'Where are you going?' he asked.

'To have a bath.'

'A bath? Now?'

'Yes, now. I feel dirty. Or do you want me to get out of this room too?'

'Let me help you then.'

'Leave me.'

He let her be, poured another drink, went to sit by his desk at the window, the burn of the whisky starting to soothe him.

He heard her turn on the giant taps, the hollow clunks resounding somewhere deep in the pipework as the water came gushing in. He cursed himself for hurting her. But it was true what he had said – happiness was not enough for him right now. It was meaning he craved. If he wanted happiness, he could just stay here, existing only in the present, in this village, at this hotel, in this room, with Sumiko, without a care for what had been in his life or what would be. But if he wanted his life to have meaning, to have some kind of narrative arc, he needed to think about his future as well.

Somewhere out in the darkness, he heard an owl call. He leaned forward, pulled aside one of the curtains. It was a clear night, a half moon in the sky. He could just make out the hotel boilerhouse with its giant chimney, the tennis courts, the path that led through the trees to the waterwheel. He thought of how he used to write there in the late summer, how beautiful the light was as it filtered through the trees, spread out over the pond, illuminating the orange-gold backs of the carp languidly swimming to and fro. Sumiko would bring him out tea and biscuits on a lacquer tray, sit with him for a few minutes, just the two of them, silently, listening to the waterwheel filling and emptying its troughs in a gentle flow.

It was the warm ooze around his stockinged feet that alerted him. At first, he thought he'd spilt a cup of tea on the carpet, the tea on the lacquer tray that had formed part of his reverie. Then through the pleasant numbness of his alcoholic haze, he realised what was happening. He rushed to the door. But it was locked. He banged his fist hard on the wooden panelling. 'Sumiko,' he cried. 'Sumiko. Open up.' Silence. Except for the gush of the taps.

He tried the door again, shook the handle. It was only a snib on the other side. He took a few steps backwards then hastened forward, shoulder first. The lock gave away easily and he was through.

He stood in a slush of water, mist filled the room. He could just see the upper half of Sumiko's naked body slumped in the bath, one arm draped over the side, her bandaged ankle propped between the taps.

'Sumiko!' he screamed. He rushed over to her, knelt down in the puddles of water, grabbed her shoulders, shook her gently. 'My God. What have you done?'

No response.

He slapped her lightly across her cheeks. Her head jerked and she breathed out a moan.

'Thank God,' he said. He dipped both his hands into the warm water and under her body, scooped her up and out of the bath. Somehow he managed to stand her upright, balance her limp body against his own so he could reach out, grab a towel, wrap it around her. Then, careful not to slip on the wet floor, he carried her into the bedroom, laid her gently down on the bed.

'What have you done?' he asked again.

Her eyes flickered open. '*Nan desu-ka?*' she whispered.

'Did you take something? Some medicine?'

'*Hai*,' she said drowsily. 'Before I came. The hospital gave me. Because of the pain. It makes me sleepy. Sleepy in the warm bath. So sleepy.'

'You fell asleep?' he said.

'*Hai*,' she said. 'The taps, Eddie-chan. The taps are still running.'

He went back into the bathroom, turned off the water, let the bath drain. When he returned to the bedroom, she was fast asleep again. He found her *yukata*, spread it across her towel-wrapped body, lay down on his back beside her.

CHAPTER SEVENTEEN

Hakone, Japan • 2003

He had arrived early at the Hakone Open-Air Museum with its twenty-six works by Henry Moore and the exuberant paintings, ceramics, sculptures and tapestries displayed at the Picasso Pavilion. He wanted to locate the meeting place at the Shikanai Plaza, stroll around the sculpture exhibits and installations on the lawns, visit the works of Miro, Calder, Bourdelle and Dubuffet in the main gallery, then return to the plaza in plenty of time to cool down and relax from his exertions. To sit waiting as a calm and unflustered gentleman, resting on his cane, enjoying the fresh air, at one with nature on this dull afternoon. Only a few hours previously, Takahashi had supplied the answers to the questions he had wanted to ask ever since he had arrived back in Japan: 'Do you know what happened to Sumiko? Is she still alive?'

'Why, of course she is.'

Edward had actually felt his heart quicken to this piece of information. A double beat. A skip of joy. When had he last felt joy? Pure joy.

'And how is she?'

'I can tell you she is in very good health.'

'That's pleasing to hear.'

'She left her employment at this hotel many years ago but in recent years she has chosen to live close by.'

'My goodness. She lives here in Hakone?'

'Only ten minutes or so from the hotel.'

'Only ten minutes.'

'By car.'

'Ten minutes by car. Is that all?'

'Yes, very close by.'

'Do you think it would be possible to see her?'

'Absolutely.' Takahashi had leaned forward across the table. 'I hope you don't mind. But I took the liberty of calling her earlier. Before I came here for our little chat. She asks if this afternoon at the Hakone Open-Air Museum would be convenient. At three o'clock?'

It was quarter to three now. He shivered on his bench, clasping his scarf tighter at the neck, observing the elderly Japanese gentleman sitting in a wheelchair opposite, mummified in a tartan blanket. This poor soul must have been abandoned by his relatives or carers as they sought to explore the gardens unhampered. So there the old man sat, staring straight ahead through thick lenses, no one to wipe the dribble off his crumpled chin, lined up opposite like some medieval jousting companion. Edward shivered again, dismissing any comparison with his fellow senior citizen. After all, he had been able to fly halfway across the world. He had taken bullet trains to Tokyo. He had wandered these grounds under his own volition. He had even managed a half-mast erection in the bath. Try doing that, old man. Just trying doing that.

As if to prove his point, Edward stood up, tapped his cane loudly on the tiles in the direction of the wheelchair, before taking another little tour of the gardens, humming as he went. That same damn tune. He had been sure it was the national anthem. But perhaps it really was the melody for the Tokyo Olympics. Da, da, da-da-da. He had left Japan long before that event had taken place. But he remembered watching it on television. Black and white. Fuzzy. Via satellite. Such a concept in those days. As was this open-air museum in these days. This environmental art. This artistic environment. He would re-visit the Moore sculptures and, if there was time, the ceramics at the Picasso exhibition.

He was aware of his calmness despite the impending meeting. But that was often the case with these dramatic and traumatic moments in his life. It was as though his nerves were so overwhelmed by the thought of meeting Sumiko again, they switched him into some kind of serene state, a higher plane, a second spiritual wind. As a marathon runner must experience after the first ten miles or a climber at high altitude pushing over 14,000 feet. Accelerated heartbeat, a struggle for breath, dizziness, nausea and then... the barrier is crossed. Overdrive. Less revs per minute. Fifth gear. Cruising. That was how he felt now. It was how he had felt when he had taken his driving test, married, knelt before the Queen. An inner calm. His own secret weapon.

The Henry Moore sculpture garden. So appropriate to let these huge bronzes lie back, legs wide apart, and breathe the mountain air, their undulating forms so reflective of the nature around them. So organic. So fluid. He just wanted to reach out and touch, run his palm over the speckled bronze mounds. The knees. The breasts. Crying out to be caressed. What could they do to him for such a sin? Arrest him? He was sure Henry wouldn't mind. Not that he knew the man personally, although he did recall attending some function with him years ago. In the Seventies. A garden party? He remembered marquees, waiters drifting among the guests on the lawns, noble Henry among them, the miner's son made good. From hewn coal to sculpted bronze. No, Henry wouldn't mind. And anyway who would know? There were no cameras. No guards. Just a discreet slide of the hand. Like that. The metal chill to the touch. So smooth.

'Eddie-chan. Eddie-chan. There you are.'

His hand leapt off the sculpture. He twisted around in the direction of the voice. And there she was. Not exactly running towards him. But walking quickly. With those small steps of hers. Both arms outstretched. Not in a kimono but wearing a knee-length plaid skirt and a green blazer. Looking as if she had just won the US Masters. What a strange thought to creep into his mind at a moment like this. He didn't even like golf. She was closer now. Her figure the same. Not filled out, but trim. Perhaps from playing golf. He believed it had become a very popular sport here. Those two hands out to greet him. Then noticing his cane, only one hand. So awkward. What to do? What to say? And then his fingers plucked into hers, his skin memory tingling to her touch, causing another shiver through him, and the smile spreading weblike around her eyes, and the hair streaked with grey and the mouth exactly the same, kissing him warm on one cold cheek and then the other. She stood back and looked at him as if she were measuring up a cabinet for her living room, and he wondered what she thought about this shrivelled up, pitiful old man with his walking stick and his few strands of hair and his crumpled-up suit trying to look so calm and dignified and unflustered and noble like Henry Moore at a garden party, yet feeling the opposite with his flimsy heart banging around inside of him, and his frail lungs struggling to say this one word:

'Sumiko.'

'Oh, Eddie,' she said, a scolding tone in her voice. Scolding him for what? For never contacting her in more than forty years? For being so decrepit while she remained so vibrant? 'I am so happy to see you.'

'As I am happy to see you.' He held on to her hand, so tiny in his grasp, clinging desperately to this lifeline back to that wonderful part of his past when he had so much energy and passion, when there was so much to do, to be achieved. 'You look beautiful,' he added.

'I look like an old woman.'

'Nothing of the sort.' His turn to playfully scold as he tried to make the calculation. She would be sixty-nine, seventy at most. 'You are a young beauty.'

'Enough flattering,' she said, squeezing his hand before she let it go. 'Let me take you for tea. There is a lovely *chaya* down by the pond. We can sit outside if it is not too cold.' He was surprised when she linked her arm in his, perhaps in nostalgic affection, or perhaps just to support him. But he felt a tingle from her closeness. A tingle that went all the way down to his abdomen. He started humming again.

'Tell me, what is this tune? I cannot get it out of my head.'

'Oh, Eddie. Is that all you can say to me after all this time?'

'No, seriously.' He hummed a bar. She giggled. So he hummed another. 'It's not your national anthem, is it?'

'No, it is not. It sounds like that song for the Tokyo Olympics. Da da da–da–da.'

He smiled and continued humming the tune as they walked.

The *chaya* was set in such a lovely spot on the edge of the woods, nestling up to a pool, accessible only by a bridge. The water brimming with carp, of course. Despite the cold, it was hard to resist not sitting outside at a table, each one shaded by a pale-orange umbrella. He would have preferred to be inside but here by the pond it was so – he had to admit it – so romantic. He had actually put ambience before his own personal comfort. When was the last time he had done that? Sumiko off to freshen up as she put it. Her English so fluent. That was a surprise. After his departure he would have expected her to be sucked back into a Japanese world of waitresses and chambermaids, her English discarded like love-letters on a flame. Here she was now, bringing out their tray of tea-things, just as she used to tend to him as he sat by the waterwheel. And as he watched her graceful approach, he felt something he had not felt for a long time. Gratitude. Towards some universal force, or God, or deities, or Nature, or whatever else made this world spin round. Yes, he felt gratitude for being allowed to live long enough to enjoy these poignant moments.

'You should be ashamed of yourself,' she said, laying out the cups and saucers on their little table. 'Coming back to Japan after all this time and not contacting me immediately.'

'I didn't even know if you were still alive.'

'You just needed to ask.'

'I didn't know who to ask. I was frightened to ask.'

'Frightened, Eddie? Is that really true? Or were you just ashamed?'

'Why would I be ashamed?'

'That such a famous writer should have known such a lowly chambermaid?'

'You could blame me for many things but not that. I was never ashamed of our relationship. Secretive, maybe. But not ashamed.'

'Then why frightened to ask?' She began to pour out the tea, first into his cup and then into her own. Then a glance at him, a smile. A smile that was hard to interpret. 'Did you think I would want to scold you?'

'I thought you might be dead. That it would be too late.'

'Why should you care now? You had more than forty years to find out about my welfare. Oh, look what I've done...' She had spilt some tea on the table. He passed her a paper napkin from his plate. 'I am sorry,' she said.

'An accident.'

'I mean I am sorry for my comments. They are very harsh. I am not being very polite. I must stop behaving like a stupid schoolgirl. The past is the past.'

He placed his hand on hers. Could almost feel her jump to his touch but she did not withdraw from his grasp. His white-haired, liver-spotted hand covering her smooth, unblemished skin. 'You have nothing to apologise for,' he said, taking his hand away.

She sat down, gathered herself into a stiffness. 'How was your trip to Tokyo?'

'Takahashi-san told you?'

'No.' She looked away from him, then back again. 'Jerome did.'

'Jerome? You still know Jerome?'

'I married him,' she said flatly. 'He didn't tell you?'

A strange laugh erupted in his throat, a sound he did not recognise as part of himself. Jerome and Sumiko. Sumiko and Jerome. He shook his head. 'He mentioned there had been a marriage to a Japanese girl. He just didn't tell me it was you.'

He waited for her to say something. But she remained silent, began touching things on the table. A salt cellar, a sachet of sweetener, a small vase with a plastic flower.

'Well?' he said. 'Don't you think that's strange? I mean we were standing in his office together looking at a photograph of you. You and me in Kamakura.'

She shrugged. 'Not really. After all, we don't see each other very much these days. We have a Japanese divorce. For the sake of form, we are still married. But the reality is that he spends all his time in Tokyo. And I live here in the mountains where I am happy. Jerome is very kind to support me in this arrangement.'

'How long did you stay together?'

'It doesn't really matter.' She picked up her cup, sipped at her tea, all the time looking at him over the rim. 'What did you expect me to do? After you left me I was devastated and I was... I was soiled goods. Jerome was the only one to pick up the pieces when I realised you would never come back. When there was not even a letter. What right do you have to...?' She sucked in her breath, held up her palm towards him as if to ward off his evil presence. 'No, no. I said to myself I will not be angry. I will not be angry.' She wriggled her shoulders, shivering herself into more of a calmness. 'Sugar? Do you take sugar in your tea, Eddie? See, I have forgotten, if you take sugar in your tea.'

'One,' he said, reproaching himself for feeling a certain satisfaction at the sudden shrill in her voice.

'Would you like to try a piece of this cherry cake?' she asked, her tone changing again, more gentle. 'It looks very delicious, don't you think? And then you can tell me why you have finally returned to our hotel in the mountains.'

He didn't want to tell her why he had come back. All she needed to know was that he was happy to be here right now in this tearoom. The reality of the moment. It felt so relaxing just sitting by this pond in the crisp mountain air. The waning sun. Branches lifting and settling in a light breeze. Modernist sculptures beckoning his eye from various niches on the hillside. Tea warming his belly, spreading heat through his veins. No current aches or pain he could speak of. Sumiko seated across from him. On the bridge, a young child, her face drawn into concentration in the realisation of her power to attract the carp simply by throwing crumbs into the water. He picked up his fork, carved out a piece of cake from the slice Sumiko had placed on his plate. The moist sponge mingled in his mouth with the sticky-sweet ripeness of the cherries. She was right. This cake was delicious. He looked up and watched as she dabbed her eyes then her lips with her napkin, leaving stains of red on the dimpled paper.

'It's all right, Eddie. There is no need to explain.' And this time it was she who reached out, touched his arm, her tiny fingers so pale against the dark wool.

'Did you ever read my book?' he asked. 'Did you read *The Waterwheel*?'

'I started it,' she said. 'But once I saw you named that stupid *panpan* girl after me, I put it down. How could you do that to me?'

CHAPTER EIGHTEEN

London • 1957

For the first time in his life, Edward flew. From Tokyo to Anchorage to Copenhagen to London on a Scandinavian Airlines DC7C. Whatever that was. As long as the shiny, noisy metal tube was robust enough to sustain him these many, many hours aloft, he didn't care what kind of aircraft he was in. This was the newly inaugurated Polar Route and he had decided to take it, needing to move quickly, not languish for weeks on the deck of an ocean liner playing quoits. Publishers were interested. Editing had to be done. He was willing to cough up the cash for the ticket, pack up his fear for a day or so, knock back a few whiskies and let the shining-blonde Scandinavian crew with their perfect teeth and their DC7C perform their shuddering, juddering airborne tasks. He had slept for large segments of the journey, but woke for the excitement of passing over the Arctic, of witnessing the white cowl of the world. The floes shone blue in the holy hum of the eerie night and he half-expected to see Amundsen's frozen Norwegian flag down there somewhere marking the spot. After this first rush to the window, he ordered another drink, tried to relax into the majestic monotony. The empty landscape would take hours to cross, blank pages needing to be filled.

It was hard to believe that only a short time earlier he had been standing in the hotel forecourt having his photograph taken with the staff. Ishikawa-san had made a speech, presented him with a signed and bound history of the hotel. Sumiko lingered in the background. Then her co-workers came forward to offer small gifts and kind words. Sumiko eventually approached in the wake of her colleagues, head bowed as she gave him a copy of Kawabata's *Snow Country*. Before he had time to thank her, she had turned and was already hurrying back to the servants' quarters. It was the last he saw of her. There was no inscription either. He opened the book, translated the first two lines in his head.

"The train came out of the long tunnel into the snow country.

The earth lay white under the night sky."

He quietly mouthed the words again, remembering how Sumiko would do the same as she lay on his bed with the novel propped up against the pillow. As if by somehow reading the words aloud, the story became more alive in her imagination. He slipped back the curtain, looked down at the icy expanse. At this, his own snow country. The earth really did lie white under the night sky. This frozen tundra. Tundra. Such a cold and lonely word. To accompany such a cold and lonely journey. He would sleep restless from now on to Copenhagen. For if this DC7C were to crash, it would smash harsh and brutal on the tundra. A wreck of tangled metal lying isolated on the permafrost. And there was still the add-on leg from Copenhagen to London to come.

His feet might have stepped on to the tarmac but his soul was still airborne, in that rushing, droning, pressurised cabin, hurtling along at however many hundreds of miles an hour a DC7C was capable of generating. Body-grounded, soul-flying, he was gliding through a new vocabulary of travel – gates and ramps and passport control and luggage collection and conveyor belts and customs. Whoosh through the swing doors. And there was Aldous, standing at the end of the walkway, wearing the same long raincoat he had worn to see him off at Southampton, leaning against a concrete pillar, smoking a cigarette like some spy come to pick up his contact, striding over towards him, arms ridiculously extended. "Hello, my dear boy, so wonderful to see you. How was the trip over the Pole? Come, I have a car." Then the two of them walking across the newly tiled lounge and out of another set of swing doors into the brisk air. "The car is just over here, yes, I learned to drive since you have been away, what is so strange about that? I am not a total incompetent when it comes to machinery you know, I'll take your suitcase, I'll just open the door for you." And there was a backseat passenger, just a silhouette, but Edward recognised her immediately.

'Hello, Eddie,' she said, her voice coming to him out of the past, down some windblown tunnel.

First one ear popped, then the other, and Edward suddenly could hear the noise of the airport all around him, like a brass band struck up just for this occasion.

'What the hell are you doing here?'

Macy patted the leather upholstery and he noticed his treasonous body slipping in beside her even as his heart and mind tried to cope with the turmoil. Perhaps this was what the more experienced flyers called 'jet lag'. This disembodiment. This detachment. His spirit still soaring above, observing this little play. That was it. He was in a kitchen sink drama. Aldous, the audience, moving in to his seat up front with a suitcase as a passenger, engine starting up, eyes on the road, ears pricked, waiting for the first lines to be said.

'I don't have to have a reason for everything I do, Eddie.'

That was his cue. Access the anger. The resentment. 'So you can just sail out of my life without a word of farewell?'

'You hit me.'

Edward glanced at Aldous whose head had turned at the remark. 'There are no secrets, young man,' he said. 'I've always said men were beasts.'

'I hardly touched you.'

'Jesus Christ, Eddie. You punched me.'

'I didn't punch you. It was a slap.'

'I don't stand for that. I saw enough of it with my father and mother. I won't let it happen to me. I just won't.'

'You hurt me too.'

'Look, I didn't ask you to get involved with me. I told you right from the start. Our relationship was to be on my terms. If you didn't like it that way, you could have baled ship anytime you wanted. You could never say I misled you. I was very clear. You just didn't want to listen, that's all.'

He felt hot. His body had been grounded less than an hour and here he was dredging up the past as if Japan had never happened. He unbuttoned his coat, wound down a gap in the window, wiped a sleeve across the misted glass. London dreary in the early afternoon drizzle. Dreich. His father's word. The comforting hiss of the tyres licking up the wet roads. The bowler hat and brolly brigades marching along the pavements. Macy, shrill and brittle beside him, Aldous at the helm, leaning back, mouthing words.

'Now, now, children. Let's have a little truce.'

'Can we, Eddie?' she said, touching his arm.

'When did you two become such great friends?' Edward grumbled. 'You used to be at each other's throats.'

She leaned forward in her seat, scratched her fingers through Aldous' hair. 'Oh, we made up long ago.'

And Edward felt the cut of jealousy in his stomach as Aldous wriggled his neck under her touch. 'America not to your liking then?' he said.

'I fell out with Mother. Again.'

'So it was a case of run back to Daddy.'

'He won't have me either.'

'How are you surviving?'

'Turns out there's huge interest in abstract expression now. Since Jackson got himself killed in that damn car crash. My paintings are selling like hot cakes, as you Brits would say. Got myself a nice little apartment-cum-studio in Kensington.'

'How long have you been back?'

'Must be nearly two years. I got in touch with Aldous to find out where you were. But you'd packed up and gone to Japan.'

'I needed to get away from you.'

'I thought I was the one to leave you.'

'You know what I mean.'

She sighed and dropped back into her seat. Crossed her legs so that her coat fell away to reveal black-stockinged shins and a glimpse of cream-silk petticoat beneath the hem of her dress. 'I've read the manuscript,' she said, adjusting her coat. 'It's pretty good.'

'Christ, Aldous. You betrayed me.'

'And why not? It's an excellent piece of work. I have booked lunch at the Savoy to celebrate its imminent publication.'

'What? Now?'

'Yes, my dear boy. Now. A civilised way to spend an afternoon, don't you think? As the rest of the world grinds away at its daily toil.'

Edward was still flying. Macy chatting away to him, reassuring him with her fingertips on the back of his hand, with her body-nearness, her body-warmness, as Aldous eased their vehicle out of the Strand traffic into that discrete lane boasting the Savoy in all its art deco, glassy-glossy, illuminated splendour. He was still flying as the car doors were snapped open and he stepped lightly on to the wet courtyard, coat-tightened and scarf-wrapped, Macy joining him, arm-linking and laughing at something Aldous had said, the two of them on either side of him now, balancing him, book-ending him, somehow making him feel whole and happy on this dreary afternoon, as they swept him into the reception area, where they stopped him dead in his tracks on the black-and-white tiles. For in all his heady joyfulness, Edward was the last of their little group to notice the veteran Right Honourable Member of Parliament for Woodford standing alone on the chessboard floor. A despondent king deserted by his subjects.

It was Churchill. Winston Churchill. Soldier, statesman, writer, painter. Knight of the realm and Nobel laureate. A confidant to kings and queens, premiers and presidents. Not ten feet away from Edward stood the greatest Englishman alive, blue eyes peering out world-weary from under his hat brim. The complexion was pale but pink-stained in the cheeks, no doubt fired up from a good Savoy Grill lunch of raw oysters, petite marmite, roast beef and vegetables, a fine glass of red. The mouth no longer defiant and wittily cruel but curled down at each corner by… what? Regret? Sadness? Disappointment? The depression he used to call the Black Dog? Or just by the gravity of old age? He would be well in his eighties by now. One hand in his pocket, the other hanging loose with a dead cigar stub wedged between these two famous fingers.

Aldous and Macy let go their grip. Edward felt like standing to attention, saluting. Or bowing. Before what the Japanese would call a Living National Treasure. Before this embodiment of so much human achievement. No doubt there would be an abandoned table of illustrious guests back in the Grill and there would be darling Clemmie waiting for him at Chartwell, but for these few moments the great man stood alone, fingering impatiently at coins in his pocket, ignored by the staff in their awe or politeness. His fickle public had receded, his military comrades were long dead, kings and presidents buried in all their pomp, while he too was left to ponder his increasing senility, the decaying organs and diminishing faculties, the journey he would eventually have to make unaccompanied. Take away the Homburg and the cigar, replace it with a flatcap and cigarette, and this was just an old man facing his own mortality.

A uniformed commissionaire arrived, saluted and informed the former Prime Minister his car had arrived. A nod of acknowledgement, fingers pressing coins into a palm that would have happily waved away the tip, the touch of greatness better than any reward, and then he was gone, leaving behind the cold draft of his presence.

Macy was the first to speak. 'What is it with you and me, Eddie? First it was the dead king. And now it's Sir Winston bloody Churchill.'

The sighting of Churchill had affected them all. It blessed their little lunch, invigorated them, made them drink too much champagne, laugh too loud, suck back too many oysters at Aldous' expense. Edward felt as if a magic dust had been sprinkled over them, that the weight of history had rubbed off on them, catching them in its vortex, fleetingly for this afternoon. He was still contained in his fuselage of space and time, the rest of the world pushed out, irrelevant. It was just the three of them in their afternoon hideaway, eating, drinking, laughing. And so he continued in his tubular shell, driven back to Kensington in a taxi, Aldous too drunk to drive, through a clear night of stars unveiled just for them. Edward's body suddenly weary, limbs desperately heavy, hard even to make the few steps to the flat. Sleep was all he wanted. To drift away. His mind surrendering to the demands of his drunk, jet-lagged body. No resistance. He could feel the cool of the sheets. At last, a pillow. Such a welcoming softness. His body still travelling. Over blue snow and frozen tundra. The quiet engine hum sustaining him. Ice flows splitting and cracking, giant continents ponderously knocking against each other. A Norwegian flag. Spitfires flying over the Savoy. Churchill waving a two-fingered victory salute. He awoke in the middle of the night. He was still in his clothes. As was Macy who slept in his loose grasp, the straps of her dress slipped off to her forearms, her buttocks shoved tight into his groin. As was Aldous, behind him, snoring softly. He eased himself out of their wedge, went over to the window, open to the cold night and the rain. He could see Kensington Palace, the Gardens, the Royal Albert Hall, lit up in the slick of the night. He was back. Sumiko and Japan seemed very far away.

CHAPTER NINETEEN

Hakone, Japan • 2003

Sumiko had a car. A rather large, sleek, metallic-silver, executive-type of vehicle. Japanese, of course. Edward recognised the marque. If only he had put his inheritance into that company all those years ago, he would be sitting pretty by now. Actually, he was sitting pretty, embraced by all this luxurious, top-of-the-range, grey-suede upholstery as Sumiko effortlessly swung her monster of a machine down the steep roads from the museum.

'Do you remember when you took me there?' she asked as they passed yet another spa resort.

'Yes, I do,' he said, tapping the floor between his legs with his walking stick at the sudden flush of memory. 'Bathing in hot springs is such a sensual experience,' he added, trying to make the sentence sound matter-of-fact. But he knew he was testing her, reminding her of their intimacy, probing to see whether even with Jerome Fisk's ring still on her finger, he could provoke her into a nostalgia for their sexual history.

'It would be good for my arthritis,' she said. 'I have so much trouble with my left hand. Look at these fingers.' She lifted the offending appendage off the steering wheel. 'It is like a... like a claw. What am I to do with something like this?'

'Perhaps we could visit one again.'

'Please stop it.'

'Stop what?'

'You know what I mean. Making plans for us.' She drove faster, her stare fixed straight ahead, the tyres screeching slightly on the bends. And then he saw she was crying.

'I'm sorry,' he said. And he truly was. He had got carried away.

'You can't do this, Eddie. You can't just walk back into my life and pretend everything is fine.'

She swung the car into the hotel forecourt, and immediately there was the familiar beetling of the bellboys around the vehicle, busy hands opening doors, searching for luggage. He waved them away, took her hand. 'Would you like to come inside? Stay for dinner?'

She sniffed, nodded her head.

'Good. That's settled.' He dragged his legs out of the seat, hobbled to his feet on his cane. The car was whisked off, leaving this empty space between them in the forecourt. He waited as she tied a silk scarf around her head.

'Do you know what would be nice?' she said, her eyes puffy from the tears but smiling now. 'If we could take a walk in the garden. Could you manage that?'

'The azaleas are very beautiful,' Edward remarked, as they wandered slowly along the pathways. 'I remember you were fond of them.'

She knelt down, the hem of her plaid skirt grazing the ground, placed her palm under one of the drooping heads, pulled in closer to the scent. He observed the still-graceful curve of her neck and seemed to recall watching her perform the same action those many years ago. Had he been truly happier then? Or was it all just an illusion? If he could go back to the past and place himself exactly on this path with Sumiko, would he have been the young writer full of ideals and passion and ambition he recalled with a wistful melancholy or would he be just the same sad and disillusioned human being he was now? He held out his hand and awkwardly helped her to her feet. They walked the rest of the way to the waterwheel in silence.

She let out just the slightest squeal when she saw it. 'Oh, Eddie-chan. It's still here!'

'Yes, it is. Although it's actually a rebuilt version of the old one. Look at how fresh the wood is. You can almost smell it from here. The substance has gone but the form still remains.'

'We Japanese are very good at doing that.'

He sat down on the low wall and she came to sit beside him. He closed his eyes, breathed in slowly, trying to grasp some kind of internal feeling for her presence. The chill of the air chafing his cheeks, he could feel that, and the sound of the breeze sifting through the trees, lifting the leaf-laden branches, creating that wonderful rush-reedy sound.

'Eddie-chan. Are you listening to me?'

'Forgive me. What were you saying?'

'This place brings back so many memories.'

'For me too. I was happy here.'

'Then why did you leave?'

'I had to.' These words seemed so weak now. But it was what he had always believed. A crossroads in his life. Stay in Japan with Sumiko or return to England to be a writer. That was his choice and if he hadn't taken it then, he would never have had another chance. Only Aldous had sown any seeds of doubt on that decision. 'If you were meant to be a writer,' his friend had told him many years later. 'You would have become a writer whether you had stayed in Japan or not. Destiny will always work itself out. Even if mere mortals like yourself want to fuck it up. Destiny will always win.'

Sumiko stood up, straightened her skirt. 'I understood you had to go,' she said. 'I just don't know why you didn't take me with you.'

'Ah, Enid. Forgive me for having abandoned you. Please let me introduce you to an old friend from this hotel. Sumiko, this is Enid.

The woman I cannot live without.' He saw that Sumiko looked confused. 'My personal assistant,' he added. The two women nodded to each other. Sumiko with a certain politeness. Enid, he noticed, with just a shiver of disdain.

'I have had more than enough to occupy myself,' Enid said. 'And when I had a few free moments, Mr Takahashi was kind enough to arrange for a guide to take me down to Hakone. The marquetry is quite exquisite. I bought some lovely souvenirs.'

'Hakone is blessed with so many different kinds of trees,' Sumiko said. 'Did you buy one of the puzzle boxes?'

'Actually, I preferred the mosaic bowls and dishes. Now, Sir Edward, I need to talk to you about a more important matter.'

'I'm afraid it will have to wait. I have promised to escort Sumiko to dinner.'

'It really is most pressing.'

'Later, Enid. Now if you will forgive me again, I'm sure my chatter with Sumiko about old times will bore you.'

'It is quite all right. I am happy to dine quietly in my room.'

The evening sparkled. His conversation sparkled. Sumiko sparkled. And when Takahashi joined them for coffee, Edward was so proud of her, this former chambermaid, holding her own so eloquently in English with the manager of this grand hotel. He sucked shamelessly on his cigar, savoured his peaty malt, absorbed the warmth of it all. He could almost say he was content. It was a state of being he had never really wanted to achieve until about two minutes before he was ready to die. After all, what kind of life was there to live in a state of contentment? A boring one was all he could imagine. Life was all about the struggle for fulfilment, the desire to fill the void. 'All creativity comes from loss.' But once the void was filled, what else was there? Yet, in this moment, he felt very close to that state of being.

'It has been a great pleasure to converse with you, Sir Edward,' Takahashi said, rising from his chair and bowing. 'It has reminded me so much of the old times. The once great days of this hotel.'

'The dining room looks quite full to me. It seems you are still doing very well.'

'Ah yes. But there is so much competition these days. And it is hard to attract the...' Takahashi coughed lightly into his closed fist. 'The same exceptional quality of clientele as we used to.'

'Takahashi-san. I am sure you understand I would like a few quiet words with Sumiko before she leaves.'

'Of course. How unthoughtful of me. Yes, I must go. There are matters to which I must attend. Sir Edward. Sumiko-chan. Please enjoy the rest of the evening.'

'He is a very kind man,' Sumiko said, once the manager had left. 'But such a busybody, don't you think? Busybody. That is the right word, isn't it?'

'Yes, it is the right word.' He drew on his cigar and observed her through a cloud of his own making. 'Tell me. Are you happy now?'

'You mean, now at this moment? Or now in my life?'

'Both.'

'Yes, I am happy to see you again. And in my life? Well, I live with my two dogs in the mountains, Jerome is very generous, and I was the lover of a famous writer who named a prostitute after me. That is not bad for a poor Japanese chambermaid.'

'Not bad at all.'

She picked up her napkin off her lap, folded it neatly. 'Eddie. It is getting late. I must go.'

He rose with her, escorted her into the foyer.

'I have taken the same room,' he told her.

'The Fuji Suite?'

'Yes, the Fuji Suite. Would you like to see it?'

He gave her the key and she went on ahead of him, almost running down the corridor in her excitement. Hobbling after her, he felt as if he was following in his own ghostly footsteps, their ghostly footsteps. By the time he had caught up with her, she had already pulled back the curtains. She opened and closed the door of the walk-in cupboard.

'See,' she said. 'The light goes on automatically when you open the door. Just as always.'

He felt so happy watching her, but also so immensely weary. He sat down on the side of the bed, slipped off his shoes and jacket, loosened his tie. She had gone into the bathroom and he could hear her turn on the taps just to delight in the clunk and gasp of the old pipework. He felt as if his world was closing in on him and all that was left for him was this room, a tiny speck of warm light in a universe of cold darkness. With difficulty, he managed to bring his legs over on to the bed, laid his head down on to the coldness of the quilt. He felt Sumiko's presence.

'Are you all right?'

'I am fine. Just tired. So tired.' He raised his head slightly from the pillow. 'Please lie with me. Lie with me and hold me. Just for a few minutes. Hold me, Sumiko. Please.'

CHAPTER TWENTY

London • 1958

'The Americans, my dear Edward, will hate it,' Aldous said, leaning back in his office chair. On the desk between them lay the final proofs for *The Waterwheel*, edited heavily in red. 'Absolutely hate it. Bugger them for their insecurities.'

'Well, I'm not changing any of it. Not a damn word.'

'I'm not asking you to, dear boy. That's what I like about the book. The uncompromising way it humanises the Japs.'

'I just want to remind the Americans we drop bombs on people. Not on abstract targets.'

'Unfortunately the Yanks will not be reminded as I doubt they will be reading it. But from where does this sense of fair play emerge? This great sense of outrage against our American cousins? Methinks you spent too much time consorting with the natives.'

Edward shrugged. 'I've just never understood how you could wipe out so many people just like that. Even listening to the news about it on the radio at the time, I felt that way. You'd think they'd have some kind of conscience about it all.'

'It's still too raw.'

'It's been thirteen bloody years.'

'It could be fifty years ago and they'd still be in denial. You've got to understand the Yanks, dear boy. They're all about glitz and glamour. They're not interested in introspection. While what I am interested in is their export market.'

'Is that important?'

'Oh yes, very important. It's not enough to sell well nationally these days. The international market is just as vital. And America is the big one. Roland has done remarkably well across the pond.'

Roland. Roland Earnshaw. Not only Aldous' latest lover but also his sole client. Roland and his wartime yarn *The Adventures of Private X* had sold close to one million copies on both sides of the Atlantic, mainly on the basis of one quite sexually graphic scene that had managed to escape the censor's attention. Aldous' commission from these sales had paid for the refurbishment in Regency style of *The Londinium* offices in which they now sat. Red and cream striped wallpaper matching the upholstery on the chairs, brass wall-lights, sconces, heavy furniture, all topped off with a chandelier at the centre. The room looked like an upmarket brothel.

'Well, Macy liked the book. And she's American.'

'I wouldn't call Macy your typical reader, dear boy. First of all, she's been your lover these past few months. And secondly, she's bound to like anything that would annoy her father. After all, Jack Collingwood was a prosecutor in Japan during the Occupation.'

'Like I said before. I'm not going to soften my stance. Anyway, the bombings are only a small part of it. There's a love story as well.'

'Then I think we might have to adopt a different approach.'

'Which is?'

'Well, if the Yanks won't like it, then perhaps the Japs will. And there are what? A hundred million of them? Not quite as big a market as the States but that's still a lot of potential eyeballs on pages. We could have it translated into Japanese. What do you think?'

'It's not a bad idea.'

'Not a bad idea? It's a bloody brilliant idea. You couldn't handle the translation, could you?'

'Afraid not. My Japanese is nowhere near good enough.'

'Well, do you know someone who could?'

Edward thought back to his time in Japan. It had only been months but it seemed like a lifetime ago. A lifetime ago with another person altogether in the starring role. 'Actually, I just might. There was someone at Tokyo Autos when I was there. Kobayashi his name was. Not particularly good at Japanese to English. But he was pretty good the other way around.'

'Can you get in touch with him?'

'I suppose so. These chaps stay in their jobs for life over there.'

'Excellent. Do what you can to bring him on board. I'm sure I can arrange a small fee. But do it quickly.' Aldous rose from his chair, walked over to the window. Outside the rain was sheeting down, rattling off the panes. 'And how is dear Macy?' he asked, lighting a Balkan Sobranie, the black-papered, gold-tipped cigarettes being his latest affectation. 'I've hardly seen her since you've returned.'

'Well, don't blame me. I haven't seen much of her either. She's been too involved with her damn exhibition.'

'Ah yes, the exhibition. That would distract her.' Aldous turned from the window, blew a lungful of smoke high into the chandelier. The smell thick and sweet like liquorice, reminding Edward of his father's pipe tobacco. 'But everything is all right between you?'

'You never know with Macy.'

'That is very true. But her sojourn in America changed her, don't you think?'

'I haven't noticed. Being with her is still as much of an emotional rollercoaster as ever.'

'But that's what you need. She keeps you on edge. Stops you slipping into complacency. Into ennui.'

'Unlike you. Who has slipped into a life of domestic bliss with Roland.'

Aldous smiled. 'That is a different scenario altogether. After all, I am an older man. My needs have changed. Domestic bliss, as you call it, suits my middle-aged temperament. And my reduced libido. While you, my dear Edward, require a woman who can keep you on the back foot. On the front foot, I fear you could be quite cruel.'

Edward was never sure about these remarks from Aldous. Either they were meant to be terribly profound or otherwise just throwaway bits of nonsense.

Macy's studio was a vast concrete space, once the top floor of a textile factory hosting several rows of looms beneath the vaulted glass-panelled ceiling. What used to be the workplace for a whole colony of weavers and seamstresses struggling to feed hungry mouths in post-war Britain was now home to a solitary artist. Macy loved the natural light of the place, even on a grey day such as this one. With just one paraffin heater sputtering in its hopeless attempt to keep the room warm, a kettle constantly simmering on top of its metal casing.

'Do you think I'm cruel?' Edward asked her.

She stood at the centre of a large canvas stretched out on the concrete floor, her face, hair, overalls and boots splattered with different coloured paints. He reckoned her body and clothes could be as much of a representation of her abstract expressionism as her paintings. She was breathing heavily from her exertions, misting the cold air.

'Yes, I think you are.' She drew herself up, folded her arms, scowled at him. Surrounded by her work, this moat of paint standing as a barrier against him, she was untouchable.

'Why do you say that?'

'Because you have just interrupted my work mid-flow. By walking into my studio asking stupid questions.'

'I'm sorry.'

'Just like my father.'

'Meaning what?'

'Not giving a shit about my work.'

'Oh, for God's sake, Macy. Stop whining about your father.'

'There you go,' she said, raising her arms wide, appealing to some invisible audience. 'As God is my witness. Just as I said. Cruel. A goddamn cruel bastard.'

How did she do that? How could she take just one moment of insensitivity on his part and turn it into a major issue? So that he stood there shaking, trying to control the shameful venom that had risen up inside of him. Instead of trying to find sympathy for her. He knew the exhibition was important to her. It was her first in two years, the first since Pollock had died. And now she felt herself to be among the anointed, one of the heirs to the great man. One of the carriers of the dripping trowels, sticks and knives of existentialist American art.

The kettle steamed and bubbled on its hotplate, distracting both of them, allowing him time to swallow down his own heated-up temper.

'I realise you're anxious about the exhibition,' he said.

'What would you know?'

'It's the same for me. Putting my book out there. Making myself vulnerable. A target for criticism.'

Her expression softened. She exited her painting with a giant stride. 'Maybe you're right. I just feel so exposed.'

He followed her to the sink where she was wiping her brushes, put his arms around her, kissed her neck.

'Leave me,' she said. 'I'm not in the mood for you.'

But he persisted, moving his hand to cup one breast through the spattered workcloth. She leaned back, opened up her neck to his kisses.

'Stop it.' But he saw the flush in her neck, felt her rump pushing back into him as he slipped his hand under the bib of her overalls. And he knew she would respond to his touch. That they would use sex to ease out the tension between them. She had bent her torso down level with the sink, using her arms to push herself back at him, and he thought this is how he would enter her. If he could figure out the clasps and studs of her workclothes. But suddenly, she turned on him, her face hot, pushing him back, taking control, forcing him to step backwards. Pace by pace until he tripped on the edge of her canvas, fell over on to the still-wet paint. He waited for her screams and accusations. But instead she was on top of him, tearing off her clothes, his clothes, as they squirmed and writhed on the gooey, gluey surface, his body slithering, skin slipping, the two of them gulping for breath. Creating swirls and smears from the rub of her breasts, the twists of his buttocks, her legs flaying, his fingers squeezing at the thick globs on the canvas. She pinned him down by his shoulders, drew her face in close, cheeks and forehead oily with green paint. Warpaint.

'Do you get it?' she said, lips to his ear.

He understood. That this was her intention. That this was a natural extension of her work. The subconscious working at a raw sexual level. Together creating. Letting the art come through. He eased off the pace of his lovemaking, his initial thrust gone, the frenzy somehow absorbed into the pores of the canvas. He felt a tenderness overtake him, the touch of his lips and fingertips became slower, gentler. She moaned and moved lazily in his embrace. He found compassion in his heart for her, for her anxiety, for her feelings of worthlessness. This lovemaking was no longer about him, but his feeling for her. He became lost in her. Mind-less, body-less, ego-less.

Later he sat with her by the heater in the dying light, wrapped in blankets, paint caked hard on his skin, smoking one of her cigarettes, drinking coffee, admiring their joint effort, joking about what it should be called.

'*Body Rhythms*,' he suggested.

She laughed. '*Body Rhythms Number One*.'

'First of a series?'

'Could be.'

'That gives me hope.'

'Don't get too complacent.'

'You should exhibit it.'

'I've been thinking about that. It's not half bad.'

'Aldous would like it. He should be able to afford a Collingwood original these days.'

'Maybe I'll offer it to him. As long as you promise not to tell him how it was made.'

'I want a credit though.'

'Not this time.'

'That's not fair.'

'I think you have to be the person on top to get the credit.'

It was his turn to laugh. He felt close to her. They had reached a point of balance, poised for a moment in perfect equanimity on their usual tightrope of emotion. He leaned over, touched her bare thigh. She grasped his hand, held it there.

'I'm sorry,' she said.

'For what?'

'For always attacking you. I just want you to know it is the only way I have of defending myself.'

'Against what?'

'Against me falling in love with you. And then you finding out what I'm really like.'

'But I know what you're really like.'

'And you're still here?'

'Yes. I'm still here.'

She reached over, stole his cigarette from between his fingers, sucked in deep, her eyes staring unblinkingly at him from behind her shield of smoke. 'Well, marry me then.'

'What?'

'Yes, Eddie. Let's do it. Let's get married.'

'I never thought you could be so spontaneous,' Aldous said.

'It feels right.' Edward scrutinised his friend's face, trying to discern some sense of approval among the usual creases and frowns of exasperation.

'You are aware what you're letting yourself in for?'

'Marriage will settle her down.'

Aldous laughed at that remark. 'You don't want Macy to settle down. You love those fabulous highs she gives you.'

'Perhaps marriage will keep us on a permanent high.'

'For the first two years maybe. Until the good sex runs out.'

'And what then?'

'Then you should prepare yourself for the lows, my dear boy. Prepare to plumb the depths.'

He married Macy in a registry office in Marylebone. Jack Collingwood had not been invited or had turned down the invitation — Edward was still unclear which. Aldous was the only guest. They had to haul someone else in off the street to be the other witness. Dominic Pike was his name, retired teacher was the occupation scrawled in the register. Although Aldous said he was just a homeless bum who happened to be sitting on the steps of the building at the time. Dominic's breath stunk of ale and there was concern whether he was sober enough to act in a legal capacity. The registrar didn't seem to mind. Aldous found the whole event thoroughly amusing and even invited Dominic to the celebratory lunch at the Savoy.

'If we can't have Sir Winston,' Aldous announced as Dominic swayed and saluted at the mention of the name. 'Then we can have Dominic.'

'Corporal Pike is grateful. But must unfortunately decline due to the lack of proper attire.'

Aldous thanked him anyway, slipped him ten shillings. Macy blew a kiss as Dominic stumbled away. She had worn black for the occasion. Black polo, short black skirt, black stockings, black shoes. The only items she wore reflecting any joy was Edward's wedding gift – his mother's silver evening-watch. After the Savoy lunch, Edward returned with Macy to the three-storey house with small walled garden they had purchased in Chelsea, with views of the Thames, the riverboats in their moorings. Funded from the success of her exhibition, the remains of his inheritance and the potential sales of his book. For although initial interest in *The Waterwheel* in Britain was poor, Aldous had been spot-on about Japan.

Kobayashi at Tokyo Autos had proved a worthy translator, delighted by the commission, finished it in three months, jokingly calling it *Kobayashi's Revenge* as a response to all the edits of his English translations he once had to endure. And then without being asked, Kobayashi had passed on the Japanese manuscript to his brother, who was a commissioning editor at a major Tokyo publishing house. The brother loved it, stumped up a decent advance. And the novel was proving a success, inspiring renewed interest for the book back in Britain.

'Entry has been through the back door,' Aldous was fond of telling Edward. 'But we got there in the end. Your fame and my fortune are secured. Thanks to Japan. And to *Kobayashi's Revenge*.'

Macy went upstairs to get changed from her black bridal wear.

Edward poured himself another glass of champagne, wandered out into the garden. Bloated from the lunch and feeling quite drunk, he eased himself down into a deckchair, almost spilling his drink in the process. He heard an upper window slide open, saw Macy's head appear as a bit of a blur. She dangled something in her hand. It took him a few seconds to realise it was her brassiere.

'Hey, husband,' she called out. 'Come up here and do your duty.'

Instinctively, he looked around to see who might be listening. High walls thankfully blocked out the other gardens.

'Give me five minutes,' he called back. It had taken such an effort to ensconce himself within the swinging canvas, he wasn't ready to drag himself upwards again, even with sex as the lure. He heard the window slam shut.

It was that beautiful time of the late afternoon, just before dusk, as the sun threw out its last shadows and Nature hummed with its pre-darkness activity. Some kind of bird was twittering away in a tree above him. He actually had a tree in this garden of his – not just one, but several – a remarkable achievement, he thought, for a boy raised in a Glasgow tenement. Although he had no idea what kind of trees they were. And there were plants and flowers he would also have to learn the names of. And ivy trailing up his walls. He raised his glass to his new home.

'To *Kobayashi's Revenge*,' he whispered. Then he shivered. Not from that sudden dip in temperature as the sun disappeared behind his trees. But from the thought of his novel circulating throughout Japan. And wondering again if Sumiko had ever read it, curled up in her bed as the snow fell.

CHAPTER TWENTY-ONE

Hakone, Japan • 2003

He awoke to the sound of a woodpecker. Such wonderful, hollow, industrious drumming, filling his mind with the mossy freshness of the forest. He was still fully clothed. Curled up behind him, her head resting between his shoulderblades, Sumiko breathing sleep. He held his own breath so he could feel her life-presence heaving into him, warm and rhythmic. Slowly, he turned with a groan towards her. And still she slept. She was wearing the hotel's *yukata*, belted close around her. Her features soft in the half-light, still retaining a girlishness and a prettiness, remarkable how little she had changed. He experienced that same overwhelming sense of gratitude he had felt at the *chaya*. Having the chance to lie with her again, to observe her sleeping, dreaming, his whole being alive to her closeness. He stroked her cheek, the skin powdered, soft. She blinked awake.

'Good morning,' he said.

'What time is it?'

'I don't know. Early.'

She muttered into the pillow, then screwed up her eyes at him through the fringe of her hair. 'How early?'

'Five o'clock maybe.'

She mumbled something in Japanese, then turned round and away from him. He draped a hand around her stomach, feeling the bones of her hips against him, the folds of belly-flesh under her robe. How long had it been since he had felt a woman close like this? Years. He breathed in deep, tried to capture the sense of the moment in whatever reserves of memory still remained to him. He let two of his fingers slip inside her robe, stroke the bare skin, remarkably smooth compared to his own desiccated flesh. His hands were trembling.

'What are you doing?'

'Holding you. Is that so bad?'

'I'm a married woman.'

'I thought you had a Japanese divorce.' He continued to stroke her and he felt himself stir. 'Sumiko?'

'What'

'Please turn round.'

'Eddie. I am seventy years old. What do you want from an old woman?'

'To kiss you.'

He heard her laugh. 'I can't believe I have to push men off at my age.'

'Don't push me off.'

She turned round slowly, used her drawn-up knees against his thighs to keep her distance. 'What's got into you, Eddie-chan?'

He stroked her cheek again, then drew her face in close with both hands. He could smell her breath, not sweet as in his memories, but sour with a morning staleness. He tried not to think of his own breath odour expelling from his rotting lungs. He pushed himself forward and kissed her full on the mouth. Her lips were dry while his own mouth was over-salivated from his excitement. There was no passion, just a sense of senile desperation. But it was a kiss to be savoured nevertheless. She pulled away. Her eyes wide-awake now, he tried to understand what he saw in them.

'I want to touch you,' he said.

'No.'

'Please.'

'I'm too ashamed.'

'Let me try.'

He put his hand over one breast, closed his eyes, the skin memory of his palm aching to recall the firmness, the tautness that had once so excited. He opened his eyes to see her looking directly at him. He held her gaze as he caressed her withered dug, felt the hairs around the nipple tickle his thumb, saw her wince with unexpected pleasure. He managed to release his other arm from under his body, brought it into play with her other breast. He lay like this for some time, fondling her, listening to the woodpecker, sensing her body in slow arousal, the quickening of his heart, the stickiness between them where their flesh touched, the opening and closing slam of a door in the hallway. She touched him for the first time, grabbing a handful of shirt and skin just above his hip, drawing his awareness away from her body to his own. The layers of belly flopping over his flaccid penis and his shrunken testicles. The skinny legs, the flaky skin, the itching underarm, the hairs in his ears and thick in his nostrils, the toenails needing to be cut, the wheezing breath, the over-excited heart. He released one hand from her breast, stroked downwards, felt the hollows around her abdomen, followed the curve underneath, fingers extended, expectant for the first brush with her pubic hair. She grabbed the exploring hand.

'I'm not ready for this.'

'Why not?'

'Why not? I'm not some *panpan* girl.'

'I'm sorry.' He turned away, then over on to his back. Bodies separate now. Staring at the ceiling. He listened to her breathing, coordinating his lungs to her rhythm, sharing the beat of this life force. Such an aching emptiness. "Love comes from desperation." Aldous again.

'Are you all right?' she asked.

'I am fine, thank you. For a man of my age.'

She moved closer to him, leaned her head on his chest. He felt uncomfortable with her weight, but he did not want her to move.

'Why did you come back, Eddie?'

The woodpecker had gone. He could feel her heart beat against his ribs.

'I came back to where I was happy,' he said. 'That winter I spent here with you, cut off from everywhere by the snow, living together in this room, writing my novel.'

She moved up the bed, stroked his face, placed little kisses on his scalp. 'Now it is still early. Please go back to sleep.'

'But I am not tired.'

'Oh, Eddie. Just rest.'

'No. I would like to get up. And do you know what I would like to do? I would like to relax in a hot pool. Takahashi-san told me the hotel *onsen* has been refurbished with Italian marble. That is what I will do. You go back to sleep. I will go for a soak.'

CHAPTER TWENTY-TWO

London • 1963

Edward's assessment of himself in these early years of both his career and his marriage was that he was content. Or at least he experienced moments of contentment – a fleeting balance between the meaningfulness he drew from his writing and the happiness he drew from Macy, which affected him so profoundly it obliterated any doubts or fears he may have otherwise possessed. It was, he thought, a precarious state to be in. An inner state that reflected the condition of the outer world as well. For everything was changing, nothing was sacrosanct. The earth was no longer the last frontier, presidents were no longer invincible, governments were no longer immune from scandal. The world was all shook up, he was all shook up, every day was a challenge just to know where he fitted into the scheme of things. To know his place in these tumultuous times. For without a sense of place, without a stance, without a perspective, how could he continue to write?

It was in this mood of reflective agitation, he watched Macy wriggle into the sequinned flapper dress she was wearing to Aldous' New Year party. The Roaring Twenties was the theme to welcome in 1964. And if he had to choose a favourite decade it would have to be the Twenties. Of course, he had been born then and for that reason alone he could have said he felt the shadow of that era imprinted on his soul. But if he could choose to be a young artist caught up in the creative spirit of the times, those times would definitely have to be the shimmying, shimmering Twenties.

'Human beings are at the peak of their creative abilities in their twenties,' he said, admiring his black and white Oxford shoes, which along with his white suit, were meant to make up his Gatsby look. 'And likewise in the lifespan of a century, the most creative decade will also be the Twenties.' He began to prove his point by effortlessly counting off that era's many great artists. F. Scott Fitzgerald, the inspiration behind his costume. Then Picasso, Miro, Hemmingway, Kafka, Pound, Proust, Ernst, Miro, George Bernard Shaw, Thomas Mann, Woolf, Colette, Chaplin, Jolson, Garbo, Gershwin, Ellington, Armstrong, Joyce, Eliot.

'Uh? What makes you say that?' She was in front of the mirror now, stretching a gold-tissue skullcap into a fit over her newly shorn locks. This devastating pruning of her hair for the sake of fashion had been a shock to him. He had loved her dark waves just the way they had been – thick, long, lustrous. A scented forest to be lost in. Now there was only a spiky thatch that left his fingers dangling.

'Because one is old enough to have absorbed the knowledge of what has been, yet young enough to reject it and create something truly original.'

'And you cannot do that in your thirties?'

'By then, the freshness has gone, conditioning has worn you down. You can only be derivative after that. You can only admire the new talents of those coming up behind you.'

'How depressing. So you and I can only be derivative from now on?' She licked a finger, dampened down a curl on to her cheekbone.

'That's what I'm saying.'

'No more abstract expressionism for me. And *The Waterwheel* will be your only truly original work?'

'Probably.'

'Oh, I don't think so. I think I could squeeze another brilliant novel or two out of you yet.' She came over to him and literally squeezed him. Two arms around his waist, clasping behind him, pulling him in towards her, so that he could feel all those threads of beads squashed against him. He loved her when she said things like that, when she made him believe in himself, when she was on his side. 'Anyway,' she went on. 'I think you are underestimating the exciting times we are living in. There is so much happening now. In art and music and politics. Even fashion. Don't you think the Sixties will be as every bit as creative as your Twenties? Don't you feel the excitement, Eddie?'

What he felt was the excitement of her. But perhaps she was right. Perhaps the Sixties could be every bit as creative as the Twenties. They certainly had been iconoclastic up until now, clearing the way for what he did not know.

'I worry my creative peak has passed,' he said. 'I do not feel such things.'

'Bullshit,' she said, using the one American profanity he had respect for. 'You're spending too much time with Aldous. You're beginning to sound like him.'

'Ah, Edward and Macy Strathairn,' Aldous said, answering the door to them in a wide-shouldered dinner suit with a pink rose embedded in the lapel. The only item that differentiated his outfit from his usual attire was a black eye-patch with the word "Tony" embroidered on it. 'The bright young things.'

'What's the deal with the patch, you old faggot?' Macy asked, kissing Aldous on the cheek as she passed.

His one blue eye brightened. 'Can you not guess?'

'Ask my husband here. He's the clever one.'

'Go on, Eddie. Help out this ignorant American broad.'

'A character from F. Scott Fitzgerald's *The Beautiful and Damned*. The dissolute Anthony Patch.'

'Very funny,' Macy sniffed. 'Well, I'm the beautiful. Which one of you is the damned?'

'I'm afraid I must answer to that description,' Aldous said, before moving on to receive another pair of guests. 'I am totally damned.'

Edward followed Macy as she weaved through Aldous' flat – a space which made no accommodation whatsoever for the guests.

The bedroom door was open to a strangled twist of sheets and blankets, the lounge boasted piles of books serving as hazardous perches for ashtrays and glasses, tins of cat food yawned dangerously at anyone stretching for a peanut. Nor had there been any accommodation made for the music of the dress period either. The Beatles' *She Loves You* blared out from the record player on a never-ending three-minute Yeah–Yeah loop. There were at least two other men dressed in white suits and spats. Then there was an Al Capone. A Ghandi. A Valentino. Lots of flapper girls. An attractive woman in flying goggles. 'Amelia Earhart,' she told Edward, as he slipped out of her grasp of his lapels. In the kitchen, Macy snatched at a bottle of red, poured herself a large glass.

'What's the matter?' he asked. 'You were fine when we left the house.'

She sashayed up to him, and said too loudly: 'It's the curse.'

'I thought it didn't affect you like other women,' he whispered back. 'You told me you got away lightly in that department.'

'It is not the pain. It's what it represents.'

'What's that supposed to mean?'

'Nothing. Forget it. I am more concerned for our friend. Don't you think Aldous looks awful?'

Aldous always looked so pale, it was hard to tell whether he was sick or just normal. Skin the colour and contours of the moon, the man shied away from the sun.

'He looks the same to me.'

'Same to you? You just have to look at the way that suit hangs on him. He's lost a lot of weight. I think he's ill and he's not telling anyone.'

'He would tell me.'

'Don't be so sure.' She plucked a cigarette out of the silver case she kept in her purse, screwed it into a holder.

'Allow me.' A silver-plated Zippo appeared between them. And then a face Edward recognised.

'Hi, Eddie,' the familiar countenance said, his fingers sparking a flame into life. 'And you must be Macy. The author's glamorous wife. I'm Jack. Mortimer.'

Edward had met Mortimer before at some literary do. Another writer. With a punchy, confident prose sprung from his journalist roots that had helped rack up three consecutive bestsellers on the spy game.

'Is that Jack Mortimer or Mortimer Jack?' Macy asked, pulling her head back from the snap of the lighter.

'The former,' Mortimer said with a tolerant grin. 'I've seen some of your stuff.' He made this remark as he clawed the air with his lighter-free hand. A tall, blonde woman in a gold lamé dress, looped over with strings of pearls, responded to the summons. 'And this is my wife, Vena.' A protective arm around her waist. 'Edward Strathairn. And his wife, Macy.'

Vena nodded a smile that displayed a smear of red lipstick on one of her front teeth. An endearing smudge, Edward thought, on the presentation of an otherwise flawlessly beautiful woman.

'My stuff?' The words came out of Macy's mouth in a swirl of smoke. 'You hear that, Eddie. He's seen my stuff. What stuff have you seen, Jack?'

'You know. The Pollock stuff.'

'Well, Jackson had his stuff. And I have mine. And he's dead now. And his work's worth a fortune. So maybe I should do the same, Jack. Get drunk and wreck my car. Or maybe I should just slash my wrists. What do you say to that? Jack?'

'I would say that is your artistic choice.'

'Touché. And what about you, Vena?'

'I have no idea what you talk about,' she slurred, her accent noticeably Nordic. 'But I would like another gin. Will you bring me one?' She purred her request into Jack's shoulder.

'In a moment. I want to finish this...'

'Come on,' Macy said, taking Vena's arm. 'I could do with another one myself. Let's leave these men to their men-talk. To their stuff.'

Edward watched the women go, their scent remaining somehow as a warning of their not-too-distant presence. Jack rocked back on his heels. 'She's a tough one, that.'

'Yours or mine?'

'Yours. Mine's a softie. Behind that cool exterior.'

'Nothing wrong with that.'

'Depends how you like 'em.'

Edward felt as if he was talking to a character in one of Jack's spy novels. The succinct, snappy, dialogue of men who held their cards close to their chest.

'How do you like them, Jack?'

'Intelligent and attractive. In that order.'

'And that's Vena?'

'No. Vena's just about sex. And Macy?'

'Intelligent and attractive. In that order.'

Jack grinned. 'Got another book in the pipeline?'

'Mulling around a few ideas.'

'Second one's the hardest.'

'You think so?'

'Proving you're not a flash in the pan.'

'How did you manage it?'

'Not so difficult in the thriller genre. Just give 'em much of the same. Flawed hero. Good plot. Lots of military hardware. Bit of sex.'

'You're making it sound too easy.'

'It can be. But literary fiction's different.'

'Why's that?'

'Got to show 'em more of your inner substance. The big ideas. You've got to have something to say. Do you have more to say, Eddie?'

'It's a pressure. But I'm working on it.'

'Yeah, well I hope you come up with the goods. I kind of liked *The Waterwheel*. We all need to do a bit of soul-searching. Especially now.'

He knew what Mortimer meant. The British press had tried to distract with Keeler and Profumo in the New Year run-up but it was the images from across the Atlantic that still prevailed. The golden Dallas afternoon, the slumped Kennedy, the pink princess in her pill-box hat scrambling across the boot of the moving car, the widow and the saluting son. The world would never be the same.

America would never be the same. But what would it become? Even with Aldous' themed trip back in time, there was no getting away from the present. A hole had been blasted into the world. Everyone was shell-shocked. He could see it in the frantic drinking, hear it in the high-pitched voices, he could smell it in the air. It was visceral.

He moved away from the kitchen to find Macy. She was dancing with Vena in the lounge, the two of them lassoed by Vena's pearls, silk-rubbing themselves against each other, breasts to breasts, belly to belly, hips to hips, skirts riding high. Men watching, leering, clapping, yeah-yeahing. He grabbed her away, forgetting about the strangle of pearls, the string snapping, beads all over the place, Macy screaming about the cut into her neck. No blood, hardly a scratch, just a red mark, but her giving him a really hard time about it anyway. This was not how he wanted to bring in the New Year. But later, Macy softening with her drinking, until she had forgotten all about the neck burn, and she was snuggling against him, draped in his arms, smooching to Sinatra. She had done it to him again, given him that roasting, rollercoaster of an evening, stretching his emotions this way and that until he was just relieved, just sheer grateful, that she had calmed. That she was still with him. The countdown came but she stayed locked in his arms. And when the first bell struck she lifted her head from his shoulders, looked at him with wet eyes.

'I want a baby, Eddie. I really want a baby.'

'I do too,' he said, mouthing this thought for the very first time. But knowing it was true, knowing that this was his desire, to create another being from an intimate union with this woman in his arms.

'We are trying to get pregnant,' Edward politely told the cleaning lady, the vicar, the postmistress, his friends, anyone who asked about his wife. Such a wonderful phrase, such a wonderful euphemism for sex, which allowed him to verbalise in public the vision inside his head that had him making love to Macy at every opportunity and from every angle. Macy demanding his sperm, desirous of it, desperate for it. He had never felt so needed. His work also beginning to blossom from these pollination attempts as he churned out page after page of his latest draft with remarkable ease. He had the opposite of writer's block. He had 'writer's flow'. 'Writer's ejaculation.' And he found himself happily immersed in a period of total creativity and procreativity.

His second novel, the proof he was no flash in the pan, was about the homeless and rootless. Not just the beggars in the streets, the vagrants sleeping under bridges along the embankment, but the broader political issues. The slum landlords, the housing shortages in central London, Tory policies that created a climate of profiteering in an unrestrained property market, the exploitation of the working class. Where he had got the inspiration from, he wasn't exactly sure. Perhaps now that he was no longer homeless and rootless himself, he felt he could start to tackle such topics. But his book was not preaching from the pulpit, a rant against social injustice. Instead, he was focused on the plight of just one man, Dominic Pike, a schoolteacher, happily married, living in a three-storey terraced house in North Kensington. Dominic Pike, who fell through the cracks. Who lost his job, his savings, his wife, his home, his friends, in that order. Until he was picked up off the streets by a bunch of well-meaning volunteers steeped in good Christian values who ran a hostel for the single homeless. And where was this hostel? In North Kensington. In fact, it was a conversion of Dominic Pike's former home. There was the front door he had painted, the boiler he had clad, the cracks he had plastered over, a set of shelves he had put up for his ex-wife. Mr Pike was now homeless living in his own home. Edward finished and delivered a polished draft to Aldous in just under a year.

But while he was satisfied with his writing accomplishment, he had failed to find similar success in dispatching his sperm to fertilise Macy's welcoming eggs. After months of vain attempts, the sheer quantity of sexual intercourse had given way to a more considered, quality approach. No more recreational sex, just strictly organised copulation. It was now a question of optimum times, menstruation cycles, body temperatures and preferred directions of flow. Masturbation was strictly out of the question. There was pressure, stress and even the apportioning of blame. He now wanted a child more than anything. He wanted a child because Macy wanted a child, he wanted a child because he wanted a child for himself, for his dead parents, for his marriage, for the void left by his finished novel. He no longer said 'we are trying to get pregnant' because the emphasis had changed from 'trying' to 'pregnant'. One year before, 'trying' had meant 'playing' and 'pleasure' and 'constant sex'. Now it meant a legs-up-in-the-air disaster.

'I am a failure,' he confided to Aldous. 'To fertilise an egg with my sperm is a simple, natural, male function yet it is the one thing over which I have no quality control. I can fail my exams because I didn't study enough. Or I can fail to lift that weight because I didn't train enough. But I fail to impregnate Macy because...?'

Aldous was standing at his easel by the window, still dressed in his blue-silk robe and pyjamas at two in the afternoon. His paintbrush was poised between palette and canvas as he observed the carefully prepared tableau. Two solid silver goblets, a decanter half-filled with port, a linen napkin threaded through a gold ring. A simple arrangement had it not been for the brace of dead pheasant. Not real pheasant, but stuffed imitations acquired from a friend of Aldous' who worked in the stock department of some film company.

'I am dying, Eddie.'

'What?'

'I am dying. I have cancer.'

'Christ, Aldous. What are you telling me?'

'I am telling you I am on the way out. End of story. *Finito*. No cure.'

'It can't be.'

'Don't worry. Your reaction is normal. Disbelief, denial, as you try to absorb the information. I would try and make it easier for you but I do not know how. I have entered the land of the dying. You may come and visit me from time to time, that's all you can do.'

A few moments of silence. Then the rattling of a bus as it throttled past the window. The port rippled in the decanter.

'Oh, Aldous,' he said as he walked over to his friend. He attempted an embrace but the intrusion of the palette and brush made his action awkward. Instead, he gently patted Aldous between the shoulderblades, his hand moving upwards on the third tap to touch the back of his friend's neck, the skin cold. He noticed the weak sunshine outside the window, St Paul's in the distance, some dried-up geraniums in the flower box. Suddenly all these details very important.

'Thank you, Eddie. But please, just sit down. It is better that way.'

'Yes. Yes, of course.' He took a chair from against the wall, brought it up close to the easel, away from the light. Cleared his throat.

'Why do you paint this stuff anyway? These inanimate objects. It doesn't seem to be your style.'

'Because it is not my style is precisely why I do it. It is important to notice the details normally overlooked. The light on the glass, the precise coloration of the wine, the pattern of the feathers, the reflection on the silverware.'

'But you could do that with landscapes. With portraits.'

'Still life isn't about people.'

Aldous' cat Macavity slipped into the room, padded listlessly over to purr at the feet of his master. The poor creature should have provided a welcome distraction but at sixteen years old Macavity was at death's door himself. Aldous bent down, scratched the animal's neck with the point of his brush.

'What do the doctors say?'

'Kidneys. I was pissing blood. That's what alerted me. If it stays where it is, I've probably got two years, tops. If it starts wandering, it could be a few months.'

'Is there pain?'

'Nothing that can't be controlled. Later, I'll just go into a morphine haze.'

'Christ, you're only fifty. It's so unfair.'

'Fifty-four. But I wouldn't say it's unfair. My health has never been too good. That's what kept me out of the war. I could have been blown to bits on a Normandy beach. Now that would have been unfair.'

Edward watched Aldous dabbing his brush on the canvas. He could see the thinness of the man, the bony wrists and ankles, the chest hollow in the 'V' of his robe, the pallid colour of his skin, the hair lank. But the blue eyes still shone. How long would it be before they sank back into their sockets, became lustreless? He loved this man. Not in the way that might be desired of him, but he loved him nevertheless.

'How am I going to tell Macy? She'll be devastated. She really loves you, you know.'

'I've told Macy already.'

'What?'

'I'd originally thought of getting her to tell you instead of me.'

'Why would you do that?'

'Because I'm a coward. And I wanted to avoid this little scene.'

'There is no little scene.'

'Oh, for fuck's sake,' Aldous shouted as he threw the paintbrush across the room. Even Macavity stirred at the outburst. 'I don't want this. All this polite tiptoeing around. I've got cancer. And I don't want one patronising word out of you, do you hear that? I will be dead soon. Fact. Just no pity, please.'

'Whatever you want.'

'You see. There's been a little scene.'

'No, there hasn't.'

'Yes, there has. There are tears running down your cheeks.'

Edward left soon after so that Aldous could lie down. He imagined this was how it would be from now on. Little bursts of energy, periods of brightness, windows of hope, of thinking that somehow the illness would be manageable, that it would be stable, that this was as bad as it would get. And then these disappearances to lie down, to suffer, to recover. These periods of absence growing longer and longer, until being with Aldous would be just one long period of absence. London didn't help his mood either with its cold wind spiking the drizzle against his cheeks, spraying it down his neck between his collar. He walked down to Oxford Street and waited half an hour for a bus, toes and fingers freezing in the bitterness, London Transport living up to its reputation by finally sending down two Number 78s at once. He let the crowded first one go by, hopped on the second, went upstairs for a cigarette. The greasy, vinegary smell of fish and chips amid the steaming coats and open newspapers cheering him up slightly, although he wasn't sure why. Life going on as usual, he supposed. He closed his eyes and mentally triggered himself to wake up before his stop.

Macy was beaming when she answered the door, her cheeks all flushed, her arms in a fling around his wet neck.

'I'm pregnant,' she shrieked. 'We're pregnant. You're pregnant. I've just come from the doctor. We're going to have a baby.'

He wanted to dance but his feet felt glued to the steps. He wanted to exclaim his happiness but his heart was heavy. And then he realised that what he really wanted to do was laugh. Not with an irony. But with joy. Sheer joy. Birth, death, birth, death, birth. The cycle of life. And for a moment, he saw himself back in a Japanese garden, the waterwheel dipping in and out of the dark water with just the merest flashes of gold from the carp swimming below the surface.

'You don't seem too happy.'

'It's all right.'

'He told you, didn't he?'

'Yes.'

She let out a little yelp like a trodden-on puppy. 'He was going to let me do it.'

'I know.'

Eight o'clock in the morning a few Sundays later, while Edward lay in bed recovering from a hangover, the phone rang. It was Aldous.

'I would like you to take me to a football match,' he demanded.

'Is that why you called at this ungodly hour?'

'This is not an ungodly hour. In fact, it is very much a godly hour when all good Christians should be up and about in preparation for the worship of their Maker.'

'You are not a good Christian, Aldous.'

'Nevertheless I would like to go to one of these football matches.'

'Don't be ridiculous. You've never been to a game in your life. Why start now? You'd hate it.'

'I believe this country will soon be hosting something called the World Trophy. I would like to be more informed.'

'It's called the World Cup.'

'World Cup it is then.'

'Well, at least let's wait until spring is here. This is the coldest winter I can remember. I have a headache. I'm going back to sleep.'

'Eddie.' The voice weak but the tone firm. 'I have no time to wait.'

'All right, all right. I'll take you to see Chelsea. They might be playing at home next week.'

'And where is home?'

'The ground's not far from here.'

'That sounds excellent. Now, tell me, does this ground have seats? Or do we have to stand in those terraced places?'

'I'll try to get tickets for the stands.'

'You're not listening. I don't want to stand. I will need to sit.'

'Just leave it to me, Aldous. I will organise the tickets.'

Chelsea were playing at home the following Saturday. Against Leicester City. Aldous turned up swamped in a fur coat with matching hat, clutching a thermos.

'I laced the tea with whisky and honey,' he said.

'Very thoughtful. Now you're going to have to let me buy you a scarf. The fans will skin you alive dressed like that.'

'I will do whatever I am told to blend in with the masses. Anyway, that Chelsea blue goes well with my eyes, don't you think? Onwards and upwards, my dear boy. Onwards and upwards.'

Edward took his friend's arm, feeling how thin it was even through the thick coat, helped him up the steep steps, guided him through the thongs of beery, pork pie-chomping supporters inside the stadium until he found the entrance up into the stands. Then up those last few steps to where the pitch was suddenly visible. And in that precious moment, Edward was glad he had come, glad Aldous had wanted this experience. For what was a life if it had not felt the wonder of entering this gladiatorial arena for the first time?

'Oh, Eddie, this is so exciting,' Aldous gasped. 'And the grass... it is so... so… I don't know... so exquisitely green.'

They found their places and they settled. It might have been a freezing hard pitch but it was not a hard battle. They spent more time out of their seats than in them, cheering a succession of Chelsea goals. And despite the cold and his illness, there were patches of colour on Aldous' cheeks, a glint of joy in his eyes. But by midway through the second half with Chelsea four–one up, Edward saw the poor man was exhausted, took him back home to Macy who wrapped him up warm in blankets on the sofa in front of a stoked-up fire.

'Look at him,' she said, bringing in some more cushions. 'He's shivering to death.'

'It was his idea.'

'I suppose you'd listen to him too if he told you to jump off Westminster Bridge.'

'I will not have you two arguing on my account,' Aldous interjected. 'I'm still quite responsible for my actions.'

'Well, I won't have you going out again in this weather in your condition.'

Of course, Aldous didn't listen.

So Edward watched him plough through the next few weeks with all the vigour of a much younger man, with all the desperation of a dying man. And he was glad to connive and conspire in all his friend's adventures. A special time for them both, each moment highlighted by the shadow of death, as they searched out London's little jewels. The Impressionists at the Courtauld Gallery, the Reading Room at the British Museum, the Royal Academy, another Chelsea game – this time against local rivals Fulham, afternoon tea at the Savoy, a shoe-shine in Burlington Arcade, an arm-in-arm stroll down King's Road, smoked salmon and cream cheese bagels at a kosher deli down Brick Lane.

'Now what are we going to call this new book of yours?' Aldous asked as he chewed away on his sandwich. Edward noted that speaking with his mouth full was something his friend never used to do. Impending death, it seemed, had rid Aldous of his manners.

'I don't have a title. That was always your advice – if you say you've got a title, you'll never write the book.'

'Very good advice. But I do need one now. The book is written. Publication is imminent. Dominic Pike and his story of homelessness and social injustice. You must have some idea.'

'How about *Address Unknown*?'

'Too bland.'

'*Between the Cracks*?'

'Too vague.'

'*The Fall of Dominic Pike*?'

Aldous smiled. A piece of smoked salmon shone pink in a wedge between two of his yellowing teeth. 'Yes, yes. That's the one.' He then took another eager bite of his bagel, chewing as he spoke. 'You know, of course, Dominic Pike was the name of that man we dragged in to witness your wedding?'

All thoughts of the publication of *The Fall of Dominic Pike* were put on temporary hold with the news of Churchill's death. The whole country came to a stop. For Edward, it was like King George VI's passing all over again. Except it was so cold he wasn't sure he would attend the funeral. But Aldous was insisting.

'I must pay my respects to the old warrior. We may never see the likes of such an occasion again.'

'Don't be so stubborn,' Edward countered. 'You'll freeze to death out there.'

'That could be a blessing,' Aldous replied.

'You're not going,' Macy said. 'And that's that.'

In the end, all three of them went, taking a taxi as far as they could until the traffic and the crowds made it impossible to go on. Then by foot up to Tower Bridge, where they watched the draped coffin carried on to the launch Havengore for its journey down the Thames to Waterloo. A piping party played the coffin on board, then a seventeen-gun salute split the bitter, grey day, each boom a wartime reminder of other explosions that used to sweep the London sky. Some of the crowd stood and saluted, others wept. Aldous clung to Macy's arm while Edward knocked back whisky from his flask. He could not help but remember their own sighting of Churchill waiting alone in the foyer of the Savoy, and think that this whole ceremony, these kings and queens, princes and presidents in attendance, this mobilisation of regiments, of armies and navies and airforces, these Archbishop blessings and the prayers and tears of a nation, were all directed towards that one man. And then as the launch pulled away from the quayside, one of the most moving sights he had ever seen. The cranes across the river at Hay's Wharf slowly dipped their jibs. On whose script had this stage direction been written? Was it at the command of some royal master of ceremonies or merely a spontaneous gesture from the crews manning the docks? For amid all the pomp and ceremony, here was the working man's salute to the great leader and it pierced Edward's heart.

'It has been a bad time for deaths,' Aldous said. 'First TS Eliot and now Winston. This has been the cruellest of months.'

Since he had discovered Macy was pregnant, Edward played secret games inside his head. The scales were ever so slightly tipped in favour of the male. But he would never, ever have admitted to that. He would have loved a girl just as much. Of course he would have.

First there were the warning signs. The abdominal pains. The spotting. The bleeding. And then in the night that awful scream. That awful, awful scream wrenching at his heart, splitting open his whole being. The rush to the bathroom. Macy lurched over the toilet basin, the red crotch stain on her nightgown. For one horrific moment, he thought she had slashed herself. And then the realisation. The hissing of the cistern filling. Shhhshhhhssssssss. How would he ever forget that sound?

'Oh my God!' she howled. 'I've flushed it down the toilet.'

It should always be a male, he thought. Let it always be a male. Because no human being should have to endure this. No human being should have to give death to their own child. He knelt down beside her. He placed a hand on the clammy skin of her shoulder but she shook it away.

'Leave me alone,' she sobbed. 'Just leave me alone.'

Two weeks later, Aldous died.

CHAPTER TWENTY-THREE

Japan • 2003

The corridors were silent. Except for the sound of his too small, blue, terry towelling slippers flapping against the soles of his feet. Too early even for the maids and their cleaning trolleys, the porters with their newspapers and shoeshines. He liked it that way. All the guests wrapped up secure in their temperature-regulated rooms. Generators humming, reception clerk barely awake at his desk, night porter making sandwiches in the kitchen. Everyone asleep, safe and sound. Like these nap sessions at school. 'Fold your arms, children. Heads down. Close your eyes. Fifteen minutes.' Drift into sleep. Protected by the teacher's watchful eye and diligent time-keeping. To this day, when he took naps, they would last one quarter of an hour. Not a minute more or less.

He had his towel and his toilet bag, his body cloaked in a complimentary *yukata*, his naked skin protected from public gaze only by this thin swathe of cotton. He was ready to wash and bathe. To soak. It was one of the things he had missed most about Japan. This ritual bathing. If only he could find the *onsen*. All these long corridors running from the main building to the annexes. He was completely lost again. That familiar sense of panic beginning to crawl over his skin. A sudden memory of his mother in the kitchen, counting matchsticks, checking totals, testing herself. He came to a crossroads in his wanderings, fumbled for his glasses in a non-existent pocket, before he realised they hung on a cord around his neck. He moved up close to peer at the signs on the wall. An arrow left to "The Library". An arrow right to "*Onsen*/Hot Baths – The Chrysanthemum Pool". Ah yes, the library. He swivelled on his cane. Onwards and upwards, Aldous. Onwards and upwards.

He pulled down the brass doorknob with the handle of his stick. At first, there was no release, but the click reluctantly came and he pushed open the heavy wooden door with his shoulder. He was greeted by total darkness and the oily-thick smell of furniture polish. He ran his hand up and down the wall until his palm found the nipple of a switch. Several lights came on at once. Not from some central fixture in the ceiling but from reading lamps at various tables scattered around the room.

There they were. All lined up on the shelves. First editions, specially bound in green leather, in both English and Japanese, with corresponding paperbacks laid out on the shelf underneath. Set out in chronological order, starting with *The Waterwheel*, of course. He was used to seeing collections of his work in bookstores, libraries, airports, even on the shelves in friends' houses. Sometimes, he even sought them out, checking which titles, if any, were still popular in the current literary climate. But he had never seen such a comprehensive display as this. Not even in his own library. It was so meticulous. So respectful. So flattering. He was quite overwhelmed. To be confronted with his oeuvre laid out in such a manner.

He picked a leather-bound copy of *The Waterwheel* off the shelf, opened it to the title page. There was an inscription in his own hand. "To Ishikawa-san and all the staff. September 1959." He had completely forgotten he had sent the hotel a copy, surprised to discover his arrogant young author-self had possessed such a thoughtfulness back then. The book he held was probably quite valuable now. First edition. In English. Signed by the author. He noted the date. It was just before the translation by Kobayashi, the passing of the manuscript to his brother at the Tokyo publishing house that led to the book's success in Japan.

Kobayashi. He hadn't thought of the man for years, not set sight on him since the days of Tokyo Autos. He remembered his tiny, wriggling moustache, the one ill-fitting suit, the bad breath, his fawning nature. He recalled all the negatives, yet had never given the man any credit for the fact his whole literary career had rested on the translator's fortuitous intervention. Without Kobayashi, *The Waterwheel* would have probably died a slow death. When he thought of the many contributors to his literary career, he would of course always single out Aldous. But Kobayashi? Never. And then there was the man's gift of the *himitsu-bako* – the secret puzzle box. He still had it, always travelled with it, had brought it with him now in his suitcase. A present from Hakone. From just a few miles from where he stood. He had to lean back against an armchair, so weighed down did he feel by this sudden remorse. He had written so passionately in *The Waterwheel* about his sense of injustice over the treatment of the Japanese, yet had completely ignored his own unsung hero. He doubted he had ever sent him a signed copy of the book. He certainly had never acknowledged his contribution publicly. The man had made this one significant gesture then just disappeared from view without receiving a single word of gratitude. He couldn't even remember if there had been a one-off payment for the commission or if Kobayashi had at least collected translation royalties over the years. Could he possibly still be alive? He would be in his eighties now. Perhaps he could get Enid to track him down. He would visit him. Shake his hand. 'If it hadn't been for you, dear friend...' Christ, he didn't even know the man's first name.

What was he thinking of? It was all too late. Too late. He had made his imprint on this world and there was no going back. As Aldous would say: 'Life's beginning will mould you, it's ending will judge you. You can do what the hell you like in between.' There must have been many Kobayashis in his life, just as there had been many Macys and Sumikos. He stood off from the chair, wiped the sleeve of his robe across his forehead. What he really needed was a glass of water. He ran a finger along his other titles on the shelf. It was like flicking though a psychiatrist's file. Which part of himself would he like to prise open? He hadn't really read any of his books again since their publication. He could respond to questions about them. He had his answers down pat. But read them again? He didn't think he could bear that.

By the window with its closed velvet drapes, he spotted a desk with a pen, a bottle of mineral water, an opener, and a glass. The sign of a good hotel, anticipating his every need. He picked up as many of the first editions he could manage and carried them over to the desk, repeating the trip until he had cleared the shelf of its hardbacks. Breathless, he sat down, rewarded himself with two full glasses of water. Then from the stacks he had constructed, he drew down the first book. It was another copy of *The Waterwheel* – Japanese edition. On the title page, he wrote. "To my dear friend Kobayashi-san. With much gratitude for your outstanding contribution. Edward Strathairn. March 1960." The next novel off the pile was *The Fall of Dominic Pike*. His London novel as the critics used to call it. *London Life* as the Japanese felt obliged to title it. A bit of social realism to follow up *The Waterwheel*. Just to confirm his credentials as a Sixties radical. Made into a rather successful film with a couple of those up-and-coming working class actors of the era. He would dedicate this one to Enid. For her long-suffering service. He then plundered his literary booty for another copy of *The Waterwheel*. English edition. He opened the book, held his pen in a few moments consideration over the blank title page and then wrote: "To Sumiko. For the happiest time. Love, Eddie. July 1957 – March 1958."

The *onsen* was empty. But the pool still steamed away, ready to welcome its bathers into its hot mineral embrace whatever the hour. He couldn't remember how the room had looked during his first stay, he wasn't even sure if the location was the same. Certainly there would not have been these large, beige, Italian-marble tiles and the fancy art-deco sconces. In the washing area, the mirrors and taps were set low in the wall, only a foot or so from the floor.

He was going to have to ease himself down on to one of those tiny plastic stools to clean himself before entering the pool. How he would raise himself up again, God only knew.

He hung up his *yukata*, placed his toiletries conveniently on a shelf, lowered himself slowly on his cane as far as he could, before having to drop his buttocks the last few inches on to the stool. The stool-legs rocked ever so slightly and for an instant he thought he would topple. But the seat steadied under his weight. He crouched over and managed to reel in a small plastic basin with the crook of his cane, filled it up with hot water from one of the taps by his shins, and poured it over himself. Sheer bliss. He repeated the process twice more until he was fully soaked. Apart from his own toiletries, the shelf above his set of taps was littered with bottles of soaps, shampoos, lotions and other unguents. He lathered himself up. What was it that Sumiko used to tell him? 'However much time you spend washing your body at home, multiply by four. Then you can enter the common pool.' He poured the scalding water over himself again. He could almost feel it scour away the flaky layers of his skin. He wiped away the mist from the mirror glass. The little sprouts of his remaining hair were plastered against his scalp. His face and sagging breasts blotched red and pink. A comical sight. He laughed and soaped himself up again. He could only guess at some of the contents of the bottles. Shampoo? Soap? Conditioner? It was all the same to him as long as they produced a fresh-smelling lather. He threw a basin of cold water over himself this time. Just for the hell of it. That was what the Finns did, didn't they? Slapped himself hard. Then hot and cold again. He looked in the mirror. He was smiling and baby-clean. 'Look at me now, Sumiko. No longer the filthy *gaijin*. I am ready for the common pool.' He raised himself up on his cane, reached about halfway in a crouch, knees bent, but-tocks sticking out awkwardly, when the cane-tip slid on the soap-and-water slicked floor. He fell sideways over the stool, his left side slamming hard on to the Italian marble.

He opened his eyes. How long had he lain there? Seconds, min-utes, hours? Pain along his side. Had he hit his head? His vision seemed clear. Or as clear as it usually was without his glasses. 'You may take my body, dear Lord, but please keep my brain intact.' He felt his skull. No bleeding. Just a slight tenderness above his left temple. He searched for his cane but it had skidded off somewhere leaving him to flounder like a beached whale in puddles of his own soaked-down filth. There was some piped music. He hadn't noticed that before. An annoying electronic twanging meant to represent the sound of a Japanese *kota*. Pling, pling, pling, plong, pling. He kicked out uselessly with his legs. The best he could hope for was to slide along the tiles to the low wall around the edge of the pool. Perhaps then he could raise himself up. But his left side on which he lay was too painful for such an exercise. He would have to turn over on to his other side. That would mean first on to his back. He tried to roll over but he just couldn't do it. There was no purchase on the wet floor. He could only stay where he was with this soapy drain by his cheek and the damn pling, plong, plink of the music. It was all so hopeless.

'Sir Edward. What has happened?'

He turned his head as much as he could, strained to look upwards, imagining himself as that beached whale opening one fearful, watery-white eye to witness the harpoon-raised arm. Instead, he saw the hotel manager also swathed in a hotel *yukata* standing over him, over this white, naked, flabby, pathetic creature stranded on an *onsen* floor, surrounded by loofahs and lotions and back-scrubbers and overturned stools and basins.

'Are you hurt?' Takahashi asked.

'I don't know. I can't move. I can't stand up.'

Takahashi crouched down. 'Before I help you to stand, let me just check your legs.'

Edward felt Takahashi stretch and bend one leg. Then the other.

'Is there pain?'

'My thigh. My shoulder.'

'I believe nothing is broken, Sir Edward.'

'What about my head? Can you see any damage?'

He sensed the brush of Takahashi's breath close to his scalp. The smell of tobacco.

'Hmm. Nothing I can see. Did you hit your head?'

'I'm not sure.'

'Well, there doesn't seem to be any... I don't know the word.'

'Bruising.'

'Yes, yes, bruising. Therefore, I shall now help you to stand. Here is your stick. I shall pull you up on this side. Please try to support yourself with your cane on the other as I do so.' Takahashi draped an arm over his shoulder. 'Now. Together. Push.'

Edward levered hard on his cane, glad to be rescued, glad to be righted, but so uncomfortable with Takahashi's clothed body close to his own nakedness, with the hotel manager's witness of his shrivelled penis tucked under the folds of his belly, the thickly veined thighs, the pink-blotched pouches of his breasts.

'Can you stand by yourself?'

'I think I can.' And he pulled himself up straight on his cane. 'I do believe I am all right.' He looked down his left side. The skin under his rib cage, over his hip and along his thigh was already patched bluish. 'Apart from a few bruises, I think I have survived intact.'

'It might be a good idea to soak in the pool, Sir Edward. The hot water would soothe the hurt muscles. Prevent some stiffness. Let me assist you.'

'No, no. I can manage,' he said, waving away the attention. 'Please let me be. I can do this by myself.' He wobbled towards the pool, grabbed the handrail, grateful for the broadness of the steps, the slight angle of descent. He placed a foot in the water. He had forgotten how boiling hot these *onsen* could be. It was almost unbearable. He waited until a slight tolerance for the heat had been achieved then waded in thigh-high. Again he waited, this time until any feeling for the temperature at all had been scalded out of him. He then paddled over to the edge where there were layered shelves and eased himself down into a sitting position, chin-high in the water. His skin was now numb from the heat, except for where it throbbed with the bruising. His heart was pumping crazily, a thermostat out of control. But he began to settle, to adjust, to let the heat take over. That was the secret. Not to resist. Just give in to the sensation. Allow the blood to boil, the organs to bake, the muscles to loosen. He turned to look at Takahashi. But surprisingly the man had left. Never mind. He needed this time alone. To collect his thoughts. He closed his eyes. He felt his body as a mass of heat. He let his mind play with words, juggling syllables and meaning until he had finally composed a *haiku*.

Winter's ice is here
Children skating without fear
The old man stumbled.

Lifting himself out of the pool, washing again, towelling dry, pulling on his robe. All these manoeuvres, he performed slowly and with great care. The muscles on one side were stiff and painful, the rest of his body loose and limber. Such a strange combination. His right side with its weak hip was what usually needed the support of his cane. Now it was the left that demanded the attention. With very small steps across the slippery tiles, he managed to reach the exit but even that small journey had tired him. He doubted he had the strength to negotiate the long passageways back to his room. He wondered if there was some kind of emergency bell he could ring for assistance. He opened the door to the hallway. A bellboy stood waiting with a wheelchair.

'What happened?' Sumiko screamed as she ran across the room, knelt down by his chair. 'You took such a long time. And now this.'

'It's all right. I am fine. Just a small fall.'

'A small fall? There is no such thing as a small fall at your age.'

'Please stop fussing. Do you have any money? I need to give this boy something for his trouble.'

'Yes, yes, of course.' She raised herself from her crouch, went in a search for her purse, found it on the bedside table. The lad accepted the tip with a gracious bow.

'How dare you let him see me here,' she snapped as soon as the door was closed. 'It will be all over the hotel I stayed here in your room. Like a common prostitute. Takahashi-san will know.'

'Oh for God's sake, Sumiko. You are an old woman. Why should you still care what people think?'

'I see. Suddenly I am an old woman. You didn't think that a few hours ago.'

'Please calm down.'

'Calm down, calm down. That is all you can say. You were always selfish. I forgot that. That's what forty years can do. Wipe away the bad parts. But now I remember. Selfish, selfish, selfish. I am the one who has to live here. I am a married woman, Eddie. Just remember that.'

'Will you please help me out of this chair? I need to lie down. I have such a headache.'

'I should just leave you there, you know that. Like some old... some old... I don't know.'

'Wreck.'

She pulled out a handkerchief from her bag, wiped her eyes. 'Yes, wreck. That is what you are. Now let me push this old wreck close to the bed. And how is this old woman supposed to lift you? You will have to help me.'

CHAPTER TWENTY-FOUR

London • 1965

Are You really out there?
If So, Answer Me
Do You really care?
If So, Answer Me
Do You hear my prayer?
If So, Answer Me
Do you see this tear?
If So, Answer Me

That was all Edward had managed to write – the title page for his third novel. Yes, he already had a title. *If So, Answer Me*. Along with a dedication to Aldous. "All creativity comes from loss." And if that were true, he should now be in a period of phenomenal endeavour. For the essence of life had been denied his unborn child, and it had been taken from his old friend. Future loss had also been accounted for. Macy had told him she would never be able to carry a pregnancy to completion. *The Fall of Dominic Pike* had also abandoned him, taking its first independent steps, stacking the bookshops on the back of enthusiastic reviews, establishing for itself a public life of its own over which he no longer had any control. It was time to create something new. To cherish Aldous' memory at least. But he was totally incapable of writing anything else beyond that first page. For all that was left to him was a numbness. He couldn't even say he felt numb, for that would have implied he still retained some ability to feel. He didn't feel anger, remorse, sadness, compassion for Macy, or even sorry for himself. There was just this senselessness. A blank, black, stony coldness.

For Macy it was different. She could lose herself in her art. For the first time in her artistic career, she was not derivative of Pollock. The sense of self, of woman, of daughter, of would-be mother, of apprentice, of self-conscious artist, that had somehow interposed itself between her brush and canvas was gone. Was dead. She now worked in a fluid frenzy, creating her best ever work. She entitled them her *Void* series. *Void Number One, Void Number Two*, right up to *Void Number 14*. When she finally found the energy and the courage to exhibit them, these were the paintings that would make her world famous.

For the first few months, Macy had wept. Then she raged. Against him, against herself, against God. Then she envied. Other pregnant women, women with babies, advertisements with babies, clothes for babies, toys for babies, food for babies. She avoided playgrounds and nurseries, closed the windows to the sounds of passing schoolchildren. There was a whole world out there he felt he had to shield her against. Then she started to blame. Herself. God. And finally him again.

'I can't believe you never cried over the loss of our child.' She had just come down to the kitchen from her studio at the top of the house. Her boots were splattered with multi-coloured drops of paint. Sometimes she wore those boots on the rare times she went out socially. Friends often commented on their hippie trendiness.

'I did mourn,' he said. 'In my own way.'

'You're just heartless. Always were.'

'That's not fair. Along with Aldous' death, it was just too much. One of us had to stand firm, or we would have both just drowned in sorrow.'

'I would have preferred if you had joined me in my grief.'

'I told you. I wanted to be strong for you.'

'Like I said. You're just cold.'

'Do you think I didn't hurt too? Do you think you have a monopoly on the mourning of our unborn child? Just because I don't spend every waking minute under a blanket crying my heart out doesn't mean I don't feel anything.'

'Well, you could at least do something constructive. Rather than just sitting around in your pyjamas all day, reading newspapers. That's not going to solve anything.'

'You know I can't write anything.'

'Can't write, can't write, can't write. If I can paint, you can write. What's the problem, Eddie?'

'Writing is more cerebral. The way you paint is much more emotional. That's the difference.'

'Well, maybe you should try being a bit more emotional about your work.' She collapsed into an armchair, fumbled in her overalls for a packet of cigarettes. He rose from the sofa, went over to the sink, filled the kettle with water. He noticed his hands were shaking.

'Tea?'

She didn't reply so he was forced to turn round to look at her. She sat in her chair like a man, sunk down, legs splayed apart. A lit cigarette dangled between her fingers. He thought she looked ugly. Not ugly physically. But ugly as a person.

'How will we manage now?' she asked.

'What do you mean?'

'How will we manage without a child? How will we manage to get through all these fucking years to come just on our own?'

'I thought our love would see us through.'

'Sure, Eddie. If that's what you think.'

But she was right. Where was the glue for their marriage without children? All these milestones that bound other couples together. The name-choosing, the nappies, the sleepless nights, the first word, the first step, the first day at school. He had so wanted a child he could end up blaming Macy for not giving him one.

Perhaps that was what Macy was doing now. Pre-empting him. Punishing him before he blamed her.

He took her to Scotland. He thought the trip might cheer them up, might help their marriage if they spent some time out of London, away from their grief, to where there was space to breathe. It would be his first visit since his parents had died. They trained it up to Glasgow, hired a car for a trip to Oban and the Western Highlands. It felt good to be back, his misery humbled into insignificance by the craggy summits, chastened by the wildness of it all. Macy stayed silent for most of the journey until they approached the small town of Inverary on the shores of Loch Fyne.

'Hey, look at that,' she said pointing to a small herd of Highland cattle. 'Big shaggy dogs with horns.'

The cows were grazing in a field bordering the driveway up to Inverary castle. He could see the towers and turrets of the Duke of Argyll's grand residence just above the treeline. And he suddenly realised he had been to this place before. With his parents. There had been a photograph, the one his Aunt Cathy had sent him to Japan. The three of them sitting on a tartan blanket, he in the middle in his school uniform, the hairy head of a Highland cow straying comically into a corner of the picture. He had to pull over into a lay-by, stop the car. He stared out at the placid waters of the loch, holding on to the knot of grief tight in his stomach, Macy quiet and stiff beside him. He needed her, really needed her to say something, to touch him, but she could not or would not respond. And he realised that his grief was just as much about her as it was for the loss of his parents.

'What has happened to us?' he said, not sure whether he was asking himself or Macy. 'What the fuck has happened to us?'

At first, she didn't say anything, just picked away at the fringes of the travel blanket she had pulled around herself. Then eventually:

'I don't want to sleep with you anymore.'

'Christ, Macy. You certainly choose your moments.'

'It's better you know the truth about how I feel.'

'And what about me? About how I feel.'

'I no longer consider myself responsible for your emotions.'

It was his turn to remain silent, to soak in these leaked pieces of information, these new boundaries for their relationship. And that was how it was for the rest of the trip. A few sentences meant to inflict wounds on each other and then a period of respite, letting the hurt sink in and be absorbed. Each new utterance marking their progress into the remoteness of the Highlands like verbal postcards of hate. By the time they had reached the tiny island of Iona, walking as strangers among the headstones in the abbey's sacred burial ground, she had defined their relationship to him thus. She would move into her own bedroom, which by virtue of being next to her studio meant she would occupy her own separate section of their Chelsea house. She did not consider herself obliged to eat with him, sleep with him or go on holiday with him. However, regarding friends in common and other shared social and professional engagements, she would be happy to accompany him if he wanted her to. For the sake of appearances. She did not want a divorce.

'Why not?'

She shrugged. 'I saw my parents go through it. Guess I just don't want to do the same to myself. But it's up to you. If you want one, I'll go along with it. I wouldn't blame you.'

His first reaction was to go for the divorce, just to spite her more than anything else. Yet he found himself backing down from that idea, not because he harboured some secret notion he could somehow make everything right between them again, but because he didn't know what else to do. He was so bruised and battered inside, so utterly defeated, all he could do was hang on to the little she was prepared to give him.

'You can take lovers,' she added. 'I wouldn't object.'

'I suppose you already have one. Is that what this is really about?'

'I'm sorry to disappoint you, Eddie. But my despair is all about you and nobody else.'

'I should feel flattered.'

'Don't be. We just weren't good for each other. You should have stayed in Japan. With your little chambermaid. She would have made you happy.'

'How would you know?'

'I just have to read *The Waterwheel* to see that.'

As parents live through their children, Edward felt he had lived – and was living – through his books. How he truly felt, what he truly believed, his shadows and his demons, his fears and his hopes, his pride and his shame, it was all there in his novels, in his characters and the conflicts he created for them. His living, breathing, everyday self was only a pretence. The artist was in the painting, the musician was in the song. If anyone wanted to know who he was, the real Edward Strathairn, all they had to do was line up his novels and read them from start to finish. There he was. On the shelf. For everyone to see. *The Waterwheel* – a love story between a British translator and a *panpan* girl as well as a plea for America to do some soul-searching in the aftermath of Hiroshima and Nagasaki. *The Fall of Dominic Pike* – his stance against social injustice that fed into a fear so many people felt when confronted with the homeless: there but for the grace of God go I. And then came *If So, Answer Me*, the one the critics said was his masterpiece even though *The Waterwheel* would remain his best-known work. Macy had been right. He had needed to bring more emotion into his work and *If So* was the novel that did just that. It was his scream of anguish. He wrote it in the five years after Aldous' death and Macy's miscarriage, carried it with him all that time in his heart and in his head. He had thrust his hand into the mire of his life, raked around inside and come up with gold. If *The Waterwheel* had given him intellectual respect in the eyes of the literary world, if *The Fall of Dominic Pike* had identified him with worthwhile social values, then *If So* gave him emotional integrity.

CHAPTER TWENTY-FIVE

Hakone, Japan • 2003

As if through the revolving door in some West End farce, Sumiko departed his bedroom just before Enid entered it. She was crying when she left. It amazed him to think he still had the capacity to make women weep. A tearless Enid now stood by his bed, copying down his choice of lunch from the hotel menu.

'I think I should call a doctor. Just to check you over.'

'It will not be necessary.'

'Mr Takahashi says there is a fine doctor living in the village.'

'That must be very pleasant for him.'

Enid sucked in her breath. 'Is there anything else?'

'Please draw the curtains. The morning sunshine hurts my eyes.'

'Do you have a headache?'

'I have a splitting headache. There are some aspirin in the bathroom cabinet.'

Enid returned with a silver-paper strip of aspirin and a glass of water, which she placed on the bedside table. She then went to close the drapes.

'Do you need anything else?'

'Ask Takahashi to send me in a bottle of whisky. He knows the one I like.'

'I will do no such thing. Please get some rest. I will call you in a few hours.'

As soon as Enid had left, he rang Takahashi at reception. Ten minutes later, a sullen bellboy arrived with the whisky on a tray, positioned it on the already crowded bedside table. The bottle was only one-third full. A note from Takahashi on the hotel's headed notepaper explained:

"This is all we have left of your favourite whisky. If you would like some more, but of a different brand, please let me know. We have some very fine Japanese malts."

He propped himself up on two large pillows, pushed out two tablets into his palm, washed them down with a large glass of malt. He breathed out deeply and noisily as the liquid hit his stomach, released its fiery glow. His head throbbed. This fall had shaken him, really rattled him up. His whole left side hurt. He took another sip of whisky. Enid had surprisingly left a crack in the curtains and a shaft of light slanted through. All the way from the sun, all those millions of miles, just to arrive in this place. And to die here. Such a remarkable journey. And for what purpose? To illuminate for a few moments his notebook lying open on the desk, on the same mahogany desk he had written his famous novel so many years before. So many light years before. Time and space. Space and time. All mixed up.

The ring of the telephone woke him. His hand fumbled over the bedside table, knocking over a glass, finding the receiver, the tangled wire knocking over something else... a bottle, the thudding fall cushioned by the deep pile of the carpet. His head, heavy, thick. His voice throaty, dry.

'What is it?'

'Sir Edward?' A woman's voice. 'Is that you?'

'Yes, this is Sir Edward Strathairn.'

'I'm sorry but it doesn't sound like you.'

'Who is this?'

'It's Enid.'

'Enid? Where the hell are you?'

'I'm in my room. Upstairs.'

'Yes, yes, of course. What time is it?'

'Five o'clock.'

'Christ. I can't believe I've slept so long.'

'I thought I'd let you be. But we need to talk.'

'Fine. Talk to me.'

'I'd prefer to see you.'

'Give me ten minutes then.'

He looked around the room. The light through the curtain crack was grey. A lacquer tray clustered with the dishes of an untouched lunch lay on the desk. He pulled back the covers, manoeuvred his legs off the bed. His left side was stiff now rather than painful. He considered that to be an achievement in his body's test of recovery. Stiffness he could manage. Stiffness he was used to. He hobbled over to the desk, gulped down a bowl of cold miso soup, followed by four pieces of fried tofu, several spoonfuls of sticky rice, a slice of salmon in a delicious soya and ginger sauce, then two small cupfuls of green tea. The blood that had pounded inside his head when he awoke had now diverted to his stomach. He could almost feel whatever proteins, fats, carbohydrates and vitamins he had consumed begin their march through his veins. He burped healthily and began searching for the bottle of whisky. Just as he spotted it poking out from under the hem of the duvet cover, there was a knock on the door. He slipped back into bed before he called for her to come in.

'Enid. How are you?'

'I am coping as usual. And you?'

'I am in fine form. Just a little stiffness in the limbs.'

'You've been drinking.'

'I have not been drinking.'

'What am I going to do with you, Sir Edward?' Her eyes scanned the room for the incriminating evidence. 'I can smell your breath from here.'

'All right. I had one glass. Just to help me sleep.'

'Well, in that case, you will be rested enough to listen.'

'Go ahead.'

'I'm afraid there have been some developments.' Enid brought out her notepad, flicked it to the opening page. 'Her autobiography has now hit the shelves.'

'What is this need people have to bore us with made-up tales of their lives? Such egotism. Such crassness. What's it called?'

'What is it called? You want to know what it's called? Oh, let me see. Yes, here it is. It's called *Macy Collingwood – Not So Abstract Expressions*.'

'I suppose that's OK. What else?'

'Well, it's only been released in America so far. There have been some reviews, mainly in the art magazines, culture pull-outs in the papers, that kind of thing.'

'What does she say about me?'

'I haven't received a copy yet.'

'Enid?'

'Only what I've seen on the Internet. There have been the expected allegations. A few of the American broadsheets have picked up on those.'

'What do they say?'

'I would say that the main theme is on the subject of your hypocrisy.'

'Well, I was never popular in the States anyway. What about back home?'

'Nothing seems to have reached the press yet.'

'Well, that's not too bad then.'

'There's something else.'

'Go on.'

'It's not good news.'

'For God's sake, Enid. Just spit it out.'

'The BBC called to say they were re-considering their offer regarding the interview series. The producer was very nice about it. She said she didn't want to rush into any rash judgements. But Sir David would like to have a chat with you. I'm so sorry.'

'I see.'

'What do you think we should do? I could put out a press release. Denying the allegations.'

'I keep telling you, Enid. There is nothing to deny.'

'But it was so long ago. And what about your reputation?'

'What can I do? As Aldous used to tell me: "Life's beginning moulds you, it's ending will judge you. It doesn't matter what you do in between."'

'But you've done so much in between.'

'I appreciate your support, Enid. But I've heard enough. I think you should go now.'

'I still think you should fight back.'

'We came here to get away from all of this nonsense. Not to fight it. I'm feeling very tired now.'

'Yes, yes, of course. Let me take away this tray. I'll leave you till the morning.'

'Thank you.'

He fixed himself another drink, this time diluted with a little water from his aspirin glass, just to stir up the flavour. The bottle was almost empty. He moved over to the writing desk, switched on the table lamp. Through the gap in the curtain, he could see the darkening sky over the treetops. He rose again and walked stiffly over to his suitcase on the stool-rack, rummaged around inside until he found Kobayashi's puzzle-box, brought it back to the desk. There it would sit, a marquetry tribute to the woods of its birth lying beyond the window. How appropriate. Now he was ready.

He would write. Not some pithy *haiku* but the seeds of something substantial. He had not thought about writing a novel for years. Surely ideas had been backing up, building up, bubbling up. Another wee dram should start to open up the sluice gates. He gulped down his drink and picked up a pen. Sketch down some thoughts. He listed his more important novels chronologically with their subject matter attached. His famous three. His triumvirate: "*The Waterwheel* (injustice). *The Fall of Dominic Pike* (the dispossessed). *If So, Answer Me* (spiritual void)." All so bloody serious. So bloody heavy. What he needed was to write a comedy. A humorous look at life. A conversation with a wise clown.

How would you like to do a series on that, Sir David? When was the last time a great writer had written comedy? Apart from Shakespeare. And Cervantes. Nothing in the last four hundred years. That was it. If he were to carry the massive, ever-changing structure of a novel inside his head for the next few years, let it be light, let it be joyful, let it be funny. He finished off the bottle. He felt truly inspired. He wrote down the word "Comedy" on the page. 'Aha!' All he had to do now was think of an amusing theme. To begin the process, he would order another bottle of malt, have a shower, let the hot flow massage the ideas inside his head, let his thoughts percolate.

'Eddie-chan, what are you doing?'

He didn't have an answer. His brain had done that quick-flick memory-scan kind of thing and come up with a blank. He did not know what he was doing. All he knew was that he was standing in a corridor, back flat-pressed against the wall. His skin felt cold, damp on the surface but inside he was hot. Sumiko was in front of him, unfurling his fingers, extracting something from his grip.

'Why are you carrying around an empty bottle? And what is this sticking out of your ear? Oh, dear. It's a cotton bud. Oh, Eddie. A cotton bud. And your robe is wet. Have you just come out of a shower?'

Yes, he remembered that. There had been a shower. The hot pinpricks of water reviving him. Such a pleasant sensation. As was the touch of Sumiko's fingers gripping his hand. Leading him where? Back to his room, of course. The Fuji Suite. She drew him to the centre of the room, made him wait there, then she was back tut-tutting, stripping off his robe, rubbing him down with a large towel. Yes, he liked that.

'What would you do without me?' Rub, rub, rub. 'Shiver to death.' Rub, rub, rub. 'And look at all these bruises. You have to be careful.' Rub, rub, rub. 'You just can't go wandering around like this.'

She dressed him in a fresh robe, made him wait again as she skilfully sorted out the sheets, plumped up the pillows, just like the chambermaid she had been. He eased himself on to the bed, stretched out his legs.

'Would you like something to drink? I can make a pot of tea.'

He nodded. And waited. All these sounds. The steaming kettle. The washing of cups. A voice outside in the back courtyard. He imagined the chef, sneaking a cigarette, scolding a kitchen boy. *Nan dayo. Nan dayo.* A hot cup placed in the clasp of his hands. 'Can you manage that?' He nodded again. The scent of the tea the same as her body perfume. He had to concentrate. That was what his doctor had told him. 'You must try and focus on everything you do. Tell yourself what you are doing as you do it.'

I am holding a cup. I am watching Sumiko bring over a chair to the side of the bed. She is picking up her cup in those delicate hands of hers. She is talking to me. I can see her mouth moving, chattering away into the tea-mist.

'... You are so stubborn. Stubborn, stubborn, stubborn. It is a miracle you ever managed to get here. How you made it to see Jerome in Tokyo I will never know. What are we going to do with you, Eddie-chan?'

'You know, Sumiko. I still cannot seem to get that tune out of my head. Dada dada da. Are you sure it is the song from the Tokyo Olympics? I thought it might have been the national anthem, but you would know your own anthem, of course. Perhaps it is something else altogether?'

'Oh, Eddie.' He watched her stand up, take his cup, lean over his body to adjust the bedcovers. 'You should try to sleep.'

Her neck was so close to his face. He remembered how she used to wear her sleek hair pinned up with long needles in a bun, just like a little maid all contrary, come from a ladies' seminary. Now it was cut shorter in a bob. He could see some grey underneath where the dye had faded. The Paisley pattern of her blouse. He grabbed her arm as she moved away.

'Sumiko.'

'Yes?'

'I would like to go to Kamakura. Can we visit there? It is not very far. We had such a great time there the last time we went.'

'Yes, yes, we can go there. Let us see how you are tomorrow. If it is a fine day and you are feeling better, I will take you there.'

'Thank you.' He heard her footsteps as she padded away from him, the click of the light switch, the door closing. A tickling sensation as he felt the solitary tear on its stop-start journey down his cheek.

CHAPTER TWENTY-SIX

London • 1971

Edward had been going through a polite and pleasant patch with Macy. A truce. A state of *détente*. His career was going well, as was hers, and they were being just a little more generous and gentle with each other. Now that it was summer, Macy would even come downstairs some mornings, join him for breakfast in the garden of their Chelsea house where they would pour each other cups of tea, open their respective posts, share a comment or two about a certain newspaper article or chat distractedly about how well the fruit trees were faring this season. It was on one such occasion she informed him her mother was very ill.

'I am going back to New York,' she said.

'For how long?'

'A few weeks. A few months. I will stay until she dies.'

'Perhaps I will join you for a while. Give you some support.'

Macy lowered her newspaper. He saw a softness in her look towards him he hadn't seen for years.

'That's mighty nice of you, Eddie. Why would you do something like that?'

He felt embarrassed. He wasn't even sure himself why he had made the suggestion, this getting on with Macy over the last few weeks catching him out. 'I don't know. It feels like the right thing to do. What do you think? I won't come for long. Just give you a bit of company. I've never seen New York. I've never even met your mother.'

'I just hope she's well enough to know who you are.'

'So you think I should come then?'

'If they'll let you in.'

Giles Morgan, his publisher, was delighted.

'We've always wanted to push you in the States, Edward,' he said. 'This is a great opportunity to test the waters. And New York is a fabulous place to kick off. The Big Apple. We'll take a nice big juicy bite out of it. You'll see. It shouldn't be difficult to set you up with a few readings, interviews and signings around the city.'

Giles rose from his swivel chair, moved over to the window with its expansive view of the Thames, his chubby cheeks glowing like a couple of big rosy apples themselves. Edward noted that while his publisher wore the customary pinstripe of his profession, the shirt, however, was lavender and the tie floral. 'It's just brilliant,' Giles said to his rainbow reflection in the pane. 'Just bloody brilliant.'

Edward had always liked Giles' exuberance. It was probably the reason why he attracted such high profile clients, this infectious enthusiasm that made his insecure writers feel valued and loved. And it wasn't just froth either. That was why Aldous had recommended him. 'Giles delivers,' his old friend had once told him. 'Giles definitely delivers.' Edward wondered if they had been lovers.

'I still don't think the Yanks have forgiven me for *The Waterwheel*.'

'Oh tosh. That was centuries ago. The world has moved on since then. They've got Vietnam to worry about now. Anyway, it's *If So* we'll be pushing. *The Waterwheel* won't even be mentioned in dispatches. And the Macy connection should help too. You know, husband of the celebrated American painter, Macy Collingwood.' Giles rubbed his hands together.

'I think we should play down the Macy connection. She's over there to see her dying mother. And we're not exactly the perfect couple.'

'Yes, yes. Of course. Play down the Macy connection. Play it down. Play it cool. Play it oh so cool. But it's all just brilliant.'

The Americans weren't so impressed by the proposal. Edward's visa was refused. No reasons given.

As Edward sat waiting in Jack Collingwood's office, he tried to recall how long it had been since he had seen the man who was still in all legality his father-in-law. It must have been at least fifteen, perhaps even closer to twenty years since they had met in that gallery in Albemarle Street where Macy had exhibited the very first of her paintings. Then there was that disastrous dinner in Soho when Macy had stormed off in a fit of pique at something her father had said. Jack had stayed on in London, eschewing an international career in the diplomatic corps or even in American politics, for the sake of his love for a junior attaché from the Spanish embassy. At least that's what Macy had told him. She had met them both once, bumped into them as a couple walking through Mayfair, hand-in-hand, happy as larks, she reported. Macy had hardly spoken to her father since.

Looking around at the bare walls, Edward wasn't sure what building he was in, never mind which office. No signs at the grey concrete entrance, just a number. And a couple of stiff security guards. A bland reception area. No signs either to indicate which department or office was located on which floor. All he knew was that Jack Collingwood was high up in the building and high up in the US Government.

The door burst open and Jack swept in. Hair pure white now, the face more lined, Mount Rushmore craggy, but still that confident, easy, American way about the man. Shiny cheeks, shiny suit, shiny smile. Edward felt immediately ill at ease.

'Well, well, well, Edward Strathairn. My famous son-in-law. You are still my son-in-law, aren't you?'

'I'm afraid so. Macy never wanted a divorce.'

'She always was a stubborn bitch. Just like her mother. Doing quite well for herself now, I see. I even bought one of her paintings. Don't tell her that though. She'll probably ask for it back or something. So what can I do for you?'

'I need a favour, Jack.'

'Yeah. Go on.'

'I've been refused a visa for the States,' Edward said, trying to sound casual. 'I thought you might be able to help.'

'Macy sent you?'

'No. My own initiative. She doesn't need to know.'

'Have you any idea what I do here, Eddie?'

'Not really. No. No, in fact, I don't. I just thought you might have some clout. You know, after twenty years with Uncle Sam in the United Kingdom, you might be able to help out family.'

'Well, you're not exactly family. You are the estranged husband of my estranged daughter.'

'Let's not be estrangers then.'

'This is not a laughing matter.'

'You're right, Jack. Macy's mother is very ill. She's gone out to be with her. I thought I'd tag along, lend her support.'

Edward could see the information had caught Collingwood off-guard, the confident sheen dulling momentarily, a light going out from under his tan.

'How bad is she?'

'Don't know exactly. Macy is staying out there until she dies.' He hadn't meant the words to come out so cruelly. After all, he had no idea what kind of relationship this man still had with his ex-wife.

'I see.' Collingwood cleared his throat, then shivered himself back into confidence mode with a straightening of his tie. 'Well, you're not exactly the easiest person to smuggle into the old US of A. A bit of a *persona non grata*. Couldn't stand your book myself. And unfortunately there are a lot of war veterans who feel the same way. Some are probably even in government now. Possibly even in embassies and consulates around the world, stamping visas into passports.'

'I don't want to argue with you, Jack. You've got your take about what happened in Japan. And I've got mine.'

'I'll see what I can do.'

Collingwood came up trumps. The visa was granted within forty-eight hours.

It was the sheer scale that impressed. Larger than life. Take a London building, a London street, a London store, and double it. No treble it. Quadruple it. Take it to the power ten. And that was New York. Skyscrapers blocking out the sun. Avenues running wider and deeper than the Thames. The people were bigger too. Louder. Ruder. More vibrant. The whole place exciting Edward from the off, filling him with a feeling he hadn't experienced for a very long time. Wonder. As soon as he had slid into that fat yellow cab at the airport and the driver had turned and asked: 'Where to, fella?' It was just like being in a movie.

His American publishers had booked him into the River Plaza Hotel on the Upper West Side. His room was twelve floors up with a view over the Hudson, across to New Jersey. Macy's mother's apartment was just two blocks further uptown, a thoughtful convenience. He called Macy as soon as he arrived. The news was not good.

'She's just been transferred to a hospice,' she told him. 'It can't be long now.'

'I'll come over. You're only five minutes away.'

'Kind of you to offer. But I'd rather be on my own tonight, Eddie. I need to adjust to all of this. Why don't you leave it until tomorrow? You're probably dead beat.'

'I've got some kind of event to do late morning. I'll come over afterwards.' He clicked off the phone, let the receiver hang there in his hands. He felt closer to Macy than he had done for a very long time.

He slept late, wasn't ready for the mid-morning arrival of the diminutive but sharply turned-out Miss Desai at his door. He had to greet her in his big fluffy white bathrobe while she stood before him in a black suit with creases like razors, black shoes, black briefcase and hair so black it was almost blue. He felt like a giant polar bear stooped over a penguin.

'I'm sorry, but I'm running a little late,' he said.

'True,' she said.

'Why don't you sit down? There's some coffee in a pot there.'

'I'll just wait, thank you.'

He went back into his bedroom, dressed quickly, returned to find Miss Desai standing exactly where he had left her.

'Right,' he said, rubbing his hands together, trying to sound cheerful. 'Lead on.'

He felt her nervousness as they travelled down in the lift together, saw her fingers nipping away at her trouser creases. He thought at first it might have been his lateness that had upset her, or he even presumed to think his reputation might be a factor. It was only in the taxi he discovered the real reason.

'I'm afraid there's been a bit of a problem,' she confessed, looking straight ahead.

'What kind of problem?'

'With the reading.'

'It has been cancelled?'

'That could have been an option. But we've decided to proceed.'

'Look, Miss Desai. Will you please just tell me what is going on?'

She wriggled herself even straighter. 'The bookstore has received a number of phone calls. There have been accusations. Accusations that the store is being unpatriotic by hosting your event. Yes, that is what they are being accused of. And, of course, we too are being accused as your publishers. Of being unpatriotic.'

'Oh, for Christ's sake,' was all he could manage.

Miss Desai ignored his remark and continued, all the time staring ahead as if the licence details of the driver, one Nikos Loukanidis, was of immense importance to her. 'We have contacted the New York Police Department, but there is nothing they can do. It is not as if there has been a direct threat or anything like that. And we can't very well interrogate the customers entering the bookstore. After all, it is an establishment open to the general public. America is still a free country after all. So the show must go on.'

'Yes,' Edward sighed. 'The show must go on.'

He had half-expected there to be a knot of protestors waiting outside the store just like the anti-Vietnam War demonstrations he had seen on the television, but he was able to walk straight in unheeded and unhampered in the wake of the purposeful Miss

Desai. The reading was scheduled to take place in a large public area in the basement where there was a small stage, a couple of chairs, a table with a microphone, several stacks of hardback copies of *If So, Answer Me*. He was pleased to see there was an audience of around sixty eager souls, already seated. He scoured their ranks for anyone he might be able to identify as an outraged Pacific War veteran. What was he looking for? Someone in army fatigues, crew cut and bandana straight out of 'Nam? They all seemed a perfectly pacific bunch to him. He began to relax.

Miss Desai carried out the introduction. She did so quite eloquently, without notes, encapsulating with great knowledge and insight his literary career to date. It suddenly occurred to him that behind her sharp exterior, Miss Desai might have even been a fan.

He stood up to such hugely generous applause he felt quite overwhelmed, heard his voice quiver slightly before he launched into his usual *spiel*. But he soon found his stride as he began to outline the tragic events that had led to him writing his *If So* novel, the necessity to fill this void with some creative endeavour. 'All creativity comes from loss,' he said after a long pause and he saw several members of the audience nod gravely in agreement. It was a gentle preparation he knew that could not help but gain a certain amount of sympathy. He then read from four different sections of his novel, sat down to loud clapping and even some enthusiastic whistling. 'God bless America,' he thought. 'Why did I wait so long to come here?' Miss Desai took questions from the floor, nothing he hadn't been asked at least twenty times before. But he delivered his responses as if he were doing so for the first time, adding in a little well-rehearsed humour if he could, always trying to remain humble.

'You're that guy who wrote *The Waterwheel*, ain't you?'

Edward scanned the room to his left where an extremely obese man was struggling to his feet.

'Yeah, you,' the man panted, finally able to rest his bulk by grabbing the back of the empty seat in front of him. Small head, small moustache, huge body swaying inside a sweat-stained shirt.

'Yes. That is true. I did write *The Waterwheel*. Many, many years ago. It was my first novel.'

'Apologist for the Japs, that's who you are.'

'Sorry?'

'Yeah, a fucking apologist for the Japs,' another voice yelled, this time from the other side of the room. In Edward's eyes, this man looked more like the genuine article – close-cropped white hair, biceps bulging from a T-shirt with "Property of US Marines" printed across the chest. Miss Desai sat stiffly, smoothed out the papers of her introductory speech. A fresh-faced shop assistant standing to the side of the stage, turned to Edward, his eyes wide with fear.

'If we hadn't dropped the bomb on these little bastards, I wouldn't be here now,' the fat man said, his face shining with sweat. 'That was me over there. Island-hopping in the Pacific. Just a kid I was. They'd have cut my head off, eaten my liver for breakfast, without so much as a by your leave.'

'Yeah,' the other man shouted. 'Yeah. For breakfast.'

'The Japanese were ready to surrender after the first bomb dropped on Hiroshima,' Edward tried to reason. 'Dropping the bomb on Nagasaki was a cruel and inhumane act against innocent civilians that served no military purpose whatsoever.'

'Yeah? Well, it saved the lives of a million American troops,' said the fat man.

'That figure's a myth,' Edward protested. 'Thirty thousand, maybe forty thousand at the most. And those were the estimates if there had been a full invasion. Which would have been unnecessary after Hiroshima anyway.'

'Yeah? And how many Japs were killed in the bombings?

'More than two hundred thousand civilians, if you include radiation poisoning.'

The fat man laughed. 'That sounds pretty fair odds to me,' he said looking smugly around his audience.

'Yeah, fair odds,' shouted Mr Property of US Marines. 'Five of their civilians to save one of us soldiers. That's more than fair. You tell him, Louis.'

Fat man Louis dabbed his forehead with a handkerchief. 'What I'm trying to get across to you, mister, is that you gotta stop talking about these Japs like they're the victims. These little bastards carried out horrific tortures. Not only against us Yanks. But against you Brits too.'

'Oh, for Christ sake,' Edward said. 'I was not trying to make them victims. All I was tying to do was to humanise them. To make my readers see that dropping an atomic bomb wasn't some abstract act happening on the other side of the world.'

'I'll tell you about some real acts on the other side of the world.' It was back to Mr Property of US Marines. 'We were in a fucking jungle out there. Mosquitoes as big as your fist. Malaria. And these Japs if they captured you. They'd boil you alive. We should have dropped more of those bombs. Wiped out the whole lotta them. Stopped them building their little cars, flooding the market, putting us out of jobs. With these tiny cars. Ain't that right, Louis?'

Louis began to waddle forward, knocking aside a few chairs with his sheer girth. 'Yeah. Putting us out of jobs. We should just drop a bomb on Vietnam too. That would save a lot more American lives too. Isn't that right?' The audience started a slow handclap. Edward wasn't sure if this was in support or against this Louis fellow. The young store clerk approached, whispered in his ear.

'There's a way out back, sir. If you'll come with me.'

Edward pulled at Miss Desai's arm. 'Come on,' he said. 'Let's go.'

As he eased himself down off the back of the stage, he felt something whizz past his head, then strike a row of books in front of him. The eggshell clung to one of the spines, releasing its viscous fluid down its length. As he watched the progress of this yellow-white slurry, he also noticed the title of the book – *War and Peace*. Then he heard Miss Desai push back her chair, address the audience through the feedback from the microphone.

'I'm sorry but Mr Strathairn will be unable to sign copies of his book at this present time. But thank you for coming.'

CHAPTER TWENTY-SEVEN

Hakone, Japan • 2003

Edward wasn't well enough the next day to travel to Kamakura. More from a hangover than anything else. But a full twenty-four hours spent in his room sleeping, resting, bathing and the occasional thought for his new idea of a comedic novel, had done him wonders. The following day, he was up early, refreshed. The bruising and stiffness still lingered but his mind was remarkably clear. He ate a fine continental breakfast in the dining room, took a short stroll in the garden up to the waterwheel and now waited in the foyer for Sumiko to collect him in that sleek car of hers. Courtesy of Enid, who disapproved of this outing, a brand new fully-charged mobile phone bulged in his inside coat pocket like a gangster's gun.

'It is so good to see you up and about again, Sir Edward.'

'Ah, Takahashi-san. Yes, thank you, I feel wonderfully revitalised this morning. There is something about these crisp autumn mornings that cheers the spirit.'

'The drive down to the station should be particularly colourful at this time of year. And, of course, you are going to Kamakura. One of my favourite destinations. Will you be visiting the Giant Buddha? Such an excellent example of Japanese bronze-casting.'

'It is first on our list.'

'As I am sure you already know, Sir Edward, a tidal wave was unable to move the statue from its spot six hundred years ago. Although it did destroy the hall in which it stood. It has survived many storms and earthquakes since, including the Great Kanto Quake, when I believe it was seen to rock on its base. Apart from that brief episode, it has remained immovable.'

'Actually, I didn't know about the tidal wave. If I recall, the statue is quite a distance inland. I am surprised a wave could reach that far.'

'I think it is about a mile from the shore, Sir Edward... Ah, there is Sumiko-chan. Shall I escort you to the vehicle?'

'Thank you, but I would like to manage on my own.'

Sumiko had already stepped out of the car to greet him. She wore a fawn suede coat with matching boots and hat, all trimmed with fur.

'I like your outfit,' he said.

She patted her hat, made some adjustment. 'Just some old things.'

He opened the passenger door, she took his cane and he eased into the seat. As they drove off, he turned to see Takahashi in the forecourt picking a leaf off the gravel. He tapped on the window with his cane. The hotel manager looked up, and instinctively managed a bow, even from his crouched position. He felt like telling Sumiko to stop the car so he could exit the vehicle, haul the man to his feet and embrace him. But the moment passed, the hotel disappeared out of sight, and he was left with just a hint of regret hovering at the edge of his general feeling of well-being.

'I thought I'd drive to Odawara and we'd take the train from there,' she said. 'It is so much easier than crawling through traffic, don't you think?'

He mumbled his consent, his attention drawn more to the autumn scene through the glass. Takahashi was right. The colours were mesmerising. What wondrous hues. Brown, yellow, burnt orange, copper red. A last brave hurrah from Nature's palette before winter set in. He could almost smell the decay. But then feeling his seat belt strapped too tight, he needed to loosen the buckle. And it was too hot. He must flick these plastic vents open or roll down the window. Why was he panicking now? He could even feel his heart pick up a pace. Perhaps he was ill. The fall. The bang on the head. Or just this drive down the hill, around these continuous bends, making him nauseous.

'Eddie-chan? Are you all right? You look pale.'

The press of a button. A mechanical whirr. And the window by his head opened. He could feel the chill cool the sweat on his brow. He captured a couple of deep breaths, placed a hand on his chest, felt the pounding ease.

'I'm fine. Just a little... I don't know... motion sickness perhaps.'

'I'll slow down. All these bends can be... Oh look, Eddie. Look over there.'

Through a sudden gap in the trees, he could see Mount Fuji in the distance, so totally dominating the horizon it was hard to believe he hadn't seen it on his visit until now. Completely devoid of clouds, shimmering, hovering like a spaceship in the cool blue sky. Just the merest of glimpses before the peak disappeared behind the foliage.

'You can close the window. I feel better now.'

'Good,' she said, as she ground down a gear. 'The sight of our sacred mountain can be very uplifting. Autumn is the best time to see Fuji-san, of course. For the summer tourists, it is always too cloudy.'

Sumiko bought one of these disposable cameras at Kamakura station and then they caught a taxi. She made the driver take a longer route so they could pass along the seafront. The city had changed drastically. Edward could see that immediately from the myriad convenience stores, parking lots and fast-food outlets that had sprung up in his absence. The usual urban blight. The vending machines offending him the most, row after row of them, armies of garish, round-the-clock robots to consumerism. But something of the old Kamakura still remained, the sacred untouchable grounds of the many temples and shrines preventing the municipal planners from completely running amok. He spotted a *tori*, the rust-red gateway in the shape of a giant Greek letter *pi*. And over there the curved tiled roof of a shrine, a narrow lane of market stalls, a wooden house peeping out from behind some concrete monstrosity. Each sighting representing a small victory to him. The taxi turned on to the coast road and he had to screw up his eyes to meet the glare of the sun off the water. Sumiko put on a pair of sunglasses. He experienced that sad, deflated feeling of a seaside town in winter. A faded postcard of closed shutters, peeling paint, empty beaches. A brace of fishing boats languishing on the sand, seaweed flapping on drying racks, giant crows foraging in wire baskets, a couple of surfers bobbing in the water, boards raised like lances. Sumiko told the driver to stop, they got out for the obligatory snapshot and then moved on.

The Great Buddha. He recalled the one photograph Jerome had shown him in his office. Sumiko standing in front of the forty-foot structure, awkwardly confined in his arm. He noted now with a certain irony that the enormous bronze statue failed to reflect one of the more important aspects of Buddhism – the one of change. So much else had moved on in this country yet the Great Buddha had remained exactly the same. But he didn't feel awe in the constancy of its presence. Just old.

'Come on, Eddie. A photograph. For old time's sake.'

'Yes, yes,' he said, rising on his cane. 'For old time's sake.'

He wandered over to where she stood. To that ideal spot where the background of the Buddha presided over them in perfect symmetry. A young Japanese girl in shredded jeans and black leather jacket with the words "TOKYO CHICK" emblazoned on the back, did the honours, handling the throw-away camera with all the casual contempt of youth. He put his arm around Sumiko, and she moved in close, the fur collar of her coat tickling his chin. Click. Frozen in a different time.

She took him for lunch in a tiny, heavily timbered soba shop, which made its own buckwheat noodles on the premises. Post-war Japan had hardly touched the place. They sat in a cold, dingy corner where a paraffin stove provided the only heat. The menu was a faded piece of yellow paper pinned to the wall offering a limited choice of soba. He opted for a noodle soup, more as an additional source of heat than anything else, although Sumiko assured him the quality of the soba was renowned throughout the Kanto region. He also asked her to order a flask of warm sake. The waitress – a tiny, ancient woman with knobbly hands and fingers like dried-up pieces of ginger-root – brought two small glasses, then filled them to the brim with the hot rice wine straight out of a giant teapot that she struggled to hold steady.

The broth when it came was delicious, its saltiness balanced nicely by the slight sweetness of the sake. He watched with amusement as Sumiko in all her finery noisily slurped at her noodles. And in this dark nook where the lack of daylight could forgive the passage of time, he remembered her as she used to be. Exquisitely beautiful. Her pale moon face peering out between a curtain of straight black hair. Her eyes, lively, curious, trusting. A loving, wondrous creature.

'We came here before,' he said.

'Yes. With Jerome.'

'It's strange I should remember that day so well.'

'The three of us together. It felt special.'

He put his hand into his overcoat pocket, brought out the wooden puzzle box. 'I want you to have this.'

Her eyes widened. 'Oh,' she said, bringing her fingertips to her lips to cover her surprise. 'I remember you used to have one of these on your desk. Is it the same one?'

'Yes. It was given to me on my first visit to Hakone. By Kobayashi-san. He was a translator at Tokyo Autos where I used to work before I met you. We were all on a company outing together. That was also the first time I came across the hotel. And do you know something else? I remembered this in the car when I saw Fuji-san again. I always thought it was you who told me that only a person who stays in Japan for a long time sees Mount Fuji uncovered by clouds. But it wasn't. It was the tea girl at the company. She told me that on the very same trip. I even remember her name. It was Mie. How can I remember all of this when I can't even remember what I had for breakfast?'

'Oh, Eddie,' she said, turning the box gently in her hands. 'This is very sweet of you… oh wait, there is something in it.' She shook it close to her ear. 'I can hear something rattling.'

'There is a secret compartment. But I can't remember how to open it.'

'What is inside?'

'I don't recall that either.'

'*Honto?*' She shook the box again. 'Surely you must remember what you put in there. It sounds like a small stone.'

'I don't know. Can you open it?'

'What? Do you think I am a magician?' she said, laughing. 'The next time I am in Hakone, I'll ask at one of the tourist shops. I am sure they will have instructions for it. These things never change. Some of them go up to over sixty moves. But this one is a simple one, I am sure. Six or seven moves at most. I just can't believe you don't remember what's inside.'

'It can't be very important.'

'Then why hide it away?'

He shrugged.

'You never gave me anything before,' she said.

'I gave you *The Waterwheel*.'

'The story of a stupid *panpan* girl?'

'It was a bit more than that. I just wish you had read it.'

'I will, Eddie. I promise.'

'There's a copy in the hotel library.'

She slipped the box into her bag, drew out a compact, screwed up her mouth in a look at the mirror. 'Now, where would you like to go next?'

'I don't care. As long as it is with you.'

'You are impossible,' she said, snapping shut her compact. Then, more kindly: 'The Museum of Literature is nearby. I believe there are some manuscripts by Kawabata-sensei in its collection. I thought you might like to see them.'

'Do you remember how Jerome and I tried to find his house for you? You sprained your ankle and we had to carry you back to the car.'

'I felt so stupid to spoil our wonderful day. But I don't remember where the house is. Or even if it is open to the public.'

'I would like it very much if we try to find it.'

'I can ask at the museum.'

'He committed suicide. You know that, of course?'

'Yes, I know.'

'Gassed himself. He didn't even leave a note. He was seventy-two years old. What kind of man kills himself at the age of seventy-two?'

The Museum of Literature was at the top of quite a steep hill. He struggled with the slope, leaning on Sumiko for support, stopping often just to catch his breath and to rest his limbs.

'It's too much for you, Eddie. We should go back.'

'Don't be ridiculous. I can manage.' But nevertheless, he was glad to reach the entrance gateway, to sit down on a bench in the gardens by the ticket booth. To take in the view of the sea beyond the rooftops of Kamakura. To enjoy the winter cherry blossom, the yellow leaves of the Gingko trees. To live in the breathless moment.

'It is such a pity it is so late in the season,' Sumiko said, bringing him his ticket. 'The rose garden here is quite spectacular in the early summer. So many different colours. Each one with its special scent. Do you think you can manage these final steps?'

'I have come this far, haven't I? Onwards and upwards.'

The museum sat in its own private valley, overlooking the gardens from the top of the long flight of steps. It was a two-storey art-deco manor house with pale yellow walls and a blue-tiled roof, its frontage crowded with large windows, greedily swallowing up the sea views from every angle. At one time, it must have been a magnificent private home. But as a museum, with its barren rooms – except for their glass exhibition cabinets – it was a cold and unwelcoming place. He let Sumiko wander off at her own pace as he hobbled from exhibit to exhibit. There was a handful of other visitors spread out around the house, but for the most part he was left alone.

He found a glass case displaying a couple of items relating to Kawabata. A black and white photograph, a simple head-shot of the frail man with his small, pointed features and remarkable swept-back mane of hair. The hair was everything. It was so thick it seemed to have sucked up all the power of its owner through its roots, leaving the rest of the man weak and fragile. The case also contained a page from the original manuscript of *Snow Country*, complete with edits by the author. And that was it. Here was Japan's first recipient of the Nobel Prize for Literature, yet hardly a mention compared to the other Kamakura literati honoured in the room. It had to be the stigma attached to the suicide. What else could explain this paltry shrine to such a great writer? In a Museum of Literature of all places. He peered back into the case, saw his own image reflected there, an eerie spectre between himself and the photograph of Kawabata. He felt Sumiko's presence beside him, saw too her reflection in the glass.

'I want to leave,' he said.

'I have Kawabata-sensei's address,' she said, inserting a folded-up piece of paper into his jacket top-pocket. 'One of the guards told me. The house is closed to the public but we could still walk by and take a peek. It is not far.'

'Good. We can complete that journey we started so many years ago.'

The walk back down the hill was perilous with the damp leaves underfoot and he had to use his cane just to keep from wobbling ahead of himself. Sumiko took his arm again, kept him steady on his feet.

'What is that noise?' she said, tugging him to a halt.

He could hear the wailing, mixed in with the tinny bark of urgent instructions. He was reminded of the air raids on the Clydeside shipyards as a child. 'Sirens,' he said. 'I can hear sirens.'

'They usually only have them for earthquakes. I didn't feel any tremors, Eddie. Did you?'

CHAPTER TWENTY-EIGHT

New York • 1971

Edward abandoned a slightly ruffled and apologetic Miss Desai on a crowded street corner, took a taxi to his hotel but decided against going up to his room. Instead, he chose to walk the two blocks north along the tree-lined avenue by the river to Macy's mother's apartment. It was a miserable afternoon harbouring a blue-less sky and a spitting rain. A couple of enormous barges slipped past low and silent on the grey, swollen waters of the Hudson, the sight for some reason filling him with an enormous sadness. Then a police car swooped into the avenue, its yowling siren and frantic lights shattering his sombre mood. The rain came heavier now. Umbrellas went up as pedestrians hastened by and he cursed himself for not letting the taxi take him these two extra blocks. His head ached and the acids in his stomach burned from lack of sustenance. His late rising had forced him to skip breakfast and his hurried departure from the bookstore meant he had missed out on the scheduled lunch with Miss Desai and his publishers. Despite his protestations that the incident at the bookstore had not affected him, the reality was quite different. Never before had he experienced such a violent reaction from his reading public. Any previous criticism had always come in the form of a review, a newspaper article or even a letter. But never this. This aggressive link between himself and his audience as symbolised by the thrown egg. He felt violated. As if he had been dealt an actual physical blow.

Another police car screamed by. Then a fire engine, its silver ladders swaying as the red monster weaved through the traffic, belting out seal-like honks in pursuit of its escort. A drop of water from an overhanging awning slithered down his neck. He tried to push back his memories of the reception at the store. New York felt like a very hostile place to him as at last he reached the grand, marble-pillared entrance that bore the number of his destination.

Given the plush foyer, the uniformed doorman who asked to be called Tony and an elevator laid with thick, thick carpet, he had half-expected a butler to be first in attendance at the massive double doors of the apartment. But no, there was Macy, her cheeks flushed, swaying in uncharacteristic girlish fashion with her back against the brass door handle as she beckoned him in.

'Welcome to New York,' she said. 'You finally made it.'

He kissed her on one hot cheek. 'So this is your American life,' he said.

'That's me. A New York gal.'

'How strange to discover this part of you so late on.'

'Well, you know whose fault that was.'

'Let's not get started.'

'Come on. I'll show you around.'

The view was virtually the same as from his hotel room. But the apartment was absolutely enormous. A couple of the reception rooms boasted chandeliers and tall gilt-edged mirrors that wouldn't have been out of place in the Palace of Versailles. He didn't actually feel he was in an apartment at all, just in some rambling house that went on forever on the same level. He couldn't help but think that this chunk of Manhattan real estate must be worth a fortune.

'Can I make myself a sandwich?' he asked. 'I haven't eaten all day.'

'Oh, poor Eddie,' she said. 'You must be in a foul mood then. Don't worry, I'll sort you out.' She poked her head inside a giant fridge. 'Chicken OK?'

'Chicken's fine.'

She brought out a plate with slices of white meat, then a couple of beers, uncapped them on an opener on the wall, passed him one. Macy was the only woman he knew who drank beer. And straight from the bottle at that. She took a deep swig then told him her news.

It was cancer, of course. Now passed the stage of whether it could be contained, spreading fast, killing her mother molecule by molecule, second by second. The hospice was a wonderful, peaceful place, she reported, even saying she wouldn't mind dying there herself when the occasion arose. And it was only a few blocks away. She could walk there to see her mother whenever she wanted.

As the afternoon light began to fade, they moved on to hard liquor. The apartment hosted a cocktail bar full of the stuff. Macy stuck to her usual gin and tonic, while Edward fussed over the choice of malts. She took him through to the lounge with its panoramic views of the river, sofas as long as railway carriages, and he could swear that was a Miro original hanging on the wall opposite a couple of Macy's own canvasses. He dropped down into an armchair, the drama of his morning's performance slowly fading. Macy sat curled up on a sofa opposite, sipping her drink, the crystal of her glass sending out sparks of reflections from the flames of the imitation coal fire. Her hair streaked grey-white, stark against the black of her polo neck. A handsome woman in her mid-forties. That was how he would describe her if he had to write her into one of his novels. Handsome. Still attractive to him. Even after all these years. Even after all the hurt.

He watched her as she worried at a thought, the two lines of concentration between her eyes reflecting her unspoken concern. He considered all his intimate knowledge of this woman garnered over the years in the pendulum swing of their relationship. Her body smells, her body cycles, her pruning and plucking and scraping and scrubbing, her fingering and fucking. After all, she was only skin and blood, bone and tissue, muscles and organs. That was all. A piece of warm decaying matter pulsing away there on the sofa at 98.6 degrees Fahrenheit. Yet what an impact she had made on his life. On his own piece of decaying matter.

'There's something I need to tell you, Eddie.'

'Uhuh?' He was tired now. Jet-lagged or just emotionally drained or just a bit drunk. He could happily sink back in this mammoth chair and be swallowed up in sleep.

'I don't know what it'll do to you.'

'You have nothing left to say that could possibly hurt me.'

'Don't be so smug.'

'Look. I'm tired. The reading was not a particular success. And I don't want a fight with you. Can't we just be friends for the few days I'm here? Let's leave this until tomorrow.'

'I need to tell you now.'

'It's that important?'

'Yes. Right now. While I still have the courage.'

'All right, all right.'

'Thank you.' She ran her finger around the rim of her glass as if she were casting a spell on the conversation. Creating a sacred space with the slight hum of the friction. She spoke softly.

'You know when you're a kid and you try to draw a spiral on a piece of paper. You start in the middle and you draw outwards and in a circle, and you make this little bump on the page so that when you come round again that little bump would become bigger, bigger and bigger each time till the whole damn thing goes out of control, loses its shape, runs haywire.' She stopped for a breath, looked across at him.

He sort of half-shrugged in his chair. 'What are you telling me?'

'I'm telling you there was one thing that happened in the past I never told you about. And that one thing just grew bigger and bigger until everything between us went out of shape. Became a lie. It was all my fault. And yet I punished you for it.'

'Go on.'

'Do you remember after those first few months we met, I left to go back to America?'

'Of course.'

'Did you ever think why I left so quickly?'

'I thought you'd had enough of me. Because of that argument we had down in Brighton.'

'The fight we had. You hit me really hard. '

'It was just a slap.'

'It was violent abuse.'

'Whatever you say. It was a long time ago.'

'Well, it made my mind up.' She paused, took a sip of her gin.

'Come on, Macy. About what?'

'I was pregnant, Eddie. I found out the day after Brighton. And after what had happened, I decided not to tell you. Instead I went back to America for an abortion. Mother arranged it. But there were complications. The surgery, if you could call it that, scarred the walls of my uterus. That was why I could never have children again. That was my bump on the page. I killed our first child without telling you. Then I lost another one because of the surgery. Then I spent the rest of my life blaming you for it. I couldn't help myself. Until here we are. Resentful of each other. Snatching a few moments of peace. But bitter nevertheless.' She drank back the rest of her glass in one gulp. 'Can you forgive me?'

He set his own glass down on a side-table. He noticed that he did this slowly, that his hand was steady. He then stood up. He felt cold. As if all the anger inside him that had raged so intensely during her confession, had ended up totally consuming itself. Until there was nothing. He walked over to where she sat on the sofa. Again he did this with remarkable control and clarity. She looked up at him, a slight smile flickering on her lips. Then with a quickness that surprised even himself, he hit her. Hard. A vicious, slashing slap to the face. The crystal glass flew out of her hand, smashed on the wooden floor. He remembered thinking that if it had only landed a few inches shorter, the rug would have probably saved it. He felt the sting of the slap on his palm and fingers. Macy's head had jerked to the side with the blow, and there she held herself, displaying her cheek, red with the welt. He was frozen in the moment, as was she. Such a profound moment, this irreparable rip he had just made in their lives. There was no going back from this. He felt anger and relief all in the one ball of emotion.

'Why the fuck didn't you tell me?' he roared.

She turned to face him. Her mascara had smeared, leaving dark smudges under her eyes, reminding him of one of her paintings. His handprint scarlet, like an ugly birthmark, across her cheek.

'Now I remember.' Her voice came out in a snarl. 'Now I remember why I didn't tell you. Because underneath all your self-righteousness, you're a violent, violent bastard.'

He hit her again. This time on the other cheek. With such a force that she fell off the sofa on to the floor. 'Go on,' she taunted from her prostrate position. 'Why don't you kick me now? Go on. Do it.'

He looked down at her sobbing body. Then calmly he turned, walked slowly out of the room, careful to avoid the broken glass. He searched around for his coat, found it lying over a chair in the hallway. As he moved to open the apartment door, he felt something sharp glance off his forehead. He looked round to see a small object spinning gold on the marble floor.

'Take it,' Macy shouted from her stance in the lounge doorway. 'Fucking take it.'

He stooped, picked up the ring. He wanted to say something to her, something final and dramatic. But looking at her, her hair matted against her wet cheeks, her skin still blotched from his blows, her mouth distorted by tears and anger, he realised words were pointless. He left the apartment, left the building, left New York, left America, left Macy for good.

CHAPTER TWENTY-NINE

Kamakura, Japan • 2003

'Do you know where you are going?' Edward asked. Since they had heard the sirens, she had been dragging him from one empty sidestreet to another without a word. He had a constant shooting pain down his left leg and he was sweating under his heavy overcoat. His body was telling him to return to the hotel, soak in a hot bath. But he was determined to see the house.

'You have the address,' she said.

'I do?'

'Yes, I put it in your pocket back at the museum. Wait. I'll ask someone.'

He was grateful to stop walking, to rest against a gatepost while she crossed the street to speak to an elderly gentleman sweeping leaves off his driveway. The man wore a pair of spotless blue overalls, the open collar revealing a shirt and tie underneath. He leaned gracefully on the handle of his brush as he listened to what Sumiko had to say, then he pointed down the street.

'The sirens,' she said on her return. 'It's a tsunami warning.'

'It can't be very serious. If he's still brushing up leaves.'

'There's been a huge earthquake in the Pacific. I don't like it. I want to go back to the station.'

'We must be very near the house.'

'The gentleman said about ten minutes.'

'Well, let's go there first.'

'But I want to leave Kamakura now.'

'We'll just walk past the house. Come on. We don't want to miss out again.'

'It's no use. We need to keep listening out for the news bulletins. We might have to move up to higher ground. These things scare me.'

'But it's only a warning. Even if it were real, these waves can take hours to cross the ocean.'

'Eddie,' she said, stamping her feet. 'For once in your life, can you stop thinking of yourself.'

'But we're nearly there.'

'I cannot swim. All right? Does that satisfy you?'

They found a taxi in the next street. The driver had his radio on and Sumiko relayed the news as they travelled back to the station.

'The tsunami will hit Chile first,' she said. 'Then Japan. Hawaii. California.'

The driver leaned forward in his seat, turned up the volume, grumbled loudly at what was heard.

'About two hours,' Sumiko reported. 'Two hours before it reaches here.'

Suddenly, he heard that tune again. Da, da, da, da, da. Da, da, da, da. What was it? The Japanese national anthem?

'Eddie. I think that's your phone.'

'Christ, so it is.' He tried to fish it out of his pocket but the seat belt was trapping it inside his coat. Da, da, da, da, da. Da, da, da, da.

'Here, I'll get it.' Sumiko slipped her hand under his belt, inside his coat, pulled out the phone. She punched one of the buttons, handed it to him.

'Hello? Hello? Sir Edward. Is that you?'

'Yes, Enid. I am here.'

'Is everything all right? Takahashi-san told me there are tsunami warnings all along the coast.'

'I am fine. We are on a taxi to the station. We will be leaving Kamakura shortly.'

'Please don't come back to the hotel.'

'What?'

'I've booked you in somewhere else. If you pass me over to Sumiko, I'll give her all the details.'

'What's going on there, Enid?'

'Oh, Sir Edward. It's the tabloids. They've picked up on the story.'

'Just tell me. What are they saying?'

'You don't want to know.'

'For fuck's sake, woman. Tell me.'

Silence.

'I'm sorry, Enid. I apologise. I realise you are trying to protect me. But please, I want to know.'

'All right. Here's one headline. It says: "*Who's In Denial Now, Sir Edward?*"'

'Any more?'

'"*Famous US-Berater Exposed As Wife Beater*".'

'I don't think "berater" is a word. Go on.'

'The Sun runs with "*Yankee Ex-Wife Nukes Novelist Sir Ed*".'

'I see.'

'There's been hundreds of emails. And I don't know how they tracked you down but the hotel has been inundated with phone calls. You shouldn't come back here. Reporters are on their way for comments. Oh, Sir Edward. I'm so sorry.'

He hung up, closed his eyes, listened to the frantic Japanese chatter on the radio. He found it quite soothing. He knew enough about tidal waves to appreciate that all this excitement would probably be about nothing. Yes, a thirty-foot monster of a wave could assault the beach at Kamakura but more than likely the quake would turn out to produce little more than a swell a few inches higher than normal. Out there in the Pacific, this potential tidal wave would be just a broad energy pulse flashing deep through the ocean away from the epicentre of the quake, running faster than a bullet train. Yet a boat in its path would hardly feel a thing. Just a ripple, as if a giant whale had passed under its hull on the way to tastier targets. A woman might rock slightly in her stateroom bed, a cocktail glass might slip an inch along the bartop, an alert sailor might raise his head momentarily from his navigation chart. But that was all. It was only when that pulse honed in on land, when the ocean bed reared up shallow, when the coastline swept up the pulse into its grasp, that the same energy could be squeezed into a dark wall of water. Into a moving mountain of raw, destructive power. He opened his eyes, looked out of the window as the taxi eased through the traffic. This was not a city in panic. This was no rush for the last helicopter out of Saigon. This population was sitting back calmly waiting for the false alarm to pass.

But he could see straight away that the situation at the station was different. While residents could flee if necessary to their evacuation points, tourists were abandoning Kamakura altogether. Yet there was still no rush or urgency. Just a well-behaved crowd massing at the station entrance, quietly obeying instructions barked through megaphones by Japanese Railway employees.

'I have the tickets,' Sumiko said. 'Try to stay close.'

The task facing them was to enter this stream of bodies in its flow to the mid-point of the tunnel under the station where either of the two main flights of steps would lead them up to the platforms. He hardly had to do anything, just give himself up to this crowd as it swept him along. His hands were pinned to his side, his cane useless, his feet hardly touching the ground. Sumiko had been pushed slightly ahead of him, but he kept her fur-trimmed hat in sight. His situation was not unpleasant, surrounded as he was by warm, supportive bodies, guiding him to his objective like a departing football crowd happy with their team's result. It was only when his little posse drove him past the entrances to the stairways did he realise he might be in trouble. He could see Sumiko's hat bobbing up the flight of steps, but he had already gone past the opening. He was on his way out of the tunnel through the opposite exit and there was nothing he could do to stop himself. Even a younger man would have been impotent against such a tide of humanity. He had no choice but to go with the flow. Go with the flow. Not to panic. Just go with the flow. Towards the light at the end of the tunnel. Go with the flow. Until he was deposited breathless outside the rear entrance.

It was quieter on this side of the station. He brushed down his coat, blinked in the light of the sun disappearing behind the hills. He loved this time of the day, this suffusion of colours that the dusk brought. Especially in the autumn when the sky was shot through with that pale, pale blue. And there was always a certain melancholy to these November sunsets tinged as they were with the approach of winter. He bought a bag of chestnuts from a nearby vendor who had set up a little brazier of hot coals outside the station. Just one bite through the shell into that bitter-sweet softness was enough to draw him back for an instant to his childhood.

'*Doko desu-ka?*' A taxi driver shouted to him through the open window of his cab. 'Where you go?'

'One moment, please.' He put his hand into his jacket top-pocket, plucked out the piece of paper, handed it to the driver. The man scanned the sheet.

'*Abunai-desuyo. Tsunami ga kimasu.* Very dangerous. Back way only.'

'Back way only?'

'No seafront.' The driver held up four fingers. '*Yon-sen en.*'

Four thousand yen. That was twice the amount he'd been charged for the journey to the station.

'All right then. *Yon-sen en.*'

As if by magic, the taxi door flew open and Edward lowered his tired limbs on to the plastic sheeting covering the back seat. The door closed by itself, followed by the clunk of the locks. The driver bent forward, muttering close to his windscreen as he edged his vehicle though the crowds until he could finally break free and shift up the gears.

'*Tsunami ga kimasu,*' the driver said, leaning back now to talk to him half over his shoulder. 'Tsunami come. Back way only.'

'Back way only,' he repeated with a tired sigh that he hoped would discourage any further conversation. The driver nodded and turned his attention to the road. The piece of paper with Kawabata's address was wedged into a heating vent on the dashboard, vibrating in the flow of warm air.

The 'back way only route' was quite pleasant. Dark lanes skirting the base of the hills surrounding the city. Earthy embankments. The smell of burning leaves. Temple gates. Roadside shrines. Sometimes even a temple itself lit up by rows of lanterns. It felt good just to sit back and relax. Perhaps, he should tell the driver to continue on like this all the way back to the hotel. Or just to keep driving on. Driving on in the back of a taxi. Forever. Such a comforting thought in its own way. He bit into another chestnut. Delicious.

'*Kochira ni narimasu,*' the driver said, pulling to a stop in the middle of a residential area. 'We are here.'

'Where is the house?'

The driver tapped his finger on the piece of paper. 'Here I know.' And then he shrugged. 'House I don't know.'

Yes, of course. He had forgotten the Japanese way of organising addresses. Houses were numbered according to when they were built within a particular area rather than according to their order in a particular street. Sometimes these two elements would coincide and a Japanese street would be numbered like any other street. But more often than not, they didn't. Then it would be a search on the basis of time rather than space. He would have to get out and ask or otherwise just look around. He paid the driver, thanked him, took back the piece of paper.

'One hour,' the driver said, holding up a nicotine-stained digit. '*Tsunami kimasu. Tsunami* come one hour. *Kyoskete-ne*? Be careful.'

It was dusk now. Streetlights blinking on. The wind had picked up, the temperature had dipped. He buttoned up his coat, tightened his scarf. Sirens still wailing somewhere in the distance. He stood all alone in a residential area, not a soul on the streets, not a light on in a house, a single piece of paper flapping in his hand. He searched for his glasses, tapping each of his pockets. He thought back. He must have left them in the *soba* shop, lost them in the tunnel. He walked over to a street lamp, held out the paper in the glow. He could just make out the numbers of the address. 2-6-3. Assuming the sequence moved left to right as it narrowed down the location, the house number must be '3'. He walked over to the gatepost of the nearest residence. A sign on the wall said 2-6-21. 'Good', he thought. 'I am on the right track.'

The street appeared to continue in a regular sequence – 2-6-20, 2-6-19, 2-6-18 – and he felt heartened at the prospect of being so close to his destination. Yet these houses were quite modern, bungalows in the European style, too modern, he worried, to be around in Kawabata's time. Too modern to accord with what he imagined to be Kawabata's aesthetic. Whatever that was. Something exquisitely carved and crafted, full of light, full of ancient pottery. By house number 2-6-9, the street began to narrow. Ahead of him, he could see a thin wedge of two-storey wooden buildings looming in the dusk, forming a narrow lane. He stopped at the entrance to this alleyway. There were no more street lights. He was tired now, hot and out of breath. He could hear the sirens wailing louder. Perhaps he should have remained in the taxi, instead of embarking on this wild goosechase. He gulped in some air, wandered into the lane.

There were only six houses in this short narrow stretch, three on either side, tall wooden structures shutting out any natural light. No lights either from any of the windows. An airless little alleyway, impossible to see any house numbers, hardly possible to see where he was going. He was glad to emerge from the other side. But instead of any continuation of the original broad residential street, he realised he had arrived at the seafront.

First there was the coast road and beyond that the beach. Not a car in sight. Not another person in sight. Traffic lights jammed on green. A full moon high in the sky. Loud speakers on lamp posts spewing out siren sounds intermingled with tinny warning messages. 'Please move to higher ground. Please move to higher ground.' He wandered across the road to the railings separating the pavement from the beach. Where he was confronted by an awesome sight. The sea had retreated. Not just drawn back as at low tide. But sucked out so far that the ocean bed stretched bluish and exposed as far back as he could see, as far back as the horizon. The huge bay was empty of water. That's what chilled him. It was like coming across an empty swimming pool. But on a vast scale. This void where there should be the fullness of the ocean. This silence where there should be the lick-lapping of the tide.

He stepped on to the beach, his feet heavy in the sand, struggling for balance on his cane. He could hardly believe this was the same place he had stopped by earlier where surfers had bobbed in the deep water. It was like walking towards a battlefield littered with corpses, a river gulch full of sun-bleached bones. Shapes rose out at him from the night. Beached boats. Bundles of fishing nets. An anchor. Seaweed drying racks. A loose umbrella, half-shut on broken spokes. An uprooted chair. Which he set upright, this rusted-metal frame lashed with broad strands of plastic. But still strong enough to take his weight, as he sat down, facing the sea.

This would have been Kawabata's beach. An early morning venue for that frail, lonely, detached man. Why did that poor soul, who loved beauty so much, commit such an ugly death? Inhaling those filthy, toxic fumes escaping from the mouth of that brown rubber hose. At least Mishima had the courage to go the way of the elegant sword. At least that death was an act of beauty in itself. But to gas yourself? At the age of seventy-two. This writer who with great sensibility had expressed the essence of the Japanese mind. This writer who had not even penned a note of farewell.

He plucked the bag of chestnuts from his pocket. The little nuggets cold now but again that taste reminding of his childhood. His father and the knife with the ivory sheath. His mother stoic and uncomplaining, showering him with dust from a yellow rag. These thoughts interrupted by a police car driving along the empty highway blaring out its bulletins. He ducked from the glare of the headlights, the twin beams casting elongated shadows across the empty bay and then disappearing. He was alone again.

Again the ringing from his phone. Da, da, da, da, da. Da, da, da, da, da. He plucked it out of his pocket, switched it off, tossed the contraption as hard as he could, watched it skid across the wet sand. The night stretched wide before him. Pagan moon. Blue seabed. Distant stars. An icy gust hinting at the arrival of snow. He shivered. What was out there in the dark, raging ocean, gathering tide-blood into its wake? A puny ripple that would do no more than lap at his toes? Or a mountain of water building its sheer walls higher and higher until it blocked out the eerie moonlight? He smiled in the face of his fate. He would wait. For death was the greatest denial of them all.

SELECTED EXTRACTS FROM

THE WATERWHEEL

BY SIR EDWARD STRATHAIRN

1928–2003
(Missing, Presumed Dead)

We were ten minutes out of Yokohama before anyone said a word. It was the soldier next to the driver who turned round. The one who had given the order for the jeep to stop and pick me up. I could see his rank. And the tag. Feldman. Captain Feldman.

'Where you from, lieutenant?' he asked.

That was the question the Yanks always put first. Never your name. They wanted to place you. A state, a city, a town, a zip code. Then the inevitable follow up jibes about the Mets, the Redskins, the Cowboys, the Bulls, the Bears. Stuff like that. Friendly but never intimate. It was an illusion I knew all about.

'England.'

'I can see that from the outfit. Where 'bouts?'

'London.'

Feldman had a pleasant face. Tanned. From lazing about sunny Okinawa, no doubt. A couple of days' stubble. Skin slack, like an old hound–dog, giving him a weary but kindly look. He scratched his cheek, thoughtful, as if he were scraping up a memory.

'I was stationed near Oxford couple of years back,' he said. 'Before this gig. London was a great place for R&R.'

'Still is,' the corporal beside me said. Large man, all crouched up in the small space, rifle between his knees. Black skin. Sleeves rolled up tight to reveal bulging biceps below the two stripes. Red-eyes. Faint moustache. Skin pocked like the road we were on. The name "Winston" on his tag. 'I'm from Atlanta,' he told me as if this somehow explained his presence in the jeep. 'Atlanta, Georgia.'

'Georgia's always on his mind.' Feldman half-sung the words.

'Good jazz,' Winston muttered softly so only I could hear. 'Them clubs in Soho.'

'You know where the fuck we're going, Sam?' Feldman shouted at the driver whose skinny head was bobbing in front of me.

'I just keep going north, captain,' Sam shouted back. 'We'll hit Tokyo soon enough.'

'Just follow the smell,' Winston said.

The smell was the rank odour from the shanty towns sprung up along the road. Corrugated iron structures propped up with salvaged pieces of wood. Futons airing in the sunshine. A few weedy patches of vegetables. It was where the first survivors would have reached before giving up and deciding to live where they stopped. Must be a river nearby. Others following until a makeshift village was born. Six months later and it would be a town I'd be looking at. Children poured out of these hovels to run after us.

'Give chocolate,' they shouted. 'Give chocolate.'

'Fuck off, you little brats,' Sam shouted back, snaking the jeep over the road in a shake to get rid of them.

'Lay off, Sam,' said Feldman. The words came out friendly but it was an order nevertheless.

'Give chocolate.' One little boy was right up racing beside me. He must have been about eight years old, yet he had the face of an old man. Wrinkled forehead. Ancient eyes. Two front teeth missing. A cigarette stub tucked behind his ear.

Corporal Winston reached into his breast pocket, pulled out some sticks of gum and tossed them. The chasing horde stopped for the pickings.

'So what's your business in Tokyo?' Feldman again. 'Or is it all top secret?'

'Nothing so exciting,' I said. 'I'm a translator. Seconded to GHQ from the Foreign Office.'

Feldman laughed. 'Did the General send for you then?'

'Something like that.'

Winston poked me gently. 'Well, say "hi" to ol' Douglas Mac-Arthur for me when you see him,' he drawled. 'Tell him old Billy Winston here would be mighty pleased to meet the supreme commander's noble acquaintance.'

'Oh, stop jawing back there,' Feldman said.

But there was no need for the captain to silence his man. We had fallen into speechlessness anyway, letting the road jostle and shake us into witnessing what was before us. The shanty towns had petered out and we were into some razed flat-lands. It wasn't like any other bombed-out city I had seen. I knew London from the blitz. And so must Feldman and Winston. The Germans had left craters where whole streets might have been. Tenement buildings blasted open like dolls' houses to reveal their innards. Gaps in what I could still see was a city. London with holes in it. But a city nevertheless. Here there were no gaps. Or at least just one big gap. For this was it. Miles and miles of rubble with the occasional scorched pillar or post still standing. Unobstructed. Occasionally a clue that human beings had once inhabited this place. A blackened safe. A burned-out oven. What were once the outskirts of Tokyo were now a petrified forest. Flies everywhere. My God, I thought. If this was Tokyo after the fire-bombings, what must Hiroshima and Nagasaki be like?

Feldman took off his cap. Military crop flecked with white. He wiped the back of his hand across his brow. 'Christ,' he said. 'What have we done?'

I was glad this hadn't been my war. At least, that was how I saw it. The Brits might have been slugging it out with the Japs in Burma, Malaya, Singapore, Sumatra and Borneo but over here on mainland Nippon this was Uncle Sam's backyard mess. I wasn't losing any sleep over the pulling of any bomb-hatch trigger on the

Enola Gay. And I wasn't taking any responsibility for this either. This was heavy-handed stuff. Typical Yankee bullying. So let the poor bastards see the result of their handiwork. They deserved to.

As we moved closer to the centre of Tokyo, I noticed the men in the jeep begin to relax. Sam the driver started to whistle while Feldman, and Corporal Winston beside me, waved casually to a few of the people who had stopped to watch our passage. Some pedestrians waved or bowed back, expressionless, politely, their faces wan and drawn, their clothes hanging loose from under-nourished bodies. The scene was still very much one of devastation but at least a few buildings had survived the fire-bombing. These were the concrete structures of ministries, banks and office blocks, walls blackened and charred, windows blown out and boarded up, metal signs twisted from the heat. Not the flimsy wood and paper houses of the poorer people that had served as mere kindling for the ferocious onslaught. Over one hundred thousand people had been burned alive that horrendous day in March, the smell of bar-becued flesh even wafting up to filter through the bomb-hatches of the B-29s circling above.

Now, where building blocks had been reduced to ashes, resi-dents had planted meagre rows of vegetables as they tried to eke out survival from the sooty soil. I saw beggars on the streets, pave-ment hawkers with a few precious possessions laid out in a barter for food, a lane of stalls where a thronging black market had sprung up. Skinny, hollow-chested urchins too weak even to chase us in the usual pester for gum and chocolate. A few leafless trees. Not a bird in the sky. Black clouds overhead. It was hard to believe the sun would ever shine on this city again. And if it did, people would probably retreat indoors from the heat.

Sam pulled up outside the Imperial Hotel. So Frank Lloyd Wright-famous, even I had heard of it. The building was an amaz-ing feat of architecture, a bizarre combination of *faux*-Mayan and art-deco design, stretching back in layers of yellowish brick from the portico to a seven-storey tower at the centre. The bombing had roughed up the facade, but the hotel still boasted a faded grandeur. Feldman insisted we all got out and have our picture taken by the pool in front of the entrance. No fountains flowed and the water was sooty black. Sam fumbled with the Brownie as Feldman and Winston took up position on either side of me. They held up their hands in a Churchillian victory-salute as I tried to manage a smile.

'It's a wonder it survived,' I remarked to Feldman as we walked back to the jeep.

'It outfoxed the Great Kanto earthquake as well,' he said, pushing back his cap, smiling at me. 'Designed by a Yank, of course.'

We all settled back into the jeep and Sam drove us towards Supreme Allied Command HQ somewhere in the heart of the city's financial district.

'One of the few areas left standing,' Sam said. 'I guess we need the money machine to get things rolling again.' He had been there a few times as part of his duties, ferrying personnel arriving to and from the ships at Yokohoma.

Winston plucked out a cigarette from a packet wedged tight in the pocket of his uniform shirt, flicked open the lighter cap, thumb-sparked a flame into existence. Took a deep inhale, offered me one as an afterthought. I refused, even though I was dying for a smoke.

'So what are you men here for?' I asked Feldman.

'Winston and me are assigned to ferret out the war criminals.'

'You mean government ministers, generals, people like that?'

'Naw. We've already got these slimeballs locked up. We're after the ones who captured the bombing crews. The B-29 guys, shot down on their missions, but managing to bail out in their chutes. Some are POWs but God knows how they've been treated. We've got intelligence saying others were executed. Heads cut off with ceremonial swords.'

'Livers gouged out, fried and eaten for dinner,' Winston added on a slow exhale of smoke.

'Bastards,' Sam hissed.

THE WATERWHEEL, CHAPTER 4

I arrived too late at SCAP headquarters in the Dai-Ichi Insurance building to be assigned barracks, so Sam took me in the jeep to a *ryokan*. A tiny windowless room, blistered *tatami* mats, lumpy futon, but the bedlinen was spotless. I went out to find something to eat, couldn't find a hotel with a restaurant still open, and ended up among the ramshackle black market stalls that had sprouted out of the debris. With the farmers and fishermen selling direct to these places, what was available to the ordinary citizen was negligible or way out of their price range. But the Yankee dollar could buy anything. In my case, a bowl of noodles flavoured with some dried fish and a small bottle of rice wine. I probably could have had a side of Kobe beef with chips if I had wanted.

My mood was upbeat with my hunger gone and my head swimming with the rough sake. I decided to take a walk down by the river and it was there that I first saw her, standing half-in and half-out of the shadow of the bridge. I couldn't see her face, just the trail of smoke from her cigarette, the dark slacks and a blouse covered by a loose cardigan over her shoulders. The style of dress confused me and I wrongly assumed she must be a Western girl.

'Hey, soldier,' she called, her voice at first weak and throaty. Her face emerged slowly from the shadow, like a pale moon from behind clouds, a red scar of lipstick, hair loose past her shoulders, not pinned up in the Japanese style. A *panpan* girl. 'Hey, soldier.' Her voice stronger this time.

I looked around. The street was empty. I would just saunter over, exchange a few words, it had been so long since I had spoken to a young woman. Yet such a strong current of excitement ran through me as I approached her. Not just a sexual thrill. But the thrill of power. So seductive of my pathetic male sexuality. I could have her just like that. For less than a dollar. For the price of a bowl of rice, some dried fish and a half bottle of rice wine. These young women sacrificed for my comfort by this defeated nation, thrown up by the Japanese authorities like barricades against the invading foreign hordes. To protect the nation's virgins by feeding them prostitutes instead. There were official brothels full of them. Sponsored by the government's Recreation and Amusement

Association. But who was this freelance woman of the street? A war orphan? An eldest sister forced to feed her family? Or did she just give pleasure in order to find her own pleasure in what a few dollars could buy?

'You not GI?' Her face was heavy with make-up. Unnecessarily, I thought, since she was quite beautiful.

'British.'

'*Eikoku-jin*. Why you here?'

I didn't know if she meant here in Japan or standing here in front of her. I decided on the former although I wasn't going to tell her I was a translator. Better she tried to communicate on my terms.

'Americans want me for work,' I said.

'Americans want me too.' A half-smile. Sad eyes lowering. She continued to suck on her cigarette, no inhalation, just light puffs kissed into the air.

I dismissed the stupid questions rushing into my head, stood there dumb, wondering what to say. I didn't want to pay to have sex with her but I didn't want to leave her either. I suddenly realised how lonely I was. How alone we both were. A large crow swung down in a black flap from the parapet and we watched as the bird struggled to unearth a scrap of food from among the reeds on the river bank.

'Can I buy you something to eat?'

She dropped the cigarette, scrunched it out with the heel of her shoe.

'One dollar,' she said.

'I don't want... I don't want sex.'

'Not sex. My time.'

'You want me to pay you so I can buy you something to eat?'

She smiled again. This time her eyes lit up. 'Take it or...' And then she screwed up her mouth in a search for the words. 'Take it. Or leave it.'

I fell in love with Sumiko at that moment. I didn't know anything about her – who she was, what had driven her to the streets, how many men she had slept with, whether she was a good person or a bad person. But even within her despair, she had exhibited a brightness, a playfulness, a hopefulness that in my own loneliness, my heart found irresistible.

'I'll take it.'

'Good,' Sumiko said, linking her arm in mine. 'I am hungry. So very hungry.'

THE WATERWHEEL, CHAPTER 5

I watched as Sumiko hurriedly scooped up a few more strands of noodles with her chopsticks. I was not used to seeing a woman eat in this way. It both shocked and amused me to see the tails of soba flick against her chin before being slurped noisily into her mouth. Like rats disappearing down a drain. I passed her a napkin and she reluctantly dabbed the stock from her lips.

'When did you last eat?' I asked.

'Yesterday morning. *Batta*. I don't know how you say.' She wiggled her fingers in insect-like fashion.

I knew but didn't say. Grasshoppers. A breakfast of grasshoppers.

The owner of the stall put down two small cups and a flask of warm sake on the counter in front of us. Beneath his peaked worker's cap, his tiny eyes stared out fiercely at us. He said something to Sumiko, which I couldn't hear. Her reply told him I was English not American. He shrugged and left us.

'What did he say?' I asked.

'He said his pride hurt to see Japanese girl with American soldier.'

'What do you think about that?'

'I am not Recreation and Amusement girl.' She picked up the noodle bowl, tipped it up high and drank down the last of the contents. In the bald light of the one bulb hanging from the rafters, I could see the darker flesh of her neck as it stretched uncovered by make-up from the collar of her blouse.

'I didn't think you were.' I knew that the RAA prostitutes worked out of licensed brothels rather than try and pick up soldiers off the street. 'So what are you then?'

'I am an *onrii* lady?'

'And what is that?'

'*Onrii. Onrii* one.'

'Only one?'

'Yes. Only one man.'

'So where is he? This one man.'

'Go back to America.'

'When?'

'Before one month.'

'And left you to eat *batta*?'

She picked up the flask of sake, filled my cup to the brim. 'I have no father, sick mother, two young sisters.' She put the flask down and counted out her responsibilities on three of her fingers. 'Only food is black market food. Too expensive. GI good to me. Sugar, salt, chocolate, cigarettes from PX. Even soap. That is Japanese life now. He give, I give. Good deal. Do you have wife?'

I shook my head.

She took my hand, began to massage the palm. 'Skin soft,' she said. 'Office soldier, yes?'

The simple act aroused me. In fact, everything about her aroused me. The smell of her cheap perfume. The touch of her rough fingers on my skin. The rocking closeness of her bare foot next to mine on the counter stool. But this was no subservient Japanese girl of the streets. There was a defiance about her. A pride. I might have had the commercial power, but she had the sexual power.

'Yes. Office soldier.'

'British office soldier can go to PX?' She let go of my hand to refill my cup.

'I don't know. I think so. I need to report tomorrow. I'll find out then.'

'OK. Which hotel you stay? Nomura? Dai-Ichi? Imperial?'

I smiled. From what I had learned from Sam the jeep driver, she had just reeled off the three main accommodation facilities for GIs and Westerners. In ascending order of luxury.

'I will find out tomorrow.'

'So where you stay tonight?'

'A *ryokan*. Near here.'

'A *ryokan*,' she sneered. 'Show me.'

I paid and we went out into the street. The market was still busy despite the hour, with stalls lit up by paraffin lamps and lanterns floating off like fireflies into the darkness. I wanted Sumiko close by me, not to lose her in the crowd, but she kept stopping at displays of goods laid out on upturned boxes or just spread out on hand-kerchiefs in the dirt. And it wasn't the usual trinkets I would have expected to catch her eye but pots and ladles and spoons and tunics and badges and military blankets. The city was devastated yet here was the fresh bacteria of commerce clinging to the rotting corpse, ready for cultivation into a new economy.

'You buy me this?' she asked, holding up a pair of silver-plated teaspoons she had snatched up from a cloth on the ground.

'No.'

'Why not?'

'They're useless.'

'They're pretty.'

'I'd rather buy you some rice.'

I pulled her away from the skinny boy who seemed to be responsible for these, his only, pieces of merchandise. She kept up apace beside me now, clinging roughly to my arm. We passed a group of men warming their hands around a fire burning high and greasy from an oil drum. One of them spat towards Sumiko as we passed. I made a half-hearted display of wanting to respond but she pushed me ahead.

'Poor soldiers,' was all she said.

Taking my bearings from the bombed-out remains of Shinjuku Station, I managed to find my way back to my *ryokan*. I waited with her outside as she smoked a cigarette.

'I can't go in,' she said.

'Why not?'

'Too Japanese.'

'Can I see you tomorrow?'

'Perhaps.'

'By the bridge?'

'Perhaps.' She passed her cigarette over to me and I squashed it
out under the heel of my shoe. 'Now I must go home.'

As I watched her disappear into the black hole of the night in
this bombed-out city, I tried to imagine where her home might be.

THE WATERWHEEL, CHAPTER 6.

I was billeted at the Nomura. My room was tiny, cramped, but I
was just grateful it wasn't one of those cordoned off into cells by
blankets – which is how most of the GIs slept. I was also given access
to the PX, where I bought some essentials for myself, a bag of rice
and a few bars of chocolate for Sumiko. That night I waited three
hours for her by the bridge but she never came. I repeated the vigil
the following night and the next with the same fruitless outcome.

By coincidence I had been assigned to work with Feldman, the
captain who had given me a run into Yokohama when I first arrived,
together with Winston, the corporal from Georgia who liked jazz.
Feldman was the chief interrogator in an investigation into the deaths
of a bailed-out American bomber crew allegedly murdered in cap-
tivity. Six of the poor Yankee bastards survived being shot down
over Southern Japan only to be captured and then eventually driven
out into the woods by a group of fishermen and shot. A blood-lust
revenge just one night after news of the second bomb dropped on
Nagasaki had reached the village. The murderers of all these thousands of innocent civilians now seeking justice for the death of six air-
men. My heart wasn't it. I didn't think Feldman's was either. He had
just finished a law degree when he had enlisted. Four years later and
these interrogations were his apprenticeship. It was hard to eke out
justice from a bunch of simple fishermen who never really believed
they had done anything wrong. War was war was war. Their victims
surely understood that. The issue was not whether the crew had been
shot but that they had taken their punishment honourably. With stoic
dignity and acceptance. Stories had circulated that the dead men's livers had been ripped out and served as a delicacy to officers at a local

army base but I was sure these tales were just meant to throw fire on to the frenzy. The autopsies proved me right. We were just one of several war crime cases on the go, right up the scale to the highest ranking officers and military commanders. This was America's Nuremberg in Japan. There would be a few showcase trials to demonstrate whose law and morality now ruled the roost and to satisfy the press back home. Then they would peter out.

But for now I spent day after endless day in a windowless interrogation room that reeked of sweat, cigarette smoke and hopelessness watching a skinny, scared peasant realise that *bushido* was irrelevant to his captors. My mouth and throat parched dry from the hours of translation and interpretation in the summer humidity as a heavily perspiring Feldman, thorough and patient, went over events again and again with his prisoners. At night, I was desperate for human company that didn't involve a bewildered and unrepentant fisherman, Feldman or Winston, a cabaret or a crate of beer or a quick fuck with a *panpan* up an alleyway by the hotel. I had been told half the Occupation Force had already contracted syphilis or gonorrhoea. Penicillin was the biggest selling drug on the market. Tokyo was just a big black hole for me, both literally and emotionally, and it was swallowing me up.

It must have been nearly two months after our first meeting when I finally saw her again. The girl who ate grasshoppers. I was crossing the road outside the Imperial when she emerged with her co-workers on the arms of a bunch of American officers in their dress uniforms. The whole lot of them were like a gaggle of geese, pouring out into the street, all het up and excited, cackling and flapping, necks wriggling in all directions. She saw me too, a flash of a smile, before she drifted on up the road with her giggling flock.

I took heart from that brief acknowledgement and went back to the bridge the following night. I only had to wait ten minutes and then she turned up. The proud spark in her I remembered from our first meeting had gone, and her whole body sagged with a certain weariness. We exchanged pleasantries.

'You are a kind man,' she said, running her finger lightly along my forearm.

I wasn't sure if she was making a statement or asking a question. I shrugged. 'All I did was buy you a meal.'

'Can you drive?'

I nodded.

'Can you get jeep?'

'I don't know. Yes, perhaps I can. Why do you need a jeep?'

'I want you to take me out of here. Out of Tokyo. To the mountains. To Hakone. Just one day. Can you do that?'

THE WATERWHEEL, CHAPTER 7

It was easier to get the jeep than I had first thought. A few forms to be filled in at the motor pool and that was all. The reason for the requisition? To visit witnesses to take statements. I had the authority to do that. Finding the extra petrol was the problem. I had almost given up on the whole adventure when finally I found some *yakuza* chap from the Kanto Ozu gang with a horde of the stuff behind a stall in the Shinjuku market. He was willing to part with a couple of jerry-cans for a few dollars if I threw my sunglasses into the deal. I filled up, drove off to pick up Sumiko at the bridge. My driving was rusty and I struggled with the double-declutching but at least the Japanese drove on the left the way I was used to. I made it to the bridge ten minutes late, quite proud of myself for only stalling twice on the way. She was wearing a bright *kimono*, pink with the pattern of cherry blossoms. I noticed her musky green-tea scent as she slipped in beside me. She hardly wore any make-up. I took that as a compliment.

The first few miles were awkward, both of us hardly speaking as I drove through the city, or what was left of it. But the regeneration that was under way in the shanty towns sprung up around the charred remains gave us reason to talk. There was scaffolding everywhere, concrete mixers, bulldozers, giant lorries hauling in bricks and girders, building crews hammering and welding, bent-backed peasants growing vegetables in fields of soot around the sites. Human beings were bloody resilient, I had to give them that.

The roads were in remarkably good condition, re-surfaced no doubt for the military ferrying supplies between HQ in Tokyo and the naval base down in Yokosuka. There was little civilian traffic, and the few other military vehicles we came across honked us wildly on seeing a soldier out with a Japanese girl. You wouldn't have known when Tokyo became Yokohama but once we had moved on south passed Ofuna, the countryside began to spread out green and clean in front of us. The air was fresher, sweeping in off the sea, and I began to breathe easy. This was my first day of R&R since I had hit Japan. I had a jeep and this little Japanese sweetheart by my side. I was ready to enjoy myself.

'I thought we might see Mount Fuji from here,' I said.

'Only person who stay in Japan long time see Fuji-san,' she said, turning to smile at me.

'Well, that rules me out,' I said, pumping the pedal a little harder. 'Where shall we go?'

'Ashinoko.'

I turned inland from the coast at Odawara and then up and over a mountain pass. The roadways became trickier, pretty rough with more potholes than macadam in patches, sharp bends and steep inclines, and I had to concentrate hard on just changing through the gears, with not much time for my passenger or the scenery. Over the summit and it was plain sailing after that, just cruising in neutral most of the time down to Hakone. Lake Ashi would have been pretty unremarkable compared to what I was used to back home had it not been for Mount Fuji sitting off in the distance. Unburdened by clouds, the sight of the volcano's absolute symmetry was astonishing, hard to believe it had been carved out so perfectly by nature rather than by human endeavour. I could understand why the Japanese accorded this mountain divine status. And given my unfettered view, I guess I was scheduled to stay in Japan a long time. A fact Sumiko didn't hesitate to tease me about.

We had lunch in a restaurant by the lake where she was more attentive than I could have ever wished. She filled and re-filled my sake cup, laughed at my stupid jokes in Japanese, hung on to my

arm as we strolled, insisted on buying me a small box inlaid with
the local marquetry as a souvenir. She then told me there was somewhere else she would like me to take her.

The hotel was one of the most impressive buildings I had ever
seen. I had just pulled out of a bend entering a small village and
there it was. So unexpected, just spilling out of the mountain side,
easy as you like. That was its architectural strength. Its organic
nature. Summing up in an instance all that was exquisitely beautiful
about Japan. Grace, elegance, subtlety, attention to detail, respect
for the natural form. I drove into the forecourt where a few other
military vehicles were parked. Christ, there was even a staff car
flying the Stars and Stripes. Perhaps the old Supreme Commander
himself had stopped by for a cuppa. A couple of white-gloved flun-
kies took the jeep, leaving me and Sumiko standing in awe in front
of the building. I thought of myself, Feldman and Winston stopping
off on my first day in Tokyo to get our photographs taken outside
the Imperial Hotel. That Frank Lloyd Wright edifice was magnificent but what I stood staring at now really moved me. I didn't
know why. Perhaps it was the romantic in me. I brushed down my
uniform ready to escort my lady through the swing doors.

'No, no,' she said, looking quite shocked. 'I want the gardens.
Will you take me there?'

It turned out her father had worked at the hotel as a gardener
before the war. She had grown up nearby with her mother and
her two sisters, often coming by to play in the grounds but never
going into the hotel itself. That was strictly off limits for children
of the staff. She skipped ahead of me now, running out of sight. I
followed her through an avenue of trees, brushing aside the strands
of cobwebs left in her wake. I came out into a clearing where she
stood by a dried-up pool. As I approached, I realised she was crying.

'It was once so beautiful,' she sobbed.

I had to admit the place could have used a good gardener. Weeds
overgrew the whole area, branches needed pruning back and the
pond area either needed to be refilled or dug over altogether. Half
the plants were dead, the rest struggling to survive in whatever
light filtered through the overhanging foliage. There was an old

waterwheel rotting away on the side of a small mill deeper into the hillside where the stream had clogged up on its fall down into the pool. The wheel would have been an intricate structure of excellent craftsmanship in its time, but many of the struts hung loose, its hoppers were filled with mud, and right at the top a bird's nest. I let Sumiko cry her heart out into my chest, then led her back to the hotel. I felt her trembling beside me as we spun through the swing doors and up the carpeted stairway. I was mentally going over my excuses to the sergeant at the motor pool as I checked both of us in for the night. We were given the Fuji Suite.

THE WATERWHEEL, CHAPTER 8

My job was coming to an end even if nothing official had been said. The American desire to persecute or prosecute the Japanese for what had happened was beginning to wane. Most of the interrogations had been completed and my superior, Captain Feldman, was now involved in the trial procedures. But even these cases were half-hearted affairs with most of the sentences of the high-ranking military men and politicians being downgraded from death to life imprisonment. Other prisoners on shorter sentences had already been shown the gate to the Tokyo streets. My turn was coming round too, time to pack up the uniform and head off home before the Yanks started getting tough on Korea. I was English–Japanese bilingual with a lieutenant's pip on my shoulder and I didn't think work would be hard to find on Civvy Street in the new world order.

My relationship with Sumiko had blossomed. If that was the right word to apply to a liaison between a *panpan* girl and her customer. She was my *onrii* lady. I was her *onrii* man. Or at least I hoped I was.

The hotel in the hills outside Hakone had become our favourite haunt whenever I could wangle a jeep out of the motor pool. We would go there on special occasions, birthdays, anniversaries and the like. The staff had come to know me well and I always chose the Fuji Suite. We cherished that room with its views on to the hillsides. And the walk-in cupboard with the light that went on and off automatically with the opening and shutting of the door. Sumiko just loved that. As if that simple contraption summed up the most decadent luxury. The hotel was also blossoming, restoring its reputation as a haven for foreigners, long experienced as it was in the ways of the Western visitor. Sometimes a famous guest would add a certain magic to our stay. We bumped into Nehru once in the gardens on a stroll out to the waterwheel.

The waterwheel had been restored now. The whole area where it sat cleared up to create a perfect little hideaway. I would sit there often and contemplate the structure, be lulled into pleasant meditation by its constant cycle as I watched the hoppers deliver or extract their loads to and from the pool. A symbol of life. A symbol of reincarnation. I would sometimes bring a small bag of breadcrumbs from the dining room. Sumiko would delight in watching the carp rush and hustle to suck up the tiniest morsel. That was what she was doing now as I sat on the low surrounding wall, smoking a cigarette.

It wasn't often I felt pleased with myself. For I had done nothing of significance in this mediocre existence I could call my life. But as I watched Sumiko feed the fish, I would like to think I had restored a little goodness into her life. I had brought her back to the place she used to play happily as a child while my financial contributions continued to keep her family alive. And in her own way, Sumiko had given me what she could. A little bit of tenderness to a man so hardened by the atrocities witnessed in the past few years. I might have been fooling myself into thinking there was something more than my money that had bought me this little bit of happiness. Or perhaps I had learned something from my American paymasters after all.

THE WATERWHEEL, CHAPTER 16

J. David Simons is the author of two previous novels as well as a number of short stories and essays. His first novel, *The Credit Draper*, was shortlisted for the McKitterick Prize. He has also been the recipient of a Creative Scotland Writer's Bursary and a Robert Louis Stevenson Fellowship. A former lawyer, cotton farmer and journalist, he also worked for seven years as a university lecturer in Japan. He now lives in Glasgow, the city of his birth.